He lowered his ... across hers. His l... her head, angling it so he could deepen the kiss. His tongue tangled with hers, and yet at the same time seemed to explore every nook and cranny as though each held a treasure. It was fire and brimstone, desperation and hunger. A panther on the hunt. As though they'd both gone without sustenance for far too long, and now at last were free to enjoy the feast that had been prepared in welcome.

She curled her arms around his neck, scraping her fingers along his scalp, threading them through the thick strands, while he wrapped his arms around her and held her tightly, her breasts smashed against his chest, the rest of her body pressed against his firm and sturdy length. She didn't know how she remained standing when her legs had grown so weak. If not for his hold on her, she suspected she might have collapsed to the floor.

He broke away from the kiss, his breath wafting over her cheek just before his tongue outlined the swirls of her ear. Delicious. How was it that there were so many parts of her that felt as though they'd been awakened from a long sleep?

"Do you want more?" he asked.

She nodded.

"I want to hear you say it."

"I want more."

By Lorraine Heath

The Counterfeit Scoundrel

The Chessmen: Masters of Seduction

LORRAINE
HEATH

AVONBOOKS

An Imprint of HarperCollinsPublishers

THE COUNTERFEIT SCOUNDREL. Copyright © 2023 by Jan Nowasky. All rights reserved. Printed in the United States of America. No part of this book may be used or reproduced in any manner whatsoever without written permission except in the case of brief quotations embodied in critical articles and reviews. For information, address HarperCollins Publishers, 195 Broadway, New York, NY 10007.

First Avon Books mass market printing: February 2023

Print Edition ISBN: 978-0-06-311463-0
Digital Edition ISBN: 978-0-06-311464-7

Cover design by Amy Halperin
Cover illustration by Victor Gadino
Cover image © Sean Pavone | Dreamstime.com (furniture)

Avon, Avon & logo, and Avon Books & logo are registered trademarks of HarperCollins Publishers in the United States of America and other countries.

HarperCollins is a registered trademark of HarperCollins Publishers in the United States of America and other countries.

FIRST EDITION

23 24 25 26 27 BVGM 10 9 8 7 6 5 4 3 2 1

For Alex and Karen
As you journey through life together
May the years be generous and kind
May all the dreams you share be fulfilled
And when you are wrinkled with age
May you still hold hands and
Smile at each other in the same way that you do now.
With my love always,
Mom

*When playing the game of seduction,
the queen is always the most powerful
piece on the board.*

The Counterfeit
Scoundrel

CHAPTER 1

*B*LACKGUARD *Blackwood.*

David Blackwood decided a man could be called worse. Sitting at the mahogany desk in his grand library, perusing the latest gossip sheet, he was astounded by how quickly and decisively a man's reputation could fall because of scandal. Two transgressions that had become very public the previous autumn were being rehashed in the gossip rags as a warning to the latest batch of debutantes and other ladies in search of a husband: a liaison with him was bound to bring about ruination. While he was not the only one to have made that damning list, it seemed he had secured the top position as the one to be avoided at any cost. Thankfully, he was more amused than insulted because he wasn't on the hunt for a wife. Not this Season nor the next nor the following fifty. He understood all too well the pitfalls of marriage and intended to avoid being shackled until he drew his last breath.

"Sir?"

He glanced up to see his slender, silver-haired butler standing as rigidly as a poker just inside the doorway. "What is it, Perkins?"

"I apologize for disturbing you when you are about your work, but a Mrs. Mallard wishes an audience."

Slipping his golden timepiece from his waistcoat pocket, he glanced at the hour. A little after seven. At nine was a meeting of the Chessmen, a moniker given to him and his three firmest friends—while they were studying hard and wreaking havoc during their time at Oxford—because of their ruthless strategy when it came to investing. That ruthlessness was the reason he was presently able to do anything he damned well pleased without worrying about Society's censure. "I'll see her, but do have the carriage brought round as I'll be departing once our business is concluded."

The second his butler disappeared, he put away the newsprint as well as the numerous reports that outlined various investment opportunities he was considering. When his desk was tidied to his satisfaction, he shoved back the sturdy leather chair, stood, and moved to the center of the gigantic chamber. He'd purchased this ridiculously large residence because his father had wanted it, and Bishop had made it his life's ambition to deny his sire anything he desired.

Now he waited patiently for his guest. Nothing good ever came from rushing into judgment, and he'd long ago learned the value of biding his time until all aspects of the situation presented themselves.

Only a few minutes passed before Perkins returned. A woman who lived up to her namesake waddled in behind him. Small of stature, she wore a frock of dark blue buttoned up to her chin. Her blond hair was tucked beneath a narrow-brimmed hat, its crown decorated with only a few light blue flowers and a sprig of green.

"Mrs. Ava Mallard," Perkins announced gravely, and the lady gave a startled jerk as though he'd reached around and pinched her bum. She looked to be preparing to take flight at any moment, with the merest encouragement to flee. A loud noise. An unexpected action. The flickering of one of the gaslights.

Ensuring his strides were leisurely, long, and unthreatening, he crossed over to her. "Mrs. Mallard, how may I be of service?"

She looked at Perkins, then shifted her attention back to him. In a barely audible whisper, she asked, "Are you the bishop?"

"It's merely Bishop, a sobriquet my mates bestowed upon me when I was at school. I must say it rather stuck." A nickname given to him because at the time he'd been destined for the clergy. Until he'd discovered he was more suited to other endeavors.

"Mrs. Winters said you helped her last autumn."

"I did indeed." The assistance had cost him five thousand quid when Mr. Winters had sued him for damages, but he'd considered the money well spent and his coffers hadn't mourned the loss. "Why don't you join me by the fire, and we'll discuss the reason you've called?"

Gnawing on her bottom lip, she glanced around. "Upon further reflection, I probably shouldn't have come."

"You're perfectly safe with me, Mrs. Mallard. Perkins, have tea brought in."

"Yes, sir." Having never been entirely comfortable around the ladies who frequently visited and being terribly unskilled at hiding his disapproval of their presence, Perkins made a hasty retreat.

Bishop backed up several steps. "I think you'll find this chair over here the most cozy. I'll stand by the hearth, shall I?"

She gave a half nod before shuffling over to a large stuffed wingback chair. He stopped by his decanter table and poured himself some scotch before walking over to the massive marble fireplace, leaning against it, and studying the woman fidgeting so nervously before him. "I take it that you've come to me because you wish to obtain a divorce."

She gave a jerky nod and clasped her hands tightly together. "He is not unfaithful, but neither is he a kind man. He has incredibly high expectations and when they are not met—"

In commiseration, he shook his head. "I don't need to know the particulars, Mrs. Mallard. That you desire to be free of him is reason enough."

"I do worry that I've delayed the inevitable for too long. I think he wishes to be rid of me, possibly to have me committed . . . or worse."

Hearing the rattling of china, he held a finger to his lips. In order to meet with success in helping these women gain their freedom, he found it necessary that no one know of his true involvement with them.

Holding a tea tray, a young woman he didn't recognize walked gracefully into his library. Her hair, the shade of the honey he poured over his scones at breakfast, was tightly secured into a neat knot beneath her white mobcap. Her eyes—a mesmerizing bright blue, like the delphiniums his mother had taken such delight in growing—were alert with an inquisitiveness that seemed to take in her surroundings and catalog each aspect. Wearing a simple black frock and frilly white bibbed apron, she required no adornment to make her one of the most strikingly beautiful women he'd ever laid eyes upon. Perkins handled all the hiring and letting go of servants, and Bishop generally paid them little notice. But she was somehow different, demanding attention by simply existing. She set the tray on the small table nearest to Mrs. Mallard.

"Have we been introduced?" He wasn't in the habit of asking questions to which he already knew the answer—if he had ever crossed paths with her in the hallway, he'd not have forgotten—but he required something innocuous and *who the devil are you* didn't seem the way to go.

Her attention had been on his guest, but she quickly shifted her focus to him and bobbed a shallow curtsy. "No, sir. I've been employed here less than a sennight."

"Your name?"

"Daisy."

He furrowed his brow. She didn't look at all like a Daisy to him. The name sounded too common, and he suspected she was anything but typical. It was the confidence with which she spoke and met his gaze. Unlike most of his staff, she appeared neither intimidated by nor in awe of her employer. He wanted to question her further, but now was not the time. "Prepare some tea for Mrs. Mallard."

During his conversation with the maid, his visitor had relaxed a tad, perhaps because she no longer felt she was being scrutinized. He preferred it when the women who came to him didn't have a nervous constitution. The maid struck him as someone who didn't. With a great deal of efficiency, she set about preparing the tea.

"Milk and sugar?" she asked in a soft voice that held a hint of gentility. While he'd not been born into the nobility, he had friends who had been. He'd accompanied them now and again to aristocratic affairs and been introduced to enough of their acquaintances to recognize refinement when he heard it. He wondered how it was that she'd come to be a servant.

"Please," Mrs. Mallard said.

He shouldn't be mesmerized, watching the delicate, unblemished hands pour tea, then milk, into the china cup decorated with pink roses—all his china reflected his mum's favorite blossoms—before adding two lumps of sugar and stirring all the contents. With a soft smile, she handed the cup and saucer to the married lady before turning her attention to him. "And you, sir?"

He lifted his glass slightly. "I prefer my beverages with a bit more bite to them."

"Shall I pour you some more before I take my leave?"

No. That's what he should have said. He needed to get her out of here so he could finish his business with Mrs. Mallard. After all, he had an appointment to keep. What he heard escaping his mouth, however, was *yes.*

What the devil was wrong with him? He'd once had no control in his life and now he maintained power over every aspect of it. He certainly never said what he did not mean. Yet he stopped silently castigating himself the second she was near enough that he could inhale the soft fragrance of sweet violets and was reminded of his mother pointing out the delicate blossoms on their walks through the forest and the many times he'd plucked them as a gift to her. Their home had always smelled of violets.

As she took the tumbler, her warm bare fingers touched his, and he went completely still, not even breathing, his eyes locking with hers, not so much from the shock of such an inappropriate encounter but the awareness it stirred to life, as though he could sense how glorious her entire body would feel nestled against his.

Then the glass was gone, as was she, along with his wits. He couldn't recall any woman ever having such a disconcerting effect on him. He watched her stroll to the sideboard. She removed the stopper from one decanter, gave it a sniff, and returned it to its proper place before giving another a try. That one she poured into his tumbler. She knew her liquors then. Expensive ones. She wandered back over to him and extended the glass. Taking more care in removing it from her grasp, he ensured no part of his hand touched hers.

"Will there be anything else, sir?" she asked.

"Not tonight." He nearly slammed his eyes shut at the implication that there might be more on another night, *more* that was not within her realm of duties. The slow stroke of his hand along her spine, a brush of his lips over her throat, a lick of her skin. Dangerous journeys all. Forbidden. Treks he wouldn't enjoy because he did not take advantage of his servants. Ever, under any circumstances.

"Very good, sir."

"Close the door on your way out." He hated that he sounded so brisk, nearly cross, but he wasn't accustomed to being unsettled by a mere slip of a woman.

"Yes, sir." If she noted his brusque tone, she gave

no indication. She gave another quick bob of a curtsy before wandering slowly from the room, and all he wanted to do was trail after her.

Jesus. He tossed back the scotch, noticing that she'd left some of her violet fragrance on the tumbler. Or maybe it was simply that the scent now permeated the room. Unfortunate that, because he needed to stop thinking about her.

"Are you suddenly unwell?" a quiet, hesitant voice asked out of the ether.

He jerked his attention to Mrs. Mallard. He'd completely forgotten about her. It was unlike him to lose his train of thought. What sort of spell had the captivating maid cast over him? "No, I'm fine. Where were we?"

"My husband's threats?" she replied meekly, although the high pitch of her voice at the end made it sound as though she wasn't entirely certain she was providing the correct answer.

At that moment, he hated the man for his ability to mentally beat down this woman until she possessed no confidence whatsoever. He wanted to see the blighter rot and her liberated from him. "Right. Have you children?"

"No."

He was glad of that. Children and the custody of them brought additional complications. Not to mention the mental anguish they suffered when too young to fully understand what was happening.

"How will you provide for yourself, Mrs. Mallard? He will not be required to pay alimony since you will be the one found guilty of infidelity."

"I've made arrangements to serve as an elderly

widow's companion, should this come about so I gain my freedom. As we get along famously, she will wait to fill the post until I know my fate."

He was impressed that she'd considered her financial position. The women he aided usually either returned to the bosom of their families or found employment. One had been squirreling away her pin money, and after her divorce he'd helped her invest it, so she received enough in interest to live modestly but happily.

He made a motion to move toward the chair across from her, and her eyes widened in alarm. "As I mentioned earlier, you have nothing to fear from me, but I need you to understand what is at stake, and my not hovering over you will make the discussion easier."

A nod, a sip of her tea, and he imagined she was striving to position herself so she could toss the hot brew on him if the need arose. He was actually grateful for that bit of rebellion.

He crossed over to the chair, sat, and, holding his tumbler with both hands, leaned forward, resting his elbows on his thighs. "To be clear, this will not be a pleasant experience for you. Divorce is granted only when adultery is involved. It could take weeks before your husband discovers what we are about, but in order to meet with success, we will have to convince him and the courts that we were engaged in an illicit liaison. It will no doubt be reported in the newspapers. All of your family—parents, siblings, cousins—will hear of it. Your friends. Enemies. Strangers. It is likely to bring you disgrace. You need to think long and hard about the consequences and be certain you wish to tread this path."

In her hands, the teacup sat still and unmoving on the saucer. Not a single vibration. Not a single tremor. "If I do nothing, I think I will run mad. I have already given it considerable thought, Mr. Bishop—"

"Just Bishop."

She gnawed on her lower lip again. Sitting this close to her, he could see the slight scarring from previous gnawing. "I feel I have no choice."

"Are you certain he isn't having an affair?"

"Quite certain. But even if he was, a woman must show two causes for divorce, while a man need show only one."

As she was familiar with that condition of the regulation, perhaps she'd already spoken with a solicitor or Mrs. Winters had explained the unfairness of the law to her. Bishop had articulated several times to his friend the Duke of Kingsland about the need to amend that portion of the act so women were not required to have more reasons to end a marriage than men. But the gents who enacted laws feared if they made it too easy for a wife to dissolve the arrangement, more fellows might find themselves turned out. Bishop thought that particular worry had an easy enough solution: don't be an arse to the woman you took to the altar. "You've indicated he's not treated you well. Would you go so far as to say cruelly?"

She nodded. "How do I prove it? It is merely my word against his. The servants will not speak out against him. He is a barrister and has far too much influence and power. But even if they did side with me, I haven't the necessary requirements to seek a divorce because, as I mentioned, he's not been unfaithful."

Perhaps not bodily but to his vows to love, honor,

and cherish. With a sigh, Bishop leaned back. "But you think he will seek a divorce when he discovers your infidelity?"

"I'm rather certain his pride will insist." Angling her head slightly and lowering her saucer to her lap, she studied him as though he were a new breed of puppy. "Why do you do this? Help women out of unpleasant circumstances? He is bound to sue you for damages for having criminal conversation with what he considers his. Other husbands have. What do you gain?"

Without answering, he tossed back what remained of his scotch and shoved himself to his feet. "Give it grave consideration, Mrs. Mallard. If you are still of a mind to carry through with this plan, find an excuse to leave your residence without your husband and return here at nine in the evening Tuesday next, at which time our affair shall commence."

The cup did give a slight rattle against the saucer then. "Mrs. Winters assured me—"

"Nothing shall actually occur between us, but we will give all appearances that it has. Once your husband begins to suspect, he will no doubt hire a detective to solicit proof. You are free to tell the truth and deny that we are involved. But you will not be believed. My reputation will ensure it."

AS INSTRUCTED EARLIER by the butler, Daisy sat in a brocade armchair at the end of the hallway waiting for the man everyone, including staff, referred to as Bishop to finish with the woman behind the closed door so she could retrieve the tea service and tidy up. No doubt pillows or cushions from one of the sofas tossed onto the floor. Perhaps even broken china or porcelain figurines. Although their encounter was certainly quieter than she'd expected.

Serving as an inquiry agent, a private investigator, she knew all about David Blackwood, was here because of his reputation. Her most recent client, Martin Parker, was relatively certain his wife was engaged in an adulterous liaison with the man. Therefore, Daisy had hired on as a maid to catch the vixen in the act. Wednesday a woman had arrived a little after nine in the evening. Daisy had managed to catch a glimpse of the lady before Bishop had escorted her up the stairs to his bedchamber, and she wasn't the wife for whom Daisy was searching. But that didn't mean Mrs. Parker wasn't one of his paramours. Last year he'd been the adulterous party named in two divorce proceedings. Now, having seen him with a second woman in this residence, she had to wonder how many he needed to slake his lust.

So here she was, hoping her client was correct and her time wasn't being wasted. Also hoping she could resist the allure of Bishop. The man was far too handsome, with features that appeared to have been chiseled from stone. Although a bit rough around the edges, they formed a fetching landscape, like that of a majestic mountain with interesting crags and hollows that begged to be explored. Dark hair and dark eyes, eyes that saw too much. Tall with remarkably broad shoulders that could no doubt carry any burden, he wore his clothes well. Obviously, he had a fine tailor and was very particular about his attire. When she'd fetched his glass, she'd noticed the unique buttons on his waistcoat. Black onyx inlaid with a golden *B*.

Most employers paid scant attention to their servants. When he'd asked her name, her heart had sped up, and she'd feared her ruse had been discovered. But apparently, he'd been only curious. Yet tiny tremors had continued to undulate through her as she had prepared tea for his guest. She'd been grateful the china hadn't rattled. The concentration with which he'd watched her certainly hadn't helped matters. No other gentleman had ever studied her so thoroughly. She'd felt as though she'd been naked. Not that he had leered, but the intensity of his gaze had made her feel as if he could see her clearly, could uncover all her secrets.

The library door finally opened, and the woman stepped out followed by Bishop, who immediately swiveled his head Daisy's way, as though he'd been struck by her presence as forcefully as she had by his when he'd appeared before her. Why the devil was she so aware of him?

"Daisy, what are you doing there?" His deep, rich, and melodic voice made her wonder if its hypnotic power was partially responsible for his ability to lure women into his bed so easily.

Quickly she came to her feet. "Mr. Perkins bade me to wait until you'd completed your . . . business so I could collect the tea service straightaway."

"Mmm, I see. Well, I'm going to escort Mrs. Mallard home before carrying on to a meeting. Hopefully Perkins remembered to have the carriage waiting for me."

"I'm rather certain he did, sir. He's quite efficient."

"Yes, he is." He studied her for a full minute while Mrs. Mallard looked on, more in curiosity than jealousy. She supposed, based on his reputation, women knew they'd be sharing him and there was no point in being bothered by it. "Right, then, see to your duties."

Without even touching his guest, he escorted her toward the large foyer that fed into stairs and hallways. If Daisy was involved with a man, she'd want him unable to keep his hands from her person. But then she'd also expect loyalty.

She wandered into the library, struck immediately by his bergamot and orange fragrance and beneath, the softer rose scent of his visitor. She hadn't expected everything to smell so crisp and fresh, assumed the activity surrounding a sexual encounter would taint the air somehow. Not that she'd ever experienced the process in order to know precisely, but she did understand the mechanics of it. A dear friend had explained things shortly after she married, and the way of it—the pain, discomfort, and embarrassment—had made Daisy decide it was something to be avoided if at all possible.

Although perhaps her friend's experience was unique. Since Daisy had made her living for the past two years in part by discovering if women were indeed having affairs, she was flummoxed as to the reason they would seek out an encounter with another man if it was truly a test of endurance rather than a gift of pleasure. Perhaps if it was the right man, with the right woman? But how was one to know when any sexual congress before marriage was to be avoided?

She'd shared a few kisses in her lifetime. The first when she was twelve and a stable boy had talked her into a bit of wickedness. She'd even let him undo one of the buttons on the bodice of her frock. She might have agreed to more if, in his haste, his clumsy fingers hadn't caused that one to go flying into the hay he'd spread out in the stall. It had taken them a good ten minutes to find it, so she could sew it back into place—using the lad's small sewing kit—before returning to her uncle's manor. The entire time she'd been terrified that her misbehavior was going to be found out, and she'd be forced to wed the lad.

Were these women who had illicit affairs terrified? Was the terror of being caught part of the appeal? Or was it love that drove them to another's bed?

Glancing around, she could find no evidence of anything that needed to be straightened. Even the cup and saucer had been returned to their proper place. With a sigh, she lifted the tray.

Based on the heat in his eyes when he'd studied her earlier, she'd expected to find scorched furniture. If they hadn't engaged in sexual relations, why was the woman here?

Daisy shook her head. It didn't matter. No one had paid her to care about Mrs. Mallard. She was to confirm that Mrs. Parker was involved with this Bishop fellow. She did hope the woman made an appearance soon.

Her gaze shifted to the desk, over to the door where no footman stood guard outside, and back to the desk. She was quite alone. Other than the thudding of her heart and the ticking of the mantel clock, she heard no other movements.

After walking over to the large structure, she set the tray on the corner. Several newspapers rested evenly on one side. They were of no interest to her. She released the latch on an elegant wooden box to reveal correspondence. A quick glance through missives indicated they were related to business not paramours.

She'd hoped for a treasure trove of love letters written by women who might have enjoyed his company, in particular one from Mrs. Parker. It would have been worth gold. A stack of ledgers was off to the other side. They would be related to business as well, no doubt. Still, she thumbed through the first to reveal columns of numbers. She lifted the second, her breath catching as her gaze fell on the third. In gilded letters was written *Appointments*. It couldn't be that easy to gain what she needed.

Licking her lips, she glanced again toward the doorway. No one about. No shadows wavering beyond it to indicate someone's imminent arrival. No distant sounds to be heard.

She set the diary in the middle of the desk. Between pages, a slender blue silk ribbon trailed out from the top. Using it as her guide, she opened the book to the present day, Friday. Each day was given its own page, and along the edge of the paper was listed various times. Today's date showed *9 p.m. Chessmen Twin Dragons.*

So that's where he was headed. He'd be late to his appointment because of Mrs. Mallard. Had she been an unexpected visitor then? Had they previously engaged in a lover's tiff? Had she come to straighten things out with him? Had she visited for another reason? Although Mrs. Mallard was not her concern, Daisy possessed an inquisitive mind, and questions constantly tumbled through it whenever she was presented with anything new or baffling. She always enjoyed deciphering any sort of puzzle.

She glanced at the day before. Thursday. Nothing in the evening. If he'd gone out, she hadn't been alerted to it, but then her present duties involved assisting the upstairs chambermaid. That she'd been asked to deliver a tea service this evening had been unexpected. She turned the page back to Wednesday. *8 p.m. Blue-Eyes.*

That would have been the woman she'd seen going up the stairs with him. She was disappointed he didn't use names. Although perhaps it was only with this particular lover. Tuesday was dinner at Knight's. Monday he'd gone to the theater with Rook. Chess pieces. Were they aliases as well? Could they be other paramours? Now she was curious about his future appointments.

She turned to Monday next. *9 p.m. Raven.* Mrs. Parker had black hair. Could he be referencing her? On Wednesday he had another appointment with Blue-Eyes. Thursday evening had a notation of F&S. Was that another lady or a club perhaps? Surely not the Fair and Spare. The notorious establishment catered to bachelors, spinsters, and those no longer married who sought companionship or more—a sexual partner—for the evening. What need had he to seek out a rendezvous when ladies were coming to him? Was he that insatiable?

Daisy heard approaching footfalls. Quickly she closed the book and returned it along with the others to their places. She'd just picked up the tray when Mr. Perkins strode in and gave her a suspicious look. "The master left some time ago. What are you still doing in here?"

"I was simply tidying up as ordered. A few items were scattered hither and yon."

"Bishop doesn't like us messing about his desk. That's not where you put the tea tray, is it?"

"No, but it's where I found it when I returned to the room." She'd become quite skilled at lying convincingly.

"Strange, that."

"Perhaps his guest moved it to prepare herself another cup of tea."

"Perhaps." He jerked his head back slightly. "Come on then. Once those are washed, all the chores will be done and we can retire for the night."

"Yes, sir." With hasty steps she followed him out. By Monday, with any luck, she'd have the answer she sought regarding her client's wife. The challenge would be proving it.

"YOU'RE UNUSUALLY QUIET this evening."

Bishop glanced over at the Duke of Kingsland—King—who occupied the chair to his right. Knight and Rook were also in the circle, seemingly curious to hear his response to their friend's question. They were all situated in a corner of the library within the Twin Dragons, a club that had once been known as Dodger's Drawing Room and had been the domain of men. But its new owner, Drake Darling, had expanded it to include women.

For some reason watching the ladies moving about had reminded Bishop of the new maid. He wondered if she ever visited here. He doubted it. He paid a good wage to his staff, but she didn't strike him as someone who would spend frivolously on memberships. If she belonged to any club at all, it was probably Aiden Trewlove's that accommodated women's whims. Or perhaps she was a member of Griffith Stanwick's Fair and Spare. But if she was a member of the latter, he'd never seen her there. And he would have noticed her. He tended to notice everything. "I have a lot on my mind lately."

"Anything you care to discuss?" Rook asked.

Have you ever had occasion to set eyes on a woman and feel as though she had branded herself on your mind, a woman you can't seem to stop thinking about? Who sends a thousand questions tumbling through your head like petals caught in a gusty breeze, like a whirlwind of discarded leaves traveling through the park? And makes you think in poetic phrases when you never have before? "No."

Eyebrows went up at that, and Bishop knew it was because he wasn't normally a man of few words. He relented. "If you must know, I'm contemplating a daisy."

Rook laughed. "For what purpose?"

"As an addition to my garden." At a table, sipping tea, in a yellow frock, wearing a wide-brimmed straw hat. One he would remove so the sun could kiss her cheeks. He suspected as a child, she'd had freckles.

"You already have one of the most elaborate gardens in London. I know of no other that has as many varieties of flowers as yours."

"But it has no daisy."

"I wondered if perhaps you were mulling over your latest unflattering appearance in the gossip rags," Knight said. "I assume you saw the damning article."

"I did indeed. *Blackguard Blackwood* has a poetic ring to it."

"Gentlemen are usually quickly forgiven their transgressions," King said. "It's been months since yours came to light. I'm unable to determine why the gossipmongers continue to harp on them."

"I wasn't born into their ranks, so absolution isn't so easily granted. I'll understand if any of you wish to no longer associate with me." To be honest, he'd been surprised to find them waiting for him, a tumbler of scotch resting on the table before the empty chair when he'd arrived.

"Don't be bloody ridiculous," Knight said. "Your affairs are your business. Certainly, I know of worse offenses."

He appreciated the loyalty, especially because he'd never told them the truth about his affairs. The fewer who knew the better. "Being seen with me could tarnish your own reputations."

"Don't make us take you outside and beat some sense into you," Rook said.

"As though any of you can match me when it comes to fisticuffs." At an early age, he'd learned the value of being able to deliver a decisive blow. He glanced over at the man who had become his first friend at Oxford. "You have a wife to consider, King."

"Penelope will be the most loyal of us all. She never sits in judgment, doesn't even peruse the gossip rags." He grinned. "She prefers scouring through financial reports."

He'd married a woman who, like them, excelled at investing. Anxious to turn the conversation away from gossip, Bishop asked, "How is marriage suiting you?"

It was a ridiculous question because they all knew the duke was madly in love with his wife, had been long before he'd realized he was.

"I find it very much to my liking. You should give it a try."

"I'm not sure marriage is something one should *try*.

Rather, I think it requires a commitment, one I'm not willing to make. Unlike you, I have no title, require no heir." Even if his current reputation didn't make him unsuitable as a husband, he had a past he wouldn't wish to inflict on any woman or offspring. He'd leave his fortune to various charities.

"It's good that your wife lets you out occasionally," Knight teased.

King scowled. "I'm not a pet to be let out. Besides, Penelope took a friend to the theater." He glanced at his watch. "I'll leave in half an hour to pick them up. With my short duration here in mind, has anyone heard of any good investments lately?"

The talk shifted to various opportunities they'd heard about or been invited to join, but Bishop listened with only half an ear because his thoughts began to wander back to the maid, and how she'd looked somewhat forlorn when he'd first clapped eyes on her sitting in the hallway waiting for him to finish up with Mrs. Mallard. Then she'd appeared incredibly alert and a tad guilty. He wondered if she'd been engaged in naughty musings about some gentleman, because surely a man played a role in her life. Servants were not usually married, so she had no husband. But perhaps she fancied someone. Regardless, she was not for him. To flirt with her at all would be a disservice to her. She was in his employ. However, it was more than that.

He'd always enjoyed women. The discovery of what they offered was one of the reasons he'd decided to forego a career in the church. A man of God shouldn't be a sinner.

However, as someone who grew easily bored, he

couldn't envision himself being content with one woman for the remainder of his life. As a result, he'd never pursued a lady with the notion of anything permanent. He wasn't certain how one even went about it, which was perfectly fine as he had no plans to go about it.

CHAPTER 2

⟨⟨⟨~⟩⟩⟩

THE following morning, with a heavy sigh, Bishop glanced at the reports spread out over his desk, the reports he'd been studying for the past hour, striving to determine if he should invest in any of the companies asking for an assist. His neck and shoulders ached. He knew better than to spend so long in one position. He needed an interruption. Perhaps a walk in the park or—

Reaching back, he yanked on the bellpull and then began rubbing on his neck as he waited for his butler to appear. A few minutes later, Perkins entered the room.

"You rang for me, sir?"

"I could set my watch by your punctuality, Perkins."

"I'll take that as a compliment, sir."

"As well you should. Have some tea brought in."

His brow furrowed, Perkins glanced around before leveling his dark stare on Bishop. "Are we expecting company?"

"No, why?"

"You don't drink tea, sir. You have gone so far as to threaten to have me dismissed should I ever have it served to you."

"Unless I request it. Now I'm requesting it. Have that new girl, Daisy, bring it in."

Normally at this point, Perkins issued a quick, "Yes, sir," and dashed off to tend to whatever business Bishop required of him. Now he opened his mouth, closed it, blinked. An odd movement of his jaw followed, and Bishop could have sworn he heard teeth grinding. "Is there a problem?"

"She is rather innocent, sir."

"However, she knows how to pour tea, does she not?"

"Yes, sir, but perhaps"—he glanced around again at the room devoid of visitors—"a footman should bring it up?"

Ah, he was worried about the young woman's reputation in light of his employer's. There were times when his willingness to help a woman escape her tyrannical husband's clutches did place him in a bad light. As his servants were sometimes called upon to serve as witnesses, he let them believe the worst of him so they could tell the truth as they saw it, rather than have them risk perjury. "Have you ever known me to take advantage of a female staff member?"

"No, sir, but neither have I ever heard you call for one by name."

Bishop released a long, drawn-out sigh. He paid this man good wages, more than some earned working for the nobility, and he shouldn't have to put up with his actions being questioned. Nevertheless, he had to admire Perkins for his protectiveness toward the staff. "The door shall remain open, and you can stand guard at the threshold to ensure I'm on my best behavior, if you like. My head is aching, and I thought perhaps some tea might help."

He gave a short bow. "Very good, sir. I'll include a dash of cook's powder that is known to relieve one's head pains."

Then he was gone, and Bishop refrained from getting up and pouring himself a scotch. He didn't know why he wanted to see the chit again. For some ungodly reason, he couldn't stop thinking about her. It wasn't her pretty features that occupied his thoughts, but her mannerisms. She had seemed to be taking in the tableaux of the room, to have been studying him and his guest. Every servant he'd ever known, including the few in his father's residence, had gone about their business without appearing to care about anyone else's. She cared. He'd been able to detect the questions fairly running through her mind. *Who is the woman? Why is she here? What's she to you?* He wondered if he should advise her to never play a game at a card table.

In the distance, he heard the soft tinkling of porcelain dishes. Even as his heart gave a hard thud against his ribs, he opened his ledger, dipped his pen in the inkwell, and hoped to give the impression that he hadn't been anxiously awaiting her arrival. To ensure she understood he recognized her as a servant and not someone to be wooed, he would not stand.

Then she was walking into the library, no Perkins in her wake, thank goodness. He didn't need his butler to serve as his guard or her chaperone. He was fully capable of controlling his desires. It wasn't as though he yearned for her. She'd merely aroused his curiosity. Although knowing what curiosity did to the cat, calling for her could prove to be a regrettable mistake.

"Where would you like the tea, sir?"

"On the same table you used last night, but I'll have a cup at my desk here."

"Very good, sir."

She set down the tray and looked over at him. He wished he'd pulled back the draperies so the sunlight filtered over her, and he could see her more clearly, but he concentrated better when no distractions hovered at the edge of his vision. He worked diligently to avoid anything that interfered with his focus. She was a distraction he didn't seem to mind.

"How do you take your tea, sir?"

"Prepare it however you enjoy it."

Her eyes widened slightly, not in alarm, but in surprise before she went about doing as he'd asked. He watched as milk and sugar—dear Lord, was that five lumps?—were added to the brew in the cup. She stirred gently, and he had the impression she was humming a little ditty in her head. She seemed at peace, content, and yet an alertness about her remained as though she was constantly gauging her surroundings, was aware of everything around her, and could probably even tell him how many ledgers were spread before him, as well as their contents.

After lifting the saucer upon which balanced the teacup, she glided over and set both on the corner of his desk. "Anything else, sir?"

"Yes. Is it Margaret, Marguerite, or Margarette?"

She went still, so visibly still, that he wasn't certain she even breathed.

"I beg your pardon?"

Interesting. The words came out crisp and demanding. The courteous, obliging servant had disappeared and before him now stood a woman who didn't like to be questioned. No, it was more than that. Wouldn't tolerate being questioned. "I doubt very much that your mother named you Daisy. Marguerite is French for daisy, and so I'm curious as to which version of the name she gave you."

Pressing her lips together, she studied him through narrowed eyes before giving a little nod. "Marguerite. She was French. My mother. She was the only one to call me Daisy, although recently I've begun using the moniker as a way to remember her."

"Was?"

A couple of quick, jerky nods. "She died when I was younger. As did my father. I was an orphan, raised by my father's spinster sister."

"My condolences on your loss."

She lifted a slender shoulder as though to shrug off his words. "It's been twenty years now. I've grown accustomed to their absence."

"We may adapt to their absence but that doesn't mean we don't still miss them."

"Your tone implies you speak from experience. Are you an orphan?"

"Not completely. But I did lose my mother when I was at a tender age." Still too young to have prevented the tragedy that befell her.

"I'm sorry."

He didn't know how to respond. He didn't usually tell people about his mother because he always felt a modicum of guilt that he'd not been able to save her. In spite of his youth, he should have been able to do *something.* Before he fell down that dark hole of regret, he reached for the cup, took a sip of the concoction, and returned the china to the saucer. "Oh, God, that's dreadful."

Her delicate brow furrowed. "Too much sugar or milk?"

"It's the tea. I've never fancied the bloody stuff."

"Then why did you ask that I bring it to you?"

"It's been a while since I've had any, and I thought to see if it's as appalling as I remember. It's more so." Why was he explaining himself? One didn't justify one's actions to servants. And did he have to sound so blasted chagrined?

"Oh, I see." She took a single step back, and he decided she really did see. It wasn't the tea he'd wanted but her presence.

"I'll also admit to finding you intriguing. Your diction is more suited to upstairs than down. You strike me as being too independent to take orders. You're accustomed to giving them."

"What makes you think that?"

"I'm not sure. You bring to mind a mine that is played out, but the owner is trying to sell it by insisting it is still of value." He shook his head. "No, that's not quite right. You're more like something of value striving to appear that it isn't. Which makes no sense. Yet still, I'd invest in you in a heartbeat."

"I can't decide if I've been complimented or insulted."

"There." He winked at her. "A servant wouldn't be so bold as to respond to what I said. Would have simply asked if I required anything else. Last night . . . you know your liquors. Most maids don't."

"How many maids have you had pour you a drink?"

He released a quick burst of laughter. "None."

"Therefore, you may be judging me by what you think a servant does rather than what one actually does."

"I grew up with servants."

"As did I."

"That does not surprise me. Why seek employment as one?"

She glanced around the room.

"I'll know if you're lying."

Her gaze came back to him and nearly skewered him. "Will you?"

He gave one brisk nod. "You don't have a face for playing cards. Your expressions are far too easy to read."

Her sigh of surrender would have lifted a kite and sent it soaring among the clouds. "My aunt gave me an ultimatum—marry or move out. I chose to move out. I needed a position quickly, and, well, some household is always in need of a servant."

"You could work as a governess. I would think that occupation would better suit you."

"With all due respect, sir, I don't believe you know me well enough to know what suits me."

I'd like to. But even as he had the thought, he squashed it. She was employed in his household, and he wasn't going to be like the man who'd raised him and cross those boundaries. He also had his scandalous reputation to contend with, which, until that moment, he'd never considered a burden, but it wasn't going to appeal to a woman such as she and would only serve to do what the gossip rags promised: bring her to ruination. While she might have the right of it and he didn't know what suited her, he did understand fully and completely that she was undeserving of a downfall, especially one at his hands. "You may take the tea."

"The inquisition is over?"

He grinned broadly. Damned, if he didn't like her. "A servant would never speak in such a condescending tone of voice to the master of the household."

"Seems I have a lot to learn." She took the saucer with its cup and gave a quick bob of a curtsy. "Good day, sir."

She deposited the china on the tray, picked it up, and began strolling from the room.

"Good day, Marguerite," he called out.

She stopped, held still for a heartbeat, two, before carrying on. He wondered what retort had been on the tip of her tongue. Probably *go to the devil*.

NEVER DO ANYTHING *to make him smile*.

Good God, but his grin had been devastating, had made him look unburdened, carefree, and fun. Had made her want to reach out and touch his mouth, his cheek, his jaw.

Then the way her Christian name had rolled off his tongue . . . She'd never liked Marguerite. It had seemed too pretentious, too large for the girl she'd been, but his deep voice had made it sound as though she fit it perfectly. She'd never be a great beauty like her mother but in that moment, she'd felt seen, appreciated, and lovely. And terrified because no man had ever made her feel as though he had a true interest in *her*, all of her, not just the shell that came with a dowry. Part of the reason she'd never felt she fitted properly within Society was because she wanted to be viewed as more than the overseer of a household and the bearer of children. Hence, much to her uncle's chagrin and her aunt's disappointment, she'd set up her own business rather than move about in their social circle of lords, ladies, and the elite.

She considered giving her notice to Perkins and then informing her client he needed to hire another sleuth. But she'd never been one to accept defeat, especially as a result of something as innocuous as feelings stirred to life by a brief meeting. Bishop's charm was such that she fully understood why women were falling into bed with him. But her moral fiber was such that even the thought of succumbing to his allure was revolting—or should have been. Instead, she wondered if he grinned at a woman while debauching her. She rather suspected he did, and it would be as intoxicating and pleasurable as the finest wine.

She also wondered why he went through lovers with the ease and frequency that most men changed shirts. Did he grow bored? Did he require a constant carousel of new ladies to hold his attention? Or did ill feelings arrive when the husbands sued him? Or perhaps the women were disappointed he'd not been discreet enough and their liaison had been discovered.

Not that any of it really mattered. The man was a devilishly handsome Lothario, and she would do well to remember that. No more fluttering heart, quivering stomach, or warmth whispering along her skin whenever she encountered him.

Still, as the days rushed toward that all-important Monday, she found herself hoping she'd run into him.

In one of the many hallways. Or in one of the chambers that she was tidying. From what she'd been able to gather, he spent most of his day and early evening in his library. Breakfast, luncheon, and dinner were all served to him on a tray delivered by a footman. She'd considered volunteering to handle the chore, but didn't need the distraction of him, and she was striving to be as unnoticed as possible. No one paid him a visit on Saturday or Sunday.

However, Sunday night from her bedchamber window, she caught sight of him strolling about the gardens, and she couldn't help but think that he struck her as a solitary, perhaps lonely, soul. She was unable to take her attention off him, even considered slipping out and joining him. Her curiosity regarding him seemed to know no bounds, even as she knew time spent in his company would come to no good. She had to remain impartial and distant because once she'd gathered her evidence, she would speak out against him in court. She couldn't experience any remorse at betraying him, and she wouldn't be riddled with guilt if they shared no confidences, if their relationship remained as it should: employer and employee.

Yet it seemed such an odd thing to see him wandering about alone when he had women aplenty seeking his company. She wondered if he was reminiscing about one of them, absurdly would have welcomed him ruminating about moments spent with her.

She was grateful when Monday finally arrived, heralding what could turn out to be her last day of mixed sentiments where Bishop was concerned. As usual, before a single ray of sunshine peered over the horizon, Mr. Perkins called the servants together in the room in which they took their meals so he could alert them to any additional requirements for the day. Daisy didn't see how another hour in bed would hurt. She was rather certain they'd still have plenty of time to get their chores done, and probably with a good deal more efficiency because they'd be bright-eyed with no cobwebs filling their heads. But the butler was a stickler for routine.

"All right then," he began, his tone stern and uncompromising. She wasn't certain he was capable of emitting a laugh or demonstrating a smile. "We have a busy day ahead of us. Following his dinner—as is his customary habit with a tray delivered to the library— the master will be enjoying the company of a friend. Mrs. Karson, he has asked for a platter of strawberries, a bowl of your chocolate glaze, and a few other sweets of your choosing, along with some cheeses, to be delivered to his bedchamber shortly after nine. Tom, you'll see to the delivery."

"Yes, sir," the footman answered sharply with military precision. Daisy was surprised he didn't salute.

"Today's flower is to be lilies and baby's breath. Sarah, ensure all is in order upstairs."

"I always do, sir."

He gave the tiniest of scowls before nodding. "Everyone else, carry on as usual. Remember, you are to clean without being seen."

As the servants began to scatter, Daisy was relatively certain Perkins had his final words embroidered on a framed sampler hanging over his bed, because he ended any directions or discussion with them. She followed Sarah to the linen cupboard and held out her arms for the fresh sheets the chambermaid handed to her.

"I was wondering," Daisy began hesitantly, "if the

lady tonight might be the one I saw on Friday when I delivered tea to the library. A Mrs. Mallard." Although she thought it unlikely. That woman had been fair and in no way resembled a raven.

"Ah, no," Sarah said, as she began marching up the back stairs. "Monday is Mrs. Parker."

Daisy's breath caught. "You know her name?"

"Yeah. Tom heard it once when he carried a tray into the bedchamber. He told me."

"Have you ever caught a glimpse of her?"

"No." She winked. "I clean without being seen."

Daisy smiled. "Perkins really does like saying that, doesn't he?"

"We're supposed to be quiet, unobtrusive. Lord of the manor isn't supposed to know he has servants, is he? We're like the cobbler's elves, aren't we, coming in and getting the job done, leaving people to think it's all magic? But he pays well, so I never complain. Although Tom does often enough."

"What has he to be unhappy about?" Daisy asked, well aware that crucial information could come from the most unexpected of places.

"He considers it beneath him to cart a tray about. Thinks it's a chore best handled by maids. He sees it as an absolute waste of his talents . . . as well as those strong muscles of his." She smiled sheepishly. "I can think of better uses for those lovely muscles."

"Such as?"

Sarah laughed lightly. "Carrying me up these stairs for starters."

At the landing, in front of a door, was a table. "Place the linens there," Sarah said. "We'll change Bishop's bed once he's up and about."

She opened the door that led into the wide and elaborate corridor of bedchambers. Daisy followed Sarah's lead, dusting and polishing and sweeping. She was gathering up the flowers in the vases that adorned several of the tables in the hallway when the door to his bedchamber opened and he stepped out. Halted. Stared at her.

But then she'd stopped as well. As had her lungs. She'd forgotten how devilishly handsome he was, dark hair, dark eyes, dark brows. She hadn't seen his valet go into the room. Did he even have one? However, he was freshly shaven and immaculately attired.

"Good morning, Marguerite."

Her arms full of wilting blossoms, she gave a quick bob. "Sir."

"You probably believe me to have an inordinate number of flowers in this residence."

"It does seem odd to have so many up here where few people see them."

"My mum loved flowers. When I was a lad, I'd help her plant them, water them, and keep the weeds away from them. Having the blossoms about reminds me of her. I suppose in a way they are a tribute to her."

"It's lovely that you have such a special memory."

"What of your mother? What did she like?"

With regret at having nothing to share, she shook her head. "I can't think of anything." Then something tickled the furthest recesses of her mind. "Singing perhaps. I remember her singing me a lullaby, something about angels guarding me all through the night. She had a lovely voice. I'd forgotten that." She hadn't many fond memories of the woman who'd given birth to her but didn't want to dwell on the reasons for their absence.

"We'll have to find a musician, see if perhaps he knows it and can give you the tune and lyrics. Do you play the pianoforte?"

"My aunt insisted I learn."

He smiled. And she wished he hadn't, because it was like the moon drawing the tide and she wanted to step nearer to him, to be within reach of his embrace. "I'll have to keep that in mind. Have a productive day."

Then he was loping down the steps as though late for an appointment, and she wondered why he would care at all if she knew how to guide her fingers over a keyboard.

"Clean without being seen," Sarah whispered harshly beside her, nearly causing Daisy to leap right out of her skin.

"What was I to do? Duck into a room?"

"You should have been listening for him. If he complains to Mr. Perkins—"

"He's not going to mention anything to the butler." She didn't know how she knew it, but she did. She also knew that no matter what servant he'd encountered, he wouldn't have been bothered enough to tell anyone.

"You finish with the flowers," Sarah ordered. "I'll see to his chamber. As he had no guest last night, it won't need much tidying today."

As the chambermaid disappeared into the room, Daisy wondered how it was that a man who seemed to idolize his mother could treat women as playthings and couldn't be satisfied with only one.

CHAPTER 3

⤳⤳⧢⧢

$\mathcal{T}$HE advantage to the tryst beginning at nine was that Perkins had dismissed all the servants for the night, except for the cook and Tom. While Daisy knew she was expected to trot off to her room, she'd found an excuse to linger in the kitchen, claiming a megrim and sipping on the Earl Grey, in which Cook had added a powder she guaranteed would cause her pains to melt away.

Leaning against the counter, she watched as Mrs. Karson arranged the tray on the worktable while Tom sat at the far end of it, engrossed in reading *David Copperfield*.

"Everything is laid out so beautifully," Daisy told the cook. The strawberries, stems removed, were arranged in a circle around a porcelain bowl filled with a chocolate glaze. Little tea cakes were lined up like soldiers down the center of the tray. On the other side were scattered small chunks of cheese. Everything was designed to be eaten with fingers. No cutlery needed for any of it. "You're practically an artist with your creation."

With a blush rising in her cheeks, the cook glanced over at her. "Thanks, ducky. I've always believed food should look appealing, and I suspect he'll be feeding all the nibbles to his guest himself."

Daisy's cheeks warmed as she envisioned the intimacy of such an action and wondered if he'd do it in bed. "It's a shame for them to mess it up by eating any of it."

"No shame to it at all. It'll please me if they gobble up every last bit after my going to such bother."

Mr. Perkins suddenly strode into the room. "She's here. He took her upstairs straightaway."

The massive foyer didn't provide any hiding places, and Daisy hadn't been able to determine how to get a good look as the woman entered the residence. Spotting Blue-Eyes had been serendipitous because Daisy had been sent to light a fire in the parlor, but no such chore that would place her in the right spot at the right time had been given to her that evening.

"Very good," Mrs. Karson said. "I'm almost done here."

"I'm off to take up the wine." He disappeared.

"It's quite a production when he has a guest," Daisy said.

"You don't know the half of it," Mrs. Karson muttered.

"Does a maid assist her . . . afterward?"

"No. I reckon he sees to the matter himself, putting her back to rights."

"Does she stay all night?"

Turning slightly, with her hands on her hips, the cook scowled. "You've a lot of questions."

"I've never been employed in a residence where such goings-on took place. Or if they did, people were much more discreet."

"What goes on upstairs is none of our concern. You keep it to yourself, or you'll find yourself let go without a reference."

"I completely understand that. I was just curious as to whether she'd be there in the morning when Sarah and I begin our chores and how it might affect them. I suppose I should simply ask Sarah."

Cook turned back to her work. "She'll be gone long before then. He usually escorts them home before midnight."

Perhaps she could stand on the front lawn behind a tree and catch sight of the woman then. But in the dark, how clear might she be? Even with the lamplights along the drive, Daisy might have difficulty identifying her.

Mrs. Karson stepped back. "There it is, Tom, all ready for you."

He looked up from his book and studied the clock on a shelf. It showed a couple of minutes past nine. "Bit early yet. He likes it delivered at a quarter past." He turned his attention back to the story.

"I'd be willing to carry it up," Daisy offered.

Cook's brow furrowed. "What of your aching head?"

She lifted the teacup. "It's much better now, thanks to your marvelous concoction."

"You should get to bed then. It's Tom's job to deliver it."

"I don't mind."

"To bed with you."

Disappointed, knowing she would raise suspicions if she argued further, she set the cup aside. "Pleasant dreams."

But when she was out of the kitchen, rather than

going to the stairs that led to the servants' quarters, she went to the back stairs she knew Tom would use to reach the bedchamber hallway. And waited.

She wanted, needed, to see the woman in order to verify that it was *her* Mrs. Parker, her client's Mrs. Parker. He'd given her a small photograph of his wife so Daisy could recognize her, but the challenge was to get a clear enough glimpse so she could identify her. Parker was too common a name, so she couldn't assume the guest was the correct one.

A short time later, she heard footfalls and smiled at Tom when he came around the corner. "You looked to be enjoying your book and are probably anxious to get back to it. I'm happy to deliver the tray for you."

He glanced back over his shoulder, as though fearing being caught doing what he ought not, and then returned his attention to her. "It is a good read but—"

Wanting to cut off his rejection before he voiced it, she reached out and squeezed his upper arm. "Truth be told, Tom, it seems like such a menial task for a man as strong as you. I've never felt muscles so firm." She batted her eyelashes, something she'd never done before because she considered it a ridiculous flirtation maneuver, but Tom fairly preened with her praise.

"'Tis a waste of me abilities."

She released her hold on him. "I so agree. It's a shame you have to spend your time doing something that is more suited to a woman." A wink. A lift of her shoulder. "Let me handle this for you, so you can attend to more important matters. Like your book."

"Perkins won't like it."

"I'm not going to tell him. And Bishop certainly won't mind. His attention is no doubt on his lover.

What does he care who brings up the tray as long as it's brought?"

He furrowed his brow. "Are you sure you don't mind?"

"Not at all. I so hate seeing you not being fully appreciated. As I'm new to the household, a chore so inconsequential really should fall to me, not to a strapping, competent lad like yourself."

With his chest puffing out at her latest bit of fawning, she was surprised his waistcoat buttons didn't suddenly pop off. "Right you are. The task is simple enough. Just knock on the door, take it in, and leave."

Excitement thrummed through her as he transferred the tray. It had been far too easy to get him to relinquish the chore, but since her arrival he'd struck her as the sort willing to do as little as possible and based upon what Sarah had shared that morning, she'd hoped he'd prove to be a fool for flattery.

She headed up the stairs, clearing her mind of everything but the image of Mrs. Parker in the photograph. A narrow face. Sharp chin. Black hair, according to her husband, as well as brown eyes. Her nose tipped slightly on the end, as though as a child, she'd kept it pressed against a toyshop window, longing for what was inside. Although perhaps Daisy was merely recalling her own childhood, of wishing for things that always seemed beyond reach. Before she could travel that path, she refocused on tonight's goal.

She arrived at the landing where that morning she'd laid the linens, linens that were now spread out over his bed. Where presently the couple might be cavorting. She carried on down the hall and rapped on the door.

"Come."

That deep, resounding voice sent what felt like little bubbles of pleasure cascading through her. Taking a deep breath, she regained her focus.

Shifting the tray slightly, she used her smallest finger to turn the latch. It put a painful strain on her hand. The things servants endured. She'd never take staff for granted again. The door finally clicked. She pushed it open and stepped into the room.

Lounging on a settee, he wore only boots, trousers, and shirtsleeves, the buttons undone to the middle of his chest, the parted linen revealing flesh and a scattering of dark, springy hair. She was so surprised by the sight of him practically naked that she nearly didn't notice the woman he was easing off his lap. When he was free of the lady, he shot to his feet. "Where's Tom?"

"Oh . . . uh." She'd never seen so much of a man bared before. Her fingers wanted to touch, to glide from the dip at his throat all the way down to the secured button. Perhaps give it its freedom and travel farther. He seemed more muscled and toned than Tom, and she had an inclination to put her theory to the test and squeeze his upper arms. Unfortunately, she feared she wouldn't be able to stop there, but would want to explore the entire landscape of him. "He was indisposed, had something important to attend to. Where shall I place the tray?"

Her voice sounded like it was coming from a great distance, each word a struggle to push out. It didn't even sound like her. It was more of a rasp, as though she'd gone her entire life without swallowing a single drop of water.

"I'll take it." He strode over. He had such long strides. Had she noticed that before? He placed his hands—large hands, strong with thick, blunt-tipped fingers, the nails evenly trimmed—on the tray and gave a little tug. "Release it."

"Right."

His lips twisted slightly as though he knew she was flummoxed and he found her reaction amusing. He walked over to a small, low oblong table near the wall, set down the tray, picked up a strawberry, and dipped it into the chocolate glaze. Holding it over his cupped hand, he walked—no, it wasn't a walk, it was a prowl, slow and leisurely like a predator on the hunt—to the woman and offered it to her, touching the tip of it to her red lips. Gazing at him adoringly, she took a bite. The smile he bestowed upon her was filled with wicked promises. Then he tossed the last bit of strawberry into his own roguishly luscious mouth. Should a man's lips be so full and tempting? After chewing and swallowing, he licked from his palm the chocolate that had dripped onto it.

Daisy had a strong urge to stop him, to lick it for him. Whatever was wrong with her? She never had these sorts of scandalous thoughts. But then she'd never been in a bedchamber with a half-clad gent before.

That indecently attired man, his eyes smoldering, directed his attention to her like a fine-honed blade. "That'll be all. Close the door on your way out."

After giving a jerky nod, she rushed from the room, hating that the door practically slammed shut behind her. It was only when she reached the stairs that she realized she hadn't even bothered to catalog enough of the woman's features in order to recall exactly what she looked like.

Damn him for distracting her, for making her knees so weak she had to sit on the top step and gather her wits about her. She couldn't very well barge back in there. By now, more clothing had probably been discarded.

With a deep sigh, she shoved herself to her feet. It seemed she was going to be spending the remainder of her evening outside, waiting to catch a glimpse of the woman as she was leaving.

BLOODY DAMNED HELL. He didn't know why in the devil it bothered him that Marguerite had come into his chamber and seen him with Louisa Parker sprawled all over him like a feline lazing in the sun. He made no secret that he entertained women in here. However, for the first time, he'd been embarrassed and experienced a bit of the shame his father had berated him for not experiencing.

It was simply the shock of her arrival. He'd been expecting Tom, had needed it to be Tom, had arranged the tableau for Tom to witness. He didn't want to put Marguerite through the torment of being a witness at a divorce trial where she'd be interrogated without mercy regarding what she'd seen and heard.

"Who was she?" Louisa asked demurely.

He shook his head. "Simply a servant."

"If we were truly having an affair, I do believe I'd be jealous by the manner in which you looked at her, as though you longed to lap her up, like a cat does cream."

Waving her off, he tossed back the wine Perkins

had poured earlier and refilled his glass—although he was very tempted to switch to scotch. He needed something stronger, something that burned, warmed, and could make one forget more swiftly. "It was all merely performance. As you're well aware, within this chamber, you and I are actors upon a stage."

Only he'd been incredibly tempted to carry the strawberry to Marguerite, place the succulent fruit between her succulent lips, and watch her bite into it while he imagined she was instead nipping at his throat. "Although she wasn't the expected party, the show must go on, and hopefully she'll be tittering about what she saw to the other servants."

Except she didn't strike him as a titterer. She appeared to be someone of honor who held secrets close. As closely as he did. He glanced over at his guest. "More wine?"

She lifted her nearly full glass. "I've barely touched this."

As she took a sip, he strode over and dropped into the thickly padded dark blue velveteen chair across from the settee where she sat. "I missed our time together last Monday. How went the visit with your mother?"

"It was exceedingly trying. She spoke of all sorts of remedies to get with child—placing an egg beneath my pillow of all things, if you can imagine. I couldn't tell her that I can't get with child if my husband never visits my bed, if I've become so abhorrent to his sensibilities that he'll barely look at me. He pays me no attention at all. If he suspects I'm involved with someone else, he's given no indication. It's been two months. I thought by now . . ." Her voice trailed off as she directed her attention to the hearth where a low fire crackled.

"Perhaps we've been too discreet. We may have to do something publicly."

Her gaze jumped back to him. "Such as?"

"Attend the theater, cross paths at a museum. Go someplace where more than my servants become aware that we enjoy each other's company."

"Do we?" she asked. "Do we enjoy each other's company?"

It wasn't unusual for the women who came to him to need reassurances, reassurances they never received from their husbands. "I look forward to the time I spend with you."

"I daresay only because you often thrash me at cards."

"I do have a competitive streak I'm afraid."

She tapped her wineglass. "Let's wait a bit longer before doing anything away from here. I realize to secure the outcome I want, my behavior will be questioned and probably written about in the newspapers and scandal sheets, but I'd still prefer to have as few witnesses as possible, to embarrass Martin as little as needed."

"As you wish." He shook his head. "Has he even noticed your absences or commented on them?"

"He's usually at his office when I leave the residence, abed when I return. The few times he has been home, I've told him I'm going to visit a friend. He merely grunts. But then that is his response to anything I say." Her gaze drifted back to the fire. "Marriage to him has become so deuced lonely."

"We'll give it one more month, and then, if necessary, we'll make our affair very visible to one and all."

Her smile was angelic. "I feel for all the women who won't benefit from your kindness once you marry."

Sputtering on his wine, he nearly choked in the process. "I've no plans to marry."

"Whyever not?"

"I should think your experience would be explanation enough."

"We did not marry for love. You could."

"Why would any woman in her right mind want to marry a man with my reputation?"

"You could claim to have reformed, just for her. Her love or yours for her transformed you. The gossips would eat it up."

He shook his head. "I have no interest in love." It had killed his mother.

CHAPTER 4

⁓⁓⁓

$\mathscr{T}$HE call to rise came far too early for Daisy. She had managed to sneak out and hide behind some bushes on the front lawn, where the chill of the night air had caused her to shiver and her teeth to clatter. All for naught. When the woman had finally emerged, Bishop had been beside her, positioned in such a way that his broad shoulders and bent head as he spoke to her made it impossible for Daisy to get a good look at his guest's features.

While she was aching and sore from last night's stalking—and was having a difficult time understanding why anyone went hunting and voluntarily subjected themselves to such torment—she knew she'd remain in this employ for at least another week.

After the morning meeting with Perkins, she trudged up the stairs behind Sarah, dreading another morning of dusting and polishing. Truly how much dust could have accumulated since the day before? And apparently all the lilies needed to be done away with and replaced with peonies because supposedly they were Mrs. Mallard's favorite. The woman, apparently a new addition to his harem, was coming this evening. She hadn't been inscribed in his appointment diary, but Daisy assumed he'd not yet had an opportunity to scrawl in her name—or whatever word he'd used to notate her. She was half-tempted to sneak into the library when he wasn't about to see what moniker he'd come up with for the lady. She didn't much like that she wondered what term he might use to describe her.

She'd gathered up half the lilies when she heard the click of his door opening and ducked into the nearby bedchamber, like a coward, because she didn't want to see how he looked after a night of debauchery. She also feared that a reminder of what she'd witnessed might cause her to blush uncontrollably, and she had no desire for him to know he had any effect on her at all. His footfalls faded away as he descended the stairs.

Carrying her basket of supplies, fresh linens stacked atop it, Sarah wandered by and then backed up and peered into the room. "What are you doing in there?"

"Clean but not be seen?"

The chambermaid pursed her lips and rolled her eyes, and Daisy hoped the maid didn't discern the true reason for her hiding. "He's left his bedchamber, so we need to get to it. Set those down and we'll finish up with the flowers later. Come on then."

Daisy wanted to finish with the blossoms now, not see his chamber in whatever disarray he'd left it after cavorting about, but as the newest member of the staff, she had no say in what she was supposed to do. Therefore, she set the lilies aside and followed Sarah into his private domain. Her gaze immediately jumped to the bed. She'd expected tangled sheets. But the arrangement of the covers was no wilder than hers upon first awakening. One pillow had an indention in it, no doubt where he'd rested his head. The other looked untouched. Had the woman placed her head on his chest? Had she fallen asleep there before he'd escorted her home?

The room smelled rather fresh. She could detect his bergamot and orange scent mixed with a lighter fragrance of lavender, his lady friend's perfume. She'd expected a darker aroma, one generated by entangled bodies lost to the throes of passion.

Sarah began stripping the bed. "Will you see to the table?"

Daisy turned. The table that had been against a wall last night had been moved so it was now situated between the settee and a wingback chair. The tray was off to the side, devoid of food, but scattered over the fine woodgrain of the table were cards. They befuddled her.

"What you be staring at?" Sarah asked.

"I wasn't expecting playing cards."

"There's usually some on the table the morning after he's had company. Cook reckons they play a naughty game. Like whoever loses a round has to maybe reveal a secret or remove a bit of clothing."

"Considering how many layers a lady wears that could take all night." In addition, it hardly seemed fair to him when he'd been outfitted in so little. He'd be nude long before his company, although perhaps he didn't mind strutting about stark naked. He hadn't bothered refastening his buttons when she'd walked in.

Sarah shrugged. "Builds up the anticipation Cook

says. Don't want to get at things too quickly. You ever had a man?"

Feeling herself blush at such an intimate question, she shook her head. "No. Have you?"

"No. I was raised to be a good girl. But I rather fancy Tom and sometimes I get all warm and tingly just looking at him."

"He is rather handsome."

Sarah's brow furrowed. "Do you fancy him, then?"

"Oh, no. He doesn't make me grow warm in the least." Not even when she'd squeezed his upper arm. She could have been testing the ripeness of a melon for all the joy it had given her. Bishop, on the other hand . . .

Why would she have to be enamored of a scapegrace? Possibly it was because he *was* a scapegrace that he appealed to her. Perhaps she was like her mother, falling for the wrong sort of man, someone who would lead her to ruin. She didn't want to be like the woman who'd given birth to her, but rather she yearned to be like the one who'd raised her. God-fearing, law-abiding, boring.

Although being an inquiry agent certainly wasn't boring. Conceivably that was one of the reasons she'd chosen this path. However, when it came to men, the duller the better. Bishop was anything but mind-numbing. Yet, they'd taken time to engage in a mundane activity. "Does he play cards with all the ladies?"

Again, Sarah shrugged her slender shoulders. "It's usually chess with Mrs. Bowles. She's his Wednesday appointment." *Blue-Eyes.* "Then he played backgammon with one of them last year. Cribbage board has been out a time or two." She pointed toward a credenza upon which rested several decanters. "Store the cards in there."

While Sarah went back to taking care of the bed, Daisy stacked the cards before placing them in the hinged gold filigree case that had been placed next to the tray. She carried it over to the small cupboard, pulled open the door, and was astonished to see several card cases as well as a variety of larger wooden boxes, some with gilt lettering visible on the side to identify them as various games. Were they all part of his seduction? She couldn't imagine that he needed anything other than himself. Then she chastised herself for the thought.

Somehow, he'd managed to capture her interest—and as more than the dastardly man leading women to ruin. She wanted him filling his residence with her favorite flower. Wanted him to serve up her favorite sweet. Wanted him engaging her in a strategic game that she would lose, but in the losing would win. Because her clothes would be pooled at his feet and from there—

Her head grew light, and she swayed, nearly toppling into the games stacked so neatly. With a measure of shame, she realized she'd stopped breathing as though waiting in anticipation for everything she'd been imagining to occur. The lady last night hadn't looked in need of smelling salts. But how could she not when she'd been cradled on his lap, her fingers so close to that bare skin and those fine hairs?

"Caw, are you ill?" Sarah was suddenly at her side,

her brow furrowed so deeply she'd no doubt have permanent wrinkles when she finally relaxed it.

"I simply lost my balance for a minute." She shoved herself to standing, glad the explanation had been enough to ease the concern in the chambermaid's eyes. "Honestly, I'm fine. I'll tend to cleaning out the fireplace."

As she began the task, she gave herself a stern lecture. She needed to keep her wits about her if she had any hope at all of being successful and providing her most recent client with all he required and expected. Even if it meant dragging Bishop through the mud.

BISHOP DIDN'T USUALLY awaken in a foul mood, but this morning he'd definitely gotten up on the wrong side of the bed. He actually enjoyed Louisa Parker's company, and under different circumstances, they'd be friends. But he was more than ready for the game they played to come to an end, especially after Marguerite had walked in on them last night. When he'd delivered Louisa to her residence, he'd very nearly gone inside with her, pounded his fist on the door to her husband's bedchamber, and yelled, "I'm having a bloody affair with your wife! Pay some attention, man!" But it was his very lack of paying attention that had brought her to Bishop to begin with.

No, his upset wasn't because it was taking so long to assist Louisa in obtaining the divorce she craved. His ill humor was the result of the shock on Marguerite's face. He hadn't spied her this morning when he'd left his bedchamber. However, he'd been tempted to peer into all the other rooms to see if she was about, because he could have sworn that he'd caught a faint wisp of violets when he'd stepped into the hallway.

Sitting at his desk now, he considered calling for her and confessing that it hadn't been as it had appeared. But he couldn't risk anyone else knowing. Nor could he risk her testifying because of happenstance and wielding the truth in a courtroom.

He heard the heavier footsteps coming down the hall and knew it wasn't her delivering his morning tray, and he was hit with both relief and disappointment.

Tom strode in, set the wooden tray on the corner of the desk, raised the sterling pitcher, and carefully poured the black coffee into the cup. With a flourish, he then lifted the silver dome covering the plate to reveal a poached egg atop a buttered muffin. A bowl of fruit rested nearby as did a small platter of bacon and ham. A scone and the honeypot. A thin crystal vase holding a single violet also sat on the tray.

When Tom had everything arranged to his satisfaction, he stepped back. "Will there be anything else, sir?"

"Yes, Tom, actually." He didn't miss the flash of concern in the young footman's eyes, and he realized the words had come out a tad more curtly than he'd intended. He'd learned early on that the servants apparently lived to please him, which was something he'd never anticipated. While he wasn't of the nobility, the fullness of his coffers was no secret, and prestige was to be found in serving a man who could pay as well as he did, along with shame in being let go. He attempted to make his tone more conciliatory. "In the future, when you have a pressing engagement and are unavailable to bring a tray to my bedchamber when I have a guest, please see the task handed off to another footman and not one of the maids."

Tom looked as though he'd been bludgeoned. "Yes, sir. Sorry, sir. It wasn't an important matter, to be honest. It was just that Daisy was so keen to do it . . . she'd offered, and Cook had told her no, sent her to bed, but she was waiting on the stairs . . . and so eager to take it up, could tell I was anxious to get back to *David Copperfield*. I didn't see how there'd be any harm in making her happy. It won't happen again, sir."

Bishop held up a finger. "Wait. You were not indisposed?"

"No, sir, not in the least. But she was there—"

"Wanting to take on the chore. Rather than being done with her duties for the day."

Tom's brow furrowed and he seemed lost. "It does seem a bit odd . . . now that I think about it. Especially as she'd complained of a megrim earlier, was in the kitchen sipping tea because of it."

Bishop tapped his fingers on his desktop. Why would a maid who began her day before the sun came up not relish an opportunity to retire as soon as possible? Perhaps she simply wanted to make a good impression. Yet still he found it peculiar, especially as she had to be aware of the supposed reason behind the lady's visit. Was she merely curious? Or had she an interest in naughtiness? Was she not as innocent as he'd determined? Or could her reason for being here have something to do with his ladies? "I shan't report to Perkins what occurred last night but do keep this conversation strictly between us."

"Yes, sir. Thank you, sir."

Bishop picked up his cup of coffee. "Oh, and when you return downstairs, let Perkins know I need a word."

"Yes, sir."

He'd never known the footman to make such a hasty exit. By the time his butler arrived, Bishop had finished his breakfast and was standing by the window, gazing out on the gardens, drinking another cup of black coffee.

"You needed me, sir?" Perkins asked.

Bishop turned from the window. "How is it that you came to hire Daisy?"

"Have you found her unsatisfactory?"

"No, but I'm curious."

"Well, sir, one of the maids, Annie, had given notice but coincidentally, and to my good fortune, she had a cousin looking for employment and she arrived the following day for an interview."

"You didn't go through an agency to hire her?"

"I didn't see the point. She had a first-rate letter of reference from the Earl of Bellingham—"

"What sort of letter of reference?"

Perkins looked taken aback as though he'd asked him something everyone knew—like the color of the sun. "Regarding the duties she performed in his residence and how she excelled at them."

When Bishop had spoken with her, he'd come away with the understanding that the position in his household was the first she'd ever held. Had she misled him? Had he misunderstood? Or had she lied to Perkins? "How long had she worked in his household?"

"Two years."

My aunt gave me an ultimatum: marry or move

out. I chose to move out. I needed a position quickly, and, well, some household is always in need of a servant.

He supposed the ultimatum could have come two years ago. But during that time wouldn't she have become more *servant-like*? Had her words to him been a lie, conjured on the spur of the moment because he'd asked a question Perkins hadn't? "Bellingham has a spinster sister, does he not?"

"I've no earthly idea."

"Not important." However, he would ask King as he would know for certain, might even be able to confirm if she'd raised an orphaned niece. If Bellingham was her uncle, had she coerced a false letter of reference out of him? For what purpose? Why did she want to work here? "But she came with a letter of reference."

"Indeed. I was quite impressed with the praise showered upon her."

"Did you ask why she gave up her position in the household of an earl to work in one of a rapscallion? Or had she been let go?"

"She left willingly, out of boredom apparently. The earl has so much staff that she seldom was occupied with chores as she was quite efficient at completing them. She was searching for a position that offered more of a challenge."

"How is cleaning bedchambers more of a challenge? What did she do at Bellingham's? Sweep steps?"

"Scullery maid. Apparently, she has designs on rising to the level of head housekeeper, so she wants to learn all positions."

He could certainly envision Marguerite as being ambitious, yet still something didn't quite add up. Inconsistences abounded, in her story, in her. "Have you found her to be quite efficient?"

"I have, sir. As well as being rather industrious. Never complains. She's always offering to take on other duties. Tidying about in here, for example."

He thought he'd detected a slight rearrangement of his appointment diary. But why would she care about his schedule? An unsettling yet welcome notion began to take hold. Was it possible Louisa Parker's husband had indeed noticed her absence in the evenings and had hired Marguerite to gather proof of his wife's infidelity? Or perhaps it was Mrs. Bowles's spouse who'd become suspicious. Had Marguerite been anxious to bring up the tray last night because she'd needed to see exactly who was in his bedchamber? Was she an inquiry agent, here under false presences to gather evidence? He could certainly envision her in that role more easily than he could that of a servant. "Very good, then, Perkins. Carry on."

He was halfway to facing the window when he spun back around. "Perkins."

His butler halted near the doorway. "Sir."

"From now on, have Daisy deliver the trays to my bedchamber when I have company."

Perkins gave a brisk nod. "As you wish."

Turning back to the window, Bishop felt a great deal of satisfaction. One of his ladies would soon be on her way to a divorce if he was correct about Marguerite, if she was, in fact, as he suspected, a sleuth hired by a distrustful husband to get at the truth regarding his wife's absences. Perhaps she wasn't quite as easy to read as he'd thought. He had to admire her for possibly being incredibly conniving, but then so was he.

And if he was wrong, where was the harm? She was hiding something. He'd wager all he possessed on that. He was quite looking forward to discovering the truth of her. He was known for being willing to do anything to win a game. He intended to be victorious at this one as well.

CHAPTER 5

DAISY couldn't believe her good fortune. She'd been given the chore of carting up the evening tray because Perkins had heard it was something she wanted to do and he'd grown tired of Tom grumbling about it.

Tuesday night, carrying out her new duty, she was surprised to discover Bishop sitting opposite Mrs. Mallard, who was perched on the edge of the settee as though she wanted to slide into a pond and paddle away. Unlike Mrs. Parker, who'd worn a gown that bared her shoulders, she was buttoned up tight as a drum, with only the skin of her throat and face exposed. Daisy was astonished the woman would be so nervous around her lover, barely lifting her eyes from her gloved hands clasped in her lap. She was also taken aback by Bishop tracking Daisy's movements to the table, his gaze a continual caress along her neck.

She set down the tray with an unsteady hand, grateful no china sat upon it to rattle and alert him that she was very much aware of his presence. Of course, it dominated the chamber, but more it seemed to dominate her, to envelop her in a comforting embrace, while at the same time stirring to life embers of passion that caused those warm and tingly sensations, the ones Sarah had mentioned she experienced when looking at Tom, to ripple through her. Blast him for having that effect upon her. She refused to become one of those ninnies who fell at his feet or into his bed with the crook of his finger.

"Will there be anything else?" She was incredibly proud of her voice for not warbling, of her breath for not sliding out on a sigh.

"Not tonight."

Another night then? Her mind had become frightfully inconvenient, popping thoughts into her head that had no place being there. It was the heat in his eyes that conjured up images of naked, entwined bodies lost to rapture, like those she'd seen in paintings at the National Gallery.

With a brisk nod and a quick look at his guest, who seemed far too shy for a man such as Bishop, Daisy walked briskly out of the room. She couldn't fathom what aspect of Mrs. Mallard appealed to him. He required someone bold, defiant, and interesting. A woman who would lounge upon his lap as Mrs. Parker had done. Perhaps he enjoyed a variation in his encounters, and she wondered if it ever crossed his mind that she would provide a different experience.

Wednesday night she discovered that he no doubt did worship the notion that variety was the spice of life, because when she reached the door to his bedchamber, she heard laughter coming from the room, his deep and joyful mingling with a lighter more carefree mirth. She didn't much like the little spark of jealousy that erupted because he was so enjoying his latest paramour. In addition, she found being privy to the sound felt intrusive and prying, more so than walking in to see a woman draped over his lap.

"You are such a scamp," a feminine voice sang out. "I hardly know what to do with you."

"Oh, I think you know very well what to do with me."

Before they could begin doing anything with each other, she knocked smartly on wood.

"Enter."

She was becoming skilled at balancing the tray while releasing the latch. Although tempted to peer around the door to ensure she wasn't going to blush deep red, she carried on through because she didn't want to give him the satisfaction of knowing that he could affect her in any manner.

The couple sat on the settee, one at each end, but they were angled so they faced each other. His arm rested along the back, his fingers hanging down and trailing over her bare upper arm, up and down, lazily circling. It wouldn't take any effort at all for the woman, who sported a few strands of silver at her temples that stood out in stark relief to the auburn elsewhere, to slide up right against him and fit herself into the beguiling nook his posture provided. If Daisy had to guess, she'd put the strumpet at forty, if not a tad older. It seemed Bishop sampled all variations when it came to harlots.

"What temptations have you brought us?" the tart asked her with a bright smile.

"Am I not temptation enough, Chastity?" he asked.

Chastity? Good Lord, was there any woman with a more inappropriate name?

"Of course, you are, darling." With a heavily bejeweled hand, she patted the empty space on the cushion between them. "Why don't you place it here?"

Daisy glanced at him to see that amused smile that he wore far too often when she was in this chamber, but in his eyes, she saw the dare: Will you come this close?

Yes, damn you, yes, I will.

She marched forward like a condemned woman on her way to the scaffold, her nerves atwitter. He was once again in shirtsleeves, this time with the sleeves rolled up past his elbows, his muscular forearms on display, the hair thick and enticing. Her mouth went dry. When she lowered herself to set down the tray, she caught a peek inside his shirt, where it billowed out slightly, and saw the dark brown disk—

At the unexpected, intimate view of his nipple, she straightened so quickly that she tottered. With one smooth unfettered motion, he immediately grabbed her upper arm, while pushing himself to his feet and pulling her against his firm body to steady her. "Are you all right?"

Nodding jerkily, she stared at her hand that had come to rest against that tantalizing V. His skin was so hot, the hairs coiling around her fingers so soft. She wanted to stroke his sternum, slide her hand along what was covered by linen.

With regret, she moved her troublesome appendage away before it could engage in any wickedness—wondering why she felt as though she'd lost something precious—stepped back, and shifted her attention to where his large hand was still folded around her slender arm. Slowly his fingers spread wide, and she was free, and yet there was such exquisite joy in being his captive.

His fingers curling into a fist, he dropped it to his side. "That'll be all."

His voice was rough and raw, and she wondered if perhaps she wasn't the only one affected by their nearness to each other. She held her tongue, fearing this time she would sound breathless. She took two steps back, hit the chair across from the settee, and wobbled. When he made a swift movement to jump into action, she quickly raised her hand, palm out, to balance herself and stop him from reaching for her. Edging her way around the side and clearing the furniture, she spun on her heel and headed for the door. It took everything within her not to glance back, not to take one more look at him. Because the very last thing she wanted to see was another woman shoving a grape into his lush mouth.

BISHOP LOOKED DOWN at his chest, surprised not to find the outline of Marguerite's palm burned into his flesh. When she'd begun to remove her hand from where it had landed, he had summoned up every ounce of will-power he possessed not to press his free hand over hers and keep it in place, connecting her to him. His heart had thudded so hard that she had to have felt it against her fingertips.

He would have wagered all he possessed that she'd been as affected as he. The black pupils of her eyes had enlarged until they'd very nearly devoured the blue. Her lips had parted as though in wonder, and he'd wanted to dip his head and take possession of that luscious mouth that haunted his dreams. He was still experiencing the tremors from the force required not to do so.

How was it that she had such power over him? No woman had ever captured his attention as she did. It was ludicrous to have any interest in her at all when she was possibly here to gather information on him. Even though he wanted her to collect it because it would lead to him accomplishing his goal of liberating a woman from an unwanted husband, he was left with the impression he wasn't going to come out the winner. That the reputation he'd cultivated so carefully was about to bite him on the arse.

He needed to lower himself into a tub of cold water in order to regain his senses. But he had a visitor in need of tending, someone with whom he enjoyed spending time, her humor and ease making her a delightful companion. He turned to her now. "Where were we?"

"You were telling me how much you enjoyed goading a friend into realizing he was in love with his secretary."

"Ah, yes." King and the once Penelope Pettypeace, now the Duchess of Kingsland.

"You weren't very kind to flirt with her in order to make him jealous."

As he rejoined her on the settee, he chuckled, remembering the incident that had happened during a dinner at the start of last summer. "For a moment there, I feared I'd misjudged what his reaction might be, and he was going to plow a fist into my jaw."

"How did you know he loved her?"

"He looked at her as though she hung the moon and stars."

"Much in the same way that you looked at the maid, just then."

He glowered. "I see what you're trying to do there, to tease me as I teased him."

She smiled. "Not really. To be honest, you appeared besotted."

He picked up a grape, tossed it into his mouth, chewed, and swallowed. "I did not." His tone sounded grumpy and defensive and served to widen her smile. "I barely know her."

He knew only that she was an orphan, raised by an aunt. He'd not yet had a chance to ask King about Bellingham. He also knew that she had to be smart and cunning if she was indeed an inquiry agent. Skilled at assessing situations. Courageous, because she could place herself in danger. A cold chill skittered down his spine as he wondered if she ever did get herself into perilous situations. Additional questions surfaced: How long had she been at the trade? How did she come to be in it? Why this particular avenue of employment?

"She's rather comely," Chastity said slyly. "This Daisy you were telling me about."

Earlier he'd explained his suspicions regarding the reasons for Marguerite's appearance in his household, even if he couldn't quite bring himself to reveal the name that seemed to suit her better. It was the name he used for her, and it somehow seemed personal and private. "As you are well aware, she quite possibly seeks to see me ruined."

"Maybe she wouldn't if she knew you better."

He shook his head. "I need her to want to ensure I pay for perceived sins. Could be your husband who hired her."

"No, Francis doesn't give women enough credit to hire one for so important a matter as proving the infidelity of his wife. I daresay I look forward to the day when I am no longer about, and he discovers exactly how much I managed. His household, his business, and his life are going to fall apart. I shall laugh until my sides ache."

He grinned. "You're a vindictive wench."

"Don't I half know it. You should also be aware that tonight I'm out for revenge and intend to give you a sound thrashing at cribbage."

"Challenge accepted." He got up to retrieve the board and cards. He wondered if Marguerite played, if she might threaten him with dire consequences if he lost. If those dire consequences happened in his bed, he'd gladly pay the price.

CHAPTER 6

⤞⤝

Sunday arrived. Every servant was granted the full day off. Daisy wondered who would see after Bishop's needs and had considered volunteering to stay behind, but she'd been unable to get the feel of his chest off her hand—no matter how many times she scrubbed at it—and had decided that she needed some time away to regain her bearings. She'd not seen him since he'd come to her rescue. She wasn't quite certain that she wouldn't have been better served if she'd suffered the humiliation of landing unceremoniously on her backside. He could have laughed uproariously. She could have despised him for it, and she would have redoubled her efforts and found increased satisfaction in seeing him brought to task.

Instead, he occupied her mind in ways he shouldn't. His strong hand clutching her arm. Fingers tucking up her chin. Mouth lowering to hers. She was supposed to be impartial, was meant to have her client's best interest at heart. Prove Bishop's culpability. State clearly and concisely his guilt. She'd begun to doubt her purpose, and that would not do.

She had managed to slip into his library and glance through his diary. He had no appointments on Sunday, no indication that any woman would call upon him. Raven was again marked for an appearance on Monday night. Skittish—no doubt Mrs. Mallard—had an appointment at nine in the evening on Tuesday. Wednesday was Blue-Eyes. Where did the man get his stamina? She supposed by resting up on Sunday.

Therefore, she decided to take advantage of the free time to visit her aunt. She waited until the other servants had left before making her way to the street, where she hired a hansom cab. She didn't want the staff wondering how she could spare precious coins for private transportation rather than going with a horse-drawn omnibus or her own feet. While she was a far cry from wealthy, she had managed to earn enough that she could splurge now and then. Besides, she knew it would ease her aunt's worries if she did arrive in a cab.

Walking up the steps of her aunt's Mayfair residence, she shivered at the ghostly sensation of a tickling on the back of her neck, as though she were being watched. Spinning around, she didn't know why she expected to discover Bishop spying on her, but there was only the cabbie driving away, the trees swaying in the slight breeze, and the unlit lampposts. It was no doubt simply her nerves on edge because she'd surrounded herself with falsehoods and constantly worried that the truth of her scheming would be uncovered. She'd experienced the sensations before, when she'd needed to pretend to be someone she wasn't in order to gather necessary information. She hadn't easily accepted the dishonesty needed in her occupation.

A dog slinking out from beneath the shadows of a bush caught her attention and caused her to laugh with relief. Her spy, no doubt. Ignoring her, he scampered toward the rear of the dwelling, where a servant would probably have a juicy morsel waiting for the scraggly interloper. Her aunt had a habit of taking in strays—as she had Daisy—and this chap was undoubtedly her latest charity case. Not that she'd ever made Daisy feel a burden, but it couldn't have been easy raising her brother's daughter by herself.

Twisting back around, Daisy shoved open the door and had barely entered the foyer when the woman who was more mother than aunt came flying down the stairs.

"Oh, Marguerite, I'm incredibly relieved to see you looking so well." Her aunt's arms came around her snugly and wrapped her in love. She was a stout woman, and it was like falling into a soft, thick feather bed. Daisy had never known anyone to give better hugs.

"Aunt Charlotte, you worry for naught."

Stepping back, curling her hands over Daisy's shoulders, her aunt held her at arm's length, her gaze scrutinizing. "I would feel more comforted if you would marry. It's what we women are made for. Marriage."

"You never married."

She released her hold. "Not for want of trying, but it was not to be. However, I have the trust that my father established for me and an older brother to see to my care. You have neither of those things, dear child. Whatever will you do in your waning years?"

"I'm setting aside some of my earnings."

"I daresay it won't be enough. I shall leave you this residence, of course, but it does have upkeep and the servants—"

Before her aunt could go on a diatribe regarding her niece's lonely fate, Daisy interrupted. "Speaking of servants, how is Annie working out for you?"

In order for Daisy to get a position in Bishop's household, there had needed to be a vacancy. After discreetly observing the servants from a distance, especially the younger girls when they'd gone to market, she'd managed to catch Annie when no one was around and told her the fabricated tale that Bishop had wanted to give her a secret assignment in another household for a short period, in the household of the sister of an earl. Soon after, Daisy had delivered the excited servant to Aunt Charlotte's abode. While her aunt preferred that Daisy marry, she was also agreeable to being a willing partner when Daisy required assistance with her sleuthing. Her aunt was seldom seen without a detective novel in hand.

"Lovely girl, terribly sweet, although I've had to get after the staff not to take advantage of her. She just wants to be fancied."

"I think I'll pop downstairs before joining you for luncheon, as I'd like to have a word with her."

"Why do I have the impression that you're not telling me everything?"

"I promise you that I'm not up to no good."

"You never were, and that worried me as well. Although your *working*"—she uttered the word as though it involved touching offal—"is a bit of a rebellion. I suppose I should have been more specific regarding what I was wishing for when it came to you doing what you ought not. I was thinking more along the lines of dressing outrageously in trousers in order to ride one of those bicycle contraptions."

Leaning in, she pressed a kiss to the parchment-like cheek. "I love you, Auntie."

"Check on the girl, and then join me in the parlor for a bit of sherry before luncheon."

She knew her aunt wouldn't wait for her arrival in order to imbibe, but still she left her there and made her way to the kitchen, where she found Annie darning in the staff's main hall. Three other servants were also engaged in one sort of activity or another. Her aunt gave them all time off after Sunday luncheon was served as well as a different half day, so she was never completely without servants except for Sunday afternoon.

Annie's button-shaped dark eyes brightened at the sight of Daisy. She immediately came to her feet and bobbed a quick curtsy. "Lady Marguerite."

"Hello, Annie. My aunt is a lady because her father was the Earl of Bellingham, and while he was my grandfather, *my father* was his youngest son. Because he never inherited the title, I haven't the right to such a distinction."

Annie blinked, blinked, blinked.

Daisy smiled gently. "I shouldn't be addressed as lady, nor should I be curtsied to."

"But ye is still nobility."

"I have precedence, yes, but it doesn't truly mean anything. I'm simply Miss Townsend."

"It's so confusing."

"It is indeed. I don't know what our ancestors were thinking when they came up with this system so long ago. It's much easier to understand if you've grown up in it." She glanced around, noting that, although the others continued their chores, they were definitely more alert and listening in. "I wondered if you might take a walk about the garden with me."

"I don't know that I'm allowed."

"This was my home for most of my life, so you are allowed if I ask. You shan't get into any trouble."

"I'd like that then."

Daisy waited until they were outside and several steps away from the house before asking, "Are you happy here?"

"Oh, yes, Lady Charlotte, she's a right good 'un. Likes me darning, even praised me for it. I wanted to be a seamstress once. But I'm not fast, and you got to be fast. But I like making stitches."

"Perhaps there are some other things involving sewing that you can do around here. I'll speak with my aunt."

"Thank you, miss."

Daisy felt a great deal of responsibility toward the girl—and a bit of guilt because she'd manipulated her away from Bishop's household in order to move herself in. "You'll let me know if you need anything."

"I do miss Sarah."

"I'll arrange for you to visit with her in a couple of weeks," Daisy assured her, a promise she'd keep as soon as she left the Blackwood household.

The girl smiled as though she'd just been handed the moon.

"I was wondering . . . do you know if Bishop has a membership at the Fair and Spare?" Daisy hadn't wanted to question his staff because she didn't need them knowing exactly how curious she was about Bishop. They might get the wrong impression, but more, it might get back to him, and he could begin to suspect she wasn't there to keep his residence dusted and polished.

Annie looked around as though searching for sprites among the blossoms. Then she gave a quick nod and whispered, "Jacob told me."

"How would he know?"

"He's a footman, travels on the carriage with the coachman whenever Bishop goes out. He's seen the people going in. He says they dress fancy, and you can't tell by looking that they're off to do some sinning."

Not everyone sinned. Daisy hadn't, but then she'd only been there once. However, she was contemplating going this evening. She needed a distraction from her thoughts of Bishop, and since his calendar hadn't a notation of *F&S* for tonight then it was doubtful he'd be there. Nevertheless, she'd wanted confirmation of his membership as a preparation just in case she saw him. If so, she would scamper out.

"How is Mr. Bishop?" Annie asked. "I miss him, too. He's always so nice."

Daisy tilted her head slightly. "Is he?"

Annie nodded enthusiastically. "When I went to get a position in his household, Mr. Perkins told me I wouldn't do as I didn't seem fast enough. Or clever enough. He sent me on me way, out the back, to the mews, but I seen the flowers and went to look at 'em all. So many, so many colors. I kinda got lost in studying 'em. Mr. Bishop come over and said, 'Who are you then?' So I told him.

"Then me mam comes rushing over. She was in the carriage in the mews, but I guess she got tired of waiting for me. Told me not to bother the fancy gent and asked if I got the position. Told her I didn't think so because he said I wouldn't do. She got sad 'cuz it was the fourth time she'd taken me someplace to get a position. 'Who's going to take care of you when I'm not about?' she asked me.

"But before I could answer, Mr. Bishop told her not to worry. That Mr. Perkins had misspoken, and she was to bring me and me things in the morning so I could begin me duties. I became Sarah's assistant and in charge of the flowers in the residence, deciding what we'd have each day. 'Cept on them days when he has the ladies calling. They gets to pick the flowers then. Mr. Bishop likes his flowers. Are you seeing to 'em for him now?"

Daisy was touched by the story. How many people, particularly men, gave much thought to their staff? "I suppose I am, yes."

"He likes violets best of all."

"Does he?"

Annie nodded.

"I shall keep that in mind. We'd best get back so I can join my aunt for luncheon."

Her aunt was waiting for her in the parlor, already sipping her sherry. "Darling girl, do join me. I worry so. I do wish you'd chosen another occupation. This skulking about that you're doing is so undignified."

Aunt Charlotte wasn't the only one to find inquiry agents unworthy of respect. Few advertised because their livelihood involved uncovering and stealing people's secrets and, therefore, was considered an affront to esteemed professions. Yet those who gained a reputation for meeting with success were in demand and somehow were found, mostly through whispers carried far and wide, whenever a need for their services arose. Daisy was convinced it was only the beginning of what would become a profitable endeavor. While sometimes what she did left her feeling in need of a bath, she couldn't help but believe a desperate need for sleuths existed and that a time would come when the profession would gain some respect. It was simply new, and people didn't quite understand all that it entailed. Knowing her family disapproved was discouraging, but she refused to allow their sentiments to undermine her efforts.

After settling into the chair across from her aunt, she declined the offered glass of sherry. "How are you, Auntie?"

"I'll feel much better when you are no longer living in the residence of a debaucher. Is Mr. Blackwood as much of a scoundrel as they indicate in the papers? I rather envision him running about half-clad."

He was half-clad but only in the privacy of his bedchamber. However, if she revealed that information to her aunt, she'd no doubt have the vapors, wondering how Daisy knew what transpired in his bedchamber. "To be honest, he's a bit confounding. On the one hand, he seems considerate and kind, but on the other, definitely rakish."

"A bit like your father then. While Lionel was my youngest brother, he was very much a lost soul. Although he loved your mother, I think he married her as an act of rebellion, never quite believing Father would truly cut him off."

Her mother, Genevieve, had served as Aunt Charlotte's lady's maid. "Mr. Blackwood has no need to worry about being cut off."

"Still, it doesn't sound as though he's one to be loyal to love."

"Perhaps he's never been in love."

"Does that make it better? That he surrounds himself with women who do not hold his heart?"

"No, I suppose it doesn't."

"I've seen him at a ball or two. He's devilishly handsome."

"I hadn't really noticed." She wondered why she felt a need to lie. She'd attended a few balls but had never spied him there. She didn't think he attended them regularly. None were marked on his calendar anyway, but she supposed, based on his recent scandals, invitations were sparse.

"I wish you had more interest in attending balls. Your uncle is willing to provide you with a dowry."

Five thousand pounds, he'd told her. "I'm quite on the shelf. Besides, my mother's experience was a cautionary tale. She loved my father, but it wasn't enough to reform him."

"They loved the opium more. Such a shame. How long before your work involving Blackwood is done?"

"Another week, maybe two."

"I despair that in that time you will fall victim to his depravity."

"Trust me, I'm not attracted to him in the least." Her hand chose that moment to throb and warm, and she curled it into a tight fist as though she could hold on to the feel of the touch of him.

CHAPTER 7

⌒⌒⌒

*L*EANING against a wall in the socializing parlor, scotch in hand, Bishop was bored. He'd come to the Fair and Spare, hoping to ease some of that boredom with a willing partner. Griffith Stanwick had opened the club that catered to those in want of companionship, but what Bishop was truly looking for was an opportunity to forget the night Marguerite had come into his bedchamber, stumbled, and fallen against him. All too often he wandered through his residence, longing for a chance encounter with the intriguing woman, but his efforts had proven fruitless. All too often when he rang for something to be brought to him, he hoped she'd be the one who'd do the bringing, but he was left to suffer the disappointment that coursed through him when she wasn't. However, he refused to ask for her by name and have to deal with Perkins's damned raised eyebrow.

He rubbed his chest, the exact spot she'd touched, and wondered if she'd used it as a portal to enter his soul. It was all so deuced irritating. At four and thirty, he was far too old to be mooning about like a lovelorn schoolboy.

Upon first arriving at the club, he'd explored the

various rooms, searching for a distraction in the form of an adventurous lady. None of the members were innocent. Occasionally he enjoyed an intimate encounter with one of them. He didn't often visit the club, and new faces were usually about, but tonight none drew his interest. He'd had a few speculative glances cast his way but hadn't reciprocated. For most of the women in attendance, the reputation he'd garnered of late didn't matter. They weren't here because they were pure or expected fidelity in a relationship. Most were simply, like him, searching for a bit of fun.

A woman with blond hair caught his eye and gave him an inviting smile even as she carried on her conversation with two other ladies. All he had to do was hold her gaze and respond with a seductive grin, and she'd be his for the night. But her hair was too sandy, not pale enough. Not moonbeams gliding through the sky toward earth. So instead, after deciding he should simply be on his way, he offered an apologetic expression, shifted his attention toward the doorway, and stood bolt upright.

It couldn't be. And yet it was. *Her.* Here. Marguerite. In a low-cut gown of pale greenish blue that revealed her bared alabaster shoulders. As she glided into the room, she smiled confidently at one swell and then another, and it took everything within him not to cut a swath through the assembled horde in order to get to her and claim her as his own.

Then her blue gaze fell on him, and he felt as though he'd been zapped by lightning, like his childhood friend, Will. The lad, all of eight, had slammed into the ground, his body had seized up, and the odor of burned cloth and singed hair had permeated the air.

After he'd finally come to, it had taken him a while before he could move. That was how Bishop seemed. As though he couldn't move. Then she looked away, and he was no longer certain if she had indeed seen or recognized him.

He watched as, smiling softly and nodding, she spoke with a gent, but whatever she said must have left the fellow unsatisfied because he walked away. For the span of a heartbeat, she appeared lost, uncertain. He should still head out, skirt around her, leave her to the enjoyment of the night. Instead, he found himself striding directly toward her.

It didn't matter that the room was crowded. When he reached her, he breathed in her unique scent of violets. "Hello, Marguerite."

She blushed. "Sir."

"I'm astonished to find one of my servants here."

Her smile was small, teasing. "My aunt brought me, on my twenty-fifth birthday and purchased me a membership. She explained that a spinster should have the opportunity for at least one dalliance in her life."

His gut clenched with the thought of her engaged in a casual encounter with someone who might not appreciate her, who might not bestow upon her all the attention she so rightly deserved. "And did you? Have that dalliance?"

She shook her head. "We didn't stay very long. I believe she was striving to frighten me into marriage, to thinking that the alternative wasn't nearly as secure or trustworthy. But this evening I was feeling restless and in need of company. Although it shall be another brief visit. Perkins warned us that he'd lock up at ten, and if we hadn't returned from our free day by then, we'd end up sleeping on the stoop."

"How fortunate then that I possess a key that would grant us both access through his locked door."

She swallowed, her delicate throat working as she glanced around. "I wasn't really expecting to run into you."

He wondered if she'd browsed through his diary and noted no appointments for today, tonight. He hadn't planned to come this evening, but the residence had become too quiet, and he'd grown irritated listening to the echo of his own footfalls, especially once he'd come to realize what he was truly doing was striving to hear hers. "May I fetch you something to drink?"

"A red wine would be lovely, thank you."

"I won't be but a tick." He made his way through the crowd to the barman, where he had his own scotch replenished and secured a glass of wine for her. Turning, he was disappointed to see her carrying on a conversation with King's younger brother. Deuced inconvenient that. He couldn't very well plow his fist into his friend's relation. But that didn't mean he had to offer a warm greeting when he returned to her side. "Lawrence."

The young man seemed surprised to discover that frost hadn't actually formed on his face, but then he grinned cheerily. "Bishop. Is that for me?" He nodded toward the wine.

"No. It's for Miss—" Damnation, he didn't even know her last name. How had that come about? Because Marguerite had seemed sufficient, all that was needed.

"Townsend," she said, taking the wine from him.

"It seems I'm intruding," Lawrence said.

"You are," Bishop responded curtly.

He lifted an eyebrow. "I'll take my leave then." But not before he lifted the lady's gloved hand and placed a kiss against her knuckles. He could be as deuced vexing as his brother. "Another time, perhaps."

With an irritatingly shrewd wink at Bishop, he finally wandered off, and Bishop knew Lawrence was going to relate this encounter to King, who would no doubt use it as means of torment at their next gathering.

"You were rather rude," Marguerite said softly.

"He'd have expected no less. Feel free to traipse after him if he intrigued you."

"Not after you went to such bother to obtain me some wine." She took a sip, licked lips that he wanted to taste.

"You seem to know people here," he said.

"I grew up among nobility and am no stranger to a few of them. Lawrence, for example."

"Yet, you now work as a servant in my household."

"I wanted to escape that life, and where better than someplace where few will recognize me? Even here, a good many of the members are commoners who have risen above their humble beginnings, and I feel at home among them. I like this club because we're all supposed to keep secret those we see within these walls, aren't we? Makes it a rather safe place for mingling about. One of the reasons I hadn't expected to cross paths with you was because you have so many women visiting your residence. Why have you a need for more?"

Her tone contained the tiniest bit of censure. He

wanted to tell her the truth, but if she was what he suspected—

"I adore women and spending time in their company. Here they do not judge, unlike slander sheets."

"The gossip rags *have* been unkind to you of late."

"You've read them, then."

"It's the best way to keep up with Society's news. And scandal."

He wouldn't mind embarking on a scandal with her. "How long have you had your membership?"

"Are you striving to cleverly determine my age without actually asking my age?"

"Yes, I suppose I am."

"You could simply ask Perkins."

And suffer through the indignity of another one of his disapproving glowers? He thought not. "Where's the fun in that? Besides, I'd rather ask you."

Her lips curled up slightly, and it was disconcerting, how much he wanted her to bestow upon him a full smile. "I've had my membership for half a year now."

She was still twenty-five then.

"Have you visited since your aunt brought you?" *Have you had that damned dalliance, if not the first night, then perhaps another? Had he been worthy of you and your attentions?* For some reason, it had never occurred to him that neophytes would come to this place to gain the experience that would relieve them of their novice status. He didn't much like the thought that someone without the proper skills would introduce her to pleasure. Even as he suspected she didn't have his best interests at heart, he couldn't seem not to have hers.

"I haven't, no. I was rather intimidated, but then this afternoon, I decided that I didn't have to do anything I didn't want to. I could set boundaries. I could enjoy a fellow's conversation and ease myself along into enjoying more."

He wondered how little, how more. Certainly, he'd been here numerous times without experiencing the more. Sometimes it was enough simply not to be alone. "Thus, your goal tonight is conversation?"

"It will all depend on how the evening goes."

She certainly had confidence. He liked that about her, a direct contrast to Mrs. Mallard. "Will you do me the honor of allowing me to show you around? We can carry our drinks with us."

"You're quite familiar with the place, are you?" she asked.

"I know every corner, especially the more shadowy ones." With his words, he was issuing a dare, and he didn't know why he felt the need to do such a thing. Still, he offered his arm.

She stared at it as though she'd never seen one before. Or perhaps a gentleman had never offered her the courtesy, although he couldn't imagine it. If she was raised among the nobility, then she'd no doubt frequented balls, although he hadn't noticed her at the few he'd attended, but then he spent most of the evening in the cardroom. For the past three years, he'd been carefully cultivating his reputation, and of late, it ensured he was seldom welcomed as a dance partner. While within these confines he'd noticed a few speculative gazes turned their way, he saw little harm in escorting her about when her presence already signaled that she didn't fear becoming tarnished. She'd chosen work over marriage, and that alone was enough to blemish her character.

Finally, she placed her hand on his forearm, and only then did he realize that he'd been holding his breath, preparing to walk away should she decline his offer. No, to do more than that: to leave entirely rather than witness her enjoying the company of another.

But she had accepted, and he could recall no other victory that had ever felt as sweet.

HIS FOREARM WAS as firm as a boulder, felt as strong as it had looked, with its ropy muscles and raised veins, resting along the back of the settee while his fingers had been stroking Mrs. Bowles. Even though he wore a coat and she gloves, she detected the heat of his flesh traveling into hers. She didn't know how it was possible that so chaste a touch could make it difficult to breathe, could awaken butterflies in her stomach, could cause her thoughts to scatter. She'd gone on strolls with men, had rested her fingers on their arms, and yet for all the impact they'd had on her, she could have been touching an ethereal being.

Bishop was anything but. He was hard, toned, and sturdy. And her hand was once again feeling as though he'd taken possession of it. This awareness of him was inconvenient. How in the world was she to speak out against him without her voice giving away her desire to know him more intimately? How was she not to recall that at this moment she'd very much like to be sitting on that settee with him in his bedchamber?

She should have walked out as soon as she spotted him. Or better yet, latched on to the first gentleman she'd neared so Bishop would have never approached her. Why had he? Why was he so willing to spend time in the company of a woman he believed to be his servant? Did she intrigue him? Or did he think she'd be an easy conquest?

Well, he was about to learn she was made of firmer stuff. She could resist his charm. She could use this opportunity to gain a better understanding of him that would allow her to ensure he paid a heavy price for encouraging women not to remain faithful to their vows. "Lead the way."

He bestowed upon her that marvelous smile that challenged her determination to defy his magnetic appeal. It wasn't fair that so simple an action could cause her to lose her head, to wish she'd encountered him here before she'd been hired to spy on him, before she knew that all the rumors about his transgressions were true. She wished he wasn't a cad and found herself wondering why he'd chosen that path, for surely it had been a conscious decision. He had to know that scoundrels weren't meant for proper and decent society, and that no father would ever grant him a daughter's hand in marriage.

But then, perhaps like her, he was content not to have a spouse or a helpmate. But why turn to a scandalous way of life, to be known as a seducer, which would force such isolation? More importantly, why did she care? Why did she want to know all the intimate details of his life, to know what had shaped him into the man he'd become? Why did she wish he was different, was someone she could respect?

He escorted her into the hallway and past the stairs. "Activities on this level are rather tame," he said quietly. "Upstairs is a bit more lively."

"I assume upstairs is where you spend the majority of your time."

"You make a good many assumptions about me, Marguerite."

"I work in your household. Few secrets about you are kept within those walls."

"I imagine there are more than you think. Just as I suspect you are comprised of an entire trove of secrets."

"I imagine there are fewer than you think."

His gaze landed on her like a soft caress. "But some exist."

"Everyone has secrets," she said.

"What would it take to uncover yours?"

"Absolute trust."

"Are they the reason you chose an occupation over a husband?"

"Are yours the reason you choose an inordinate number of lovers over a wife?"

He chuckled low. "Why do I have the sense that we are playing chess, and the winning strategy involves holding secrets close?"

"I was under the impression this club was for light flirtation, not the acquisition of in-depth understanding of another."

"So it is. This way."

They turned into another corridor and were greeted by piano keys being struck with an accomplished hand.

"I was hoping to entice you into playing for me," he said, while setting their empty glasses on the tray of a passing footman, "but it sounds as though another beat us to it. Still, let's enjoy the music, shall we?"

When they entered the musicale room, she was surprised to find this scandalous club would have such a magnificent rosewood grand piano. An older silverhaired gentleman sat at it, running his hands lovingly over the ivory, while three ladies stood nearby admiring his entertaining talent.

A few couples occupied the dimly lit room, some making use of those shadowy corners Bishop had referenced earlier, and she fought not to envision how his fingers might have played over a lady's skin with the same efficiency and purpose as the pianist's fingers worked at the gorgeous instrument or the cries and gasps that might have been emitted by those recipients of Bishop's talents. She knew he had them and used them to perfection behind closed doors. She'd seen the way two of his latest paramours gazed at him adoringly. Mrs. Mallard would eventually as well, once she grew comfortable as a sinner. Although Daisy often wondered why the woman had begun coming to him when she hadn't yet embraced the role of devotee.

How had they met? How had any of them met? Certainly, their acquaintance hadn't begun here, since the club granted membership only to the unmarried.

With his arm shifting from beneath her hold, he guided it around, so his large hand came to rest at the small of her back and, with gentle pressure, he directed her toward the piano. A harmless place. Or it should have been, but his fingers remained splayed against the silk of her gown, sending out delicious tentacles of warmth that kept her entire body aware of his nearness. His ability to stir to life sensations with so light a touch was quite possibly lethal, and yet she had no desire to seek out safety and move beyond his reach.

The tune fell into silence, and those gathered around the piano clapped lightly, even Bishop, which meant he was no longer connected to her, and she rather resented the absence of his touch. But after a few meetings of his palms, he returned his hand to her back. And her breath settled into a calm and quiet acceptance.

"I say," he began in a commanding yet low voice so as not to disturb those in the shadows who probably hadn't even noticed the music stopping, "are you familiar with a lullaby about angels guarding a babe through the night?"

Every aspect of her went still. Within this place of decadence and sinners, he was asking about a lullaby? He'd actually remembered the memory she'd shared about her mother? While it had been only a few days since that conversation, she hadn't thought he'd really paid attention to what she was saying, that it had just been trivial talk, something to fill the silence in passing, to politely listen to and forget.

"I recall a Welsh lullaby my wife would sing to our children," the pianist said.

"If you're married, why are you here?" one of the ladies asked, clearly offended that their unattached ranks had been breached.

"I'm a widower," he responded sadly before striking the first chord.

Daisy wondered if it was a recent change in his marital status, and then he was forgotten as a tune floated forth and he accompanied it with the words. She was no longer in this room, but was a small child nestled on her mother's lap, feeling safe, secure, loved. Tears stung her eyes as she remembered how she'd longed for those moments of being carried into slumber. Every night until the last night, when Daisy was five, her mother had held her close and sung those words or hummed that tune. It didn't matter if Daisy woke up later alone in her wooden slatted prison that she couldn't escape—the box in which her parents placed her whenever they went out as a means to keep her safe when their need for the opium dragon became too great.

She became aware of a warm breath wafting over her ear. "Is that the one?"

Blinking back the tears before they'd fully gained their freedom, she shifted her attention to Bishop, to the warmth in his eyes, and perhaps a spark of hope that he'd given her the correct gift. "It is, yes. I'd forgotten how much I loved it."

He smiled then, but it wasn't the one that stole breaths. It was one that returned them, soft and gentle, barely there, but filling his eyes, one that signaled this is a moment I've shared with no other. This moment is ours and ours alone.

His hand wrapped around her wrist. His finger slid into her glove to stroke the sensitive skin where her pulse thrummed. "How did she die? Your mother?"

"Opium." She remembered being hungry, cold, and scared. A phalanx of liveried footmen bursting through the door, followed by her aunt marching in like an avenging angel. A poker being used to pry the lock off her cage. "I recall little about her death except everyone garbed in black and her lying so pale and still in a box. I made such a fuss, crying and screaming. Inconsolable really. I suppose that's the reason that when my father passed a short time later, they didn't show him to me but just told me he was gone. Auntie took me to visit their resting places in the city." They'd not been interred at the family estate. It was only for those who'd actually held the title associated with the earldom. Not for a lesser son who'd brought naught but shame and heartache to his relations.

"I'm sorry," Bishop said quietly. "And I apologize for asking. This isn't the place for those sorts of memories."

"They're no longer fresh or vivid or painful. It's like viewing them through gossamer. More like something I was told rather than something I experienced." She couldn't even recall what they looked like without studying the images nestled in a locket she always wore about her neck. She refrained from reaching for it now.

"I'm extremely grateful for that mercy. I wouldn't want to do anything to cause you hurt."

Her heart stumbled, and she wondered if he'd noted it where his finger continued to gently stroke. She was going to cause him and his reputation hurt, a great deal of it, when she turned over her report, when she spoke out against him. She should leave now, leave his presence, but it was so deuced hard when his gaze was wandering intently over her features as though he longed to touch each one with the edge of his finger, the tip of his tongue, the brush of his lips.

She thought she could actually detect a longing in those dark eyes, a yearning for her.

Then the moment was gone as the pianist transitioned from the lullaby into a more spirited song. Everything seemed to fade away, except for the man beside her. She wanted him to take her into the shadows, and if he wouldn't, maybe she would grasp his hand and lead him into them, ignoring the danger to her heart that possibly awaited her there. His kindness was such a powerful aphrodisiac. In spite of her determination to resist him, she was falling—

"No, I said no."

The trembling feminine harsh whisper caught her attention, and apparently his, because he jerked his head around. When he looked back at her, his brow was furrowed. "Excuse me. I won't be long."

Stunned, she watched as he crossed over to one of those corners, but she wasn't about to wait, so she followed. A man had his hand wrapped around a small woman's upper arm, his body positioned so she was fairly caged between him and the wall.

"I believe the lady indicated she is not interested in what you're offering," Bishop said calmly with such deadly menace that a fissure of dread raced up Daisy's spine.

The gent swung his head around and glared. "I purchased her dinner."

"That does not obligate her to spend the remainder of the evening in your presence, especially when it's obvious to all in this chamber that you have become quite boorish."

"She owes me."

"You had her company for dinner. Be grateful for that. Now unhand her."

"It's none of your concern, Bishop."

"It's every gentleman's concern. Would you rather we finish this outside?"

The swell held up his hand, fingers splayed, releasing his hold on the lady. "No, I've seen the damage your punch can inflict."

"My man will see you out," a deep voice said, the tone brooking no argument, and Daisy glanced over to where the club owner stood, looking as though he were on the verge of committing murder. His wife skirted away from his side to tend to the lady in question and offer comfort. Standing behind him was the giant of a bruiser who usually guarded the entrance door. "Your membership is canceled. Hand over your card."

"Look, Stanwick—" His whine actually grated Daisy's ears.

"You're one word away from receiving that punch Bishop was threatening. You know the rules."

Appearing shamefaced rather than belligerent, he plucked his card from his pocket, tore it up, and let it flutter to the floor. Then he dutifully followed the bruiser out.

"Appreciate the assist, Bishop," Lord Griffith Stanwick said, offering his hand.

Bishop shook it. "I have no tolerance for that sort of behavior."

"Neither have I. I'll extend your membership for a year."

Bishop scowled. "Don't reward me for doing what was right."

"Fine. Enjoy your evening then." He joined his wife in consoling the lady.

Bishop watched the threesome for a few seconds to ensure all was well before turning to Daisy. "Shall we go upstairs?"

"I don't know if I can tolerate anything more exciting than all that. I truly thought you were going to come to fisticuffs. What did he mean about your punch?"

He seemed uncomfortable with the question. "I've done some boxing for sport."

Which might account for the delicious firmness she'd touched earlier and wanted to touch again. She looked to the corner. "Does that sort of thing happen often here?"

"I've never seen it before. Stanwick insists gentlemen respect the ladies' wishes. What do you wish for?"

That you weren't a rakehell my aunt would disapprove of. That you'd stop entertaining ladies in your residence, in particular your boudoir. That you would find me as intriguing as I do you. "A peek upstairs, I suppose."

He once more offered his arm, and she was foolish to welcome the opportunity to touch him again, to lay her hand on that steady support, and she wondered if his ladies came to him for that uncompromising regard. He provided an alcove where troubles could be set and, when picked up once again, wouldn't feel as heavy. The time she'd spent with him in this room alone had taken her through a gamut of emotions, of memories she seldom visited, and yet her steps seemed lighter as they walked out.

He escorted her in the slow, leisurely way he had, as though time didn't exist or clocks wouldn't move forward without his permission. While she constantly rushed hither and yon, striving to cram as many activities into the day as possible: the chores demanded of her because of her position in his household, the answers she needed to secure for her clients, the trips to the modiste so she appeared successful when in her office or didn't appear to be the daughter of a pauper when family obligations required her presence. Friends to visit, letters to pen, books to read. Life to live.

They ascended the red carpeted stairs to another floor of dim lights. She supposed questionable behavior flourished with the illusion of invisibility. He showed her a room where people dined, one where they gambled, one where they smoked. She was shocked to see women puffing on cheroots. She and he carried on to the other end of the hallway, where a ballroom beckoned. She could see within it that couples waltzed, holding each other scandalously close.

"Now that you've seen what is offered, what's your pleasure?" he asked in a low voice, hinting at wickedness.

Facing him, she nodded toward another set of stairs across from where they stood. "What's up there?"

He drew her away from the ballroom doorway and into one of those shadowed corners that he'd confessed to knowing so well. "Private rooms." His gaze was direct and heated, the fingers of one hand trailing softly along her cheek. "Up there, you'll find that dalliance your aunt warned you about."

"It was an encouragement more than a warning."

"Be sure it's what you desire, that he is the one for whom you yearn. Spend a little time in the corners first."

Somehow, without her noticing they'd moved closer together. She didn't know if she'd eased toward him or he'd come nearer to her, but their warm breaths were mingling. His familiar bergamot with a hint of orange scent, mixed with the fragrance of scotch, suddenly smelled dark and decadent, and she was aware of heat swirling through her. Every bit of her wanted to lock itself with every inch of him. How had this happened? Was it the magic of this place? That desire couldn't lie dormant? That every aspect of passion was awakened? She'd never wanted a man as she wanted now. It was exciting and terrifying.

He lowered his head until his lips almost brushed against her cheek, and his words were a sweet refrain in her ear. "I have something for you."

She knew she should object, that he was going to kiss her, and yet the words to stop him knotted in her throat because she didn't want to give them freedom. She didn't want them uttered. She yearned for what he was offering. Yearned for it and more.

Her lids were half-shuttered when a brass key appeared within her field of vision. Her eyes flew open as she stared at it, held up by his forefinger and thumb. He'd moved back slightly, enough that she could no longer feel the caress of his breath. "What does it open?"

He pressed it against her palm and curled her fingers around it. "The main door to my residence. My carriage is in the mews. You know my coachman, do you not?"

She nodded. He and Jacob resided in a small stable at the rear of his dwelling.

"When you're finished here, he'll be waiting to transport you back to the residence."

"What about you?"

"I have an urgent matter that requires my attention." His grin was nearly self-mocking. "Perkins is unlikely to force *me* to sleep on the stoop. You may return the key to me tomorrow. Enjoy the remainder of your evening." He leaned back in and whispered with a rasp, "Be very selective regarding with whom you traipse up those stairs."

In astonishment, she watched as he sauntered toward the stairway that would lead him to the floor below. His stride was long, but unhurried, as though he hadn't a care in the world, as though being in her company had been a lark, as though he hadn't been on the verge of kissing her. Hadn't experienced the same magnetic draw she had.

While her blood continued to feel like molten lava and her breath sawed in and out. How could she have been so wrong regarding what had been occurring between them? How was it she had fallen prey to his mesmeric charm?

She was angry, hurt, and mortified. He gathered women about him with the ease that a child collected flowers, but he hadn't wanted her. Because she was unmarried? But every woman here was in the same state, and yet he'd come in search of companionship so he couldn't object because she was a spinster. Why then? Why hadn't he at least wanted to kiss her?

"Miss Townsend?"

Without even noticing it, she'd crept out of the shadows and was nearer to the ballroom entrance. She looked up at the man who'd spoken. His wavy blond hair fell over his brow, nearly obscuring his blue eyes. She'd met him at an afternoon garden party some years back. "Mr. Endicott. How very nice to see you again."

"I'd not expected you to be here."

"You know how it is with spinsters. We're always in need of a bit of company." She kept her tone light, refusing to allow him to witness her humiliation, her upset. How unsettled she'd become.

Music was drifting out of the ballroom.

"I say, would you honor me with a dance?"

She wasn't in the mood for any sort of entertainment, but wasn't that the best way to get over the hurt? Pick oneself up and carry on. "I'd be delighted."

As he escorted her into the chamber, she wished he was someone else, someone he shouldn't be, someone with whom it seemed she'd been willing to follow an unwise course.

CHAPTER 8

~~~

$\mathcal{N}$EARING midnight, Daisy slipped the key into the lock of the front door. Traveling to the residence in a carriage that carried the fragrance of bergamot and oranges had certainly done little enough to take her mind off Bishop. Nor had dancing with a couple of fellows she knew from affairs at her uncle's or dancing with three she'd met only tonight. She should have enjoyed the attention but had been preoccupied wondering at the reason Bishop had abruptly left her.

It was all for the good. She knew that. They were working at cross-purposes. He was embroiled in affairs, and she was invested in ensuring he paid dearly for at least one of them.

Once inside, she headed straight for his library, and upon her arrival there, cursed herself for the disappointment that overcame her because he wasn't about. Not sitting behind his desk or lounging by the fire in the large chair with its plump cushions, glass of scotch in hand, as he nursed his regrets for having not kissed her. After he'd walked away from her, he'd probably not given her another moment's thought while she'd been riddled with questions about him.

She wondered if he was outside, strolling alone and

lonely, through his gardens. The temptation to wander out the terrace doors in search of him was frightfully overwhelming, even as she chastised herself for the absurdity of it. Although perhaps she should check the back stoop to ensure Perkins hadn't ignored any knocks out of hand. She was concerned only because Bishop had made concessions to ensure she arrived safely, and she worried that he might have had a time of it getting home.

Of course, he could have plans to stay out until dawn—perhaps with a lady somewhere. Maybe she had been the urgent matter.

Don't be a blasted ninny. Politeness had caused him to spend some time with her this evening. And he'd grown bored. Such was her appeal. She was predictable. Not enticing nor intriguing. Even the gentlemen in the ballroom had been content with one dance before moving on to someone else. Although perhaps she could have held their attention if she'd wanted, if she hadn't been distracted with thoughts of Bishop.

Thoughts that were beginning to annoy because they wouldn't grant her peace. Maybe because she clutched the key that had once lived inside his pocket, had once carried his warmth. Had been gifted to her for the evening as though she were a cinder girl on her way to a ball.

She marched over to his desk and deposited the brass in its center where he would see it on the morrow when he sat to begin his tasks. Would he hold it and take a minute to recall the time they'd spent together? Or would he tuck it away without any thought at all?

Not that it mattered. She'd soon be done with her business here. And other clients would require different information. While some might even have need of proof of marital transgressions, hopefully none would depend upon her spying on Bishop again.

Pivoting on her heel, she carried on into the hallway, directing her feet to take her to the servants' stairs that would lead her to the kitchens, and from there to the stairs that would transport her to the small bedchamber where she knew she would glance out the window in hopes of seeing him in the gardens. Just a glimpse, just to reassure herself he'd returned home safely.

But as she neared the stairs, she noted the pale light shining into the corridor through a doorway that was normally shut, a room she'd never explored because she'd had no reason to go into it as part of her duties. Also coming from it were grunts and heavy breathing.

She very much doubted a servant was cavorting in that chamber. No, it would be the master of the household, and now she knew what his urgent matter entailed. Bringing a woman here and carrying on as though no one might walk by. Of course, everyone was abed, so in all likelihood the couple wouldn't be disturbed.

For all of a heartbeat, she considered retreating to the library and sleeping on the sofa there. But what if he was with Mrs. Parker and this was Daisy's opportunity to catch them engaged in amorous congress? To witness with her own eyes—

She squeezed those eyes shut, not certain she really wanted to see him showering such intimate attention on another. Not that she'd ever allow him to shower it on her.

Opening her eyes, she licked her lips. She was being paid to deliver a service and had known from the beginning that certain aspects of it would be unpleasant. However, she needed to be able to describe an action seen not merely heard. Taking a deep breath to steady her nerves, she eased closer and peered around the doorjamb.

Her mouth quite suddenly became as arid as a desert, and her skin felt as though it had been enveloped by the sun.

Bared from the waist up, dew glistening over his skin, facing away from her, Bishop sat on the edge of a short backless bench, with one hand grasping a leather strap with what appeared to be a heavy iron bell attached to it and lifting it to his shoulder before lowering it to do the same on the other side with another bell. His movements were smooth, purposeful, quick, and she couldn't look away from his muscles bunching, knotting, and rippling with his efforts. Up, down. Up, down. Over and over.

Then he stopped. One bell raised. And glanced back over his shoulder. With his penetrating gaze, he pinned her to the spot.

Slowly, ever so slowly, he lowered that mass of iron before twisting slightly and snatching up the linen that had been draped behind him over the bench. "You returned earlier than I expected."

Had he been expecting her? She didn't think that's what he'd meant. She wasn't certain what he'd meant, however, because she could barely reason as she watched him wipe the sweat from his brow and then his throat. Had she ever noticed that a man's throat was such a powerful aphrodisiac? Not that she'd ever seen that many and certainly not so much of one, one that flowed down into shoulders and chest. Jolly good thing that men wore neckcloths.

"That's not the gown you were wearing at the Fair and Spare."

"No. I took advantage of the transportation you provided and had your coachman stop by my aunt's on the way so I could change back into my usual frock. I have little use for gowns in my current position. I hope that was all right."

He merely shrugged.

"Did you get your matter tended to?"

His smile was self-effacing. "Not as well as I would have liked."

"May I ask what you're doing?"

He stood, and only then did she notice that his feet were also bare and his trousers fit him remarkably snugly as though his legs had been melted and then poured into them. "Strength training, something I began doing when I was younger, much younger, a gangly weakling, all limbs and not much else. I was around seven when I ran across a book on strength training at a bookstall. It recommended having something heavy to lift and suggested church bells. Hence one night I crept into a church tower and stole some small ones. Began working with those. I suppose I gained some strength at that tender age, but I was thirteen, fourteen before I detected any true muscle."

While his arms rested at his side, his hand was knotted around the linen as though it held him securely there.

"You must have a formidable punch. That's the reason that fellow didn't want to accept your invitation to go outside."

"Most likely. I trust the other gentlemen in attendance treated you properly."

She nodded. *None were as interesting as you.* "I danced in the ballroom for a while." Then for some reason she couldn't decipher she felt compelled to add, "I didn't traipse up those final stairs."

One corner of his mouth hitched up. "You don't owe me an explanation of your evening."

"Of course not." She watched as a drop of sweat rolled down his chest and along the hollows of his stomach until it reached its destination and was absorbed into the waistband of his trousers. His hand flexed around that linen, once, twice. He was chiseled like a Greek statue or a Roman god. What would he do if she moved toward him and captured with the tip of her finger or her tongue the next droplet that began its journey? But doing so would compromise her integrity. Even being here now was cause for concern. As much as she wanted to stay, she had to leave. "I should abed. Chores begin early."

He nodded.

"Thank you for ensuring I do get to sleep in a bed and not on the stoop."

His response was a short grunt.

She gave a quick bob. "Good night, sir."

Another nod from him, and she was rather certain she'd overstayed her welcome. Quickly she departed, grateful for, and yet wishing she didn't now have a more revealing glimpse of the scenery the women who visited his bedchamber enjoyed. She was beginning to despise each and every one of those damnable ladies.

WITH A GROAN of agony, Bishop dropped onto the bench, his teeth clenched so tightly that his jaw ached, the hand gripping the towel throbbing with pain. Creating the torment had been the only way to keep his body from hardening in response to the way she looked at him with wanton desire. His damned trousers fit so tightly that how badly he wanted her would have been revealed.

It hadn't mattered within the shadows of the Fair and Spare. She'd not been able to see what he'd not been able to control when he'd stood so remarkably close to her while her back was pressed against that wall. Hopefully, she'd also not been able to detect how desperately he wanted to know the taste of her upon his tongue, the feel of her skin against his palms, the fit of her curves against his planes. The press of her breasts to his chest.

The need to lean in and take her mouth had nearly overpowered him. It had required a strength of purpose he hadn't realized he possessed to leave her in that shadowed corner untouched—except for the glory his fingertips had experienced trailing along her warm cheek and his flared nostrils had enjoyed in absorbing her violet fragrance.

Did you get your matter attended to? She'd asked the question so innocently that she couldn't have known the silent battle waged within him.

After leaving the Fair and Spare, he'd come straight to the residence, to this room where he'd gone to war with the bells. Pushing, pushing, pushing himself until his muscles trembled and screamed in protest. Until his mind was finally devoid of every thought of her.

But all it had taken was looking over his shoulder to see her standing in the doorway for all the yearning to come roaring back. When she'd mentioned a bed, he'd had to bite his tongue to keep himself from pleading, "Come to mine."

Then he'd had to begin reciting a damned nursery rhyme about sheep and bags of wool to distract himself in order not to reveal how desperately he wanted her. Christ, what the devil was wrong with him? She was the very last woman he should desire. She was here under false pretenses. He was sure of it. How could he trust a woman such as that? How could he long for her?

Even if he was being equally dishonest in what he was allowing her to witness. And if he had misjudged her, was wrong about her, if she truly was working as a servant to avoid marriage . . . well, then she was under his protection and care. He wouldn't dishonor himself by taking undue advantage of her position in his household. It was one thing to have a scandalous reputation as a libertine. But it was unforgiveable to gain a reputation as a man who took that to which he had no right.

Bending down, he folded his hands around the leather straps attached to the bells and began lifting them, alternating left then right. If he wore himself out, perhaps he could convince himself that it was merely the decadent atmosphere of the Fair and Spare that had inhabited him tonight and made her so appealing. The forbidden aspect of it lingering so that when he'd seen her hovering in the threshold, her eyes darkening at the sight of his bared chest, he'd been forced to battle the demons of temptation and desire in order to remain standing where he was. Tonight's excursion was the cause of it all, had been responsible for sending confusing emotions rampaging through him.

Her, there, in a place that encouraged sin.

As his breaths grew more labored with his efforts to lift the bells and sweat drenched his body, he convinced himself that the damnable club was the culprit.

Up until the moment he collapsed into his bed exhausted, and all the walls erected to accept the lies fell away leaving him to face the unvarnished truth: tonight wasn't the first time he'd wanted her. Unfortunately, he doubted it would be the last.

CHAPTER 9

⧜⧜⧜

$\mathcal{A}$ FEW minutes after the clock struck nine that Monday evening, clutching the tray until her fingers ached, Daisy repeated her mantra as she made her way up the stairs.

Focus on the woman. Ignore Bishop. Don't think about the way he'd looked at you last night at the Fair and Spare as though he'd like nothing more than to gobble you up, or the way all your feminine bits had ached for him to do so. You need to properly identify the woman. You need to get the information for your client. You need to get out of this bloody household and away from a man who is making it far too easy to understand how your mother may have been beguiled into falling for the wrong sort.

When she reached his bedchamber door, she redoubled her resolve to concentrate on the woman and then kicked the thick wood twice with her toe.

"Come."

She took a deep breath, shifted the tray, released the latch, strolled in, and came to a staggering halt. Once more he was in shirtsleeves, rakishly unbuttoned to reveal that enticing sliver of skin. The woman was nestled against the crook of his side as though she'd once been carved from it and had returned to her place of origin. Her lips curling up slightly, she was looking steadfastly at Daisy as though daring her to object. His arm circled the tart's shoulders, holding her near. With his free hand, he waved toward the low table, off to the side. "See to it."

What Daisy would very much like to *see* was the contents of the tray dumped in his lap. Last night he'd shown interest in her, made her feel special. And now he was absorbed with another woman, and while she had known it would be thus, still it hurt. Irrationally. Stupidly. She was going to look forward to telling Mr. Parker his wife was indeed a trollop, and she dearly hoped he would sue Blackguard Blackwood for every coin in his possession.

She fairly marched to the table and dropped the tray from such a height that it was a wonder the wooden platter didn't splinter. "Shall I prepare a strawberry for you?" she ground out, realizing she'd lost all objectivity and desperately needed to relocate it.

"Not necessary."

Slowly she inhaled, exhaled, and forced her face to go as neutral as possible, refusing to let him see how his actions upset her. She meant nothing to him, and he should mean nothing to her. But last night, she'd thought—foolishly as it turned out—that he cared.

Spinning about, she came to an abrupt halt halfway into her pivot as though she'd rammed into a brick wall. Her lungs refused to draw in air. Her heart pounded. Her chest felt as though it was locked in a vise.

The back of the settee was low enough that, standing behind it but slightly off to the side, she had a clear view of the couple pressing their mouths together, his hand grazing her cheek. They were kissing. Right there in front of her. The indecency of it. They couldn't have waited one more minute until after she took her leave?

Serenely turning back, she picked up the delicate porcelain bowl with the chocolate glaze, sauntered to the settee, and poured the thick, sticky contents over his head.

"What the bloody hell!" He lunged up to his feet and glared at her, the chocolate dripping onto his face and shirt making it very difficult to take his glower seriously.

"I thought she might fancy tasting you with a bit of chocolate." With that parting shot, she walked calmly out of the room and quietly closed the door in her wake.

Bishop was damned tempted to chase after the little chit and let *her* taste him with a bit of chocolate. But the giggling woman on the settee held him in place, because it would do her no good if he mucked up what he hoped they'd accomplished with that rather chaste kiss. Still, he scowled at her.

Trying to catch her breath, she gasped, "Do you think if Martin did hire her that she's going to tell him about the chocolate glaze incident?"

He bloody well hoped not. "I doubt it. She'd come across as incredibly unprofessional. If you'll excuse me, I need to tidy up."

He strode into the bathing chamber, pulled his shirt over his head, and looked into the mirror hanging above the sink. What a disastrous mess. Then he chuckled because damned, if he didn't admire her spunk. And the casualness with which she'd responded as though pouring concoctions over gentlemen's heads was an everyday occurrence for her, to be taken in stride.

He couldn't help but admit that, after giving attention to Marguerite last night, she had a right to feel ill-used and he deserved to be doused. He should have left the Fair and Spare the moment he'd spied her. Instead, he had taken actions to complicate matters.

By the time he returned to his visitor, his face was clean and his hair wet. From his wardrobe, he retrieved a shirt and donned it. He went to his decanter credenza and filled a tumbler with scotch. "Would you care for anything to drink?"

"No, I poured myself more wine while waiting for you."

He wandered over, dropped into the chair, and frowned at the chocolate decorating the settee. He'd leave orders with Perkins that Daisy—and only Daisy— was to clean it in the morning. "Did any get on you?"

"Just a tad but I was able to clean it off easily enough. It seems she's as interested in you as you are in her."

"I have no interest in her, and if she has any in me, she has a rather odd way of showing it."

Louisa smiled. "When I was younger, much younger, anytime a lad tugged on one of my plaits, I immediately knew he fancied me. Although I would say your maid was demonstrating something a little more. Jealousy. Perhaps she noticed the heat in your eyes whenever you look at her. Have you been giving her attention?"

"Not here. But we did spend some time together last night at the Fair and Spare."

"Did you kiss her?"

"No." But he'd wanted to. Desperately. More than that, he'd wanted to carry her up that final flight of stairs.

"Whyever not?"

"She'll have to appear in court, and there can be no implication of bias."

"Did you enjoy her company?"

Immensely. Rather than answer he shrugged. "With any luck, she'll report the kiss to your husband, and you'll be well on your way to a divorce."

After taking a sip of her wine, Louisa shifted her gaze to the hearth. "I know I should be ecstatic at the prospect, and yet it makes me rather sad."

A small droplet of chocolate rested on her shoulder where it curved into her neck, and if that skin belonged to Marguerite, he'd move over to the settee and lick it off. Why did he have to view everything in the context of what he would do if it involved her? It was deuced irritating.

He shook off thoughts of the confounding woman and studied Louisa's sorrowful, mournful expression. "When you first came to me, I told you that I didn't need to know why you sought an end to your marriage."

"I remember. I was both relieved and disappointed. It made it easier not to worry that perhaps you'd decide the fault was mine. But then I'd also thought it would be nice to have someone help me carry the burden."

"If you want to tell me . . ." He let his voice trail off, the invitation there if she cared to accept it. He'd come to like her, to appreciate her, and to take a personal interest in helping her.

She swallowed more wine, glanced around. "I've spent two months in your bedchamber. It seems I should be able to tell you anything."

"You spent the time on my settee, not in my bed." They shared the settee only until the tray was delivered.

"True. But there is a kindness in you that I think you are uncomfortable acknowledging."

"We're not going to talk about me, Louisa, but I'm more than happy to listen if you need that weight lifted."

She nodded. "We've been married ten years. It wasn't a love match. We both knew it. He needed a wife, and I needed security. He'd had great success with his shop, which was sectioned off into all these different departments. He was going to open another. My brother, his solicitor, had invited him to dinner. Things progressed from there. Six months later, we were wed. Over time, I did come to love him. He's an incredibly kind and generous man. Three years ago, I finally got with child. But six months later, I lost it. He took it rather hard. I knew I'd disappointed him. He hasn't come to me since. All he does is work. But if he is rid of me, he can start over and perhaps find happiness, begin a family."

Bishop got up and joined her on the settee, ignoring

the chocolate that had dripped on the brocade as well
as on her shoulder. He took her hand. "I'm sorry for
what you went through. I suppose sometimes for the
wounds to heal, we need a fresh start."

She nodded. "He and I."

Leaning in, he pressed a kiss to her forehead. "I'll
ensure that you get it."

CHAPTER 10

THE next morning, Daisy was surprised to discover she hadn't been immediately sacked—after having the audacity to pour chocolate over Bishop's head. But oh, it had felt so damned good to do so.

Upon awakening, she'd considered giving her notice and simply walking out, but didn't want to sacrifice her position until she was certain she had obtained enough information for Mr. Parker. Arranging to secure that confirmation had taken a great deal of pleading and a lie—

"My aunt is terribly ill. I'd like very much to call on her this afternoon."

"You've only just begun working here, Daisy."

"Yes, Mr. Perkins, but I've finished all my chores for the day and will return before I have to cart up a tray this evening."

Perkins had finally consented, which was the reason she now found herself in Mr. Parker's office on the top floor of his most recently opened shop, which housed several different departments, each handling specific merchandise.

Although he'd instructed her to sit in the chair near his desk, he was standing at the window, watching her cautiously as though expecting her to deliver a blow of some sort. She feared that was exactly what she was going to do.

"You have something to report?" he finally asked. He was a tall, gangly man with deep-set brown eyes that seemed to take in everything.

"I'm afraid I can now confirm that your wife is indeed having an affair with Mr. Blackwood."

"You've seen them together, then?"

Telling him the truth was going to be far more difficult than she'd expected. He seemed the decent sort. And kind. "In his bedchamber last night, kissing. Will that be enough, do you think, for the courts?"

He gave her his back, looking out the window, no doubt hoping she wouldn't see how devastated he was. "It's enough for me. That's all that matters. Thank you, Miss Townsend. I'll see you paid straightaway the remainder of what I owe you."

"I'm sorry the news couldn't have been more cheerful."

"As am I."

"I'll see myself out." She rose—

"Does he appear to be kind to her?"

Oh, God, why didn't he just ask her to flay his heart and hers? "He treats her well, I think." Except for having other paramours, but she didn't want to tell him that bit. "I have the impression she enjoys his company."

He merely nodded. And she left him there, standing alone at the window, staring out upon a world that probably appeared somewhat different and drearier now.

Once she was on the street, she couldn't bring herself to head straight back to Bishop's residence. She had no reason to return at all, except she hadn't given notice and felt an obligation to officially end matters with Perkins, since he'd hired her. She would tell him tonight, leave on the morrow, and send Annie back to him in the afternoon. For now, however, she was in need of comfort and went to her aunt's residence.

Daisy was in the parlor pouring herself a brandy when Aunt Charlotte strolled in.

"Bit early in the day for that."

She turned and her aunt's eyes widened. "My dear girl, whatever is amiss? I've never known you to look so forlorn."

"I had to give my client some rather devastating news." She dropped onto the sofa and took a sip. "It was harder than I expected it to be. I became a sleuth to help people, and right now I feel as though I destroyed a man."

"Well that Blackguard Blackwood deserves it, carrying on as he does." She helped herself to some port and joined Daisy on the sofa.

"Not him. He'll survive. It's Mr. Parker. His wife is shagging about."

"Were you peering through the keyhole?"

"No, but I saw her and Bishop kissing."

"Oh, posh, that doesn't mean they're doing the nasty. I've kissed gentlemen aplenty and gone no further than that."

"In their bedchamber?"

"Well, no. That is rather a different kettle of fish." Aunt Charlotte studied her for a minute. "Why do I have the impression Mr. Parker is not the only one personally affected and saddened by the knowledge you uncovered?"

Her eyes stinging, she got up and went to stare at

the empty hearth because she didn't want her aunt to see any tears she might be unable to hold back. "I wanted him to be better than that."

"Blackwood, I suppose you mean."

She nodded. "He's such a different person when it's only him and me. He acts interested, asks questions, and when he looks at me, I feel as though for him no one else in the entire world matters as much as I do."

"That's how scoundrels are, darling. They win us over with their charm, until we're willing to give them everything they seek, until we convince ourselves that the heartache we know is waiting on the horizon will be well worth it."

Daisy faced her aunt. "You speak from experience?"

"I do, yes. And because I do, I can assure you that the heartache is most definitely *not* worth it."

Oh, but Aunt Charlotte didn't know Bishop. Daisy couldn't help but believe that he would prove an exception to her aunt's conviction. That whatever pain he caused would be worth the price of enjoying his company as well as pleasure at his hands.

"Are you done with being a servant now?" her aunt asked.

She nodded. "I'll give my notice tonight and take Annie back tomorrow."

"I like the girl, was hoping she'd stay on."

"She has a friend she misses."

Her aunt waved a hand like a queen signaling a head was to be chopped off. "I'll hire her as well. Serve the rogue right if we steal his servants after he made my darling niece wretchedly sad."

She chuckled lightly, grateful that her aunt had a way of always lifting her spirits. "I'll talk with Sarah."

"You'll stay for dinner."

"I have a chore I have to see to at nine." As it was Tuesday, Mrs. Mallard was on the schedule.

"We have a few hours yet. We'll have an early meal. I'll fill you in on all the latest gossip that is bound to cheer you up. Besides, what are they going to do if you don't rush back? Let you go?"

"Well, you are ill, so I suppose Mr. Perkins will understand my lingering. But I do need to get back in time, so another servant isn't called upon to do my chore." Even if it meant possibly seeing Bishop kissing someone else. Only tonight she would act as though she absolutely did not care.

"If your father had only had your responsible ways. It's a position you're pretending at, and you give it consideration as though it was real."

"You taught me well."

"If I'd done that, you'd be married by now."

Rolling her eyes, Daisy finished off her brandy, wondering if she might be able to get her aunt to give her the specifics regarding how she knew about scoundrels and heartbreak.

But a few hours later, sitting in her aunt's carriage on her way back to Bishop's, she was none the wiser regarding her aunt's youth. She was also going to be late.

When she finally arrived, she didn't bother dashing up to her room to change into her uniform but instead headed straight for the kitchen. Her simple frock of gray wool and black trim adequately covered her arms and shoulders. The bustle was small enough, the train short enough so as not to be a hindrance. Reaching up, she removed the pins securing her hat, with its assortment of silk daisies and peacock feathers, and had the chapeau in hand as she strode through the doorway and into the cook's domain.

"You're tardy," Perkins immediately barked.

Mrs. Karson looked as though she'd been equally chastised, her brow deeply furrowed and her lips pressed together tightly, dipping down at each corner in worry.

"My apologies, but there was an accident—"

He quickly cut off her lie. "I don't need your excuses. I need you upstairs."

"Right." She tossed her hat onto the table and reached for the tray.

"Leave it. He doesn't want the food. He wants only you."

Daisy's heart slammed against her ribs. That didn't bode well. Had someone followed her? Did Bishop know her purpose in being here? Was he going to vent his anger, take her to task? What did it matter? She wasn't beholden to him, wasn't truly his servant—at least she wouldn't be beginning tomorrow. If he thought to rebuke or chastise her, well, she'd rebuke and chastise right back, and storm out with the parting shot that she'd see him in court. "Right."

Still, her nerves coiled more tightly with each step that brought her nearer to her destination. She wasn't looking forward to the confrontation, felt a spark of guilt for having betrayed him. But he'd brought it all upon himself with his unconscionable behavior.

When she reached the end of the hallway, she was surprised to see his door was open in invitation. She supposed he knew she'd show up at some point, but if he was going to take her to task, why not do it in his library? Did he think he'd have better success at intimidating her in his bedchamber? Or was he considering reestablishing the rapport they'd shared at the Fair and Spare? Was it seduction he intended?

Bracing herself to resist the lure of him, she marched over the threshold and into the room.

Mrs. Mallard was sitting on the settee, quietly weeping. Bishop was positioned beside her, leaning over her, gently pressing a cloth to her face, murmuring. He glanced over his shoulder. "Thank God, you're here. Will you see to her?"

Even as he spoke, he unfolded his body and stepped away, giving Daisy a clearer view of the woman. Blood trickled from her split lower lip and a red welt on her cheek would no doubt be bruised by morning. "My word, what happened?"

"Her husband." His voice was rife with disgust, and he was holding the linen toward Daisy. After taking it, she settled herself close to the woman's side, dipped the cloth in the porcelain bowl on the table he'd moved nearer to the settee, wrung it out, and tenderly patted it against the woman's lower lip.

"Why would he do this?"

"Somehow he learned I was going out at night," Mrs. Mallard replied meekly. "In the evening, I'm not to leave the residence without him."

"Therefore, he struck you?"

She nodded mournfully.

"Has he done this before?"

"It's of no consequence," Bishop responded sternly. "Mrs. Mallard, do you know where he is now?"

"Probably at his club."

"Which one would that be?"

"The Cerberus."

"I know it. Daisy, will you accompany Mrs. Mallard home?"

"Yes, of course." A spark of fear rushed through her, not for the woman, but for the man who stood there with fury undulating off him in waves, a man who gave all appearances of preparing to go to war. A man who would not accept defeat. "What are you going to do?"

"Ensure he never touches her again."

Then he was storming from the chamber, and she wanted to rush after him, urge him to take care. To possibly wait until he had a cooler head. Instead, she looked back at her charge and thought she detected the tiniest of smiles, but it was quickly gone and she couldn't be sure she'd spotted it at all. "Do you feel up to traveling?"

"Without a doubt."

As they journeyed in Bishop's carriage—after he'd given instructions to the driver, he'd disappeared to either walk or hire a hansom cab—Mrs. Mallard stared out the window. As an inquiry agent, Daisy had grown accustomed to observing and scrutinizing even the smallest of details. Something niggled at her, something she couldn't quite identify. Perhaps it was simply her worry over Bishop, when her concern should be this woman. "Will you be safe in your residence, do you think?"

Mrs. Mallard looked at her. "Once Bishop puts the fear of God in him, I don't think Bertram will bother me at all. I shall lock my bedchamber door, however, as a precaution."

"Could he not break it down?"

"I very much doubt it. It's quite sturdy." She gave a caustic laugh. "He ensured it is almost impregnable. He has always been more jailor than husband."

"Why did you marry him?"

"At the time, he seemed the best choice."

Daisy couldn't help but wonder if her mother had thought the same thing. How did one know what was truly in the hearts of men? Her line of work brought into her life many men *and* women who had trusted and been betrayed. Although she was beginning to understand why Mrs. Mallard might have turned to Bishop, sought him out as a lover. He might be a scoundrel, but he did have some good in him. She couldn't imagine him ever striking a woman. Maybe Mrs. Mallard had just needed some reassurance that there were gents in the world who wouldn't hurt her.

When they reached the residence, the woman waited in silence for the footman to open the door and hand her down. Daisy made to follow, but Mrs. Mallard gave her a shy smile. "No need to come with me. I'll be fine. Thank you for accompanying me home."

"If you need anything, send word to Bishop."

"I shall. Good night." Slowly she wandered toward her residence.

Daisy settled back against the squabs. The footman closed the carriage door. Once Mrs. Mallard was inside, the coachman urged the horses on.

Daisy banged quickly on the roof, and the carriage soon came to a halt. She leaned out the window and shouted, "Take me to the Cerberus Club."

If Bishop was familiar with the club, no doubt his coachman had delivered him there a time or two. From his perch, the fellow bent over and glared at her.

"Master's orders are to return you straightaway to the residence."

"I don't give a bloody damn. Take me to the club or I'll find my own way there."

He hesitated. "Bishop ain't gonna like it. He'll sack me."

"He'll like it even less if you leave me to wander the streets. Please. You know he's going there, and you no doubt have discerned the reason for it. If he gets hurt, he might need us. Where's the harm in making certain he's all right?"

Another hesitation, this one longer than the first. Finally, he straightened and, with a flick of his wrists, sent the beasts into a trot. She was grateful to note that they weren't traveling in the direction from which they'd come. It was silly to worry about a man who was fully capable of taking care of himself, but she'd never before seen that sort of anger, anger that had the power to destroy. She feared what he might do with it.

CHAPTER 11

⟨⟨⟨⟨⟨⟨⟨

$\mathcal{B}$ISHOP had paced outside the Cerberus Club for more than half an hour. He was far too familiar with the dangers that awaited a man who was not in control of a situation, and he'd needed for his world to return to its proper colors rather than the bright red that had invaded his vision the second he saw Mrs. Mallard's injured face. While she'd initially blamed it on a door, he recognized a beating—no matter how light—when he saw one. The fear and worry mirrored in her eyes had merely confirmed what he knew to be true: her husband had smacked her about. It was an action that never failed to bludgeon Bishop's gut and chest, as though he possessed the ability to feel every slap, every punch, every blow.

He'd thought the walking required before he found a hansom would have done the trick and reduced his fury somewhat, but he was still livid when he'd leapt out of the conveyance, and so he'd begun the task of directing his thoughts toward serene avenues: walking through fields of clover; looking up at blue skies, spotting a rainbow. But his usual haunts had failed him, and so he'd begun to think of *her*. Marguerite. At first, he'd gone to his favorite memories of her: at his side, wandering through the Fair and Spare; her soft voice; her fragrance; her dumping chocolate on him. He'd chuckled low at the last recollection, and while the heat of anger that had accompanied him to his destination wasn't totally gone, it had cooled enough that calculating control had been restored to him.

Now he strode into the dimly lit club, with its smoky haze, and carried on to the far end of the foyer where a tall man with his arms crossed over his chest was leaning casually against the jamb of an open doorway, giving the impression that he wasn't watching every table with the intensity of a hawk. Bishop stopped beside him. "Aiden."

Aiden Trewlove slid his gaze over and arched a brow. "Bishop. Been a while since you've honored my establishment with your presence. I've heard you prefer the posher clubs these days."

"I've heard your dealers cheat."

Aiden barked out his laughter. "They don't cheat anyone who doesn't deserve or can't afford to be cheated. How are you, mate?"

"Too many irons in the fire. You know how it is."

"I do indeed. One of those irons bring you here tonight?"

He gave a curt nod. "Do you know if Bertram Mallard is about?"

Aiden jerked his head to the right. "Table in the far corner, gent with the toothy grin. What's your interest?"

"He did something I don't tolerate. I'm going to relieve him of that grin."

Aiden nodded. "Break anything other than him and you'll be paying for it."

"Send me an accounting of what's owed."

"With pleasure."

Focusing all his attention on his quarry, Bishop skirted around numerous occupied tables and tried to keep a grasp on the calm he'd finally achieved outside. But it was a challenge knowing what this vile excuse for a man had done to his wife. He'd never understood how any man could deliberately strike a woman, but then he'd never fathomed what was to be gained by being unkind in any manner. He reached his mark and came to a stop practically hovering over the scapegrace. "Mallard?"

His grin bright, the man looked up. "Yes?"

"I'd like a word."

His smile disappeared; his brow furrowed. "Not now. I'm winning, man."

"It won't take long." He waved his hand over the table and stared down every player. "You gents don't mind halting your play for just a minute, do you?"

The inflection he'd used signaled that he wasn't truly asking. They would cease their activities. After each had nodded and lowered their cards, he turned his attention back to Mallard. "If you'll get up now."

"Who the devil are you and what's this about?"

"I'll explain once you're standing."

Mallard sighed in obvious exasperation. "Make it quick."

Once the man was completely out of his chair, Bishop brought his arm back and then sent his balled fist flying straight into the bastard's jaw. His false teeth soared over several heads as he crumpled to the floor. Bishop bent down, grabbed his shirtfront, and lifted him slightly. "I'm known as Bishop. Strike your wife again, and I'll see you delivered straightaway to hell. She's under my protection now."

Mallard was blinking, his eyes wobbling about as though he couldn't focus. Blood dribbled from his mouth and nose. Bishop released his grip and let the man fall back to the floor. His lids closed and he went absolutely still. But he was breathing, the air whistling through his nostrils that were no longer properly aligned.

Tugging on the hem of his waistcoat and then straightening his coat, Bishop met the circle of horrified gazes and gaping mouths. "I have no tolerance for those who harm women. If you're his friend, ensure he understands that when he awakens."

Dismissing the stares, he turned toward the entrance—

And staggered to an abrupt stop. She was there. Marguerite. Standing two tables away. Watching him. Studying him. Her face a mask of confusion and worry. He didn't bother to hide his annoyance that she would have witnessed his inability to control his anger and the precise level of hurt he was capable of inflicting. Even if the fellow had deserved the punch, it brought Bishop no joy to have delivered it. "What the devil are you doing here?"

"I thought you might have need of your carriage to return you home."

She sounded so incredibly calm and reasonable that he almost laughed. Trust her to act as though they'd merely crossed paths at the park, not that he'd just laid a man flat with a single blow. He suspected the other three women who'd recently been in his bedchamber would have been aghast. But not her, not his

Marguerite. He wondered if a time would come when he would know exactly what to expect of her, when she wouldn't take him by surprise.

With a brisk nod, he indicated she should precede him, and he followed her out.

ONCE THEY WERE in the carriage, he drew the curtains, more to protect her reputation than his. It wouldn't do at all for people to catch a glimpse of them traveling together this time of night. His hand ached like the very devil. But the anger that had driven him to the club had abated. Inhaling her fragrance helped, as did the notion that she'd come for him. Risking possible danger, not certain what she would find. Or perhaps it had been merely curiosity that had driven her to his side. "You saw Mrs. Mallard delivered to her home safely?"

"Yes. Do you love her?"

"Why would you think that?"

"Because your actions regarding her seemed rather personal."

"Personal." Slipping a finger behind a curtain, he moved the cloth slightly aside and peered out. He should ignore the inquiry. He'd never spoken of it, but tonight the past had come rushing back and he was still raw from all the emotions stirred to life. For some inexplicable reason he wanted her to know, to under-stand what had compelled him to behave as he had. He didn't seek absolution or forgiveness, but neither did he want her to believe she should fear him. "I sup-pose they were. My father's business was to import and export goods from around the world. He would sometimes take his fists to my mother. When the ships were late, or the cargo arrived damaged, or the sea stole what he considered rightfully his. As though she was responsible for the whims of nature."

Realizing the streetlamps they passed might be giving her a view of his agony as he spoke the words, he let the curtain fall back into place, finding solace and comfort in the darkness. When he was a lad, it had hidden him from his shame at not being able to protect the woman who'd given birth to him. "I was fourteen, away at Eton, when she died. I accused him of killing her. He swore she'd fallen down the stairs. The constables accepted his accounting of what happened, but I've always known it was a lie. When I delivered that blow to Mallard, I envisioned my father's face."

"I can't imagine how devastating that must have been for you—to see someone you loved hurt by someone else you loved."

"I didn't love him," he said quickly with finality. "But she did. I never understood how she could. All I wanted was to prevent him from hurting her."

"Is he the reason you began lifting bells?"

"I hoped I could become strong enough to stop him. But it proved a fruitless endeavor."

"I daresay you'd have stopped him tonight. Did you break Mallard's jaw, do you think?"

"Possibly."

"I do hope he finds his teeth."

He didn't care if the man did or not.

They were silent for the remainder of the journey. When they arrived at the residence, he disembarked and extended his hand toward her, unable to hold back his hiss of pain when she took hold of it. She immediately let go, and he offered his other hand as support while she climbed out.

"Come to the kitchen, so I can tend to your injury," she said, her tone stern.

"It'll be fine."

"Don't be stubborn. You need some ice for it."

It was late enough so all the servants would be abed, none to witness her caring for him. Where was the harm?

The harm, he decided as he sat in a chair at the cook's worktable, was how much he enjoyed her looking after him. Crouching before the icebox, she was chipping away at a hunk of ice, placing the chunks in a bowl that she'd lined with linen. When she was finished, she joined him at the table, folded the cloth over the frozen bits, and secured each end. Gently, she took his hand—red, grazed, and swollen—and supported it with hers while she placed the cold compress against it. He clenched his back teeth to stop himself from groaning.

"Do you think your hand is broken?" she asked.

"No. However, I was surprised to find his jaw was like stone." The man was probably in his late thirties. "Why did you really come to the club?"

"I thought you might get hurt or need some assistance."

He grinned broadly for the first time since Mrs. Mallard had shown up at his door, bruised and broken. "Skilled at fisticuffs, are you?"

Her mouth twitched. "No, but I thought I might be able to do something to help. Besides, I brought the footman in with me. Did you not notice him?"

He hadn't. All he'd been able to see was her. It was as though all his surroundings had bleached away, no doubt a result of his heightened focus brought on by his original anger—like a predator in the wild aware of danger. "You should have returned here as soon as you had Mrs. Mallard safely tucked away, not put yourself at risk by going to a gaming hell."

Quickly she lifted her gaze to his, then lowered it back to his aching hand. He suspected it was her touch more than the ice that was bringing him comfort. "To be honest, I was also a bit curious about the club. I've never been to a gaming hell."

"You could have gambled at the Fair and Spare."

"It's not quite the same, though, is it. Everyone's on their best behavior there, striving to make an impression of respectability and civility. I've always pictured a gaming hell as being a bit more accepting of scowls and profanity and tempers."

His temper had certainly been on display. He didn't want her recalling it, pondering it, or being frightened by it. Although he was beginning to suspect very little scared her, that, unlike Mrs. Mallard, she was never cowed. She was bold and daring. He was sitting here now with one of her soft hands holding his while she tended to it because she'd fairly ordered him about. She was a determined little minx, prepared to stand her ground to ensure he didn't brush off an injury that did indeed need looking after.

He wanted her to reveal the truth of herself, here, now, in this quiet corner of his residence that smelled of baked bread and the early mornings of his childhood. What had hers been like? Who was she really? Therefore, he decided to direct the conversation away from himself and onto her.

"How is your aunt?" Her head came up so swiftly he was surprised it didn't go flying off her shoulders and across the room like Mallard's false teeth. Her eyes were big and round in alarm, as though she'd been caught doing something she ought not. He felt a need to reassure her. "Perkins mentioned she was ill."

"Oh, yes. I was quite relieved to confirm that she's improving."

"What is her ailment?"

"Her physician isn't quite sure. Some sort of malaise. To be honest, it might be all the sherry. She does enjoy her sherry."

"Ah. And what do you enjoy?" He'd dipped his head a fraction, enough to inhale fully her fragrance. He also caught the wispy scent of her skin, unique to her. He wanted to bury his nose into all the heated hollows: the curve of her neck, between her breasts, between her thighs. Breathe in deeply and simply relish.

She licked her lips, and he wished he'd been the one to dampen them. But then he wanted to dampen all of her, to coax little sighs of pleasure from her. Now that the fire of anger had been doused, the conflagration of desire had risen. It didn't help matters that she held his hand so tenderly, that she took such care not to cause him discomfort as she gently kept the ice in place.

"Sherry. Brandy. Port," she finally said.

"And red wine," he uttered, his voice husky. Somehow their faces had come even closer together. He could sense her rapid, shallow breathing as her breaths wafted over his jaw. It wouldn't take as much as a quarter of an inch turn to graze his mouth over her cheek. If he lowered his head a minuscule amount, he could learn the softness and taste of her neck.

"Yes. Although to be honest, I enjoy any wine that is open."

"You should not be so easy to please." He could count her eyelashes, but he couldn't tear his attention away from the shade of her eyes or how they had darkened to the blue depths of a midnight sky. An hour when it was so incredibly easy to sin, when making excuses to do so required no effort at all.

"Should a lady be difficult?" she asked.

"She should require effort." *To woo.* Only he wasn't going to woo her. She wasn't for him, would never be for him, and he needed to remember that, remember her possible purpose in being here. It wasn't for him. It was for another man.

He placed his free hand over hers. "Why don't you go on up to bed now? I can tend to my knuckles. Your tender ministrations have made everything feel much better." Even his battered soul.

"I should, yes. The morning comes early." She slipped her palm out from beneath his and stood. "Good night, sir."

Suddenly they were back to employer and employee, when for most of the night they'd been something more: friends. "Good night, Marguerite."

After she left, he got up and tossed the melting ice into the sink. He'd come very close to asking her to join him in his bed, to extend her comfort. And that would never do. He prayed he was wrong about her, that she wasn't here to betray him.

CHAPTER 12

$\mathcal{S}$ITTING behind his desk, Bishop read the letter that had arrived from his man of affairs that morning.

Through a series of mishaps, including storms and damaged cargo, your father is struggling to remain afloat. Pun intended. Hoping to recoup his losses quickly, he has decided to branch out into horse racing and has made an offer on a gelding named Storm Chaser. Appropriate, yes? Please advise.

Bishop scoffed. Just like his sire to seek a quick, and what he assumed would be an easy, solution to a complicated matter. Wealth seldom arrived on the whim of a wager. Neither did vengeance.

Years ago, at the age of nineteen, when he'd first begun accumulating the funds that freed him of his father's hold over him, he'd started plotting the scapegrace's demise. He'd set out to thwart the old man's dreams and happiness whenever possible by hiring a private investigator to keep him apprised of the elder Blackwood's financial, social, and business arrangements. Eventually Bishop had the money to hire a man of affairs to whom the investigator reported, a man who took care of matters at Bishop's request.

Now he dipped his pen into the inkwell and began

scrawling out the words that usually followed the arrival of a missive such as he'd just received. *Offer double.*

He, himself, had no desire to race a horse, but he suspected it was a beautiful beast that would enjoy jaunts through the park.

A few hours later, he'd just taken a bite of the beef stuffed sandwich that he was enjoying for his midday meal when Perkins strode in and presented him with a pristine ecru card resting on a silver salver like an island in the midst of an ocean. "Mr. Martin Parker has come to call."

Two nights ago, Marguerite had seen him kissing Mrs. Parker, and the woman's husband suddenly appeared, from out of nowhere, like a magician emerging through a cloud of smoke. It couldn't be coincidence. Surely, Bishop was correct about Marguerite being an investigator. He wondered when she'd managed to get word to Parker. Perhaps the ailing aunt had been a ruse. He remembered her somewhat guilty reaction to his question. Yes, that was no doubt it. The chit was indeed duplicitous.

Setting down his sandwich, Bishop took the card, studied it, and tapped it against his desk. He suspected Parker was here to inform him about his plans to bring suit against Bishop for his role in his wife's infidelity. He wondered what it was going to cost him, not that it mattered. He tossed his napkin onto the tray. "Have this taken away and then send him in."

A short time later, a finely dressed gentleman was standing stiffly in the library. His clothing was well tailored, yet little else about him was remarkable. Bishop had the unkind thought that the gent would be overlooked in a circle of three. He hardly seemed to fit with Bishop's image of the sort of man who would stand beside the lovely Louisa Parker. Bishop didn't extend a welcoming hand because he doubted his guest would take it. "Mr. Parker."

"Mr. Blackwood." He'd expected a voice rife with anger. Instead, it reflected the tone of someone who had wagered a great deal and lost.

"Mr. Blackwood is my father. I go by Bishop. Friend and foe refer to me as such."

"Do you love her?"

Bishop felt as though the man had suddenly delivered an unexpected blow that threatened to send him reeling backward. "I beg your pardon?"

"Louisa. Do you love her? Is she happy with you?" He held up his long-fingered hand. "It doesn't matter. I want to make this situation as easy for her as possible. A married woman known to carry on with another man is ostracized. Therefore, I need to take actions that will allow her to file for divorce rather than my instigating the proceedings. I thought perhaps, based upon your reputation, you might be able to guide me toward a right proper brothel."

Stunned, Bishop could do little except stare as his brain tried to make sense of the words tossed so calmly and resolutely his way. "By its very nature, a brothel is not proper."

The man's face scrunched up as though something he'd eaten wasn't agreeing with him. "I had hoped you might know of one where my pockets wouldn't be fleeced, and I wouldn't come away from the experience diseased."

Well, this conversation certainly wasn't going as he'd anticipated. He may have misjudged a situation and a man. Not something he managed to do often. "You're not here to deliver a blow to my jaw or challenge me to a duel or inform me you intend to sue me?"

"I'm tempted to do all three but assume any one of those would cause Louisa distress, and she is unhappy enough, obviously, to have turned to you."

Why did that sound like an insult? Subtle, but still an affront. Bishop found himself liking the man, damn it. "Would you care for some scotch?"

"Desperately. Thank you."

"Take a chair somewhere. I believe we need to talk." He went to the sideboard and poured two generous glasses of the amber liquid before joining his guest in the seating area near the fireplace. He didn't know why people always gravitated toward that part of the room, even when no flames licked at log or coal. He handed Parker his glass and then sank into the chair opposite him. "Cheers."

He downed a good portion of his, watching while his guest did the same. When any woman came to him, Bishop did a bit of investigating on the husband. Parker, the son of a mercantile owner, had expanded the family business and now was proprietor of three thriving stores, each with several levels and departments. He was looking for investors for a fourth, and Bishop had been considering going in anonymously. The man had a knack for knowing what items people wanted to purchase, and the decor in his retail establishments was fine enough to appeal to those gaining wealth without making them feel that they were shopping below their station. "How long have you known she's been coming here?"

Parker inhaled deeply. "I thought from the beginning. Two months." He tapped a well-manicured slender finger against the glass. "Has it been longer?"

The question came out in a near strangle. Bishop shook his head. "No, you have the right of it."

"I know she married me for my money, that she doesn't love me."

"Why would you think that?"

"Look at me, man. I'm lanky like a scarecrow. My face is too narrow, my nose resembles a beak, and I've hardly any chin at all, whereas you look as though you've been chiseled from granite for the specific purpose of adornment. Strong jaw, deep brow, sharp cheekbones. I imagine she fell for you rather quickly and thoroughly."

"I think you insult her by insinuating she's as shallow as all that, to be turned by comely features."

Parker took a sip of his scotch. "You're correct, of course. She is so exquisite. I fell in love with her from the beginning. It wasn't her beauty . . . well, it drew me to her. How could it not? A perfect blossom. But it was her kindness that held me enthralled. And her humor. She could make me laugh, and I'd had little laughter in my life. But then when she lost the babe . . ." His voice trailed off as if he struggled with the words. "She nearly died. I cannot bear the thought of a world without her in it. You are taking precautions to avoid getting her with child, surely."

His gaze was pointed and direct. However, Bishop couldn't help but wonder if that was the reason the man was avoiding his wife's bed. The fear of losing her. Losing her to another man was more acceptable than losing her to death. Good Lord. "I assure you she is in no danger of carrying my babe."

Parker nodded as though mollified and satisfied. "I trust you will do right by her when she is free."

Unfortunately, Bishop had swallowed scotch before those words were uttered and it took extreme effort not to spew the contents all over himself and his guest. Forcing down the liquor, he nearly choked. "You mean, marry her?"

"Without question."

Bishop had a lot of questions and only one answer. Absolutely not. But he had no desire to face a pistol at dawn. "You do realize that a woman can't acquire a divorce based solely on her husband's infidelity."

Parker nodded. "Abandonment for two years or cruelty. I haven't quite decided which way to go there. I don't wish to hurt her, nor do I wish to put her through the agony of a long wait before she can be with you publicly."

"I may have an idea, but let's get the infidelity out of the way before discussing it, shall we?"

"You know of a place then?"

"I do. You'll require a witness, of course. The establishment I have in mind provides discreet peepholes. Bring your witness, and I'll arrange with the proprietress for that person to be placed in a position to watch." He thought Parker visibly paled, but still the man nodded just before tossing back his remaining scotch. "Are you available Thursday evening at nine?"

"I shall make myself so."

"You really do love your wife."

"All I've ever wanted is for her to be happy."

AT HALF SEVEN, Thursday evening, with all her chores done, Daisy feigned a megrim and retired to her bedchamber, grateful Bishop had no lady friends visiting that night requiring she carry up any trays. He'd gone out earlier, apparently to enjoy dinner with friends. After arriving in her room, she changed out of her uniform and into her simple gray frock. A few minutes later, she managed to slip out of the residence with no one the wiser and made her way to the street where Mr. Parker was waiting for her in his carriage.

Although he hadn't given her the specifics, he'd offered her a rather large amount in addition to the already agreed upon cost of her services because he needed a witness in hand for this evening. She wondered if perhaps Bishop wasn't with friends, but with the man's wife, and Mr. Parker knew where to find them so they could be caught in the act. She rather hoped, if that was the case, they wouldn't be too far into the act.

Mr. Parker had assured her that after tonight they'd have all they required so she could resign from her post at Bishop's. She didn't much like admitting her mixed feelings regarding that possibility. The rapscallion intrigued her far too much.

Every time she decided he was an absolute scoundrel, he did something incredibly unscoundrel-like. Last night when she'd gone up to deliver the tray to him and Blue-Eyes, she'd heard laughter coming from the room and had hesitated to knock, to interrupt. The sound had seemed so natural, as though they truly enjoyed each other's company. For a moment, she'd been jealous that her occupation made her suspicious of him and his actions. She couldn't simply accept a smile, or a question, or a bit of conversation without wondering at the true reason behind it. She'd become incredibly guarded with her own emotions, but her reason there was more because of her parents than anything. In addition, the untrustworthy sorts she encountered certainly didn't diminish her fear of being hurt, of trusting someone only to discover she shouldn't.

When she'd finally rapped on the door, and his deep voice had bidden her entry, she walked in to see the couple sitting on opposite ends of the settee, he again comfortably attired in little save his boots, trousers, and shirtsleeves, his long legs stretched before him. Blue-Eyes was holding a gossip rag, and Daisy was left with the impression the woman had been reading snippets from it in order to keep him amused. Without being asked, she carried the tray to the low table that always began its night against the wall and deposited the tray.

"Oh, look here," Mrs. Bowles announced. "Something about your friend the Duke of Kingsland strutting about. Speculation is that his duchess might be with child." She glanced over the top of the paper. "Is she?"

"You know I don't discuss my friends' personal lives."

Reaching out, she playfully slapped his arm. "You're absolutely no fun at all." Then tilting her head slightly, she looked at Daisy. "Don't you quite agree?"

Bishop glanced over his shoulder, pinning Daisy with a stare as effectively as if he'd shot an arrow into her and secured her against a tree. She was relatively certain he was daring her to answer the question that never should have been asked of her, a servant. She hardly knew how to respond. While she wouldn't describe him as carefree, she had enjoyed his company at the club. Other times as well. In the hallway. In his library. While she might not label their time together following the incident at the Cerberus as enjoyable, she had to acknowledge that his opening up to her had created a sort of intimacy as well as satisfaction, because she rather doubted he'd ever shared his mother's story with anyone. But he'd told it to her and in the telling had handed her something precious.

The woman moved to the edge of the cushion as though waiting on pins and needles for Daisy's response. Bishop didn't appear to even be breathing. Daisy finally decided upon, "It's not my place to say." She ensured her tone signaled a clear message that no amount of cajoling would result in a different answer, because she was reasonably certain Blue-Eyes wasn't one to give up easily, especially when mirth was dancing in those eyes for which he'd named her. "Will there be anything else, sir?"

For the briefest of seconds, it looked as though he might do the cajoling, but instead he settled back, seemingly relaxed. "No. Thank you."

She headed for the door, stopped, turned. "How is your hand?"

He opened it, closed it, flexed it again. "Much better."

"I'm glad." She gave a quick curtsy. "Enjoy your evening."

"Oh, we shall," Mrs. Bowles said, and Daisy heard her tittering laughter as she closed the door in her wake and had the absurd thought that she hoped the woman might choke on one of the grapes she'd left for her. However, Daisy's hopes did not bear fruit as she and Sarah had not needed to drag any inert forms from the bedchamber that morning.

Now as the carriage rattled along, she focused her attention on the man sitting across from her. The man who had greeted her and then lapsed into silence as the horses set the vehicle into motion.

"I love a good mystery," she said quietly after a time. It was part of the reason she'd become an inquiry agent. "Am I to deduce where we're going?"

"To a brothel."

She felt as though she'd been smacked. "Bishop is taking your wife to a brothel?" That made absolutely no sense.

"No, it's not my wife's infidelities I want you to witness, but my own."

"I don't understand."

"I wanted proof she had strayed, but now that I have it, I realize for her to have any hope at happiness in the future, I must play the villain. I have been assured that a peephole looks into the room where I'll have my liaison. You need not observe the entire encounter, simply enough of it so you can convince a court I was unfaithful."

"Mr. Parker—"

"I realize I'm asking a great deal of you. If the sum to which we've agreed isn't enough, I can provide more."

Her job was to get the results her clients were paying for. It was not to convince them that they'd gone rather mad, and yet, she couldn't be silent when she feared he was making a grave mistake. Especially when he was so undeserving of all the unhappiness showered upon him. "Are you certain this is the wisest course?"

"Divorce is not pretty, Miss Townsend, but there is no reason it must be absolutely hideous."

"I hope someday you will find a woman who appreciates you, Mr. Parker. You are too kind by half."

The carriage came to a halt, and she glanced out the window at the rather unassuming building that looked more like a residence than a place for wickedness. She wasn't quite certain what she'd been expecting. Perhaps a gentleman waving a lantern and encouraging people to come inside like a barker did at a carnival or fete. *Come see the attractions. Be mesmerized and astounded.*

Her aunt would absolutely have the vapors if she knew Daisy was on the verge of stepping into a bawdy house, and yet she couldn't deny being rather curious regarding what one looked like on the inside.

Mr. Parker disembarked and then handed her down. Together they walked along the cobbled path to the door. He hesitated. "Do we just go in, do you presume?"

"I've no experience at this sort of thing, but I should think so. It is a place of business after all."

"Naturally, you've no experience. I should have hired a man to come with me. But I trust you, Miss Townsend, to be discreet with this matter . . . at least until you testify."

"I will behave with all the appropriate decorum." With that, she opened the door and led the way inside. It was dimly lit and everywhere she looked, she saw red silk and satin, risqué paintings and statuettes. Bared marble breasts and porcelain buttocks.

Wearing a low-cut scarlet gown, a buxom woman

with flaming red hair approached. "Ah, you must be Mr. Parker. I'm Jewel, the madam of the establishment. I already have a girl waiting for you. If you'll be kind enough to follow me."

Mr. Parker audibly swallowed, and Daisy was fairly certain that his grip on the brim of his hat was going to cause that one side to permanently curl up. As she trailed after the couple, she noticed a few scantily clad women sprawled about on various chairs and settees, but no men. She assumed the gents were already being entertained. She followed Mr. Parker and Jewel up one flight of stairs and down a long hallway, the closed door of each room painted a different color.

"You'll be in the blue room here, miss," Jewel said. "Mr. Parker will be in the lilac room right beside it." Opening the door, she ushered Daisy into the chamber and closed the portal with a sharp *click* behind her.

A pale light was provided by a solitary lamp on the table across the room. And there lounging on the bed near it, with his long legs stretched out, his ankles crossed, and his hands folded behind his head, was Bishop.

CHAPTER 13

Bishop had never regretted more being correct. For nearly half an hour he'd been here waiting to learn the truth, pacing the length of the room, hoping another explanation existed for how Parker had discerned that his wife was having an "affair" with Bishop. Hoping an unmemorable gent would wander in. Someone he would forget in an instant. Not the woman he would remember for a lifetime.

As soon as he'd heard the footfalls in the hallway, he'd leapt onto the bed and struck a relaxed pose in an effort to disguise his trepidation at what he was about to discover. With the turn of the knob, his stomach had tightened. With the opening of the door, he'd ceased to draw breath. He didn't know if he'd ever breathe properly again. Because there she was, staring at him, her face gone pale. She'd been caught. Knew he knew the truth of her.

There was no escape for her. Unfortunately, neither was there any for him.

But he'd come prepared for her to walk through that door. He knew the strategy he would use to be the victor in this game they'd been playing.

"WHAT THE DEVIL are you doing here?" Daisy asked, not bothering to keep the pique out of her tone. He didn't seem at all surprised to see her. As a matter of fact, his lips curled up ever so slightly, as though he was amused by her presence. She thought it quite likely that he'd been anticipating her arrival. Had he arranged this entire sordid affair? Had Mr. Parker spoken to him? It had never occurred to her that he would. Nor had she thought to ask how he'd come up with the ridiculous notion of visiting this scandalous establishment in the first place, especially with her in tow. But Bishop seemed completely unrattled—and entirely too provocative stretched out on that bed.

"Your Mr. Parker came to me seeking advice on the best way to cheat on his wife. Since two witnesses are required for an accusation of adultery to carry any weight in the courts, being the helpful fellow I am, I decided to offer my services."

Heat flooded her. She hadn't been looking forward to watching an intimate encounter, but at least alone, she could blush in private and look away when bodies became entangled. But to view the act of fornication with him—

"I'm not sharing a peephole with you." She scrutinized the wall, covered in floral wallpaper, separating the two chambers. "Where is it anyway?"

"There isn't one."

She spun around and glared at him. "Then how are we to witness what is about to occur?"

He rolled to a sitting position, dropped his legs over the side of the bed, and held up a stethoscope that had been designed to be used with both ears. "I borrowed this from a friend. We'll listen in."

"Have you another?"

"No, but we can share." He walked over in his loose-jointed way that for some reason made it more difficult to breathe. When he was near enough that she could feel the warmth of his body, he held one of the earpieces toward her while placing the other in his own ear.

It was a terrible, awful idea, and yet she refused to display any cowardice in front of him. Shoring up her resolve, she snatched the offering and tucked it into her ear, but the tube covered in velvet was so short that she had to step nearer to him, so near that she could see the short stubble of whiskers along his jaw. She had a clear view of the delicate muscles just above his collar moving whenever he swallowed. The sight mesmerized her. She and he were practically breathing each other's exhales, and his bergamot fragrance teased her nostrils. His gaze never straying from hers, he placed the wooden bell-shaped end of the instrument against the wall.

The voices were faint, slightly muffled, and she struggled to make out the words.

"*. . . devil are you doing here?*" A man, Mr. Parker no doubt.

"*Bishop thought we should talk, someplace neutral.*" A woman.

"*Therefore, he brought my wife to a brothel?*"

Daisy's eyes widened and she whispered, "Mrs. Parker?"

Bishop merely raised a dark eyebrow and gave a barely perceptible nod. What game was he playing at? She could easily imagine Mr. Parker being stunned into inaction upon first entering the room and seeing his wife there, much as she'd been at the sight of Bishop, so she suspected she and her nemesis had not missed much of the couple's conversation.

"Did you not bring your female detective?" Mrs. Parker asked.

"When did you know about me?" Daisy asked quietly, because if Mrs. Parker knew, in all likelihood, so did Bishop.

"That's different. She is here in a professional capacity."

"Not until tonight. Not for certain, anyway. Although I'd begun to suspect the morning following the night you first delivered a tray to my bedchamber."

"That's why you had me start carting them up."

"You should be grateful. I made it easier for you to spy on me and gather the information you were there to obtain."

Nothing about being in his presence made anything any easier. Especially because it somehow seemed that with each word spoken, they'd gravitated a little nearer. The top of her head reached his shoulder. It would take only the tip up of her chin, the tip down of his for their mouths to meet.

"Besides," Mrs. Parker continued, *"Bishop said it's no longer a house of ill repute but rather a place for wayward women to take refuge and learn new skills. The proprietress merely arranged for it to look like a brothel again so you wouldn't get suspicious before entering this room."*

"That hardly makes it any better, Louisa."

Daisy didn't want to acknowledge her disappointment that it was no longer a bordello, that she wouldn't have the experience of knowing precisely what a bawdy house looked like. This room in its shades of blue was warm, comforting, and inviting.

"This is not the sort of place for a proper lady to visit nor are these the sort of women she should even know about," Mr. Parker insisted.

"Yet my husband is determined to know one very intimately. Why, Martin?"

"Because it's better to have my transgressions discussed in public than yours. Men are more easily forgiven. Women are not."

"What do you perceive as my transgressions?"

"I know precisely what they are. As you pointed out, I have a detective on the matter."

"We play cards."

"Louisa, she's seen you . . ."

His voice trailed off, and Daisy decided he'd either mumbled or couldn't bring himself to voice out loud that his wife had been seen sitting on another man's lap or kissing him. On the lap of the man whose scent surrounded Daisy, whose heat radiated out to touch her. Whose nearness made it difficult to think, to concentrate on the words being exchanged on the other side of the wall.

"Playacting," Mrs. Parker said quite clearly. *"We've never—"*

Everything went quiet and Daisy strained hard to hear. Then her gaze fell on the bell-shaped end of the stethoscope. It was no longer pressed to the wall but dangled between Bishop's fingers. She lifted her eyes to his.

"It was getting a little too personal," he murmured.

Because Mrs. Parker was going to reveal the truth of him. The rapscallion, the scoundrel, the rake. The

man married women steered clear of for fear they
might fall under his spell. The man unmarried girls
were warned would lead them to ruination. She considered the cards she gathered up on the mornings after one of his ladies visited. "You don't actually bed
them, do you? Any of them."

"If you don't step away, I'm going to do something
that we'll probably both regret." His eyes began to
smolder, his breaths coming more quickly. Those lips
of his that by their very design offered promises of
passion had parted slightly. She knew what he wanted,
knew it called for a hasty retreat on her part.

She stepped forward.

He lowered his head and slashed his mouth across
hers, tugging free the ends of the tubing joining them.
The stethoscope clattered to the floor. His large hand
cradled the back of her head, angling it so he could
deepen the kiss. His tongue tangled with hers, and yet
at the same time seemed to explore every nook and
cranny as though each held a treasure. This was nothing at all like the kiss she'd seen him give to Mrs.
Parker. It had been chaste, tame, a cat stretching in the
sun. This one was fire and brimstone, desperation and
hunger. A panther on the hunt. As though they'd both
gone without sustenance for far too long, and now at
last were free to enjoy the feast that had been prepared
in welcome.

She curled her arms around his neck, scraping her
fingers along his scalp, threading them through the
thick strands, while he wrapped his arms around her
and held her tightly, her breasts smashed against his
chest, the rest of her body pressed against his firm

and sturdy length. She didn't know how she remained standing when her legs had grown so weak. If not for his hold on her, she suspected she might have collapsed to the floor.

His mouth left hers to trail heated kisses along her throat, beneath her jaw, to her ear. "I've wanted to do that since the first moment I laid eyes on you."

The man Society believed had no restraint when it came to women appeared to possess an abundance of it. "Why didn't you?"

"You were a member of my staff. But you're not in my household at this minute."

"No, I'm not." She was in the arms of a scoundrel in a once-upon-a-time brothel.

Then his mouth was back on hers, his enthusiasm somehow not diminished in the least, as though he would never have enough of her. As though it would be impossible to ever be sated.

BISHOP HAD KNOWN it—she—would be like this. Feverish, demanding, all-consuming. It was one of the reasons he'd resisted the allure of her until now. Because he'd understood once wouldn't be enough. That he would become drunk on the taste of her, more flavorful than the finest wine. Her heat seeped through his clothing to warm his skin. He might forever feel her presence there, within his pores, coursing through his blood. He was so incredibly hard. For her.

He fought to ignore the bed with its thick blue duvet beckoning only a few feet away. After lifting her into his arms, he could reach it in half a dozen long steps, lay her down upon it, and stretch out alongside her.

He imagined the joy to be found in loosening buttons, lacings, and ribbons. Of slowly revealing every inch of her flesh.

Her low moans echoed around him while her hands traveled over him, mapping out the contours of his shoulders and back before delving into his hair and tugging on the strands, not in a manner that signaled she wished to push him away, but in a fashion that communicated her need to have him nearer.

As lust ratcheted painfully through him, he couldn't seem to escape the reality of what she was—a woman who'd come to him under false pretenses. Nor was he completely innocent. Putting on a performance each time she opened the door to his bedchamber.

But the desire was not pretend. It was true and real. Yet if he gave in to it and took full possession of her, he didn't know what he would discover on the other side of it. Would he, a man who never lost at anything, lose a part of himself? Was it worth sacrificing a pawn to take the queen?

THE PLEASURE SWIRLING through Daisy was both frightening and exhilarating. If he wasn't what she'd thought, then what sort of man was he? How much of him was merely facade? Was she a fool to relish the way his mouth moved over hers, to enjoy his hands pressing her flush against him?

The loud rapping on the door had her leaping out of his arms and flattening her back against the wall, because without him, she needed some support or she would indeed crumple. Her breaths came in mad gasps. As though unaffected by what had just transpired, casually he reached down and grabbed the stethoscope from the floor where it had landed earlier. Once he straightened, he barked, "Come."

It was the only indication she had that he wasn't at all pleased by the intrusion. But then, if she'd learned anything at all this evening, it was that he was very skilled at not revealing much about himself, his thoughts, or his feelings. Within his bedchamber, he'd fooled her completely. Perhaps he'd been doing the same with the kiss. Duping her into believing he desired her. A punishment, maybe, because he'd learned something about her tonight as well, confirmed his suspicions.

The door opened and, her face a mask of serenity, Mrs. Parker gracefully glided in, her husband in her wake. "We still have things to work out, but at least we're talking again."

She walked over to Bishop, rose up on her toes, and gave him a peck on the cheek. "Thank you for everything. I shan't be coming to see you any longer."

"I shall miss our card games. You were a formidable opponent."

"I suspect you often let me win."

"I never lose on purpose."

Daisy fought not to be jealous of the ease between them. But then she suspected they'd always been honest with each other. There'd been no subterfuge.

"Miss Townsend, would you like us to return you—" Mr. Parker began.

"I'll provide her with transportation," Bishop said. "No sense in you going out of your way when she and I are traveling in the same direction."

Mr. Parker approached and shook his hand. "Thank you, sir, for offering us the opportunity to rethink matters."

"I'm glad I had the right of it."

Mr. Parker turned to her. "Send me an accounting of what I owe, and I'll see it paid immediately."

Daisy nodded. "Yes, sir."

As the couple began to leave, Bishop placed his hand on the small of Daisy's back, indicating she should follow them. When they reached the foyer, Jewel was waiting.

"Thank you, Jewel, for your assistance," Bishop said.

"It was the least I could do to show our appreciation for your latest donation."

Daisy was beginning to believe this man was far more complicated than she'd imagined, with layers to him that a lifetime might never uncover. Yet, as dangerous as it might be, she wanted to delve into his hidden depths and discover the true Bishop.

Once they were in his carriage, sitting on opposite squabs, he pulled the curtains across the windows. "Wouldn't do for you to be seen alone with me, late at night. Especially leaving a brothel."

"Former brothel," she reminded him. "How did you know of it?"

"How do you think? I visited when I was much younger. Surrendered my virginity to a sweet girl named Sally Greene."

She could tell by his tone that he had fond memories, and she didn't want to explore why she was struck with a bit of envy. Of more interest was the fact that they were sitting here talking about his virginity. She didn't know if she'd ever heard the word spoken aloud, but he'd uttered it as though they possessed an intimacy that allowed them to discuss anything. "Why do you do it? Why pretend to have affairs with women?"

He'd not lit a lantern inside the coach, and it was black as pitch. She could make out his faint outline but couldn't see his features, couldn't discern his expression, or guess at what he might be thinking.

"Because of your mother? Because of what happened to her?"

"I don't wish to talk about it."

His voice was rough and raw, as though he was battling an unseen force, but shimmering beneath it was an undercurrent of something more powerful, something that had broken loose when they'd been alone in that room in the brothel. Something they hadn't completely left behind, something they hadn't tamed, something that still prowled.

"What is it that you wish?" she dared to whisper.

The silence between them grew thick and heavy, as words were weighed, actions considered, strategy determined. Finally, she heard a low long sigh of surrender, and then his deep voice filled the confines. "This."

Suddenly he was sitting beside her, drawing her near, his mouth moving deliberately and with purpose over hers. And she knew, *knew*, when they arrived at his residence, they were going to journey up those stairs together to his bedchamber. They would sit on that settee where he had played cards with other women, but they would play a very different game. Eventually they would make their way to his bed, and that pillow that always looked untouched would soon bear the indentation of her head.

It was what she wanted. *This.* Such a small word for something so large, so all-encompassing. Something with the power to shape, mold, redefine a person, a sensation, a belief. She was going to have her dalliance, not at a club, but in his residence, between his sheets, pressed against his body. And she knew that she would never again be the same.

Because even now it felt as though every aspect of her had come apart, and his hands moving so slowly and with purpose over her back, her hips, and her sides were creating a very different contour, putting everything where it should have been all along. Open, honest, revealed.

With his mouth devouring hers, no secrets existed between them. His growls, her moans were more honest than their words. They couldn't be contained. They couldn't omit bits that were too frightening to share. There was a truth to their murmuring, an authenticity that stripped away all deceit.

After loosening the buttons on her frock—not with the nervous fingers of a youth so one went flying but with the experienced fingers of a man, who, though eager, was not anxious—and parting the material, he dragged his mouth along her throat and lower, to her breasts, lifted by her corset for his enjoyment and hers. His mouth was moist and hot as it journeyed over the swells, slowly and provocatively.

After unbuttoning first his waistcoat and then his shirt, she slipped her hand inside, relishing the feel of his warm skin, daring to touch what she'd once caught only a scandalous peek at. When her fingers circled his nipple, one she'd blushed at glimpsing, he groaned low before dipping his tongue into the hollow between her breasts.

"This isn't enough for me," he ground out. "Stop me when it becomes too much for you."

How could it ever become too much? How could she ever utter stop?

She wanted this, wanted him. Not as early on as he'd claimed he had wanted her, not that first night. Perhaps when she'd prepared him tea. Or maybe it had been sooner, but her inexperience had caused her not to recognize yearning when it engulfed her. However, she would certainly recognize it in the future, because it swamped her now.

His mouth came back to hers with surety and purpose. No man had ever kissed her as though his life depended upon doing so, as though she was sustenance to his hunger, predator to his prey, shelter from his storm. She was relatively certain a tempest of memories raged inside of him, ones he didn't want to discuss because they made him vulnerable. How could a man be victorious if he wasn't always strong?

He brought his sturdy hand to her hip, squeezed, and moved it lower still, until he was able to guide her legs up so they draped over his lap, while she remained sitting up but bent back as he continued to devour. Then that hand, that wicked hand, slid beneath the hem of her skirt and grazed her calf.

Was this the *too much* he feared she'd object to? Because it wasn't nearly enough.

Gently, slowly, he kneaded his way up her leg, past her knee, along the inside of her thigh. Had she ever noticed how sensitive the skin there was, how it seemed to have the ability to beg, to demand more?

Her backside squirmed against his thigh while his fingers tenderly stroked up, down, and around.

He broke away from the kiss, his breath wafting over her cheek just before his tongue outlined the swirls of her ear. Delicious. How was it that so many parts of her felt as though they'd been awakened from a long sleep?

"Do you want more?" he asked.

She nodded.

"I want to hear you say it."

"I want more."

"Do you want it all?"

She wasn't quite certain what the *all* entailed, but in his capable hands, she knew it would be glorious. "I want it all."

The fingers at her thigh moved up and brushed lightly over her mound, and she unexpectedly found herself lifting her hips toward that touch. He chuckled low, darkly into her ear. "You do want it."

Desperately. But she didn't have the courage to admit that when she didn't know how to precisely make him crave her in the same manner. Oh, she knew what she wanted to do to him, what she wanted to stroke, explore, and come to know. But she didn't know if they had time for it all because they were nearing his residence surely. Patience was a virtue, although her thoughts were not virtuous. Thus, she would wait until they were alone in his bedchamber, and then she would ask all the questions of him that he'd asked of her. She would make him beg.

Like those of a clever thief, his fingers snuck through the slit in her drawers to delicately stroke the opening in her body, and in so doing, he stole her breath. She trembled and moaned, her head dropping back. One of her hands slid up to cup the side of his neck while the other clutched his strong, powerful shoulder. His fingers danced over her quivering flesh, parted the folds, and circled the sensitive area.

"So hot," he rasped. "So wet. So delectable." He skimmed the intimate length of her. "Softer or firmer?"

"Firmer."

The pressure increased and her body tingled far beyond where he touched. How could she grant him such power? Why was she not frightened of what he could unleash? Because she trusted him. He hadn't kissed her at the club because she was a member of his household, but she was no longer. They both knew it. Tonight signaled the end of one relationship and perhaps the beginning of another.

"Faster or slower?"

"Slower . . . no . . . faster . . . I don't . . . know. I can't think."

He teased, changing the pace, going from leisurely to frantic to somewhere in between. His strokes long and short, circular, winding. Pleasure coursed through her. Her body trembled as the tension built. She gasped.

His breaths grew harsh, not as harsh as hers, but she was aware of his muscles tightening as though he was following her on this journey. Then she escaped the confines of flesh and bone, and his mouth was blanketing hers, capturing her screams, holding tight as her cries turned into whimpers and she went lax in his arms while the intense ecstasy ebbed and floated away.

She had an overwhelming urge to thank him. She was grateful for the darkness, even as she resented it for not allowing her to see his face. To see if what she'd felt and experienced had transferred into him. She didn't know how she'd support herself when she got out of the carriage because her entire being felt like warm jam and she simply wanted to spread herself over him.

Carefully, he eased her legs off his lap and helped her to sit up straighter. His lips landed on her throat just before he went to work securing her buttons. "Are you all right?" he asked, his voice a low caress along her nerves.

She wanted to laugh with joy and happiness. And a measure of awe. "Very."

Finished with his task, he slid slightly away and, based upon what she could feel and detect of his movements, was putting himself back to rights. But she also sensed something else. A pulling apart, a separation, the erecting of an invisible wall.

She remembered the question she'd asked earlier, in that room that should have been tawdry, but instead was comforting, the inquiry he'd ignored in favor of kissing her. She'd let the answer go, welcoming his lips instead. When she'd asked about the affairs, he'd distracted her with his yearning mouth and questing fingers.

Suddenly it seemed imperative to hear the answer from those lips that had taunted, teased, and satisfied her. To have confirmation that she had deciphered that matter correctly. "Those other ladies, the ones you take to your bedchamber, are you the same with them as you were with Mrs. Parker? Do you simply play cards?"

She was aware of him stiffening, tension radiating out from him, and she feared she'd gotten it wrong.

That Mrs. Parker was merely the exception. And he'd just added Daisy to his list of numerous conquests.

JESUS. WHAT HAD he done?

He hadn't regretted kissing her in the bedchamber, but here in this carriage he did have regrets. He'd lost control. Knowing where they were headed, he never should have crossed over to her, taken her in his arms, been welcomed into hers, and allowed himself to be spurred on by her eagerness.

He never lost control, but with her from the beginning, he'd had a tenuous hold on it. For the past few moments, being with her had been like having the reins on a team of horses snatched from his grasp, giving them the means to send him careening over a cliff.

Even now he couldn't bring himself to return to his place across from her. Nor could he provide her with the answer she wanted. He'd already told her more than he should, more than he'd ever revealed to anyone. He had to hold everything else close because he'd given a promise to Mrs. Bowles and Mrs. Mallard. He'd see it through.

In addition, and more importantly, he'd made a vow to his mother on the morning that he'd placed a bouquet of violets on the freshly turned earth that marked her grave: he would help those who needed him. No matter the cost. At the time, he hadn't realized how steep the price might be. He wasn't quite certain that he'd actually understood it until a moment ago. When he'd had only a taste of the glory that was Marguerite Townsend. But it wasn't her place to pay for his sins. And she would if they continued on. Just as he'd told Mrs. Mallard that first night when she'd come to him, his reputation would ensure it. "I won't discuss my relationship with the others."

He could sense her studying him within the velvety dark confines of the vehicle.

"You don't trust me," she said quietly, and yet the words struck him like a bullet fired straight into his soul.

He didn't know if he trusted anyone completely, not even his fellow Chessmen. He'd never told them the truth of his relationship with his women, because he couldn't risk a stray word compromising what he was striving to accomplish. In the end, atonement was all he sought.

"How can I, when from the beginning you lied to me?"

"As though you were honest with me? I would say you went so far as to purposely lead me into believing you were having an affair with Mrs. Parker. I went to no great effort to deceive you or to convince you to believe something that wasn't true."

"You pretended to be a servant." His voice came out harsher than he'd intended, perhaps because the truth of her words struck a little too close to home. He had sought to deceive her every single time she opened the door to his bedchamber.

"I *was* a servant." Her tone carried a pique that he was unaccustomed to having women direct his way. "Up before the sun, dusting, and scrubbing, and polishing. Cleaning without being seen until my back ached."

"Gathering your information."

"Observing."

"Spying."

"Reporting what I saw. I'm not the one who created a fairy tale in that damned room, determined to entice someone into believing it. If you're looking for deception, Mr. Blackwood, look no further than yourself and your actions."

Damn her for calling him by his father's name, a moniker he never used because anything that hinted at his association with that wretched man sickened him. And damn her for calling him out on his transgressions because, between the two of them, he had indeed been the most deceptive. While he could argue for the need for it, he couldn't bring himself to do so. Because his father had been a deceitful bastard. Flirting, cajoling, and wooing his mother until she fell in love with him, causing her to believe life with him would be idyllic—not the hell it had become. Always promising the beatings wouldn't happen again. Through him, Bishop had learned that words couldn't be trusted, that truth resided only in actions.

And his actions tonight had been unconscionable.

He shouldn't have kissed her at the brothel. He'd known at the time that it was a bad idea, but standing there within inches of her, listening as she breathed, inhaling the violet fragrance along her skin, gazing into those wide blue eyes, and staring at those lush plump lips, he'd been unable to resist the temptation of her and had surrendered like an untried schoolboy. But he certainly hadn't kissed her like he had no experience. Nor had she responded as though she'd never snuck off into the gardens with a man.

For those few minutes there had been no secrets between them. She'd known he was a counterfeit lover, and he'd known she was a phony servant.

What they'd shared was probably the first honest moment between them. And it should have been enough. He should have ensured it was enough. But then, when they'd first gotten into the carriage with the taste of her still fresh on his lips, he'd wanted a little bit more. The little bit had turned into a great deal because she'd been so responsive, and he'd wanted to give her the gift of pleasure.

But now the mistake loomed because she wasn't someone who would be content with a dalliance. It was the reason she hadn't gone up those stairs at the Fair and Spare. She wanted more, deserved more.

Deserved what he couldn't give her. A man in whom she could take pride. A man with whom she could be seen in public. Any further association with him would bring her naught but mortification, would serve only to blemish her reputation. He needed to spare her that, protect her in his own fashion.

Her anger was causing her to breathe harshly and heavily. That was a good start to sending her on her way. Although what he truly wanted was to take her mouth once more and turn the anger back into passion. Her response to him had been a gift, one he shouldn't have received, couldn't accept.

DAISY WAITED FOR him to respond, to provide any sort of denial to her accusations.

"You're absolutely correct," he finally said quietly, his voice low and rough, as though he'd had to force out the words. "I play games, doing whatever necessary to win. Sometimes that involves creating fairy tales. I apologize for my earlier behavior. It shouldn't have happened."

A game. Anger and hurt rushed in to replace the pleasure she'd experienced only moments before. He'd taken something wonderful and turned it into something she regretted and resented with every fiber of her being.

"Because you lost?" she asked caustically.

In spite of the darkness, she was aware of him whipping his head around to look—no, she imagined he was glaring—at her. She feared that with her, he'd crafted another fairy tale, that nothing that had ever transpired between them had been honest and true.

"Because you weren't made for dalliances, and that's all I was offering."

She wanted to object, but the truth was, after what they'd just shared, she didn't know how anyone who fell apart in another's arms returned to a casual relationship, because even now she felt the pull of him and wanted to be nestled against him. Instead, the abyss between them was widening with each clop of the horses' hooves. She had the odd sensation of the carriage stretching until they'd no longer be in close proximity of each other.

The vehicle began to slow, and he returned to his place opposite her. "By the way, we're arriving at your aunt's residence. I thought it best to take you there."

Because he didn't have the strength to resist her if she was in his residence? Or because he didn't want her? She wasn't going to beg or weep or confess that his apology hurt because it confirmed what he'd known and stated before he'd kissed her: there would be regrets.

He regretted all that had happened. She regretted all that hadn't.

"How extremely thoughtful."

"I'll have Perkins pack up your belongings and send them round in the morning."

"No need. With the exception of the frock I'm wearing, everything I brought with me was temporary. It's how I handle things when I go into a situation where I might have to leave in haste. Staff is welcome to whatever remains. Or Perkins can toss it all out. None of it means anything to me." She wanted to add that he didn't mean anything either, but it was the dishonesty between them that had led to this awkward moment. Their relationship had been built on a foundation of lies. She'd be a fool to wish for more between them.

When the carriage came to a stop, to her surprise, he opened the door, leapt out, and reached back in to hand her down. "I'll see you to the door."

"No need. I think we're quite done with each other, Mr. Blackwood."

Straightening her shoulders, she began her trek up the drive to the residence.

She would not weep. She wouldn't mourn the loss of him. She would not repeat her mother's mistake. She wouldn't hold on to memories of him, would give him no sway over her. The gossip rags had been correct about him. He was Blackguard Blackwood, scoundrel extraordinaire, and for the briefest of moments she might have fancied him. But she was no fool. She wouldn't pine for him. She would never again think of him at all.

CHAPTER 14

⌒⌒⌒⌒

$\mathcal{F}$RIDAY was a dreary, rainy day that suited Daisy's melancholy. While she let an office with rooms above it where she resided, she had decided to spend a few days with her aunt. Especially as she was having a difficult time keeping her vow not to think of Bishop. She'd lost herself to him, and damn it, she wanted to do so again. Stupid girl. She was too much like her mother, yearning for a man who was no good for her, who would lead her to ruin.

She was curled in the corner of the sofa in her aunt's drawing room. In her palm rested her locket, open, so she could study the two miniature photographs, the last taken of her parents. Her father's portraits within the earl's residences had been moved to the attic, except for those from his youth, when he'd been included with the remainder of the family in paintings.

As for her mother, only this small picture existed, and Daisy knew a time would come when her eyes would betray her and she'd need a magnifying glass to make out the details. Neither of her parents were smiling, and yet she detected a note of happiness in the serenity of their faces and the glow in their eyes. She wished the images had been painted so she'd know the exact shade of their hair and eyes. In the portraits from his youth, her father's hair had been a sandy blond but she assumed it had shifted into a light brown. His eyes were dark. Were they the color of coffee, like Bishop's? Or were they more like tea?

Her mother's hair was fair, as were her eyes. No doubt blue like her daughter's. Daisy wished she could remember them more clearly, could draw upon the memories that the lullaby played at the Fair and Spare had invoked. She was still amazed that Bishop had remembered the phrase she'd mentioned and more that he'd thought to ask the pianist if he'd been familiar with it.

Yet, she shouldn't be surprised, because all along she'd seen examples of his kindness. She'd simply assigned ulterior motives to them, but now she was beginning to suspect it was simply his way. A man who as a boy had seen his mother hurt, and now did all he could to ensure women were made to feel special. Surrounding them with their favorite flowers and sweets. Truly listening when they spoke.

That night at the Fair and Spare, he'd already deciphered who she truly was and her purpose in his household, and yet he'd still shown her kindness.

You don't have a face for playing cards. Your expressions are far too easy to read.

In that shadowed corner had he read her longing for him, how it eclipsed her common sense? Yet last night he'd been equally easy to read. He'd wanted that kiss at the bordello as much as she. Now they were free of each other. She wondered if in the freedom hovered the pursuit of desire.

Not desire. Lust. That's all it would entail. No emotional attachment existed between them. He'd proven that easily enough.

"I don't like seeing you moping about, sweeting."

Glancing up, she smiled at her aunt. "I'm not moping. Reminiscing more like. Or trying to, but I have so few memories. None at all of Father. You seldom speak of him. What was he like?"

Frowning, Aunt Charlotte settled into a nearby plush chair. "You don't want to travel this path."

"But I do. I know he was far from perfect but there had to be some good in him for my mother to love him as she did."

"Are you striving to justify your feelings for Mr. Blackwood?"

The scoundrel had been correct. She was too easy to read. "No. But I've spent so many years afraid that I'd repeat my mother's mistake"—she shook her head—"I just want to understand. To know someone I can't remember knowing."

Her aunt released a long, tortured sigh that sounded as though it had risen up from the soles of her feet. "Lionel was the youngest, the baby. Even as a man, he was considered the baby. He came five years after me, a surprise I suspect. As you're aware, I have three older brothers, whom I adore. But they are always so serious. Lionel never was. He was mischievous and fun. Constantly smiling and laughing. A natural charmer. He could have had any lady in the *ton*, even as a son who was unlikely to ever inherit. But he fancied my lady's maid, even though she was older than he. Six or seven years, I think.

"They laughed all the time. He made her feel young. She made him feel . . . important, I suppose. To her, he wasn't the third spare. He was the one everyone admired and wanted."

"They were happy then, you think?"

Her aunt's smile was sad. "For a while, yes. But my father had told him that if he married a servant, a girl with no family, no prospects, no dowry, well, he'd be on his own. Lionel had always possessed a bit of a rebellious streak, perhaps because it allowed him to stand out and apart from three brothers who excelled at everything. School, sports, hunting, and the ladies. They all had good marriages. Anyway, he wed your mother and was cast out. I did what I could for him, but my allowance went only so far, and at the time I still resided with my parents. No one else in the family had anything further to do with him."

Daisy felt her first ray of hope. "He must have loved her tremendously then, don't you think, to have given up so much for her?"

"Still, it was an incredibly foolish thing to do, wasn't it? Marriage requires more than love. Sometimes life requires sacrifices to survive."

"Is that what you did? Sacrificed."

"We're not discussing me. You want some memories of your parents, and I can't give you anything of joy except to confirm that they loved you very, very much."

"But they left me so often. I have vague memories of that."

"Yes, I know, and I wish you didn't. Lionel took odd jobs here and there. He never stayed long at anything. He grew bored or decided it was beneath him. He hated the notion of work. I suppose he sought escape when he turned to the opium. And he took your mother with him."

Daisy had known Aunt Charlotte wouldn't weave a fanciful story but did rather wish she'd softened the harsh reality. "I'll take consolation in the fact that at least they are together, in a Romeo and Juliet sort of way I suppose. Too tragic to bring much solace."

Her aunt looked as though she'd been slapped before lowering her gaze to her fingers, knitted tightly together in her lap. "That is one way to view it."

"I have wonderful memories of time spent with you."

Aunt Charlotte smiled tenderly. "You've brought immense joy to my life. Even on a day like today when there is naught but rain, you provide the sunshine. Whether you marry a scoundrel or a saint or marry not at all, I shall not turn you out."

"Nor I you, should you marry a scoundrel or a saint."

Her aunt laughed deeply and fully. "With half a century on me, I'm too set in my ways, I'm afraid."

Daisy couldn't help but believe her father had been naught but charm without substance. Bishop was as much substance as charm. Alas, she needed to forget him and become as set in her ways as her aunt.

SATURDAY MORNING, PUSHING his body to the limit, Bishop lifted the bells one at a time. Left arm. Right arm. Left. Right. A few years back, he'd designed an instrument that was easier to hold and hired a blacksmith to forge his creation into existence. While his right hand—still tender from its encounter with Mallard's jaw—protested the abuse, he welcomed the distraction because it took his mind off *her*, for short spells at a time anyway.

He'd almost gone to the Fair and Spare last night, in hopes of running into Marguerite. Not that she'd have welcomed him, not based on the manner in which she'd stridden away from him. *Go to the devil*, her posture had said. Damned if he didn't admire her all the more for it.

So instead, during the late hours, he'd wandered aimlessly through his residence, detecting her fragrance in far too many rooms. He cursed the chit for not leaving him be. He was tempted to call on her, simply to ensure she was well. What would that accomplish, except to make her all the harder to forget?

Time, he needed time—

"Sir?"

With a growl for the interruption, he lowered the weighted object to the floor, grabbed a linen, and wiped the sweat from his brow. "What is it, Perkins?"

"An Inspector Swindler from Scotland Yard wishes a word. He's waiting for you in the library."

Mallard was no doubt pressing charges, the little shite. Turning, he gave his butler a nod. "Tell him I'll be there shortly."

"Yes, sir."

Taking the back stairs to his bedchamber, Bishop washed up quickly and changed into the proper attire that reflected a gentleman to be reckoned with. With a last glance in the mirror, he adjusted his neckcloth and headed down.

In the library, a tall, broad-shouldered older man was perusing Bishop's bookshelves. "Inspector, would you care for some scotch?"

He took his time swiveling about. "No, thank you. I'm here on urgent business."

"Tea then?"

"No, thank you."

"Very well." Bishop strode over to his desk and pointed to the chair in front of it. "Please."

Once his visitor had settled into place, Bishop dropped into the chair behind his desk, because it signaled a position of power. But studying the man across from him, he couldn't help but believe Swindler wouldn't relinquish any ground. "How might I be of service?"

"I've been told that on Tuesday last, you went to the Cerberus Club and promptly punched one Mr. Bertram Mallard in the jaw."

"Yes, I did. He'd smacked his wife about, and I don't tolerate that sort of behavior."

The inspector steadfastly held his gaze. "What is her relationship to you that you would hear of his actions or would care about her well-being?"

"She and I are . . . involved."

"How long have you had a relationship with her?"

"A couple of weeks."

Swindler nodded as though he'd already known the answer, and Bishop suspected he had. "You have a reputation for having affairs with married ladies."

He shrugged indolently. "They're convenient. A married woman isn't going to look to me for marriage, and I have no desire to be shackled."

"Where were you Thursday last?"

Bishop furrowed his brow. "What has that to do with this matter?"

"Please answer the question."

Leaning back, Bishop tapped his index finger on his desk, noting the inspector's gaze dropping briefly to his bruised knuckles. The direction of the inquiry was troubling. "I was at a brothel."

"Were you there throughout the night, until dawn?"

"What bloody hell difference does that make?"

"Were you there until dawn?"

"No. I arrived around half eight and departed a little after half ten, I believe. I didn't check my timepiece."

"Which brothel did you grace with your presence?"

"I'd rather not say as I wasn't alone."

"The entire reason for going to a brothel is not to be alone, is it not? Which one?"

Bishop shifted forward and placed his elbows on his desk. "I don't see how my whereabouts has any bearing whatsoever on Mallard pressing charges against me either for striking him or sharing favors with his wife."

"I'm not here for either of those reasons."

"Then why the devil are you disturbing my day?"

"Bertram Mallard was murdered shortly before midnight Thursday night. Your dealings with him are cause for suspicion, especially as you were overheard to vow that you'd deliver him straightaway to hell."

On Sunday afternoon Bishop sent word to Chastity Bowles to come to his residence at seven that evening if at all possible. If her husband intercepted his missive, then perhaps the man would begin to question his wife's frequent absences and she might obtain the divorce she wanted. She arrived at seven on the dot, and Bishop cursed her husband for paying so little attention to her that she could meet with him on very little notice.

He was waiting in the foyer when she arrived, as always, dressed in a lovely evening gown, her silvering hair styled to perfection and adorned with a solitary ostrich feather. She was no doubt the most punctual woman he'd ever met and possibly the most joyful, in spite of her unhappy marriage. Her smile was bright, her eyes aglow. He enjoyed her teasing manner immensely. They each possessed the ability to make the other laugh, although he suspected she'd send no giggles his way tonight.

"It was rather exciting receiving an unexpected missive from you," she said gaily. "I quite like the notion of us meeting on a night that's not usually ours."

He was rather regretful that he was going to disappoint her, but before he could respond, she carried on. "Aren't you ravishing?"

"That's a term more aptly applied to women, I think," he said with a grin.

"Nonsense. Besides, I suspect you grow weary of having the term *handsome* thrown at you all the time."

"Never." Although truth be told, he'd never understood what it was about his dark features that appealed to women. They seemed a bit rough-hewn around the edges to him, or perhaps it was that he saw too much of his father in the jagged landscape of his face. "Let's retire to the parlor, shall we?"

He offered his arm, and she stared at it as though unfamiliar with the appendage. "We're not going straight to your bedchamber?"

"Not tonight. I have a matter to discuss with you."

Her delicate brow furrowed, the light in her blue eyes seemed to dim. He'd never before truly noticed nor realized that blue eyes came in different shades. Hers were a cerulean, whereas Marguerite's, if captured just right by light, could appear almost gray, like a storm cloud on the horizon, with a brighter sky simply waiting to make its appearance. The musing train speeding down a track he didn't wish to travel came to a careening stop when Chastity finally placed her hand on his arm.

He led her into the parlor where two glasses of chardonnay—her preferred wine—were already waiting. After settling her on the sofa, he took the chair opposite her and waited while she took a swallow, two. Then she smiled. "You must have the finest wine cellar in all of England."

"Only in London, I suspect. I've never seen the point in spending money on swill. When I was younger and not quite so flush, I would save up until I could afford one good bottle of wine rather than purchasing several bottles that didn't measure up."

"I've learned more about wine during our three months together than I did during the entirety of my life before that."

He leaned forward. "That's what I need to talk to you about, Chastity."

"My enjoyment of wine?" she asked hopefully.

"No, our time together. I'm afraid we're going to need to stop seeing each other."

She smiled elatedly, not the reaction he'd anticipated. "You've fallen in love, haven't you? With that very pretty maid, Daisy. I knew you fancied her."

"What? No!" With his need to put distance between her and her preposterous words, he straightened so fast and flung himself back into the chair with such force that his wine sloshed over the rim of his glass. "No. No. I'm being investigated for murder."

The sweet and amused laughter trilled out of her. "Oh, my Lord! Only you would see falling in love to be a worse outcome than hanging."

He supposed his reaction did seem rather absurd. But love was the very last thing he needed or wanted. It would do nothing except muddle his life.

"I'm unlikely to hang. I didn't do it, but the situation does complicate our arrangement. I hate to leave you in the lurch before your damned husband has taken any notice of your frequent absences, but my footman Tom has seen you enough times in my bedchamber that he could serve as a witness at least to your visits and where they led. I'd shared with you my suspicions regarding Daisy being a possible inquiry agent, and they were spot-on. She could also testify to your presence in my bedchamber. If you were to confess to coming here to your husband, raise his ire, then he might finally take matters in hand and seek a divorce."

"Mmm." She took another sip of her wine. Then another. "About my husband . . . I haven't been entirely honest there. He died two months ago."

Blinking, dumbfounded, Bishop stared at her. "I beg your pardon?"

He'd never known her to look so uncomfortable as she nodded and managed to turn the wedding ring on her finger while still holding on to her glass of wine. "His heart gave out. While he was in bed with a woman nearly thirty years his junior. She was all of two and twenty. He hadn't the stamina to keep up with her apparently. Serves him right, I say."

"Why didn't you tell me?"

She traced a finger around the rim of her glass, her cheeks blossoming into a dark pink hue. "I enjoyed your company. You made me laugh, and I was very much in need of a laugh. And while we never journeyed to your bed, still you made me feel as though

I was enough for those few hours every Wednesday night. I've seen forty-one years, twenty of those with a man who married me for my dowry and spent that money purchasing baubles for other ladies, but never for me. At the time of his death, I'd been seeing you for barely a month, but already you knew my favorite flower, my favorite wine, my favorite authors. I wasn't ready to give up someone who appreciated the small details of me. I hope you can forgive me for my self-ishness. You are a young man who probably would have preferred spending those evenings with someone nearer your age—your fellow Chessmen whom you've told me so much about and, of course, the ladies."

Setting his glass aside, he rose, walked over to the sofa, and sat beside her. Placing his arm around her, he drew her up against his side. "Nothing to forgive. You had a need, Chastity, and I'm glad to have been of service."

"Are you quite sure you're not a little bit in love?"

"With you? Absolutely."

She laughed lightly. "No, I meant with the maid. I could have sworn there was an attraction between you, so palpable that I felt it thrumming around you."

"She was here under false pretenses and would have told the world what she saw."

"Which is what you wanted."

"Yes, but"—releasing his hold on her, he got up and stalked to the fireplace—"whoever she was, she wasn't who I thought she was."

"Not at all?"

He swung around and tried not to glare too force-fully. "Why are you haranguing me with mentions of her?"

"Because perhaps there is more truth between the two of you than you realize."

He didn't want to consider their time at the Fair and Spare when she'd known no one was waiting in a bedchamber for him, when she'd not been spying on him because there had been no information for her to gather on him at the club. Nor did he want to think about the kiss, the raw power of it, when for those few minutes she hadn't needed to snoop on him and he hadn't needed to pretend to be having an affair. The way she'd looked at him, the way he'd wanted to touch her. It had felt real, so damned real. And then in the carriage when he'd been unable to resist . . .

"Whom do they think you've murdered?" Chastity asked.

"The husband of a woman I was striving to help."

"But you'll be proven innocent?"

"Yes, of course. It's well on its way to that happening. Otherwise, they'd have already arrested me."

Although what he was fairly certain they were doing was watching him. He'd noticed a couple of fellows trailing him when he'd gone out yesterday afternoon for a visit with his tailor. And last night, he'd noticed a man smoking and leaning against a lamppost across the street. Maybe he'd been waiting for someone, but since he was there for at least a couple of hours, Bishop thought it was likely he was waiting on him.

"I should so hate for you to come to a bad end. Perhaps you should hire a detective to help you prove your innocence," Chastity said.

He offered her a mocking grin. "I suppose you have a particular one in mind?"

She laughed lightly. "Yes, as a matter of fact, I do."

"I doubt she would even see me. We didn't part ways on the best of terms."

"I feel rather certain that you can charm her into forgiveness."

He almost objected to her notion that the fault was his, but he shouldn't have brought Marguerite pleasure when he'd known he was going to deliver her to her aunt's with the hope of never seeing her again. But it was the very notion of never seeing her again that had driven him to cross over to her side of the carriage, because he couldn't bear the thought of spending the remainder of his life wondering what it would feel like to have her shattering with ecstasy in his arms. In the end he'd taken things further than he'd intended, even if she'd been more than willing to welcome him.

Their relationship had started as a game he'd been intent on winning. Yet standing there, with Chastity's raised brow and knowing smirk directed his way, he felt as though Marguerite had struck the final blow and left him on the battlefield bloodied and tattered but determined to make a last stand.

CHAPTER 15

MONDAY morning, dressed in a dark green frock that was appropriate for a woman of business, Daisy gave her aunt a hug before climbing into the carriage that would convey her to her office. She'd slept fitfully every night since Bishop had delivered her to her aunt's residence.

It hurt to discover that he didn't trust her. It made her feel as though the basis for their relationship had been a fabrication—except for their time at the Fair and Spare, the few minutes when she'd been tending to his injured hand, and those moments in the former brothel when she'd learned the truth of him, when they'd been so near to each other, when their lips had merged with the impact of molten lead being forged into something new.

That was how she'd felt. That she was no longer who she'd been but had irrevocably been altered into someone else. It had been both exhilarating and frightening.

But it had opened her up to welcoming his attentions in the carriage. It infuriated her to think that perhaps the kisses and touches he'd bestowed upon her had been exactly like the kiss he'd given Mrs. Parker:

pretense. Because he'd been continuing to play at a role, at a game.

Just as well that they'd parted on less-than-ideal terms because she no longer trusted herself to remain impartial where he was concerned. The chaotic organ known as the heart could not be relied upon. A woman needed to depend upon her head, her reasoning, her logic. All three guided Daisy toward steering clear of Blackguard Blackwood. Even if she now suspected he wasn't a blackguard at all.

The carriage rolled to a stop a few streets away from her building. After several minutes of simply sitting there, she leaned out the window. "Summers?"

He shouted down, "Sorry, miss. Appears there's been some sort of incident up ahead that's blocking the path."

Vehicles and horses getting entangled or a broken axle or something else equally inconvenient. She wasn't accustomed to simply lounging around as she had since Friday. She was more than ready to get back to the business of living—and to her occupation of searching for the answers to others' dilemmas. "I'm going to walk from here."

"Yes, miss."

The footman climbed down, opened the door, unfolded the step for her, and assisted her onto the street.

"Thank you," she said. Her time portraying a servant had taught her that occasionally gratitude wasn't unwarranted.

"I'll accompany you, miss."

"Not necessary. I walk about alone in this area all the time. The advantage to being a spinster." He scowled, and she smiled to reassure him. "I'll be fine.

I'm a working woman, not a debutante on her way to a ball." Women with occupations didn't require chaperones. She was beginning to wonder why any single woman did. Shouldn't a lady be trusted to behave without needing to have a guard about?

She marched over to the bricked pavement that ran in front of all the buildings and began wending her way through the jostling crowd. She tended to walk faster than most and was constantly skirting around mothers with their children or men taking a leisurely stroll. Usually, if she didn't sleep in her apartment, she arrived at her office before many people were seeing about their day, because she relished the early morning quiet and used the time to sort through her plans and appointments—when she had them. Her uncle provided her with a modest allowance she intended to repay at a future date, once her business was thriving.

She stopped to purchase a newspaper so she could peruse it for any opportunities to hire out her services. She wasn't yet established enough to have a steady stream of clientele.

As she was nearing her office, her heart gave a little thump when she spied the tall, broad-shouldered man, hands on his hips, staring at her door with enough intensity to bore a hole through the thick, oaken wood. She slowed her pace because she didn't particularly want to speak with Bishop. However, curiosity got the better of her. What the deuce was he doing here?

He stalked over to a window, raised to his brow the hand that had stroked her cheek, leaned in, and stared through the glass. Not that he would have seen anything beyond the backside of the draperies that she closed each evening, opened each morning. Stepping back, he glanced around. His gray beaver top hat cast a shadow over his upper face, so she could see little save the tautness of his jaw. He was not happy.

Then he turned slightly, and she knew he'd spotted her because his jaw relaxed a fraction, but more she could almost feel his gaze landing on her like a physical presence, could have sworn it traveled from the top of her hat to the tips of her toes, taking in all of her. Or perhaps she was merely associating his actions with her own in-depth perusal of him. Did he have to look so incredibly well turned out? She almost imagined that he'd gone to extra bother to ensure not a single wrinkle disturbed the perfection of his black coat and trousers that fit him flawlessly. His jacket, secured with a solitary button at his waist, revealed a dark gray waistcoat and light gray silk cravat. It was unfair that he should be so ridiculously handsome or that he had the ability to make her disloyal heart flutter uncontrollably.

Still, her step never faltered. Not even when she was near enough to see through the shadows created by his hat brim and into the depths of his dark eyes that seemed to take in all of her. "What are you doing here?"

Her tone was curt but respectful, her voice giving away none of the tumultuous emotions rampaging through her. Jolly good for her.

"Do you have any notion regarding how challenging it is to find you? You have no shingle advertising this is your place of business, nothing painted on the windows or doors. Even with your address in hand it was deuced difficult to locate."

She wondered who had given him her address, not

that it particularly mattered. Newspapers were reluctant to allow advertising from sleuths so most of her clients came to her through word of mouth. "My landlord has no respect for my occupation and threatened to double my lease fee if I identified what sort of service I provided. He thought it would lower the property values of the area."

"Paint a bloody daisy on the door then."

She hadn't considered that. She also wondered why, if he was keen to find her, he hadn't gone to her aunt's, since he'd known she was there. "Why are you here?" She reiterated her earlier question.

"I have a matter to discuss with you. Preferably indoors." He nodded toward the building.

She should go inside and lock him out. She really didn't care what he had to say, and yet she desperately did.

Retrieving the key from her reticule, primly and incredibly slowly, because the impatience shimmering off him made her smile inwardly, she approached the door. In his residence, he'd been remarkably skilled at not revealing what he was feeling, part of the reason she hadn't known that he'd already deduced who she was, but now he inhabited her dominion, and she intended to reign over the sweetness of it as long as possible.

With a turn of the key, a releasing of the latch, she marched into her sparsely furnished office and threw back the draperies to let in the sunlight before taking up her position behind her desk, standing tall, steadfast, and proud, like a general daring anyone to try and take what he had conquered. She set her newspaper on top, dropped her reticule into a drawer, and then indicated with a wave of her hand the chair in front of the desk for her visitor.

He looked at it as though someone had dumped offal in it. Rather than take the offering, he wandered over to her small bookcase.

"Why would you have guidebooks on London?" he asked, as though truly interested.

"Because sometimes I'm called upon to frequent areas of the city with which I am not familiar. Again, why are you here, Mr. Blackwood?"

Still bent over, studying her books, he peered at her, a half smile curling those lush lips slightly. He'd removed his hat. His hair, usually so tidy, had fallen over his brow. She refused to leave her position in order to brush it back because he was no doubt attempting to stage an ambush or at the very least take the chair behind the desk in order to gain the upper hand.

"We're going to be formal, are we?" he asked.

"You set the tone during our last parting."

"So I did." Straightening, he walked to the window and gazed out. "Do you normally work with the draperies drawn aside?"

"I do, yes."

He shook his head. "I'd be distracted, unable to get any work done, watching these people constantly walking by."

She'd had clients who had been a bit slow about revealing why they'd come to her. Mr. Parker came to mind. He'd been embarrassed to share the reason for his visit, the circumstances surrounding his need of her, what exactly he required she discover. But surely Bishop wasn't here to retain her services. "I find it soothing to see people carrying on about their day, and to know that what I do might ensure that someone is able to continue engaging in what they enjoy." She made a deliberate effort to soften her tone with her next words. "What brings you to my door?"

He twisted around but retained his position by the window, the sunlight filtering in creating a halo around him, an aberration because he was certainly no angel. "I don't know if you saw in the *Times* that Bertram Mallard was found dead late Thursday night."

She'd used the few days with her aunt to insulate herself from the world. Had avoided reading the newspapers. In want of an escape from all troubles, she'd buried herself in books. "Mallard? Mrs. Mallard's husband? Your Mrs. Mallard?"

"I wouldn't call her *mine*, but yes, the husband of that Mrs. Mallard."

"Fortunate for her, then, I suppose, as she'll no longer require your services or have to go through the embarrassment of a divorce."

"Unfortunate for me, however. They think I killed him."

BISHOP SHOULD HAVE known that the formidable woman standing before him wouldn't gasp or swoon or even grow pale. Her delicate brow did furrow as though she was striving to make sense of his words or perhaps puzzle out how they'd come to be. He wished she wasn't exactly as he remembered, but, apparently, he'd spent so much time studying her that his mind had painted an accurate image of her. He must have recalled it a thousand times since he'd taken her to her aunt's residence.

When he'd first spied her outside this building, he'd

cursed her for looking so remarkably lovely in green. A small hat was perched at a jaunty angle on her head. The woman in no way resembled a servant. How in God's name had he ever, for even a single second, believed she was one? Then he'd cursed himself thoroughly for being so damned relieved to see her.

"Why would you come to that conclusion?"

"An Inspector James Swindler of Scotland Yard called upon me Saturday morning and put me through a phalanx of questions."

"Swindler. I know him. He's good—he's very good. He'll ferret out the culprit. Perhaps it was Mrs. Mallard. After her husband struck her, she had reason enough."

"But not the strength. She's a tiny birdlike creature. Swindler said Mallard was struck from behind, one blow that caved in his skull."

"Someone incredibly strong then, like you."

"Unfortunately, yes. He was aware of the incident at the Cerberus."

She closed her eyes briefly as though to better view the entire situation. "Of course. Your disgust with Mallard was on full display, and there were witnesses galore. What questions did Swindler ask?"

"He wanted to know my whereabouts Thursday night."

"What did you tell him?"

"The truth. I was at a brothel."

She took a deep breath, nodded, narrowed her eyes as if in thought. "I wonder why he didn't come to me to verify your story."

"I imagine because I didn't inform him you were there. That's what I came to tell you. I didn't divulge your name, nor will I. Not under any circumstances. Therefore, you need not concern yourself with the matter."

"Why the deuce did you not tell him we were together?"

"Because it wouldn't do your reputation any favors. In addition, I couldn't explain your presence without also revealing that of the Parkers. The very last thing they need right now while their relationship is so fragile and they are in the process of reconciling is to be associated with a man who is being suspected of murdering a bloke or to be put through the gauntlet with suspicions."

With a scoff, she shook her head. "He'll find all that out when he speaks with that woman Jewel."

"He's not going to speak with her because I didn't tell him which brothel. She doesn't need the headache either, or people interfering with her good works."

She seemed at a loss for words, but he could see all the various wheels in her head turning. He'd always found her easy to read. "Look, I didn't do it, and if this inspector fellow is as good as you say, he'll figure out who did without me providing any particulars about my life or that night."

"You're blatantly holding back information. I'm surprised he didn't arrest you."

"I told him I didn't kill the man."

She waved a hand in the air as though shooing away a fly. "Oh, well, then, that's all that needs to be done. It's not as if a guilty person would proclaim to be innocent."

He was rather regretting coming to her, because she was making him realize that he might be skating at the edge of naivete when it came to how this matter could resolve itself. "He didn't arrest me."

"Swindler is incredibly thorough. He'll wait until he has sufficient evidence."

"He won't find any pointing to me."

"Don't you understand? He already has. It's the reason he questioned you."

"Daisy—"

"Marguerite."

He waited, studying her. She looked up at the ceiling, down at the floor. Shook her head. "I told you that my mother called me Daisy. Therefore, I used it as my name when I came to work at your residence because Marguerite sounded too posh for a servant. To be honest, I never really liked Marguerite . . . until you said it. Be that as it may, please tell Swindler that I was with you Thursday night and what we were doing."

"Kissing?"

A swatch of red blossomed over her face and neck. "Everything that needs to be told."

"It wouldn't make any difference. I don't know the details of how they figured it out, but they determined that Mallard died around midnight. I left you shortly before eleven."

"Enough time to get to him and do the deed?"

"Yes."

She held up a finger. "But your coachman and footman—they would have known where you went after you delivered me to my aunt's."

He sighed. "After seeing you to your destination, I got out at the next street over. I needed a walk." To stop thinking about her. "I sent them on. I don't have my staff stay up until I return home because some-times, I'm out until all hours."

"No one knows when you returned to the resi-dence?"

"I'm afraid not. Although the hour of my return would not have exonerated me."

"What time did you get back there?"

"A little after one."

"That's a lot of walking."

"I was trying to convince myself that nothing about you was real. I failed miserably at it."

SHE'D FAILED MISERABLY as well, trying to convince her-self that he'd just been playacting, and the man she knew was not the man he was. She suspected a few things about each of them wasn't the truth of them, but they were probably minor. She knew him well enough that even though he had no alibi, and he could have left her and had time to do it, in her heart of hearts she knew he hadn't.

She had worked with the police a few times and had once observed them using the temperature of the body to determine the approximate time of death. That Bishop had no alibi for the period when a fatal blow was struck was disconcerting.

"We need to figure out who killed Mallard," she stated succinctly.

"You said this Swindler fellow was clever and would determine the real culprit."

"You were evasive, which will increase his sus-picions that it's you. That's what he'll be striving to prove. We need to go to him and tell him everything."

194   LORRAINE HEATH

"No. The women who have come to me are entitled to their privacy."

"I think you're just afraid that your reputation as a seducer will become tarnished."

The smile he gave her was completely untarnished and definitely designed to seduce. She was surprised the buttons on her frock didn't simply set themselves free, granting him access to whatever he wanted. How could a flash of teeth accompanied by a heated glance be so beguiling? "Stop."

"Stop what?"

"Stop setting about to prove you are irresistible."

He began sauntering over, and it took every ounce of willpower she possessed not to retreat, not to dash up the stairs that led to a suite of rooms where she resided when not visiting her aunt. But if she did, this idiot man was not going to look out for his own well-being until he was standing in the dock. He came to a stop near enough to her desk that she could smell the bergamot and oranges.

"Why do you care?" he asked quietly.

"Because whoever did this needs to suffer for it."

"How do you know it wasn't me?"

"You'd have done it to his face, so he'd have known it was coming and precisely why. You wouldn't have bludgeoned him on the back of the head like some coward."

He looked at her with a sort of wonder. "That sentiment comes very close to what I told Swindler." Reaching out, he trailed his fingers along her jaw. "How is it that you know me so well after such a short time?"

She moved back slightly, just beyond his reach. This was her business establishment, not a brothel, not his bedchamber, not his carriage. Besides, she had no intention of being affected by any touch, glance, or smile. Trust was at the core of any viable relationship, and he didn't trust her. Unfortunately, when it came to him, she didn't trust herself. She would resist the allure of him if it killed her. "I'm incredibly observant. I know a fellow who is equally so. I suggest you hire him. I'll provide you with his information." Settling into her chair, she dipped her pen in the inkwell and began to scrawl out his name and address.

"I don't want to hire him."

She glanced up. "Don't be a fool. You need someone whose only goal is to see you exonerated."

"Then let it be you."

The words struck her with a force that left her disoriented and feeling as though she was tumbling. She imagined Mr. Mallard had experienced the same when Bishop's fist had connected with his jaw. "I don't believe that would be wise or serve your best interests."

Because she could barely think when he was near. It was deuced irritating.

"On the contrary. You know me. I should think that would give you an advantage. Especially if this police investigation runs amok. This other fellow would ask a thousand questions to which you already know the answers. I'd be ahead in the game with you."

She shook her head. "It's not a game. This situation could have dire consequences for you."

"Which is the reason I need it to be you."

"I didn't think you trusted me."

"I lied. I trust no one more."

She was grateful to be sitting, because her legs might

have given out. "Then why indicate otherwise in the carriage?"

"I'm not the sort of man with whom you should associate."

To protect her. Because that was what he did. Protected women. "Well, at least we can both agree on something."

A corner of his mouth hitched up. "Not going to argue the point?"

"I'm a fast learner, Mr. Blackwood."

"I hate when anyone calls me that. It's my father's name, not mine."

She supposed she couldn't blame him. "You say I shouldn't associate with you, yet here you are, striving to hire me."

He glanced around her office, and she wondered if he was searching for something innocuous upon which to comment. Finally, his gaze landed on her, like sunshine over the lawn. "Because you're clever. Tenacious. I don't think you enjoyed coming into my bedchamber, and yet you did it anyway. Daring. Not many women would set foot in a brothel."

"That was more out of curiosity than anything."

"Still, it involved a bit of bravery, not knowing what you might find."

She shouldn't allow him to flatter her into assisting him, and yet the truth was that she was the best one for the job. She knew him, knew Mrs. Mallard, knew Swindler. Knew the situation. "Very well, against my better judgment, I'll take you on."

"Splendid. Now is as good a time as any to negotiate the terms for your services, I should think."

She didn't want him to pay her. She simply wanted

to ensure he didn't hang. On the other hand, he could well afford the expense, and as a businesswoman, she needed to save altruistic endeavors for those in need of charity. "I don't negotiate. I have set fees."

"I have a policy of never paying set fees. I always negotiate."

She scoffed. "Even when your life is at risk?"

"Always start as you intend to go."

"Is it your intention, then, to be a difficult client?"

"It's my intention to be a client you won't soon forget."

As though she could ever forget him.

She again indicated the chair in front of her. He studied it as though it was the enemy before finally dropping into it.

"You don't like sitting on that side of a desk," she said.

"No. It's not a position of strength. On the other hand, it doesn't matter where I am in this office, my strength outweighs yours."

"Don't be so certain." She announced her fee.

He offered double.

She furrowed her brow. "I'm incredibly flummoxed to discover that you don't understand the principle of negotiation."

"I understand the principle perfectly. What you don't understand is the value I place on my life and my ability to continue to breathe. I don't want you being approached by someone with a more interesting case and deciding to skip off in pursuit of it."

She was struck by two things: his attempt to make light of his predicament and the very real possibility that he was in fact worried. "Am I to deduce by your concerns that you believe there is a chance they might decide you did the poor fellow in?"

"Unfortunately, I was rather testy with the inspector, and as you so succinctly pointed out, I have no proof I wasn't there."

"I suppose if I say I'll take two-thirds of what you offered, you'll accuse *me* of not knowing how negotiations work."

"If you take anything less than what I offered, then you absolutely have no idea how negotiations work. Always take the best proposition, especially when the gent making it can well afford it."

"Very well, that portion is settled. However, I have some conditions that must be met before I'll agree to work on your behalf."

His eyes narrowed until they mirrored a sharp-edged blade, a look he'd no doubt perfected to slice to ribbons another man's objections before they were fully uttered. There was a terrifying aspect to it, and if she hadn't spent a little over a fortnight in his household, she might have shown some alarm, but she kept her face passive, hoping, on this matter at least, he couldn't read her thoughts. "Surely during your other negotiations, you've found more than money has been on the bargaining table," she said sweetly.

A muscle in his cheek ticked. Finally, he gave a little nod of acquiescence. "What would those conditions entail?"

"Firstly, we must be completely honest with each other from this moment forward."

"Were we not before?"

The audacity, to ask such a question as though he didn't already know the answer.

"I am well aware that you were putting on a performance in your bedchamber whenever I walked in. Perhaps even at the Fair and Spare, since you'd already suspected my purpose in being in your residence."

"Not at the Fair and Spare."

And in your carriage, were you performing then? She had to bite her tongue to keep from asking, not certain if she really wanted the truth of it. "I have to be able to trust my clients, and they must trust me if I'm to deliver what they require."

"What do you perceive that I require?"

"To be proven innocent."

He gave a brisk nod. "Complete honesty from this moment forward. I can accept that. Anything else?"

"You must show me the respect and courtesy due my professional position."

"I wouldn't be here, Miss Townsend, if I didn't already respect you and your skills."

She pondered his words and the meaning of them. As well as the formality of his address. "You came here with the distinct purpose of hiring me?"

He merely held her gaze. No muscle movement. No fidgeting or acknowledgment.

"Complete honesty," she reiterated.

"Yes."

"But earlier you gave a different reason for your presence."

"I'm not accustomed to asking for assistance and wasn't comfortable with the notion of it."

"Therefore, you let the need for a sleuth appear to be my idea instead of yours. No more of that. I can't help you if you're not more direct."

"We'd not negotiated the honesty part yet."

Giving a curt nod, she had the feeling he'd always looked at her with a sort of raw honesty but suspected his words and actions had been a combination of truth and falsehoods. "And lastly, our conduct is to reflect all business."

"What precisely does that mean?" His tone contained an undercurrent of pique.

She rather regretted the last condition already, because it would prevent her from teasing him and raising his ire. From emptying a bowl of chocolate glaze over him, although the image that jumped into her mind was not of pouring it over his head but slathering it across his chest. But she knew he could serve as a distraction, and she had to remain focused on the task at hand. It would be easier to resist him if he never touched her, if he never gave any indication that he wanted her. She cleared her throat. "We are business partners and nothing else. I very much doubt you reach across your solicitor's desk to stroke his jaw."

"Do you not like me touching you?"

"That's beside the point." She squeezed her eyes shut, wishing she hadn't revealed that, but then it was part of the total honesty she needed between them. She wanted him to touch her again, which was the very reason that she needed this condition in place: to remove all temptation. "Why did you not keep your distance in the carriage? Why give the impression that you . . . desired me?"

His jaw clenched. He didn't want to tell her. Should she tell him not to sit at a card table because she was beginning to find him easier to read? Was it because he was more comfortable around her or that she simply knew him better?

"Because kissing you wasn't enough. I did desire you. I owe you an apology for"—he swallowed, but firmly held her gaze—"any impression I gave that I was not affected by what transpired between us. I've not been able to stop thinking about how satisfying it felt to have you fall apart in my arms."

She shouldn't have asked, because she'd grown warm, and his intense gaze was making tiny tremors erupt throughout her. Now she regretted asking for the third condition. But she was not going to withdraw it. "Can you not see how such behavior might distract us from remaining focused on the task at hand?"

"I'll concede your point—and you should know that I seldom concede."

Giving her the victory and acknowledging it. Good Lord, it might go to her head. "Well then, if you are agreeable to those three terms—"

"As long as they go both ways."

"That goes without saying."

"I want to hear you say it, because I'm well aware that you were playacting as well. I believe there might be the slightest possibility that you are not as easy to read as I'd originally presumed or that you let on."

Taking a deep breath, she couldn't hold back a small smile of triumph. "I shall be completely honest with you, conduct myself at all times as a business-woman, and afford you the respect of a man who is not a scoundrel."

"You don't have to go quite that far. I am perhaps a bit of a scoundrel."

She didn't think so, but with honesty between them, perhaps she'd uncover the truth of him. "Then we're in agreement. I'll draw up papers for us to sign. Half of the amount due upon signing, the remainder when I have the proof you need."

"Where do you reside?"

"What has that to do with anything?"

"Complete honesty."

Feeling as though he was going to work to make her regret those terms, she nodded to the side. "I have rooms at the top of those stairs. Although I often stay with my aunt overnight. Why?"

"If you were paying for lodgings, I was going to offer you a room in my residence as part of the terms."

"Very generous, but not necessary. However, out of curiosity, I assume the staff was told I'd been let go but not the particulars."

"I never divulge particulars."

She shot him a pointed look. "As Inspector Swindler discovered. I intend to speak with him—"

"No. Nothing is to be gained by dragging others into this."

"I won't tell him what you don't wish him to know, but we need to know what he in fact knows."

"You think he'll tell you?"

"I think he'll share what he can. I helped him with a case last year that involved a woman who was stealing jewelry from her employer. He and I got along rather well."

Bishop didn't like it, but he'd never been one to leave his destiny to chance. After Swindler had left, he'd considered seeking out Marguerite to gain her assistance, but he wasn't comfortable with his feelings for her. He could hardly go an hour without some thought of her popping into his head: if not a memory, then a musing regarding what she might be doing at that moment. "Why did you take a position as a servant in my household rather than just watching the residence for Mrs. Parker's arrival?"

"Because seeing her go into the residence wasn't proof that she was having an affair."

"What was your plan? To listen at the doorway and barge in when you heard the bed squeaking in hopes of catching us copulating?"

He shouldn't take such delight in her cheeks turning pink, but he did wonder how far the blush traveled. "Somehow, I very much doubt that you have a bed that squeaks."

"True. It is rather distracting to have something protesting in concert to your movements. So how far were you prepared to go for your proof?"

"Identifying her in the bedchamber was enough. The kiss cinched it."

"You didn't like me kissing her."

With a raised eyebrow, she tapped her fingers on her desk. "I think we've gone off topic. I also think we need to have a word with Mrs. Mallard. I suppose she's still about."

"She's the one who found her husband."

Deep furrows appeared in her forehead while she quickly leaned forward as though needing to shorten the distance between them in order to hear better. "I beg your pardon?"

"Swindler said she found him—shortly after he was killed apparently."

"Had she heard some noise?"

"He didn't say."

She held up a well-manicured slender finger. "Why was she searching for her husband in the middle of the night? If he struck her, why was she not avoiding him?"

He narrowed his eyes. "Why do you say *if he struck her*? You saw the evidence."

"I saw that she'd been struck. I did not see that he did it."

"Why would she lie?"

She sat back and held up her hands. "All of London believes yours to be a house of fornication. Why not tell them the truth?"

"Because there is a purpose to the lie." After shoving himself to his feet, he walked back to the window and gazed out. He didn't like the notion that he may have been taken for a fool. "Do you think she conspired to have him killed?"

"I don't know, but we should speak with her."

"I'm rather certain she had no role in his death. She was far too timid. If she was planning to have him done in, why come to me in the first place?"

"I suppose you make a valid point in her favor."

"Perhaps it was a robbery. Or he owed a wagering debt he hadn't paid."

"Maybe. Still, it can't hurt to at least speak with her."

He nodded. "I'd like to see her and offer my condolences."

"I suppose there is no time like the present to get started. Shall we pay Mrs. Mallard a visit?"

CHAPTER 16

$\mathcal{T}$HE Mallard home was in Mayfair not far from Aunt Charlotte's residence—which, unfortunately, added weight to the notion that Bishop would have had ample time to drop Daisy off and then make his way over there to do the deed that ended Mallard's life.

Upon their arrival, she and Bishop had been escorted into one of two front parlors to wait while the butler went to inform Mrs. Mallard of their arrival. Daisy had caught sight of a dark wood casket in the parlor across the way. In this room, the mirror over the fireplace had been turned to face the wall. Black bunting had been draped here and there. A somberness filled the house. She was astounded activity was occurring in the residence and it hadn't been locked up until a culprit was caught.

"Do you know how he made his money?" she asked Bishop, who was wandering through the room as though striving to memorize every aspect of it. If she'd had any doubts regarding whether he'd been here before, they were laid to rest. He seemed as unfamiliar with the place as she.

"He was a barrister, although a good bit of his fortune was inherited."

"He may have represented criminals or other wrong-doers in the courts, then. Do you think he could have had a falling-out with one of his clients?"

From his study of a pastoral painting, he glanced over his shoulder at her. "Bad enough to exact revenge that would take not only Mallard's life but that of the person who did him in if he were found out?"

She shrugged. "Let's say you're arrested for this crime. You hire a barrister to defend you in court. Yet still you're found guilty. Would you not place some of the blame on the man you'd engaged to ensure you were declared innocent?"

"I wouldn't bloody well pay him for his services." He scrutinized the various aspects of the room. "Still, murder seems a bit extreme."

"If you were hanged, is there no one who would want to punish him for failing you?"

He glowered. "You have incredibly dark thoughts, Marguerite."

"I have read too many murder mysteries, I suppose. I'm simply striving to determine a motive that would result in such a violent act."

Footsteps sounded, and Bishop returned to her side. She couldn't help but think that together they made a formidable alliance.

Wearing all black, her hands clasped tightly before her, Mrs. Mallard walked into the room and came to an abrupt halt, her brow furrowing. "Mr. Blackwood, I was expecting only you. My butler didn't mention that you'd brought someone with you. Are you in the habit of traveling about with one of your maids?"

"First, my condolences on your loss. While I know

you wished a divorce, I imagine the unexpected turn in the situation has been quite upsetting."

"It has indeed."

"Miss Townsend, as it happens, is an inquiry agent. She was incognito while in my residence at the behest of the husband of one of my ladies. Based on her experience, I thought she might be able to provide some insight into what happened here."

"That's incredibly thoughtful of you. However, Scotland Yard seems to have the matter well in hand."

"Still, I'm rather curious regarding the details."

"It seems fairly straightforward. Someone entered our residence and killed him."

"Where?" Daisy asked.

As though still in shock, the woman slowly shifted her gaze from Bishop to Daisy. "As I stated. In this very residence."

Daisy felt remorse at hammering the widow during such an emotional phase of her life, because, even if she hadn't wanted to remain with her husband, she surely couldn't have wished the worst upon him. However, based on her limited experience working with Swindler, she knew time was of the essence, that with each passing hour clues had a tendency to begin fading until they no longer existed. "I apologize for not being clearer. I meant in which room."

"Oh, I see. Yes, of course. The library. The police closed off the chamber, locked it, and took the key with them. They don't want us in there until they've completed their investigation, whatever that means. They took him away. I don't know when they'll return him, but I've had the casket readied. He was not a patient man, my husband. He'd be rather unhappy about a delay in his burial. He was a stickler for arriving at destinations promptly."

The widow was rambling, whether from nerves or unease or worry. Or maybe she was merely uncomfortable talking about unexpected death. "Any notion as to which door they used to break in?"

"The front."

Daisy frowned. "It didn't appear to be damaged."

"The butler carelessly left the door unlocked."

"Convenient that, to have neglected so important a duty on a night when someone was planning to do your husband in."

"I hadn't even considered the coincidence. How clever of you to notice when Scotland Yard didn't. Whomever it was must have picked the lock, then. The city is rife with criminals for whom locks are no deterrent. Why am I being interrogated? I've already told the police everything there is to tell."

"Did you mention your association with me?" Bishop asked.

"Only that we were friends. Not the particulars of our association. I didn't think it would do either of us any favors if they thought we were involved or that I wished to be rid of my husband. I did mention the comfort you provided the night Bertram struck me. It was bound to come out at some point. Best to be upfront. Again, why all the questions?"

"Because Scotland Yard suspects I might have done him in."

"Wherever would they get such a notion? It's absolutely ridiculous. I shall so inform them. Forthwith."

"It would probably be best not to say anything at

all," Daisy stated. "As Shakespeare says, when one protests too much, well, one is not likely to be believed."

Reaching out, Mrs. Mallard squeezed Bishop's arm, her eyes widening almost in alarm. "My, but you are strong, aren't you?" Quickly she released her hold. "My apologies for touching you. I wanted only to reassure you that I won't say anything if you don't wish it."

"As Miss Townsend alludes, it's probably best if you don't elaborate regarding our relationship, at least for the time being."

"Yes, I'm sure you're quite right. It goes without saying that I shan't be visiting you any longer."

"If, however, you need anything of me, don't hesitate to send word."

"You're very kind, Mr. Blackwood. I do hope Scotland Yard won't trouble you any further. Now, if you'll be so kind as to excuse me, much remains to be done."

"Of course, Mrs. Mallard. We'll see ourselves out."

Neither Daisy nor Bishop spoke until his carriage was on its way back to her office.

"The few times I saw her in your residence, she was prone to cowering," Daisy mused.

"She lived in fear."

No longer. That much was obvious, but something more than that seemed very different about the woman. Daisy couldn't quite identify what it was. She looked out the window, searching for the answer there. "Did she ever touch you before?"

"Jealous?"

She cast a scathing glance his way. "That would be like an eagle being jealous of a duckling."

He arched a brow. "You see yourself as an eagle?"

"More a lioness, but the comparison seemed to call for fowls, considering her name. Still, I can't imagine her grasping at any man."

"She was much more timid in our previous encounters, but again she had the shadow of her husband looming over her."

"I suppose. Still, the loss of a life, the loss of someone with whom you've shared a life should elicit some sorrow. I saw no evidence of true mourning in her mien."

"People grieve differently. Perhaps she grieves in private. To be honest, I can't blame her for any gladness she might feel at being rid of him."

"I suppose you have a point. But if my husband was murdered because the butler forgot to secure the door, the butler would be let go. Immediately. Without a reference. Could the butler have done it, do you think? If Mallard was unkind to her, he might have been cruel to the staff as well. A tyrant. Perhaps she wasn't the only one to fear him or want to be done with him. I'm very interested to know what Swindler thinks happened that night. I also need to review the newspaper accounts. After I'm delivered to my office, I'll be in touch when I have more to share."

"I'll be leaving the carriage with you. I'll take a cab back to my residence."

"That's not necessary. I'm perfectly capable of making my way around London."

"But having access to my carriage should make things easier for you, allow you to get about more freely and at your convenience. Might assist you in bringing a quicker end to this entire affair. Consider its use as an additional payment for your services."

SITTING BEHIND HIS desk, with his chair turned to the side, Bishop watched as the shadows moved across the far wall with the passing of the afternoon. He should have stayed with Marguerite, but he'd had an absurd notion that he could get some work done while she visited with Inspector Swindler. Instead, he'd worried that she might have been arrested or that her presence might have made her a suspect, even if she wasn't strong enough to deliver the killing blow. Ridiculous scenarios had been running through his mind. Even as he knew if something happened to her that his coachman would let him know, with each passing second, he was concerned that he'd put her in harm's way. He also feared he might be in a bit of bother regarding this situation.

"Miss Marguerite Townsend has come to call," Perkins suddenly announced.

Bishop hadn't even heard him enter, but he was out of his chair as though he'd been catapulted. "Thank God. Send her in."

He stalked over to the sideboard, poured himself a scotch, lifted a hand, and stared at all the other decanters. She'd told him what she enjoyed drinking, but which was her favorite, her preference?

Hearing the footsteps, he turned just in time to see her walking into the library, Perkins right behind her, watching her like a hawk as though he expected her to steal the silver.

"Will you stay for dinner?" Bishop asked.

She was obviously as surprised by the invitation as he was that he'd issued it without any thought, but it was nearing that time of the evening, and now that she was here, he realized he hadn't eaten all day. Had she?

Perkins seemed equally taken aback by the question, no doubt because they'd never had a guest for an actual dinner.

Bishop saw the instant that regret and a need to decline crossed her features. "I often dine with my business associates," he said as flatly as possible, as though his entire being wasn't waiting in anticipation of her company like a dog hoping for a bit of table scraps tossed its way. "I believe it helps to strengthen the trust needed for a successful partnership."

Her eyes narrowed slightly, and he suspected she was studying him intently because she hoped to slice away an untruth. But they'd already agreed to complete honesty, so finally with a nod, she said, "Yes, that would be lovely, thank you."

The relief that swept through him was a bit unnerving, but he refused to even entertain Chastity's thoughts regarding his feelings. He was simply allowing them the opportunity to become more comfortable with each other after all the deception that had characterized their previous time together. "Wonderful. Perkins, see to the matter. We'll take our meal in the dining room."

"While she is here, sir, you might ask her to stop thieving our staff."

She smiled at Perkins, and Bishop hated the jealousy that ratcheted through him. "I won't be taking any more," she said.

With a nod, Perkins marched out. She, however, glided toward Bishop as though she walked upon clouds.

"Would you care for something to drink?" he asked.

"Port."

If she was one of his ladies, he'd have quipped, "Don't you think you're already too sweet?" But she wasn't one of them, often in need of false flattery or lighthearted banter to steady nerves or build up confidence. She possessed both in abundance. He handed her the port. "Join me by the fire."

Once they were both settled in comfortable chairs across from each other, she said, "I brought the papers for you to sign."

He nodded. "We'll see to it following dinner. Did you meet with Swindler?"

"I did, yes." She took a sip of her port and looked at the low flames flaring on the hearth. "As you said, he is of the opinion the murderer must be a man. Although it seems Mrs. Mallard left him with the impression that you were jealous of her husband."

Had he not already swallowed his scotch, he might have spewed it. "I beg your pardon?"

She shifted her attention to him. "She told him a bit more than she revealed to us. She implied the two of you had been involved for a while but had only recently begun to meet here."

"That's absurd. The night you delivered tea to this room is the first time I'd ever met her."

"I assumed as much. I think whenever she came here, she may have been putting on a performance for your benefit."

"But why?"

"That's the question, isn't it?"

A movement in the doorway caught his attention.

"Dinner is served, sir," Perkins announced.

Bishop set his glass aside. "Let's leave our discussion here, shall we? Lest it upset our digestion."

DAISY WONDERED IF this was the first time that the dining room had ever been used. Unmarried gentlemen who lived alone seldom hosted dinners, because women were needed to ensure all ran smoothly. Although Perkins had no doubt overseen meals presented elsewhere as she found no fault with his management of the footmen who brought in the dishes. The butler himself saw to the serving of the wine.

She and Bishop sat across from each other on the narrow sides of the table rather than at the head and foot of it, for which she was grateful because its length was ridiculously long, meant to accommodate a large number of guests. But with little distance between them, she could see him clearly, noting the dark circles beneath his eyes. He might be giving the appearance that he wasn't bothered by Swindler's suspicions, but she would wager that they did weigh heavily on him, might have given him a couple of restless nights. He might even be uncomfortable with the notion that he'd struck a man two nights before he was killed.

When all activity ceased, and she was preparing to dip her spoon into the soup, Bishop asked, "What are you doing with my servants? Why the theft?"

She didn't miss the fact that standing off to the side, Perkins arrogantly raised a brow.

"The first, Annie, I stole away to ensure you were short on staff."

"Opening the way for you to get a position here."

"Precisely." Unlike the butler, who looked as though he was preparing to chew nails, Bishop seemed not only amused but mildly impressed. "She missed her friend Sarah, so once the Parker situation was resolved, I lured the chambermaid away as well. They now have positions within my aunt's household. They didn't come cheap, either. You pay your servants well."

"Is your uncle by any chance the Earl of Bellingham?"

"He is. How did you determine that?"

"He wrote your letter of reference."

"Ah, yes, although actually, he only signed it. I penned it. He was very grumpy about my asking for his assistance, but then annoyed with me is his usual state. He believes what I'm doing is beneath me. However, he is of a mind that to be given to a man in want of my dowry is not."

"He objects to your independence, then?"

"He worries that his guardianship of me will be brought into question. He also fears change in the social order. I truly believe in a few years, we women will come into our own. I daresay we'll even vote."

"Heaven forbid."

His tone implied horror at the notion, but his eyes reflected humor, and she suspected when the time came, he would fully support allowing women more freedom along with the right to vote. Weren't his current actions proof that he didn't believe women should be held back by ancient beliefs that regarded them as chattel?

"What made you decide to become a sleuth? Due to the spying aspect of it, the intrusion on another's privacy, it's not the most respected of occupations."

Daisy hoped *that* attitude would also eventually change. "Books. My aunt is a voracious reader of detective novels, and in so many of them, the detective is a woman. From the night she took me in, she would read the tales to me in the evenings. As I got older, she added a challenge to the readings. When we each thought we knew who the killer was, we'd inscribe the character's name on a slip of paper, along with the date and time, and place it in a box, not to be opened until the story was finished. Then we'd reveal our guesses. If we'd both guessed correctly, the winner was the one who submitted her choice first. I was correct more often than not."

"However, the author knows going in who the culprit is. The story is designed to provide clues that will lead you along the correct, albeit often crooked, path. Real life is not so straightforward."

"True, but I enjoy the challenge of not only gathering the information but determining the best way to get it."

Focused on watching his features, searching for judgment and finding only attentiveness and perhaps an increasing measure of respect, she barely noticed when a dish was removed and replaced by another. But then it had always seemed that when he was about, he managed to dominate her attention.

"I'd thought female detectives existed only in fiction," he said quietly as though they were sharing embarrassing secrets.

"I believe all fiction is based in truth, although many people hold your assumption. It's one of the reasons women so often meet with success when striving to uncover that for which they are searching. No one suspects us of having the wherewithal to be effective. Yet we are crucial in solving a good many crimes or gathering needed information—such as unfaithful spouses."

"How many adulteresses have you identified?"

"Two, not including Mrs. Parker, who doesn't really qualify for the label. And one adulterer, although I daresay there are more unfaithful men than women, but men's transgressions alone are not enough for a woman to obtain a divorce. Laws written by men tend to favor men. But someday, women shall be involved in writing the laws as well."

"You have a great deal of faith in what your gender will accomplish."

"A woman presently oversees an empire. Victoria is not the first female to do so."

With a small smile, he sipped his wine, and she couldn't help but believe that he enjoyed getting a rise out of her. "You're quite passionate about women and their abilities. I'm rather glad a bowl of chocolate glaze isn't near at hand."

She looked down at the chicken that had just been set before her, then back up at him. "I won't apologize for it."

"Nor would I expect you to. Did you attack the other men you spied leading women astray?"

"I hardly attacked you."

He placed a hand over his heart. "I was wounded to the bone."

"I seriously doubt that. What say we leave the past behind and begin anew?"

She thought if the table wasn't separating them that he'd be touching her, so incredibly intense was his stare, as though he was delving into the very depths of her soul. "There are too many moments in our past that I take pleasure in recalling," he said with absolute seriousness, his voice gentle but housing a spark of hope that she could say the same.

Which she could. And yet . . .

"But how much of us was truly us?"

"More than either of us wanted, I expect. But our current journey together will provide the answer to that question easily enough."

"We were both playing games before."

"Indeed. But just as truth resides in what is written in a novel, so it is to be found in how we play the game. The moves, the strategy. How we react in defeat is as telling as how we respond in victory."

"I wouldn't know about defeat, as I've never lost."

He dropped his head back, sending his deep laughter echoing throughout the room, circling around her, and settling into her heart. "You would say the same even if you had lost."

She grinned. "I would."

"You see? We did learn something about each other. Now we simply have to separate the chaff from the wheat. I'm quite looking forward to the exercise."

FOLLOWING DINNER, SHE consented to take a stroll through the garden with him. The large area was his favorite part of the property. It was where he came to remember. Where he came to forget. Yet no matter how many times he'd walked it since their parting, he'd been unable to forget her. The taste of her, the feel of her in his arms. The joy of swallowing her cries of pleasure, of being the one who had caused them.

And this was his favorite time of the day, when the

sun was winking its farewell and twilight was hovering, offering quiet moments before the dark.

They didn't speak for the longest while. As they walked along, her hands were clasped in front of her, his clutched behind his back. Shackled really, because if not, he was going to touch her and receive a censorious look while being asked if he linked his fingers with his solicitor's.

"I never knew flowers came in such a variety of colors," she said at last. "In your garden, you must have every type of flower that exists. This is a living tribute to your mother, isn't it? Rather like the flowers in the vases in your residence."

It shouldn't please him so much that she remembered his explanation for the abundance of blooms that adorned the rooms. "She was happiest in her garden. It wasn't nearly as large as this. Just a little patch at the back of our house. We had no gardener. She battled the weeds herself. Her husband wouldn't let her spend as much as a ha'penny on seed. She'd trade several stalks of the same plant with various neighbors for one rare find she could add to her collection. We lived at the edge of the city. In the spring, we'd trudge to a forest where she'd carefully dig up flowers that were probably weeds, but she loved them all the same. And sometimes, we'd go to a park and when no one was looking, she'd gingerly take the stem by its roots to transplant in her garden. We got caught once. Young copper. Told her she wasn't allowed to steal the flora. If he saw her doing it again—which he very likely would, because he always walked by at ten in the morning—he'd have to haul her in."

He shifted his gaze over to her and watched as understanding dawned. She smiled and he wanted to pocket it, so gentle and lovely was it, without suspicion or distrust. Like the smiles she'd given him at the club, the ones that had made him long for more.

"She avoided that hour of the morning to do her pilfering."

He grinned. "She did. Swindler reminds me of him a bit."

She stopped beside a trellis where pink roses would bloom in a few more weeks. "You never answered the question I asked after we left the brothel. Do you help these women because of your mother?"

Since he'd handled the inquisition during dinner, he supposed it was only fair that she asked the questions now. With no prevarication, she'd answered. He owed her the same consideration.

"*An ungrateful tart* my father called her on more than one occasion. There are nights when I wake up still hearing her screaming at his abuse. Divorce was not truly an option at the time. It was expensive, requiring an act of Parliament. Three years after she died, the law changed and divorces began being handled in the civil courts. While it was too late for her, it wasn't for others. A woman shouldn't live her life in misery. Sometimes her only recourse is divorce, but the law doesn't make it easy. Men are prideful creatures. If a woman wants to be rid of her husband, I try to help her find a way—within the law."

"I know of the two divorces last year. How many have you assisted?"

"Four." He offered her a rueful grin. "The first was quite by accident, three years ago. The sister of my tailor. I'd gone in to select the fabric for new attire. Call me vain, but I like for my clothing to reflect the latest fashion. I was discussing the style with my tailor when his sister came in, wretchedly unhappy, weeping. I can't tolerate tears. Her husband was lazy and a drunkard. She looked at me. 'I don't suppose you'd have an affair with me. He has vowed to divorce me if I'm ever unfaithful.' I wasn't going to take advantage of a desperate woman, but I agreed to pretend to have an affair with her. We worked out the particulars and within a year she had her divorce. The fancy buttons on my waistcoat are a gift from my tailor for helping his sister obtain a happier life. Having learned sewing at her father's knee, she went to work as a seamstress. A few months later she wrote me asking if I'd help one of her clients. And it has gone from there."

"But it does your reputation as a man to be trusted no favors."

"It does, however, drive my father to distraction, and I take great pleasure in that. He was determined that I should be a clergyman, absolve him of all his sins. I felt guilty, tainted, for taking what he provided—food, shelter, clothing, education. I decided I was destined for the church as well, to absolve me of my guilt. But while I was at Oxford, I found a circle of friends who had their own burdens to bear, who wanted to break free of their restraints as I did. To do that, we needed money. And thus we strategized together and found a way not only to gain funds but to forge our own paths. If he'd shown my mum a scintilla of kindness, I might care about his opinion of me. As it is, the more miserable I make him, the more satisfied I feel. Revenge of sorts, I suppose."

"It hurts you in the process. What woman would want to marry you?"

"I have no plans to marry."

"We're of like minds there. I would hate being forced to come to you and pretend to have an affair in order to get a divorce to correct my error."

"If you came to me, the affair would not be pretend."

Her eyes widened, and her lips parted.

"Complete honesty," he said. "Would you want it to be pretend?"

She glanced around as though searching for an escape or perhaps for an answer that wouldn't be a lie but neither would it reveal the truth. Finally, she met and held his gaze. "I believe we've violated the third rule about keeping to business. It's getting late. I should go."

It was no doubt wishful thinking on his part, but he decided her answer to his question was no. She wouldn't want it to be pretend.

CHAPTER 17

⚬⚬⚬

$\mathcal{B}$ISHOP had been surprised his offer to accompany Marguerite home, along with the promise of his carriage being made available to her the following day, had been met with what could only be described as an expression of culpability mingled with unease. He'd not liked it and had suspected the reason for it: she didn't trust him or herself alone in the carriage in the dark, anticipated a repeat performance of what had transpired when they left the former brothel.

He'd intended to be a perfect gentleman, not moving to her side until she indicated he could do so. Although he'd also expected to have her in his arms before his carriage had fully left the drive. He'd decided that they needed to face whatever was simmering between them and so he'd declared, "Complete honesty."

She'd angled that heart-shaped chin of hers up defiantly and he'd once more become aware that she was not as easy to read as he'd originally assumed. "I'm not returning to my rooms. I'm going to Mrs. Mallard's."

And so it was that he now found himself hunched behind a group of hedgerows near the locked gate of the Mallard residence. He was surprised she hadn't brought out picks and opened it so they could sneak closer. His carriage was waiting down the street, around the corner, in hopes that it wouldn't be sighted but would be readily available if they needed to make a hasty escape.

"I'm not quite sure what it is you hope to accomplish," he said, peering through the slatted wrought iron fence at the manor, darkened save for pale light visible in a solitary chamber on an upper floor.

"I simply want to see if she goes out or if anyone comes to visit her."

"Most decent sorts are abed this time of night."

"Why assume she's decent?"

"Why assume she's not?"

"She wasn't honest with us regarding what she told Swindler."

"Perhaps he exaggerated or misconstrued her words."

He was astonished her sigh of frustration didn't blow away the hedges surrounding them. "He is incredibly diligent at sticking to facts. How did she come to your attention?"

"As most women do. She showed up on my doorstep. Apparently Mrs. Winters—"

"One of the women who got divorced last year because you were having an affair with her, which I assume you weren't."

"I don't discuss the particulars of my relationships. Anyway, Mrs. Winters had suggested Mrs. Mallard pay me a visit."

"You didn't know her before that?"

"No. We never crossed paths."

"Yet within a fortnight of meeting you, her husband is dead. I find the timing suspect."

"You find her suspect."

"Yes." He heard the tiniest clatter of her teeth.

The night had grown cooler as the hours had progressed. He considered opening his coat wider and drawing her into the haven of his body, where his heat could help to rebuff the cold. But there was that damned term about businesslike behavior or some such that she'd insisted upon. He'd signed the agreement before they'd left his residence, and already he regretted not crossing out anything designed to make a gentleman out of him. He should leave her to suffer in the chill until she came to her senses and drifted closer to him, to take advantage of what he could offer. But he suspected she was determined not to acknowledge that she'd made an error with her rules. At least not after only a few hours. After shrugging out of his coat, he draped it over her shoulders.

"I can't accept this. You'll get cold," she said, even as she drew the lapels closer together, as though needing at least a few seconds of his warmth to carry her through.

Her gaze had fallen on him. Although the distant streetlamp barely illuminated her features, it was enough for him to see her true concern. Even though the brisk night air had already begun to work its way through his shirtsleeves, he said, "I'll be fine."

To hell with the complete honesty as well. Another thing to which he shouldn't have agreed. Although perhaps it would work in his favor if he told her the truth: *I want to kiss you. I've wanted to kiss you ever since I first laid eyes on you this morning. I can barely think for how much I want to kiss you.*

As though she could read the yearning etched on his

features—when had he lost the ability to give none of his thoughts away?—she looked back toward the residence and quickly straightened. "She's moving about. Or someone is. It appears light, probably lamplight, is bobbing down the stairs that lead to the entryway."

Small windows at two levels lit up and then descended into darkness. The glow finally brightened the windows on either side of the door. As though the illumination was wielded by a sorcerer with the ability to conjure, a coach came down the quiet street and stopped a short distance away.

Grabbing Marguerite, Bishop ducked down, shielding her, although with his coat around her, she was probably more invisible than the sleeves of his shirt. Thank goodness for his dark waistcoat and trousers. Peering through the foliage, he watched as a footman hopped down, raced to the gate, unlocked it, and swung both sides open. The vehicle was already moving before he jumped back on board.

"She's going somewhere," Marguerite whispered, her breath skimming along his throat from where she was tucked up against him, and he didn't know if he'd felt anything as sensual in his entire life.

"Or someone else is leaving," he said.

"Must you offer an alternative to everything I suggest?"

"You would lose all respect for me and my deciphering abilities if I didn't take on the role of the devil's advocate."

"You assume I have any respect for you at all."

"I don't think you'd be here if you didn't."

He felt the light touch of her lips along the underside of his jaw before she straightened and moved quickly away from him, causing leaves to rustle in her wake. "Where are you going?"

"I'm trying to see if it's her or someone else." She'd made it to the edge of the gate by the time he caught up with her. "It's her."

"It's a woman in a hooded pelisse. It could be a friend, a sister—"

"We need to follow."

The good news was that they didn't need to pass in front of the gate in order to retrace their steps back to his coach, which fortunately was facing in an advantageous direction. He gave his coachman the orders to move into position and follow at a discreet distance the coach that would soon be leaving the Mallard residence. As he climbed in and took his seat opposite Marguerite, he could feel the excitement thrumming through her and found himself wishing he was the cause of it.

WHAT RESPECTABLE ONLY-A-FEW-DAYS-A-WIDOW went out in the dead of night?

As the carriage clattered through the streets, Daisy knew her thoughts should be focused on determining an array of possibilities that would satisfy that question, but her mind seemed suddenly unable to concentrate on anything other than the feel of Bishop's bristly jaw against her lips a few minutes earlier. Had he commented on her brushing them over his skin, she would have lied—complete honesty be hanged—and told him that it had happened accidentally, that she'd lost her balance when she'd made to move away from him. Much as she had that night of the nipple incident. Not that she could refer to it as such to him. The settee incident. Much better.

But thus far she'd been spared the inquisition and, therefore, had run her tongue over her lips several times as though she could still taste his saltiness, feel the softness of his skin hovering beneath the bristle, waiting for a closer inspection. Nestled within his protective embrace, she'd inhaled his bergamot and orange fragrance deeply into her lungs and discovered a hint of dark scotch and leather. While she'd never enjoyed the flavor of scotch, she'd always liked the scent of it, so manly and bold. It suited him.

While she knew now that they were back in the carriage that she should hand over his coat, and she'd already absorbed all the warmth it could provide, she couldn't bring herself to give up this little piece of him. She didn't want him messing with her senses or her sensibilities, and yet she was powerless to stop him from breaching her defenses.

She yearned for another kiss and more. To be on his lap, to have his hands stroking her. It was a struggle to remember he was a client and this matter was business. To demonstrate her professionalism. When all she wanted was to climb all over him.

He'd pulled the curtains again to protect her reputation, but a lamp had been lit so they could see each other with a bit more clarity. She almost asked him to remove his waistcoat and cravat, loosen a few buttons, so she could pretend he was sitting on his bedchamber settee waiting for her.

She lifted the curtain slightly to gaze out. "I don't recognize where we are."

"My coachman will know, and he'll remember the route should you need to traverse it later."

Releasing the curtain, she studied the manner in

which the shadows played over the contours of one side of his face while the light toyed with the other. Was there a single environment in which he didn't appear devilishly handsome? "Is that the reason you didn't let him go when he took me to the Cerberus Club? He warned me that you would."

"It would take too much effort to train someone to follow my exacting standards. It's the reason Perkins has no fear of finding himself on the street. I'm not as concerned with obeyance as I am with competence. Besides, I find a bit of rebellion a good thing, a sign of an independent thinker. I value a man—or a woman—who can anticipate what I need before I ask for it."

His voice had gone low, his eyes dark, and she wondered if his needs at that precise moment matched hers.

The carriage began to slow. Once more she glanced out, as did he. They were on a street of terrace houses, and the vehicle had settled into a crawl. Because she was facing forward, she could see the coach they'd been following had stopped in front of a building and a woman was being handed down. "It's her. It's Mrs. Mallard."

Once they were past the coach, he said, "I saw which residence she went into, but I couldn't see who opened the door to her."

He let the curtain fall back into place, as did she. "What now?" he asked. "Do we bang on the door and confront her? And accuse her of what exactly?"

She shook her head. "No, I'll come back tomorrow, discreetly ask around, perhaps knock on the door as a flower seller or something. Discover who lives there. See if I can uncover anything else that might prove useful in our quest."

"You don't want to go into hiding to see how long she stays?"

She detected a bit of sarcasm in his tone. "You think it's just an innocent late-night visit?"

"I think she's a woman who suffered a terrible jolt when she discovered her husband. It had to be a gruesome sight. She was wary of me from the beginning, fearful of everything, so perhaps her inclination was to think I'd done it in order to save her. She may have even still been in shock when she spoke with Swindler and didn't choose her words carefully. Or she is prone to exaggeration."

"Perhaps. But I'm not going to wait about to see how long she stays. I'll gather more information tomorrow."

He knocked twice briskly on the ceiling and the coach increased in speed. "I don't know why you think the worst of her. You can't be jealous of her, because I didn't use her to tease you."

"Oh? Is that what you were doing with Mrs. Parker and Mrs. Bowles? Teasing me?"

After giving her that smile that captured her breath, he peered out the window. She supposed she was acting like a bit of a shrew.

"What time do you want the carriage brought round to you tomorrow?"

"It's not necess—"

He pinned her with a pointed glare that might as well have been a rapier through her larynx as it stopped her ability to speak. "We've been through this already."

"Ten," she said, after finally regaining her voice.

"See how much easier it is when you cooperate?"

"I thought you liked working with people who didn't always do as you said."

"What of you? Do you like working with people who don't always follow your rules?"

"My rules serve a purpose to keep things professional between us."

"All business as I recall."

"Precisely."

He crossed over until he was sitting beside her, his thigh brushing against hers, sending heat spiraling through her. "Do you know what I saw to this afternoon?"

She wasn't certain she wanted to know. His eyes held a touch of humor and something more, something dangerous. *Hunger.* She felt like a poor creature caught in a web with the inability to move and no chance of escape, all the while knowing it was facing peril. Somehow, she managed to unlock her muscles and shake her head. "No."

"I visited my solicitor. You should have witnessed the absolute shock on his face when I touched his cheek."

Before she could laugh at the absurdity, his warm palm was cradling her face, his gaze intense as his eyes held hers. "That was your objection to my touching you, was it not? That I hadn't touched him?"

Had she objected? She could hardly think when it felt as though his fingers were growing all the warmer, as though where their skin touched a tiny fire had been lit and was beginning to spread, to consume. She had little doubt that eventually it would reach her toes. "Did you kiss your solicitor as well?"

A flash of white teeth just before he lowered his

head, and his luscious mouth was brushing against the swirls of her ear. "Should I have?" he rasped, and flames of desire began licking along her flesh where his breath wafted over it. She would probably combust if his breath and fingers ever came together against any part of her person.

Yes, yes, yes was the answer she wanted to provide to his question, but she knew if she lowered the drawbridge, she would essentially be doing away with the third condition. That once she was no longer standing her ground in defense of it, nothing would stop him from swimming the moat and scaling the walls of the castle she'd erected in which to take shelter from all the wicked things she wished to experience with him.

She was aware of the absolute stillness of his body as he awaited her response. He wasn't going to push her into it, force her to make a hurried decision. Blackguard Blackwood the *ton* had labeled him, and it was such an inappropriate moniker for this man. "As your lips are so near to mine, I suppose it would be a waste not to close the distance between them."

She felt the spread of his smile against the sensitive skin just below her ear. His mouth, heated and moist, filled with triumph and promises.

He lifted his head, captured, and held her gaze. One heartbeat. Two. "I can't abide waste," he growled, just before sweeping in to possess what he probably didn't realize he already owned.

She had intended not to welcome him too eagerly, but as with everything where he was concerned, her intentions seldom reflected reality. It would have been foolish, really, not to make the most of this moment when his mouth slashed over hers before gentling on a sigh and a soft moan, as if now that she'd given him his freedom to possess, he wanted to luxuriate in the taking of her. His tongue traced the outline of her lips, before pressing along the seam of her mouth, urging her to open for him. And she did. Wanting—needing—to taste him fully, to have their tongues circling, roaming, withdrawing. Only to come together again.

She stroked her hands over his broad shoulders. Traced her fingers over the firm muscles of his back. She knew the strength she detected in those powerful muscles was the result of a young boy striving to develop the means to defend his mother. As a man, still he worked to protect women.

She was presently the beneficiary of all that effort. And she gloried in it.

The manner in which he pressed his large, strong hands along her back, over her sides. The way it felt to be caged in by those sturdy arms.

She wanted to clamber onto his lap, to be pressed even closer to him, along the entire length of him. She wanted to loosen buttons, remove clothing, experience the warmth of his skin against her fingertips.

Had she really thought a condition designed to avoid anything personal developing between them was going to protect her from this overwhelming urge to keep nothing from him?

Every spinster should have a dalliance with a man who knows what he's about.

Her aunt had offered that sage advice. Bishop certainly knew what he was about.

HOLY HELL! So much for that third condition. Her eagerness was burning right through it. Bishop wouldn't be surprised to look at their agreement and find that particular line scorched.

It seemed in the darkness of night, within the confines of his carriage, they could seldom travel without coming together. Was it the adventure of sleuthing, of sneaking about that made it seem acceptable to engage in the forbidden? Did it heighten senses and awareness? Did it make it impossible not to want?

Although he'd wanted her during dinner. Had wanted her in the library. Had wanted her earlier in the day when the sun had shone into the carriage. He wondered if a time would come when he wouldn't want her, when he would be content to have only the memories of her.

But he wanted those memories to encompass the whole of her.

He trailed his mouth along her throat, taking immense satisfaction in her dropping her head back and moaning as though nothing had ever felt more sublime. For him, it hadn't. Just having her back in his arms was heaven.

Taking her lobe between his teeth, he nipped and soothed. Then with his tongue, he outlined the delicate shell of her ear. "I don't want to do this in the carriage. Come back to my residence with me."

He could hear her breath sawing in and out, could feel the tension radiating through her.

"It would render me unprofessional."

"You can't be an inquiry agent twenty-four hours a day, surely. For a few hours, could you not be just a woman? With no mysteries to solve, no clues to collect. Only pleasure to be had?"

"You won't sue me for breach of contract?"

Chuckling low, he took her mouth, hard and with purpose, but briefly. "No."

Reaching up, he banged three times on the ceiling.

"What are you doing?" she asked.

"Two knocks alerted the coachman to go to your place of business. Three means my residence. I needed to let him know there is a change in destination."

"I won't stay the entire night."

"However long you stay, I shall make it enough."

CHAPTER 18

$\mathcal{S}$HE thought it unlikely that staying with him for the remainder of her life would be enough for her. That a few hours with her would be enough for him almost had her banging twice on the ceiling, signaling she'd changed her mind.

Only she hadn't.

As complete honesty now existed between them, she was grateful to know there were limitations to what he would give. While she knew it was reckless of her to accompany him to his residence, to his bedchamber—because she was very much aware they weren't going to sit in his parlor and drink tea—she couldn't seem to find the strength to reverse her course.

Had her mother felt this way when her father had asked for her hand? Had she known it was an unwise decision to say yes but been powerless to utter any other word?

The truth was she wanted Bishop. She had for a while now. She didn't know if there was a precise moment when she'd thought *I want that man*. Rather it had been a slow dawning, like a shadow creeping over the city when the sun set. One hardly noticed until it encompassed all and closed one within darkness.

Although she didn't feel confined, but rather liberated. She was never going to marry, and if she was going to give her purity away, she wanted it taken by someone she admired. And she did admire him. To assist women in need, he risked censure and a lifetime of being alone. And presently a much worse fate. But it seemed he found it all worth the cost. So whatever price she paid to be with him, if later it demanded heartache, she would pay it without remorse or regret or bitterness.

He'd offered no promises except for now, uttered no words of love. Complete honesty. That was much more than her father had given her mother. A gift, really. To know precisely where she stood. Pleasure was on the horizon, and once they reached it, they would return to business. Keeping everything neat and tidy. Never mixing the two.

After their destination was altered, he took her mouth passionately but briefly before straightening and pulling her into the nook of his side, his arm circling her shoulders, his head resting against hers. As though now it was time to wait, to allow the anticipation to build.

She still had his coat draped around her. Didn't want to relinquish it.

He sat so motionless, as though if he moved at all, he wouldn't be able to stick to his determination not to take her in the carriage. She thought she should say something but didn't want to disturb the quiet, the calm before the storm. She was rather certain that when they reached their destination and he was unleashed, she was going to be hit with the force of a powerful tempest that destroyed ships. Like him, she remained quiet, gathering her strength, determined to welcome him as an equal, to take all that he was offering.

The carriage came to a halt, and he immediately went into action, springing away from her, opening the door without waiting for the footman, and leaping out. Reaching back in for her, he extended his hand. She didn't hesitate to place hers in it.

Her feet landing on the drive should have grounded her, but it was as though she'd stepped into a dream. Everything seemed at once near and distant, solid, yet ethereal.

He offered his arm, and she placed her fingers on it. In silence, they went up the steps and into his residence. A lamp had been left burning on a table in the foyer.

He didn't bother to take it. No doubt familiar with every aspect of the rooms, able to wander through them in the dark, he led her up the stairs. The shadows began to thicken, went black as though she and he had gone into a tunnel, and then began to lighten again when they reached the landing.

His bedchamber door was open, a pale glow—no doubt provided by the lamp that sat on a small table beside the bed—spilling into the hallway to reveal the flowers.

Removing her hand from his arm, she wandered over to the first table with its vase stuffed with the blossoms. She skimmed her finger around the circle of white petals connected to the yellow button-like center. Daisies. The hallway was filled with daisies.

She glanced over her shoulder at him. "Was it your plan all along to seduce me into joining you here tonight?"

"No, but those have become my favorite flower, almost like having you here."

He held out his hand, and she enthusiastically placed her palm against his, relishing the way his fingers closed around hers. He guided her into the room where she'd tidied, brought trays, and poured chocolate on him. Become jealous, if she was honest. She hadn't understood at the time that's what she was feeling, but she acknowledged it now. It had hurt to think all those women knew him as she wanted to. Perhaps she'd insisted on that third condition because she'd thought it would give her the strength not to surrender to her wants and desires. But they were too powerful, too strong. The potency with which she yearned for him overwhelmed her.

He closed the door, and the sound of it *snicking* into place seemed to unleash a flood of desire. He flicked his jacket off her, sending it to the floor, before pulling her into his arms, and blanketing his mouth over hers. No gentle preamble to this kiss, no outlining of what he was about to taste. No need for either when she eagerly opened her mouth to him, taking what she would, what she'd wanted from the moment she'd seen him hovering outside her office door that morning.

Had it been only that morning? Not even a full day or a full night. The third condition was tossed aside, and her resolve to resist him was torn to tatters, and yet it felt as though in its place had been woven a tapestry spun in gold.

Because everywhere he touched suddenly tingled like it shone and glittered. Although he moved hurriedly, squeezing a breast, cupping her backside, mapping out the terrain of her, so also did he give the impression that every aspect of her with which he came into contact was precious, treasured.

His groans and growls were deep, tortured almost, as though each caress and stroke wasn't enough, while at the same time each was everything.

He plowed his hands up into her hair, his fingers taking on the task of locating and dislodging every hairpin that held her locks in place. She'd left her hat in the carriage when they'd begun tonight's adventures, because she'd decided its wide brim would make it more difficult to hide. When creeping about, it was best not to have objects sticking out that could get caught on things. Now she was grateful he didn't have to mess with removing it.

Her hair cascaded around her shoulders and along her back and over his forearms, because he still cradled her head. Only then did he break off the kiss. He smiled in appreciation and wonder. "Like honey."

He combed his fingers through the strands. "So incredibly soft." He trailed his thumbs along her cheek. "Your skin is as silky as a rose petal."

It was how she was feeling, as though all of her was unfurling after a quarter of a century on this earth, after so many years of being wary of the goodness of men, of living with a woman who had never married, and being the daughter of one who'd chosen poorly.

She didn't think she was following in her mother's footsteps, but if she was, she wasn't going to regret it. And for the first time, she suspected that her mother hadn't either. That she'd chosen love, for better or worse, because of moments like this when she felt treasured.

With nimble fingers she began loosening the onyx

buttons of his waistcoat. Lowering his hands, he slipped the pearl buttons on her bodice through their openings. When one task was complete, they moved on to the next, removing garments, their breaths quickening as additional skin was revealed. Their fingers growing greedy to reveal more.

When his shirt was gone, she pressed her mouth to his chest, felt his growl rumbling through him. Her frock was a pool of fabric on the floor, her petticoats beside it.

Once more he cradled her face, held her still, and captured her gaze. "Complete honesty. I want to be sure you understand that I never took to that bed any of the women I've helped to secure a divorce. I was never intimate with any of them. I would never take advantage of someone's vulnerability."

She nodded because she knew him well enough not to be surprised by the words and whispered, "I've never had a dalliance."

He smiled. She smiled. For a few minutes they simply took each other in, until finally, lifting her into his arms, he carried her to the bed, laid her down, and went to work divesting her of everything else she wore.

She loved watching how his brow pleated, the concentration he directed to the task, as though he was measuring the profitability of an investment and if it was worth the risk that it might not pay off at all. And then the wonder, the appreciation in his eyes when her corset and chemise were littering the floor and her breasts were bared. As though she was definitely worth the risk.

He lowered himself to the edge of the mattress and cupped them. "You are so exquisite."

She skimmed a hand along the corded muscles of his torso. "So are you."

He laughed and shook his head. Was he embarrassed?

Standing again, he reached for her drawers. She stopped him and sat up. "I'll do it. I want to see you. All of you."

While she wiggled out of her last bit of clothing, he saw to the remainder of his. Could *beautiful* be applied to a man? Because he was. Gorgeous and sumptuous with defined muscles that her fingers were anxious to trace, to outline, to memorize. The appreciation in his gaze at the sight of her fully revealed took her breath.

Then he was climbing onto the bed and into her arms.

IF HEAVEN EXISTED on earth, he'd just ascended to it. Here, with his body pressed against hers, exchanging heat, creating sensations. She wasn't shy. He'd give her that. Although he hadn't truly expected her to be.

From their very first encounter, he'd judged her to be a woman who knew her own mind and wasn't afraid to go after what she wanted. It was part of the reason that he'd had difficulty reconciling her as being a servant. She was bold, daring, and fearless.

Hovering behind hedges and chasing after carriages in the middle of the night.

Then setting up rules to a game he couldn't let her win.

Did you kiss your solicitor as well?

If it was what she'd required in order to welcome his mouth playing over hers, he'd have gone directly to his solicitor's residence, stirred him from his slumber, and kissed him in front of her. He'd wanted her that desperately. He still did. And he had the uncomfortable feeling that, even after they'd reached completion, he still would.

He'd had women aplenty through the years, but he'd never felt so *involved* with one. As though every aspect of her complemented every aspect of him. She challenged him. She made him consider the possibility that he'd finally encountered an opponent he might not be able to win out over. That with her, the usual strategies didn't apply.

She was exciting. Interesting. And beautiful. Every inch of her.

And she'd given his fingers the luxury of exploring those inches. He'd offered her the same, and she took advantage of his willingness to let her put her investigative skills to the test to learn all the various ways his body differed from hers.

She seemed particularly enamored of his chest and abdomen, skimming her hands over them repeatedly. Once she'd rubbed her hand over his backside and given it a quick squeeze while he nibbled on her neck. She tangled her fingers in his hair, rubbed his shoulders, his back. He enjoyed it all, relished it.

But sensed a hesitancy in her. In this brave woman.

Her hand drifted down to his hip, began drawing little circles that expanded ever wider.

"Do you know you're driving me mad?" he asked, as he lowered his hand to the springy curls between her thighs and began creating his own circles over the silk of her skin, softer than any petal he'd ever known.

"Am I?"

They were on their sides, facing each other. He looked deeply into her eyes. "Do you want to see me in torment? Wrap your hand around my cock."

"Will it hurt?"

"No, it'll be exquisite."

Her fingers closed around him, and a bolt of pure pleasure shot through him, eliciting a groan he couldn't contain. Although she smiled, her eyes darkened, and he knew his reaction was fueling her desires, her own satisfaction. "Do you see how powerful you are? If I'd been standing, you'd have dropped me to my knees."

"Drop me to mine. Like you did in the carriage after our visit to the brothel. I've not been able to stop thinking about it."

"That experience is going to pale when compared with what I'm going to do to you now."

SHE THOUGHT THAT perhaps she should have had the good sense to be frightened by the vow that sounded almost like a threat, by the hunger in his eyes that hinted he was on the verge of devouring her. Of the way his muscles bunched up and his cock jumped within her hand. It had been hard, but it grew more so.

He rolled her onto her back, balancing his weight on one arm while his other hand came up to knead her breast. Lowering his head, he took the taut pearl into his mouth and sucked, drawing pleasure all the way up from the soles of her feet.

She was struck by an odd thought. In the room where he worked with weights to increase his strength, did he also work to increase his prowess? Were there tools for that? Or routines to be done over and over? Or did knowing exactly what to do and how to do it with the right amount of pressure require a partner to give directions?

He'd asked that night in the carriage, to tell him what she needed, how she needed it. Firm, soft. Fast, slow.

But now it was as though he knew her so well that he could intuit it. Was it the way her body was moving beneath his? Squirming. Tightening. Loosening. Surely, he could feel all those little movements, just as she could feel the tensing of his muscles beneath her hands whenever she moaned or whimpered. He seemed to like both sounds equally and appeared intent on doing whatever necessary to elicit them.

While she loved his growls and his groans.

Shifting his weight, he settled between her thighs and began to move down the length of her body, leaving little love bites in his wake. Along each rib and then the expanse of her stomach. He gave attention to one hip and then the other.

His hands, folded around her sides, moved down to her hips, to the insides of her thighs. He spread her legs wide, parted the folds that hid a tiny bud. She felt as though he was unfurling petals, going straight to the heart of the bloom.

He lowered his head and with a sweep of his tongue, he caused her to gasp and blossom. He was the sun that nudged nature into awakening. Bringing up her knees, she squeezed her feet against his firm sides, creating butterfly wings with her legs while he licked and suckled. And groaned. A tortured sound as though he couldn't get enough of her, yet what he possessed provided sustenance and refuge and dreams.

It was incredibly intimate, what was happening between them. She knew how his muscles bunched with his movements. He knew how her body strained to be closer to him. Even the parts of her that weren't touching him felt as though they were. With each stroke of his tongue or glide of his finger, unheralded pleasure spiraled through her and she wanted to shout with the absolute joy of it.

She couldn't take her eyes off his dark head, nestled between her legs. Even as the sight made her grow hot and struggle to breathe. Little tremors were swirling through her, increasing in size until she wasn't certain she could contain them. Didn't know if she wanted to contain them.

Reaching up, he cradled a breast, circled his thumb around her hardened nipple. Lightly skimmed over the straining tip. His tongue, velvet and silk, pressed harder against her nubbin, then lighter. Harder again. A stroke, a sweep, a swirl.

The sensations his attentions elicited ratcheted through her, increasing in intensity.

"Oh, my," came out on a startled breath.

"Give in to it," he ordered.

Against his mouth, that secret part of her throbbed. Her feet pressed more firmly against him. Her fingers clutched at his hair because it was all becoming too much. Much more than it had been in the carriage, so much more. It was glorious and frightening and compelling.

Then her entire body unfurled as exquisite pleasure burst through her, and she knew what it was to blossom beautifully, perfect and rare.

Moving up, he gently nudged his cock against her opening. But she didn't want gentle. She wanted him.

She wanted him sharing this wonder with her, wanted to give to him as he'd given to her.

Placing her hands on his firm backside, she squeezed his buttocks as he pushed his hard length into her. The wonder of him spreading her, filling her. The discomfort was minimal, and then he was seated to the hilt. He growled low with satisfaction.

"You're still throbbing," he croaked. "You feel so damned good."

He withdrew slightly and then pushed back in. And again. Slowly at first, and she knew he was giving her time to grow accustomed to the sensation of their bodies joined. Resting on his elbows, he looked down at her, their gazes holding. She watched as his eyes darkened and smoldered while his movements quickened, while he thrust and pumped into her.

With a roar, he pulled out of her, and she felt his hot seed coat her thigh. Breathing heavily, he lowered his head and placed a kiss where the curve of her shoulder met her neck. "You've ruined me for all other women."

HE HADN'T MEANT to give voice to those words, but they'd been rumbling around his head, and he'd accepted the truth of them, and they'd spilled out.

Afterward, he'd cleaned her up, hating the spots of blood that indicated he'd caused her some pain. How could there be blood with no pain? He'd intended to go slowly, carefully, but when she'd dug her fingers into his arse, urging him on, he'd catered to her desires, grateful for the aftermath of her pleasure pulsing around his cock. It had served to heighten his awareness of her as well as his own pleasure.

Now she lounged against his side, her head nestled in the crook of his shoulder, her fingers toying with the hairs on his chest as though she was fascinated by them. He couldn't recall ever experiencing such contentment. Even if the possibility of a hangman's noose threatened his future. At present, she was all that mattered. Being here with her, enjoying her.

"Well, that was rather . . . splendid," she said dreamily, as though she hadn't fully broken free of the lethargy that lingered after lovemaking.

He chuckled low. "I'm glad you approved."

"However, I can't imagine being so intimate with a stranger. Is that the reason you told me to spend time in the shadows before going up those stairs at the Fair and Spare?"

"I didn't want you going up those stairs."

"I'm glad you're the one I had my dalliance with."

He didn't know why it bothered him that she viewed what had passed between them as a *dalliance*. The word made what had transpired seem trivial, inconsequential. Yet for him, it had eclipsed anything he'd ever experienced with anyone else. Somehow, it had been grander and more significant.

Cupping the back of her head, he tilted it until he could look into her eyes. "Why have you chosen the path of an inquiry agent rather than a wife?"

She sighed. "The law is not kind to women. Husbands still have control over a majority of their wives' financial life, but more, women are seldom allowed to keep their identity. They're absorbed into their husbands' lives as though they have no interests or dreams of their own. My aunt never married, and I've never known a more content woman in my life."

"Perhaps you're also influenced by your mother's experience."

"She loved my father, but he was weak in character. How does one avoid making such a grave mistake?"

"By getting to know the man before you marry him."

She shook her head. "But that's no guarantee, is it? Otherwise, women wouldn't have come to you."

"I don't know how well they knew their husbands before they married. I don't pry into their reasons or the particulars of their marriage. What they liked, what they didn't. What finally was the last straw."

"Pity. If you'd gathered enough information perhaps you could have written a book with tips on how to have a successful marriage. Tip one would be to take your mouth on a journey between your wife's legs."

Laughing, he rolled until she was beneath him. "Did you like that?"

She smiled, the force of it rivaling the most delicate and beautiful of blooms. "I did. But I need to leave soon."

"I'll take another journey before you go, shall I?"

Her answer was to spread herself for him. Ah, yes, she had most definitely ruined him for anyone else. And yet, he couldn't seem to regret it.

CHAPTER 19

⌒⌒⌒⌒

The following morning, much to her surprise after such a late night, Daisy was up with the sun, refreshed and energized. And a little sore in places she hadn't known she could experience discomfort. Yet even the aches were welcome and good because of how they had come to be. She regretted none of her time with Bishop, even if it meant that in complete honesty she had to scratch through a line on their agreement. Even if it meant she felt more compelled to get to the truth of what had happened to Mr. Mallard, if the weight of what she'd taken on now felt as heavy as all those bells he lifted.

She had been unwise to take Bishop on as a client, should have done her sleuthing in secret, because she now feared she would disappoint him, wouldn't find the proof needed to exonerate him. She'd never pitted her investigative skills against a murderer, had assumed it only required gathering the facts in order to be victorious. But if she was not successful, it was likely that the wrong man would be delivered to the gallows.

A man she cared about far more than was wise. A man she feared that if she allowed it, her heart would love.

But at least she had a starting point for the day. The dwelling Widow Mallard had snuck off to visit late last night, when her residence had been dark and quiet, servants no doubt abed. No one to know of her escapade save her coachman and footman. Although it wouldn't have mattered if every staff member had known of her activities. No law prevented a widow from going out.

But it struck Daisy as odd. To venture forth at such an hour. Only a few days a widow. After discovering her husband with a bloody mess for a head.

Most women would have taken to their beds for days to recover from the shock of it. But Daisy thought Mrs. Mallard's actions could not have been more surprising had she gone to the Fair and Spare and asked for a membership. Something was amiss. Even as Bishop had tossed out reasons—sensible reasons—for the woman's attitude and excursion, Daisy couldn't help but believe that something nefarious was afoot.

She prepared herself a light breakfast—egg, toast, and tea. The tea, of course, reminded her of Bishop's dislike for it. Whatever was wrong with the man not to enjoy the calmness that came with a nice cup of the brew? That first sip always righted her world, no matter what troubles might have visited her the hours before or were waiting ahead. And with a chocolate biscuit or sweet, it was absolutely wonderful. Why did he loathe it so? On the other hand, she couldn't tolerate scotch so perhaps they were even. Scotch in a glass anyway. She did love the flavor of it on his tongue.

She smiled at the memory of his returning her here last night. They couldn't be in a confined space for long without eventually kissing. And oh, the kisses they now shared. Nothing at all chaste and proper about them. She'd almost invited him to her bed.

With a chuckle, she descended the stairs to her office and took her place behind her desk. Dipping pen in inkwell, she began making a list of everything she'd learned so far about the recent death, striving to find a pattern or a clue that required a deeper exploration.

At one minute before the hour of ten, she saw the familiar carriage come to a stop in front of her building. Grabbing her reticule, she exited her office, locked the door, and placed her hand in the waiting footman's so he could assist her up.

Before she'd even settled on the squabs, she knew Bishop was there—his bergamot and orange fragrance powerful, fresh, and crisp. Sitting across from her, he was dressed immaculately, not a wrinkle to be seen. Nor a whisker. He'd obviously taken a razor to his face recently. Beginning her day with the sight of him was better than starting it with tea. "I'd not expected you to be here. Are we delivering you somewhere?"

"If you intend to confront people on my behalf, you're not going to be doing it alone."

"If you're not in favor of letting me do my job, then why even hire me?"

"You're free to do your job. I'll simply observe."

She crossed her arms beneath her breasts, watched his gaze drop before quickly lifting back to her eyes. "I shouldn't have accepted the use of your carriage. I'm fine on my own."

"I've no doubt. Let the footman know where we're going."

She should get out now and hire a cab, but truthfully,

she was a bit relieved he would be accompanying her. Last night, she'd seen little of the area she wanted to visit now but had the sense that it was one of the dodgier portions of London. She looked at the footman. "Where that coach we followed last night made its stop."

"Yes, miss." He shut the door, and the carriage rocked as he joined the coachman to relay the instructions.

The horses released neighs before the carriage was rumbling up the street.

"Don't you have business to attend to?" she asked.

"I am attending to business, the business of murder. It's hard to concentrate with suspicions hanging over my head."

For as marvelous as he looked, shadows rested in half-moons beneath his eyes, and she rather feared he'd had a restless night after they'd parted ways. He hadn't drawn the curtains on the windows—after all it was a respectable hour—even if being in a carriage alone with Blackguard Blackwood would have ruined a marriageable lady's chances at a trip to the altar. Or at the very least caused a questioning of her wisdom.

"What is it you wish to accomplish with this foray into Whitechapel?" he asked.

"Is that where we were last night?"

"Yes. As a matter of fact"—he withdrew a slip of paper from inside his coat pocket and handed it to her—"my coachman has provided the address and the house number."

"An efficient fellow."

"I hire only the best."

Feeling the heat rising in her cheeks, she looked out the window. "Surely you're not including me as I have yet to prove myself."

"I thought you exemplary at pouring tea."

Under different circumstances, she might have laughed. Instead, she gave him a woeful look. "I do wish you would take all this seriously."

"I do, more so than I'm comfortable admitting. However, I wouldn't have hired you if I hadn't thought you capable of doing what I needed."

"Yet here you are . . . observing."

"Not for lack of faith in your abilities. But rather a fascination with your methods. They're very much like striving to determine if an investment is worth the risk. Although the investment is a murderer."

HE WAS GRATEFUL she hadn't declared *complete honesty* because he didn't want to admit he feared losing her. He didn't know what he'd expected striving to prove him innocent would entail—but certainly not skulking about in the dead of night or calling upon a stranger who might not wish to be called upon. The woman was taking risks for him. He was humbled by her actions and terrified of the consequences she might suffer. "I should hire a guard or two to travel with you in case your investigation leads you to the door of whomever did in Mallard, and he takes exception to your snooping about."

"I'm fully capable of protecting myself."

He raised both eyebrows at her before turning his attention to the window, because he didn't want her to see how the fact that she knew the possibility existed that she would be in need of protection caused him more worry. He should have been relieved that she understood the reality of the situation. Instead, it ratcheted up his apprehension. He should dismiss her. Leave his fate in the hands of Scotland Yard.

"I carry a small pistol in my reticule," she admitted.

As though her being armed was supposed to reassure him? "And you would shoot a man?"

"Or a woman. I'd rather not, of course, but I wouldn't shy away from doing it if the circumstances necessitated it. In addition, when I worked with Swindler, he taught me a few techniques to protect myself. One involves grabbing an opponent's hand and leveraging his thumb in such a way that the pain fells him to his knees. It doesn't require much strength and can be quite effective. I used it a few months ago on a fellow who attempted to steal my reticule."

Someone accosted her? Her tone implied that she'd taken the attack in stride, simply a normal occurrence that needed to be dealt with. "Jesus. Why the devil don't you have a chaperone?"

"You think my fifty-year-old aunt would be better suited to fending off ruffians than I am? And what of your female staff? Do they have a chaperone when they go to market?"

"I'm certain a footman accompanies them."

"When they have free time and leave the safety of your residence, does a footman watch over them then? A working woman isn't expected to have a chaperone."

"Who makes these ridiculous arbitrary rules?" he grumbled.

She smiled softly as one did when confronted by a wayward child who was unable to see reason. "I like being able to come and go without constantly being watched. I love my aunt dearly, but she guarded me like a hawk, as though at any moment I was in danger of being spirited away. Even now, sometimes, I'll sense someone watching me, someone she's no doubt hired for her own peace of mind. I try not to resent it, just as I'm striving not to resent you being here."

He thought she'd welcome his presence, his assistance. The woman was too independent by half. During the past three years, the women who had come to him had been unable to acquire on their own what they wanted—because of the law. He'd begun to view women as always needing help. They married for security. Here was a woman who tested the limits placed on her gender. He loved her independence as much as he despised it. "I won't interfere."

"See that you don't."

He didn't accompany Daisy to the townhome in which Mrs. Mallard had disappeared the night before. But he was watching her. From across the street, while leaning against a lamppost, perusing a newspaper as though it wasn't unusual for a man to be so enamored of the articles that he had to immediately stop to read what was happening in the world, couldn't wait until he arrived at his home or place of business to examine what he'd just purchased from a passing paperboy.

After they'd disembarked two streets over, he'd instructed the coachman to traverse a route through the surrounding area that would periodically bring the carriage back around, so they wouldn't have long to wait once she was ready to depart.

Rapping her knuckles on the door, she'd decided to

take on the role of an overly inquisitive neighbor, one concerned about strange happenings in the middle of the night. Fretful, nonthreatening. Curious.

Her heart gave a tiny lurch when she heard the latch give. This was always the most exciting and terrifying part of her job. Not knowing what to expect from the person she was about to confront, hoping to gather the information she needed without giving herself away or raising someone's ire.

The door began swinging open, only to stop when a man was partially revealed, shadows playing over his features, as though he feared being fully exposed or bursting into flames should the morning sunlight reach him. Something about him was familiar, but she couldn't quite place him, which she found equally odd because he had a very unforgettable nose. It had obviously been broken at least once, possibly several times, and listed to the side, which gave his face a rather lopsided appearance. His hair—that which hadn't deserted the top of his head—was a pale blond, nearly white. She was fairly certain the wrinkles at the corners of his brown eyes were not the result of laughing but of strife, because they cut deep and aged that gaunt face.

"Daisy, what are you doing here?" His hoarse voice was that of a man who'd spent years screaming.

She might have wondered at his occupation that had stolen the smooth timbre if she'd retained her ability to decipher matters. But his addressing her by name had stunned her. Where might their paths have crossed? Had he once worked as a servant in her aunt's residence? In her uncle's? Had she met him at the Fair and Spare the very first time she'd visited? Although living in this area of London indicated he couldn't afford the club membership. However, he was immaculately dressed, his coat draping perfectly over his slender frame. "How do you know my name?"

"We met some years back. I doubt you remember. You were a mere child. Still, I would recognize you anywhere."

He would have looked younger then. Perhaps she could see the shadow of his youth.

"You so strongly favor your mother," he added, and her heart gave a hard lurch.

"Did you know her, then?"

"I did, yes."

"And my father?"

"Him, as well."

She wanted to ask for details. How had he known them? Had they been friends? Had he introduced them to the opium that had taken them from her? Had he traveled the path to ruin beside them? But she wasn't here for her past. Unfortunately, however, neither could she claim to live in this neighborhood because he might question her regarding precisely which residence was hers, hoping to become reacquainted. She decided honesty was her best approach. "I wondered if you knew Mrs. Mallard."

"I do, yes. As a matter of fact, she paid me a visit last night."

His straightforwardness surprised her. She'd expected a denial. "May I ask her purpose in coming here?"

"Would you fancy joining me inside?"

Over his shoulder, she could see naught but darkness. "No, but thank you for the invitation. I just . . .

I'm worried about her. Widows are easily taken advantage of."

"They are indeed. She's fortunate to have your concern. She came to me because I have the ability to serve as an intermediary between this world and the next. She was hoping to connect with her husband so he might tell her who killed him."

She couldn't have been more shocked. Had Mrs. Mallard truly loved her husband or was it fear that sent her in search of the culprits, dreading she might be next? Did she know why he was killed, know more than she was letting on? "Did she find the answers she sought?"

"Unfortunately, no. But we're likely to try again in the near future, in her residence, where his spirit no doubt lingers awaiting justice."

"I see." Would they invite Inspector Swindler to attend? Did he believe such poppycock? "I shan't keep you any longer."

She backed up a step. Stopped. "I'm sorry. What was your name?"

His smile transformed not only his face, making it appear younger, but himself as well, giving him a charismatic and charming air, and she understood how he could easily lure women into believing not only that he could communicate with the dead but that he could bring them back to life. "Thanatos."

"A pleasure to meet you, Mr. Thanatos." With that she spun on her heel—

"Daisy."

With a chill racing up her spine at how easily he said her name, as though it belonged to him as much as to her, she came to an abrupt halt and looked back over her shoulder.

"Be wary of the gent across the street, pretending to read the newspaper. I don't trust him." With that, he closed the door.

"HE WARNED ME about you."

Even from his position across the street, Bishop had seen her go pale, and he had nearly dashed over straightaway, but she'd raised a hand—palm out, fingers spread—so quickly that she might as well have shouted, *Don't.*

Turning down the street, she'd walked at a fast clip. After passing his newspaper and a crown to a scruffy fellow who'd been limping by, Bishop had sauntered along his side of the street until he was out of view of that residence, and then he'd crossed over to her. Immediately he'd placed his hand on the small of her back and detected the tiniest of tremors going through her. As though anticipating he was going to begin asking questions, she'd shaken her head. It had nearly killed him to hold his tongue.

Only now when they were finally in his carriage, her nestled against his side, his arm around her shoulders, the curtains drawn because it wouldn't do for anyone who might recognize her to see her in such an intimate position with him, had she spoken.

"His purpose was no doubt to unsettle you," he assured her. It seemed he'd done a bang-up job of it.

"I didn't like him. He knew my name. Knew my parents, which immediately makes him suspect, because they visited and were known in the unsavory parts of London. I think he's a charlatan, claiming to have the power to communicate with the dead. Said his name was Thanatos—"

"Like the Greek god of death?" he interrupted.

She nodded. "Mrs. Mallard wants this Thanatos fellow to ask her husband who killed him. Apparently, she visited him last night for that purpose, and he had no luck, so he's going to hold a séance within her residence. What amount do you think she's paying for that service?"

"Far more than I'm paying you for the same information, I suspect."

Twisting slightly, she smiled up at him, tentatively, almost shyly. "But you're more likely to get your money's worth."

He cradled her chin, tilted her head a fraction so he could look directly into her eyes. "Not if something—anything at all, even something as small as a splinter—happens to you."

Then he lowered his mouth to hers, another reason he'd tipped up her chin, so he could reach her lips easily. He'd been terrified and useless standing by that lamppost, when he couldn't see precisely who was at that door, who wouldn't open it fully in order to be seen. He'd almost immediately crossed over but had known this courageous woman would have never forgiven him if he'd given the impression he didn't believe her capable of protecting herself.

He didn't know if he possessed the words to make her understand how precious she'd become to him, and so he struggled to convey his feelings with another sort of language, one that cavemen had no doubt used before they'd ever learned to utter a word. As gently and carefully as he could, he'd taken her mouth as though it were made of spun glass.

Her sigh, along with her body melting against

his, had desire flaming unbidden and uncontrollably through him. More roughly than he'd intended, he pulled her onto his lap before reestablishing his dominance over his needs and yearnings. Not that she seemed to have minded his handling of her because her fingers were scraping along his scalp, tangling in his hair, tugging and directing his head to a different angle that allowed *her* to take the kiss deeper.

She began trembling again, but this time it wasn't fear. A subtle difference existed between the tremors before and those now. These were born of want and desire; these carried ecstasy over skin to nerve endings. These spoke of advancing, not retreating. These were the sort one experienced when sitting on the edge of the seat, waiting for the final move on the chessboard that would declare a winner—and already knowing who the victor would be.

He stroked his hands down her back to her hips, cradling them, incredibly tempted to turn her so she straddled his thighs, but they would soon be stopping, and it was daylight. They might not have a chance to right themselves before a footman opened the door.

He trailed his mouth over her neck, her throat. "Have dinner with me this evening?"

"I've already arranged to dine with my aunt."

"Maybe I could see you afterward."

Leaning back slightly, she held his gaze and nodded. "I'd like that very much."

"What's your favorite flower?"

A lovely smile spread over her face. "Tulips."

CHAPTER 20

Naturally he'd insisted his carriage remain with Daisy after it delivered him to his residence. She'd almost gone in with him then, for a little private time together. But she feared he was very much like opium: addictive.

If she wasn't careful, she was going to want to be in his company every moment of every day.

But she needed to tend to other matters as part of her investigation. She was grateful he wasn't going to observe, confirming it was truly his concern about her trek to Whitechapel and her knocking on a stranger's door that had led to him accompanying her that morning. It warmed her to the core to know he cared enough to want to protect her and understood her well enough to grant her freedom to go about her business without him.

"For someone who hasn't a client, you seem remarkably at peace," her aunt said now as they sat across from each other at the dining table. She was well aware that it usually took Daisy a couple of weeks to land another assignment.

"Actually, I have been hired by someone, and he is paying me rather well for my services."

"Oh, and what are you to do this time? Catch a thief, an errant husband, a stray cat?"

Her aunt provided more support and loyalty than most, but at times even she made light of Daisy's choice for an occupation. Not out of meanness, but rather a lack of understanding regarding how much it meant to Daisy to do what she did. The idea of working had never entered her aunt's head and wasn't something in which she'd have ever considered engaging. "A murderer."

Aunt Charlotte gasped and pressed a hand to her throat. Then she relaxed and laughed. "You almost had me there, but you're joshing. You're referring to a book you're reading. What is the title?"

"No, I'm serious. A man was killed, and my client is a suspect."

Her brow furrowed deeply. "What if he is the murderer? He could kill you next."

"He's not. I'm certain of it."

"Is it his carriage in which you arrived?"

"Yes, he's made it available to me."

Sipping her wine, her aunt studied her over the rim. Finally, she set down the glass. "Who is he, then, this man who has hired you?"

"I'd rather keep his name confidential." While she trusted her aunt implicitly, she also knew the news might be too tantalizing to keep to herself, and Daisy didn't want gossip running rampant that Bishop was being investigated.

She'd managed to catch a couple of Mrs. Mallard's servants while they were outside taking a few minutes to themselves. They'd never known Mr. Mallard to strike his wife. They believed her facial injuries were a result of running into a door. Daisy supposed it was possible that servants were unaware of everything that went on inside a residence—a marriage. Especially if those occurrences happened behind closed doors or during the wee hours. "I'm perfectly safe, Auntie. Scotland Yard and I are working together to resolve this situation."

Relief washed over her features. "Oh, well, if you're assisting Scotland Yard, I do hope you'll eventually share all the fascinating and intricate details. As you are well aware, I do so love a good murder."

"I daresay *good* murders occur only within the pages of books."

"I suppose that's true enough. Will you be staying the night?" A glint in her aunt's eyes alerted her that the dear woman intended to begin a campaign to get the information from her niece and her strategy would involve an abundance of sherry.

"I'm afraid I can't. I have an early appointment with Scotland Yard." Thank goodness, she didn't have a *complete honesty* agreement with her aunt, even if it did mean she suffered through a prick of guilt whenever she strayed from the truth. However, she suspected she'd give Aunt Charlotte the vapors more often than not if she knew the risks Daisy sometimes took. Nonetheless she was very tempted to express her gratitude to her aunt for advising her that she should have a dalliance. *It was the most wonderful thing I've ever experienced, and tonight I'm going to experience it again.* Although she wondered when a dalliance became an affair. How many liaisons were needed to transform the encounters into something else entirely, something that made her more a harlot than simply a curious spinster?

As Bishop's carriage rolled into the circle of his drive, Daisy saw him standing on the bottom step, and as she hadn't seen his trek to that position, she wondered how long he'd been waiting for her arrival, if it was impatience to be with her that had driven him there. When the door opened, he was the one extending his hand and helping her out of the vehicle.

"How was the visit with your aunt?" he asked politely, shifting her hand to his arm as he escorted her into the residence.

"Excruciatingly long."

He flashed her a grin as though pleased by her answer, with the acknowledgment that she'd wanted to be here sooner.

She was surprised Perkins wasn't in the foyer, but then what need had they for the butler when Bishop was already leading her up the stairs? The residence was so quiet that she wondered if he'd sent all the servants away for the night, to protect her reputation, so she wouldn't be spotted. She'd arrived not quite as late this evening as she had the night before. The coachman and footman knew of her arrival, but she suspected that he'd sworn them to secrecy regarding her presence. Or any of her destinations.

Smelling the tulips before they reached the top of the stairs, she couldn't contain her smile. When they turned the corner into the hallway, at least double the number of blossoms that usually graced the vases greeted her. "You didn't have to go to all that trouble."

"For you it was no trouble."

Looking up at him, she held his gaze. "I don't need flirtation. I need honesty."

"What makes you think I wasn't being honest? They're flowers, for God's sake. It's not as though I had to plant them, grow them, and dig them up."

She nodded. *Trust him, trust him, trust him.* He was going to compliment and say nice things. She would do the same. They'd enjoy their time together, these few hours when they had no worries about the future. When he wasn't a client, and she wasn't an inquiry agent. When he was merely a man, and she merely a woman.

He led her into the bedchamber. While he closed the door, she wandered over to the settee. The low table had already been placed before it and resting on it was a tray with strawberries alongside a small bowl of chocolate. She laughed. "You trust me with the chocolate?"

"Should be you wondering if you can trust me. Because I owe you a pouring."

Before she could question what the devil that meant, he pulled her into his arms and blanketed his mouth over hers, dispensing with any preliminary softness or teasing, his tongue delving deep to dance with hers in a ritual that was probably as ancient as time itself. She eagerly welcomed him because she saw no need to play coy or be shy. She wanted him. It was the reason she was here. They both knew it.

She didn't need him filling his hallways with flowers or feeding her strawberries coated with chocolate. She didn't need compliments. Or politeness. She needed only this, this hunger between them that was brutally honest.

Her hair fell around her. She hadn't even realized that he'd seen to her hairpins. But with that task done, it was as though a storm washed over them. As though they each realized that the skin available to them to stroke, kiss, and lick wasn't enough. Buttons were quickly loosened, fastenings undone. Clothing pooled on the floor. Was kicked aside.

When they were completely naked, they came together for a searing kiss and to relish the feel of warm skin pressed close against warm skin. Hands explored and she knew she'd never grow tired of touching him. Even though she'd thought she'd touched all of him last night, now it seemed she had more to learn. He was a combination of silkiness and roughness, of coarse hair and softer strands. She wanted to remember every inch of him.

Suddenly he lifted her into his arms, carried her to the bed, and tossed her onto it. Then he walked away. Quickly she sat up. "Where are you going?"

He didn't answer, but she watched in horror as he bent over and grabbed the porcelain bowl. She scooted back until she hit the headboard. "What are you going to do with that?"

As he prowled toward her, his smile was devilish and seductive. "You poured chocolate over me. It seems only fair I return the favor. Lie down."

Stunned, she now understood his earlier comment about wondering and trust. "You can't be serious, surely."

"Lie down."

"Bishop, sweetheart—"

"Lie. Down." His tone was implacable. She should have ordered him not to use it with her, and yet there was something else woven through it that caused his voice to growl, that hinted at desire tautly leashed, that caused her belly to quiver and warmth to pool between her legs.

"You'll make a mess." Her voice held no conviction, the pitch more invitation than scolding. Perhaps even a bit of a dare.

"I intend to clean it up." After setting the bowl on the table beside the bed, he took hold of her ankles and dragged her down, until her head landed on the pillow that had always appeared untouched until last night. When she rolled over, intending to make her escape, he said, "Trust me."

The urgency and need had her stopping. Breathing heavily, she glanced over her shoulder at him. "I don't want it in my hair."

"It's not going in your hair." He lowered himself to the edge of the bed, cupped her shoulder, and guided her over until she was flat on her back. He dipped his finger in the chocolate and then gently painted it over her lips before joining his mouth to hers.

As he kissed her, she tasted the chocolate and his dark essence. There was a sweetness to it, not only to the flavor but to the gentleness with which he savored her, groaning low.

When he lifted his head, he smiled. "There, all cleaned up."

"Not all." She took his finger, closed her mouth around it, and licked off the chocolate that remained on it. She wasn't certain any sweet had ever tasted so delicious.

His eyes darkened. He growled.

When she was done, he drizzled a small amount

of chocolate over her breast, creating a little design of swirls around her turgid nipple before dotting the hard peak. Lowering his head, he lapped at her flesh. Of their own accord, her fingers combed through his thick hair and held him in place. Never had she imagined a man would do such wicked things with her, that she'd want him to, that she would crave the attention he so thoroughly bestowed upon her.

He moved on to her other breast, careful not to pour too much, but to create a delicate pattern. Watching him caused heat to course through her, as though the chocolate turned molten and seeped through her skin and into her blood. She suspected that he'd intended to coat all of her thoroughly and to take his time doing so, but she was soon squirming with need and desire and urging him to hurry. To finish the punishment that wasn't a punishment at all.

Then there was no chocolate between them, and they both became lost in the sensations they each elicited in the other, with long strokes of a hand, the press of fingers, the sojourn of tongues over flesh. He wasn't shy about exploring every inch of her, and his actions emboldened her to do the same with him. It was so incredibly liberating, more so than taking on an occupation rather than following the path laid out for her that, had she remained on it, would have led to marriage.

When he thrust into her, she tightened around him, holding him close, relishing how perfectly they came together. They moved in tandem rocking against each other. The pleasure built swiftly, perhaps because of the chocolate. Was it an aphrodisiac? Or perhaps it was him, perhaps that was what he was to her. Because he had the ability to make her insatiable, even as he satisfied her.

This time when she fell apart in his arms, it was with his name filling her screams.

AFTER DIPPING THE strawberry into the chocolate, Bishop carried it to her mouth. She had the look of a woman well sated after their frenzied coming together. He'd been so lost in her, in the sensations she caused to course through him, that he'd remembered to withdraw from her barely in the nick of time. He'd had the absurd thought that he wouldn't mind her carrying his child. But he also knew he would do nothing to force her into marriage. No compromising situations. No limiting of choices. Because if he'd learned anything at all about her, it was that she needed to be in charge of her destiny, to decide her course. To be free of Societal restraints. Not to be hindered by others' expectations.

"What would you like for a treat to nibble on the next time you visit?" he asked.

She smiled lethargically. "You."

Chuckling low, he dropped a kiss on her lips. "I was thinking of something sweet. A woman who puts five lumps of sugar in her tea must like sweets."

"Chocolate and strawberries serve just fine."

"I couldn't believe when you dumped the chocolate on my head. I might have—" *Fallen in love with you then*. He furrowed his brow. Where had that thought come from? He was not a man to fall in love. He liked her a great deal, more than was wise with his reputation being what it was. He wouldn't allow her to be painted with the same brush, and that meant an eventual parting of their ways.

"What?" she asked. "What might you have?"

"I might have thought you were jealous."

"Cross, more like. You'd flirted with me the night before, and at the time I thought you were a Lothario."

He set the bowl aside. "And now?"

"I still think you're a Lothario, but at the moment you're mine. I suppose tomorrow evening, however, you'll be Mrs. Bowles's pretend lover."

Did he detect a bit of pique in her voice? He brushed strands of her hair back from her cheek. "She and I ended our arrangement. My current situation is rather distracting." Lowering his head, he pressed his lips to her shoulder. She had the most delicate shoulders. "And she had no further need of me since her husband is dead."

She jerked upright. "Murdered?"

"No. Natural causes, although it happened in his mistress's bed."

"Oh." She settled back against the pillow.

He trailed his finger over the swells of her breast. "You sound disappointed."

"I thought perhaps someone was killing men whose wives were having affairs. Although I don't know why one would. I was looking for a connection, I suppose. An easier task at exonerating you. The best way to prove you innocent is to find who is guilty. At the moment we have damn few clues."

He pressed his thumb against her brow, easing away the pleats that had formed there. "Don't think about it. We should leave our troubles on the other side of that door."

Lifting a hand, she cradled his jaw. "How can you not be worried?"

"We're in the early days yet and I've hired an extremely skilled investigator. You'll get to the bottom of things."

"Perhaps I'll hire that Thanatos fellow. If only it were so easy to contact the dead and have them tell us who did them in. Have you ever been to a séance?"

"No. I think it's all rubbish. He'll take her money, and she'll be none the wiser. Widows are often taken advantage of."

"Women as a whole are."

He knew that well enough. After shifting his leg over hers, so her thigh pressed against his cock, he nuzzled the soft spot beneath her ear. "I do hope you don't think I've taken advantage."

"Of what? My lustful cravings?"

He imagined she felt his wide grin forming against her silken flesh. Had he ever known a woman so comfortable in her own skin? Was it because she'd been raised by a spinster, untethered to a man, who had encouraged her to engage in a dalliance? Because she'd had no father to dote on her and warn her about men's tendencies to misbehave? Or was it simply her nature to accept and face reality?

He'd always sought to create a fantasy atmosphere for the ladies who came to him, to pamper them and to make amends for the other men in their lives, the men who had caused them to knock on his door. To spoil them as he'd wished his mother had been spoiled, had deserved to be. But all Marguerite required of him was brutal honesty. "Speaking of lustful cravings, I might die if I can't have you again."

Her answer was to nudge him gently onto his back, straddle his hips, and take possession of his mouth as though it were in need of conquering. She tasted of strawberries and chocolate. She tasted of decadence.

She wrapped her slender hands around his wrists, moved them so they rested on either side of his head on the pillow, and had her way with him. He could have broken free of her hold—easily. But he was held in place by more than skin and bone. He was shackled by the realization that no other woman had sought to give as much of herself to him as she did.

She was unrelenting fire, causing his body to burn wherever she touched. Her knees pressing against his hips. Her feet resting against his legs. Her sweet, sweet, heated core rubbing against his cock as she undulated over him, kissing his neck, his jaw, his chest, his mouth. Whatever she could reach without relinquishing her hold on his wrists.

Then she moved her hands up until their fingers interlocked, lifted her hips, and enveloped his cock in molten velvet. With a low groan of pure ecstasy, he slid his eyes closed.

"Look at me," she ordered.

How could he not obey? Anything she asked of him, he would have granted at that moment. She rode him as though her life depended on it. He felt as though his did. When had he ever been this dependent on another—for pleasure, for a place to set down burdens, for a chest in which to store secrets, for a key to unlock dreams.

Dreams that didn't involve retribution, anger, and winning. Always winning.

She was not for the future. She was for only now. Living for the moment because she was correct. They were short on clues. Disaster and a rope could be waiting for him at the end of this journey. But he would take the sight of her eyes turning a deeper hue of blue with him. The sound of her gasps and mewls. Her lax mouth. Her breasts bouncing with her energetic movements. The drop of sweat disappearing into the valley between.

The hunger in her eyes. The ecstasy that glowed around her when she arched her spine, tossed back her head, and cried out, "Bishop!"

Her glorious release was enough to send him hurtling over the abyss, growling her name, a benediction and a curse, because at that moment she owned him, body and soul.

Breathing heavily, lethargic and spent, he welcomed her sprawling over him. Her fingers loosened their hold on his. He stroked her back, once, twice, before succumbing to the depths of slumber calling for him.

CHAPTER 21

⁓⌇⌇⁓

DAISY was relatively certain when Bishop awoke and discovered her gone, he was not going to be happy with her. Might even be cross enough to never again drizzle chocolate over her. She'd enjoyed that far too much, but later as she'd begun drifting off to sleep, languid and satisfied, she'd noticed the stethoscope resting on the credenza and been struck with the notion that perhaps the séance was to be held tonight—after all, wouldn't they want to know who the murderer was as soon as possible?—and if she could get close enough to the house, she might be able to decipher precisely why Widow Mallard would go to such bother to discover who had murdered her husband.

She'd wanted to divorce him, had been fearful of him. Why care anything at all about him after he was gone?

They had no children. She was bound to inherit everything. Based on the residence alone, Daisy was fairly certain the widow would find herself with the means to live without cares or financial worries. Her life would entail relative comfort and ease.

Perhaps she merely wished to know to whom she owed her liberation.

The carriage had been waiting to deliver Daisy to her office and rooms. However, she'd instructed Bishop's coachman to bring the vehicle to a halt on a side street in the same spot he had the night before, when she and Bishop had spied on the Mallard residence. Then she'd ordered him to wait, out of sight, until she returned. He'd not hesitated, only too keen to follow her directions, relatively certain his employer would praise him for "seeing to your needs. He thinks well of you, he does."

She very much doubted Bishop was going to be as pleased as the coachman believed, but she would do all in her power to mitigate his anger, so he didn't take his frustration out on his servant. Although she suspected most of his irritation would be directed at her. Discovering something tonight would certainly go a long way toward lessening his upset with her.

It had been a mistake to get physically involved because it was a distraction. Because she could no longer view him as a client. She knew every dent and hollow of his body. She knew how glorious it felt to have him buried deeply inside her. Saving him had become personal, because it was the only way to save herself the heartbreak of losing him. Even if he wanted to call things off once they had their proof, she could eventually accept the separation. What she couldn't accept was a world without him in it.

Flattening herself against the wrought iron fence where a slender bit of darkness hovered, a narrow path that the streetlamps didn't illuminate, she crept over the pavement toward the gate. Not wanting to take the time to return to the residence in order to change into darker clothing, she'd located one of Bishop's black outer coats and was wearing it over her frock, its hem falling to her midcalf. Along with his hat that she'd donned over her pinned up hair, the attire allowed her to blend in with the shadows. In the deep pocket of the coat rested the stethoscope. Periodically, she skimmed her fingers over it, because for some reason it increased her confidence and courage. Perhaps because it symbolized that first night when they'd acknowledged their attraction, when they'd given in and kissed. The night she'd realized he wasn't a scoundrel at all, and she'd desperately wanted all of London to know the same. More so now, she wanted to shout it from the rooftops: *You don't know him. You don't know him as I do.*

She was only a few steps from the gate when a hansom cab came to a stop. Flinging herself back, she ensured she was beyond reach of the streetlamp as well as the lamp hanging from the side of the cab. A man climbed out, a man she'd spoken with only that morning. Thanatos. He seemed a little taller, perhaps because he'd been crouched in his doorway, as though fearing the sun. But even straightened, he was not nearly as tall as Bishop, probably came to his shoulder, if that. He strode with confidence to the gate, shoved open the wrought iron door, and slipped through, pulling it closed behind him.

It hadn't been locked. The widow was expecting him then. For the séance? Daisy supposed this hour might be the best for calling up spirits. Hadn't one of the ghosts visited Scrooge at the last toll of midnight? That time had only just passed.

The hansom in which he'd arrived had departed, taking the extra illumination with it. Daisy neared the gate and watched as Thanatos strode up the drive. She could see a pale light shining through the entryway windows and a strip of brightness where the draperies in the front parlor didn't meet completely.

He reached the front door. It opened. A woman was suddenly in his arms, clinging to him, their silhouettes outlined by the glow spilling forth. Turning slightly, he lowered his head. They were kissing. Not a perfunctory brushing of mouths or a bussing of lips across a cheek. No, this went on for a while, with her arms going around his shoulders and his circling her waist.

The couple broke apart and Thanatos ushered the widow inside. As soon as the door was secured, Daisy opened the gate, hurried through, and took the time to close it quietly. Then she was running for all she was worth along the lawn that bordered the drive because she didn't want them to hear her approaching.

Hedgerows lined the front of the house. Working her way between them and the brick facade, she tiptoed over until she reached the edge of the window. Removing the stethoscope from her pocket, she tucked the earpieces into place and then pressed the wooden funnel to the glass.

"—came to see me today. She must have followed you last night."

"She's trying to prove Bishop is innocent."

"It would have helped matters if you'd managed to secure one of those unique buttons from his waistcoat that we could have left as a clue near your husband's body."

"I know that was the plan, but he never left me alone. He was worse than the chaperone I had when I was a debutante. Watching, watching, always watching. Feeding me. Wanting to play cards. There were times when I feared he could read our entire plan written all over my face. Why haven't they arrested him? I'm afraid they suspect us."

Daisy felt her heart clamor. Mrs. Mallard hadn't gone to Bishop because she wanted a divorce. She'd sought him out because she needed someone arrested for her husband's murder, someone who wasn't the man she'd been kissing a few minutes ago.

"They're not going to suspect you," Thanatos said. "And they don't know about me."

"Well, that silly little inquiry agent does."

"She won't cause any trouble. I told her I was a medium you had hired to contact the spirit of your recently departed husband, so he could reveal who killed him."

"Why in God's name would you do that?"

"I had to tell her something. Although I have taken to the idea and decided we can use the falsehood to our advantage. Tomorrow you'll call upon Swindler, tell him we held a séance during which your husband visited us and declared his murderer to be Blackguard Blackwood."

"I don't like the manner in which Swindler studies me. As though he can ferret out the lies." Daisy heard the worry in her voice. "And that troublesome inquiry agent as well. The night you struck me, for a minute there, I thought she was going to discern the truth, that we wanted to raise Bishop's ire, ensure he confronted Bertram. How did you know he would?"

"I didn't choose him to take the fall without learning all I could about him." Daisy seethed at the words. "I suspected a man who helped women escape a troublesome spouse would defend her if she was not treated well. I had the right of him."

He was fairly gloating. Daisy thought she might be ill.

"Perhaps we should escape while we can. Now. Tonight. Go to France. The solicitor was here today. I have access to all the money."

"It'll leave things too untidy if we go, my sweet. We could never come back."

A rustling in the nearby bushes had Daisy's breath catching. Quickly, she glanced around but didn't see anyone. She should probably depart. She had enough information to set Swindler on the correct path. But what she didn't understand was the reason they'd chosen murder over a divorce? Granted, murder made everything happen sooner—

"Neither of us has any family here. Why does it matter if we can't come back?" Widow Mallard asked.

"Your money will restore my place in Society. At my side, you will enter the aristocracy just as you wanted, just as I promised. We simply need to follow through on the plan."

Another rustling, a bit louder, nearly made Daisy jump out of her skin. She jerked her head to the side—

An earsplitting screech suddenly echoed around her as something dark and terrifying flew at her. Reacting with lightning speed, unable to prevent her quick yell of alarm from escaping, she lifted her hands to protect her face and stumbled backward as a ball of fur slammed into her shoulder and sharp talons raked along her hands. She landed hard on her backside in that narrow fissure between pointed shrubbery leaves and rough brick. Lurching from side to side, she slapped at the feral beast until it finally scampered away.

She needed to scarper off as well. Absolutely. Because none of this had happened quietly. Unfortunately, in the foray, the stethoscope had become dislodged, lost. She hoped it didn't cost a fortune to replace because she didn't have the time to look for it. Crawling on her knees and injured hands, she made it to the opening, shoved herself to her feet—

"Well, what have we here?" a deep voice asked with a touch of amusement.

A large hand closed tightly around her upper arm and gave her a hard jerk, as though she was little more than a rag doll. When the motion stopped, she found herself standing on the tips of her toes, staring into the vengeful eyes of the god of Death.

"Unhand me." She was grateful her voice didn't quiver. She attributed her breathlessness to her encounter with the beastly cat, and hoped he did as well, rather than fear on her part.

"I think not."

He began dragging her toward the open doorway, the light spilling out around the silhouette of Mrs. Mallard, wringing her hands. Daisy dug in her heels, but she was no match for his strength. God, how many times had she told Bishop she wasn't in need of rescue? Yet, at the moment, she'd give anything for him to ride in on a white steed and get her out of this mess.

"Oh, God," Mrs. Mallard cried pitifully, resembling the cowed woman who'd first come to Bishop. "The inquiry agent. What is she doing here?"

"Spying obviously," he ground out. "Listening at the window, no doubt."

"I didn't hear anything," she lied.

"Of course, you didn't. And I can truly summon the

dead." He pulled her into the house, into the parlor, and flung her into a wingback chair.

Daisy sprang back to her feet and judged the distance to the doorway. Since he was blocking her path, she knew she couldn't make it before he was on her again. Could she survive the glass if she threw herself through the window? Would the draperies offer protection from the sharp shards?

"What am I going to do with you?" he asked lightly as though amused by her.

"You'll have to kill her," Mrs. Mallard said with the ease of one saying *you'll need to butter your bread*.

"No, I don't think I will. You're not going to do anything foolish now, are you, Daisy?"

"Nothing foolish, but neither will I stand back and watch an innocent man be accused of your crime." She was being reckless, should pretend to be frightened. Should promise anything to be set free, but she decided too much was at risk for him to negotiate with her. He knew it as well as she did. They'd not reached an impasse, because he held all the power, but she still had gumption and grit on her side. "You'll not prevent me from telling Inspector Swindler what I know."

"Don't be ridiculous, Daisy. You're not going to do anything that will see me arrested. You're not going to betray your father."

CHAPTER 22

*L*ETHARGICALLY, Bishop stretched before reaching for the woman who'd come to mean so much to him, a woman who occupied his thoughts as though nothing else in the world mattered. His hand found no hip to curl over, his fingers no warm soft skin to lure him closer. He was greeted only with cool linen.

Opening his eyes fully, he sat bolt upright and stared at the tangled emptiness, the hollow in the pillow that confirmed she had indeed recently occupied that space. Quickly he glanced around. Clothing was no longer scattered haphazardly over the floor. His was folded neatly and resting on a chair. Hers was nowhere to be seen.

"Marguerite!" he called out, already knowing it was a fruitless endeavor, and he'd hear no response from her. He scrambled out of the bed and stormed to the bathing room. The door was ajar, no light within. Still, he pushed it open wider to chase back the shadows and stepped inside, but she wasn't there. Why the devil had she left him?

Perhaps she'd been unable to sleep and had gone to the library for a book, to the kitchen for a morsel to eat, to his exercise room to lift a few weights. Disappointment ratcheted through him because she hadn't invited him along. He'd have been happy to read to her, to place nibbles between her lips, to glide his hands over her arms as they strained—

Intending to go in search of her, because surely she'd not left the residence completely, he pivoted quickly and nearly lost his balance when he abruptly changed direction because his gaze had skimmed over the credenza where he'd set the stethoscope so he wouldn't forget to return it to its owner. An instrument that was no longer there.

He raced over to the window and looked out on the drive. The carriage was gone.

He cursed thoroughly and soundly as he hastened over to the wall and yanked on the bellpull a good half dozen times. He'd have tugged on it a half dozen more if he hadn't dislodged it from its mooring so it fell to the floor, useless. Which was how he felt. Useless. She was so damned independent, so damned determined to prove she didn't need him—

He wasn't going to find her in the residence. She'd left. And she'd left without him.

Because she didn't need him, but he damn well needed her. And while he wanted to trust her, he feared she was off doing something reckless with that bloody stethoscope. As a matter of fact, he'd wager his entire fortune that she was.

He snatched up his clothes and had them donned by the time the knock sounded. "Come."

Wearing a nightcap and his dressing gown haphazardly secured to reveal his nightshirt, hairy calves, and slippered feet, Perkins stepped in, somewhat bleary-eyed. "Sir?"

"I don't suppose you saw Miss Townsend leave."

"No, sir. I wasn't aware she was even here."

"Right. Wake a footman and meet me in the library. I have a message I want delivered straightaway to Scotland Yard."

"Yes, sir."

His butler disappeared. Dropping into the chair, Bishop pulled on his stockings and his boots. He'd have to go in search of a hansom. This time of night, how long would it take him to locate one? He might end up running the entire way to his destination.

Then he was rushing down the stairs as though his life depended on it. Not his, but hers. However, they'd inexplicably become entwined, one and the same. Because without her, how could any joy remain in his world?

HER FATHER. HER *father*. Those two little words were like ice picks jabbing over and over into her mind, her memories, her very heart.

With the braided tasseled ropes used to hold back the draperies, the beastly man had bound her to the wooden arms and legs of a chair with a stuffed, brocaded seat and back. Had she wanted to be there, she might have found the furniture comfortable. She didn't.

It was his eyes, she realized now, the shape of his eyes and the mirth residing in them that had seemed so familiar. Whether in person or in a photograph, his carefree attitude showed through. How had she not recognized her own father? Perhaps because she'd not been searching for him, hadn't expected him, because they'd told her that he was dead. Because she'd visited his resting place and the first words she'd ever learned to read were those inscribed on his and her mother's headstones. She'd traced her fingers over the carved letters, memorized the outline of them.

Other than his eyes, nothing about him resembled the man in the portrait she carried in her locket, which was even now resting warm against her skin. The last twenty years had not been kind to him, not as kind as they'd been to her. He was all of forty-five, and yet he appeared more aged than his oldest brother, the Earl of Bellingham, at fifty-seven. His lopsided nose told her he'd been in more than one fight. In this lit room, she could see a small scar above his right brow, one that hadn't been visible when he'd opened his door to her because the light hadn't been able to reach all the way in.

Mrs. Mallard was perhaps even more horrified than Daisy by his declaration. With her arms folded across her chest, she stood a short distance away, staring at their captive, obviously wishing she had the power to disappear her forever. "How can you have a daughter?" she finally asked, sounding ill that the words had even formed in her mouth.

"If you don't know the answer to that, m'dear, then I now understand why you and Mallard had no children during the eight years you were married," Thanatos— no, Lionel Townsend—said drolly.

"I'm serious, Lionel. What are we going to do with her?"

"Take her with us."

"I'll fight you every step of the way," Daisy vowed, her tone strong with conviction. She considered screaming for help, but she doubted her voice would reach the sleeping quarters of the staff. Neither did she know how many servants were in residence. She'd seen only the butler, the coachman, a footman, and the two maids whom she'd spoken to earlier. Even if there were more, would any of them turn against their mistress? Would any of them believe Daisy? Would any of them choose to put their own lives at risk to save hers? She already knew that guilt at endangering them would eat at her. She couldn't place them in harm's way. She was on her own.

She was fairly certain that her father—she got lightheaded remembering that word could be attributed to this man—wouldn't take her life, but she had no guarantee he wouldn't kill others who might try to help her. She was certain he had struck the fatal blow to Mallard's skull. She was infinitely grateful that she'd snuck out of Bishop's bedchamber so he had no idea where she'd gotten off to. No matter what happened to her, he would remain safe.

Her father chuckled low, darkly. "Damn, but how you remind me of your mother. So incredibly fearless. She cast off Society's censure at our marriage as though the ugly words directed our way were naught but dandelion petals."

"Yet, you led her to ruin, to her death."

He narrowed his eyes and his jaw tautened. "Ava, darling, go pack a few things. We'll go to my residence until morning, at which time we'll visit the bank and close out your accounts. Afterward we'll board a ship for foreign climes."

"Thank God, thank God, we're leaving." She spun on her heel and dashed out of the parlor.

He walked over to a table, poured himself something dark, and then sauntered over to Daisy. He dropped into a chair, crossed one leg over the other, and lounged back. "She hasn't your mother's pluck. But she'll do nicely for now. I'll make her happy."

"Until you have your hands on her money?"

"You judge me so harshly. Although I suppose I can't blame you. You don't know me. Charlotte made sure of that. My blasted sister. Spinster. Old maid. Couldn't entice a man into loving her. Couldn't make a man be willing to saddle himself—"

"Don't speak of her like that. You left me to rot. She took me in."

"I wanted you, Daisy, but they wouldn't let me have you. My brother. My sister. The horrid witch couldn't have children of her own, so she took mine. Still, I was surprised you didn't recognize me when I opened my door to you. But it has been twenty years." He rubbed his listing nose. "And I barely resemble the portraits of my youth."

He took a sip of his drink, studying her over the rim of the tumbler, and she wondered if he saw any of her mother in her features. If he saw any of his own. She hoped not. She didn't want any part of her to be like him. All the years she'd longed for him and her mother. All the hours she'd missed them. The tears she'd shed. For this diabolical bit of rubbish, who would conspire to have another blamed for his crime. "No one is going to believe Bishop guilty of murder."

He arched that scarred brow. "If that were true, he'd not have had to hire you." He winked at her. "He has a temper . . . like his father. I remember when his wife died, the speculation that perhaps he'd done it. The police go where they're led. I'm going to lead them to Blackwood. Imagine my surprise, though, when I caught a glimpse of you working in his residence. As a servant. I knew you were up to no good, that you were an inquiry agent sniffing out something. I was very relieved to see you visit Parker. That confirmed your presence there had nothing to do with Ava. Therefore, I decided it was time to act."

She remembered those times when the tiny hairs on the back of her neck had risen. "You've spied on me."

"I've observed you from time to time. How could I not when you look so much like your mother?"

"Just like you killed Mallard, you killed her. Not with blunt force, but still you were responsible. You will pay for the lives you've ruined."

His jaw tensed, and she saw a flash of frightening anger, before he regained an icy calm. "You know nothing of it, Daisy. I loved her, you know, your mother, desperately. However, our family—yours now and mine then—cared more about image, and blood, and proper lineages than the heart. But Genni and I were happy for a time in our small, simple corner of the world."

He took another long swallow of his drink. "And then we had you. You should have made us joyous, should have made our world complete. But you were a difficult birth. She almost died then and there. Afterward, she was in so much pain. The physician gave her laudanum. It helped, but after a while, she couldn't stop taking it, even as its power diminished. It was devastating to watch her suffer. I had to help her, no matter the cost. Because I loved her, you see. With all that I was, all that I would ever be. Therefore, I took her to an opium den. For the first time since you were born, she experienced no agony. She was at peace. But it was all temporary. And thus we returned, over and over and over. Until the smoky dragon became our god and we worshipped it for its kindness. Therefore, you see, my dear daughter, if you wish to lay the cause of her death at someone's feet, perhaps you should lay it at your own."

AS THE HANSOM drew to a halt near the Mallard residence, the doors immediately sprung open because Bishop had tossed enough coins the driver's way before climbing into the vehicle to ensure no delay in disembarking once they arrived at their destination.

Bishop didn't know if tonight was when the séance was planned. And it was possible that Marguerite was at the townhome of Thanatos, but his gut had told him to come here. Because if she was going to listen through a window, she'd have more success at this residence that at least provided some cover from being seen.

As he walked briskly the few steps to the gate, he noticed the faint light that shone from inside the residence, from inside the front parlor, not fully able to breach the thickness of the draperies but providing an outline and revealing a slender slit where they were destined to meet. Someone was home. Someone was awake. Then he saw a black cat wander through a slim opening in the gate, causing it to swing slightly ajar. It was unlocked. Marguerite would have gone through it. She wouldn't have waited a short distance away because she had the bloody stethoscope and would have wanted to press it to the glass of that window that was serving as a beacon to her curiosity.

His heart felt like a battering ram inside his chest, beating unmercifully against his ribs, forcefully pumping the blood needed to make his legs propel him forward along the drive. As soon as he realized his movements were raising a clamor, he jumped over to the grass and ran like mad to the edge of the bushes that lined up so perfectly in front of the house. But a narrow gap between them was wide enough for her to scoot along. However, when he looked down its length, he couldn't see her crouching at the glass, listening. He saw no sign of her at all. Had he been wrong? Had he misread her intentions? Had she gone round to the side of the house, the back? But from his position at the residence's corner, he could see no other light except for that coming from the front room where he and Marguerite had originally waited for Mrs. Mallard.

If the communicating with the dead was happening tonight, had she invited herself inside? He wouldn't put it past her. The woman seemed to harbor the belief that she was invincible, a character in a mystery novel who would somehow survive to solve another murder another day.

Perhaps a quick peek through that part in the draperies would provide the answers or at least a clue.

He pressed himself against the wall and began edging toward that window, the sharp-edged leaves of the hedges catching on his clothing. Something crunched beneath his boot. Bending down, he felt around until he located it. The stethoscope. She'd been here. And she wouldn't have carelessly left it behind. Not unless she'd been taken by surprise.

That the erratic hard pounding of his heart didn't

cause the building to shake on its foundation was a wonder. Ignoring the bushes' determination to detain him, he moved swiftly to the window and peered through the thin slit.

Like some untamed creature, he nearly howled in fury and fear. She was there, inside, bound to a chair. Alone.

No, not alone. A man walked by her and whatever he said caused her to pale. Had he threatened her? Christ, he was going to tear him limb from limb. She looked to the side toward the entryway. Quickly, he put the stethoscope into his ears and pressed the funnel to the glass.

"—for a footman to fetch my valise." He recognized the voice, even though it was somewhat distorted. Mrs. Mallard.

"Don't be ridiculous, Ava. We don't want anyone to know we're leaving, or more importantly, that we have her. I'll get it."

With him going up the stairs, leaving the women alone, Bishop knew the moment had arrived to strike in order to ensure victory.

CHAPTER 23

"I DON'T understand," Daisy said softly, nonthreateningly, wanting to establish a more friendly rapport with the widow. "You were seeking a divorce. Why kill your husband?"

Mrs. Mallard looked at Daisy as though she was a simpleton. "It was never about getting a divorce. That takes too long and is no guarantee of freedom."

"My father struck you. What makes you think he won't do it again?"

The widow's cheeks turned pink and she glared as though she wished a hole in the floor would open up and swallow Daisy whole. "There was a purpose to his action that night. He didn't want to hurt me, but Mrs. Winters had told me that Bishop was very protective of his ladies, and we needed him to have a public confrontation with Bertram so suspicions for my husband's murder would fall on Bishop. Only for a time, only so no one was watching me. Until everything was in order, and we could leave. I daresay Bishop won't hang."

She couldn't be sure of that outcome, nor could she guarantee it. The woman was a fool to believe this mad scheme could have a satisfactory ending. Even if

Bishop was spared, the uncertainty regarding his involvement in murder would serve to tarnish his reputation to a greater degree than it already was. Daisy suspected her father's charms had blinded Mrs. Mallard to reality. "Wasn't your husband surprised to receive a blow and a threat from a complete stranger who accused him of striking his wife? Wasn't he confused? Didn't he question you?"

"He was in too much pain to do much of anything other than take the laudanum I offered him. I kept pouring it into him until the following night, when Lionel carried him down the stairs to the library."

"What a coldhearted bitch you are." The words rang out, frigid and menacing, sending an icy shiver down Daisy's spine. She jerked her head around to discover Bishop, standing in the doorway like some god of wrath.

"Lio—"

Before Mrs. Mallard could fully scream for her lover, Bishop was on the termagant, his hand effectively covering her mouth. Lifting her easily as though she was a rag doll, he flung her onto a sofa, stuffed his handkerchief into her mouth before she had a chance to recover from his unexpected rough treatment of her, and then pulled her arms behind her back. He glanced around feverishly.

"They used the drapery ties to bind me," Daisy told him.

With a nod, he stood, pulling his captive along with him. While she struggled, he managed to reach a window, where he yanked a woven cord free. Quickly, he bound her hands before grabbing another makeshift rope, lowering her to the floor, and wrapping the braided strands around her ankles. He rushed over to Daisy and began untying the knots at her right wrist.

"You should prepare to ambush him. He'll be back any—"

As though her words had conjured him, she heard the footfalls echoing along the stairs.

With a curse, Bishop sprinted to the doorway and pressed his back against the wall. He'd undone the knots enough that Daisy was able to further loosen the binding by moving her arm back and forth. She went still when her father, holding a large leather valise in one hand, appeared in the doorway. He seemed to quickly take in that something was amiss, probably because the lower half of Mrs. Mallard resting on the floor was revealed as she was striving to inch her way out in very caterpillar-like movements from behind the sofa. "What's this, then?"

Bishop leapt at him, but her father twisted around and swung the valise at his assailant's head. Ducking, Bishop still took the brunt of the assault on his shoulder, and it slammed him against the wall. It didn't escape her notice that these two dueling men each had a lover in the room, a woman they would defend to the death, that they would move heaven and earth to save—

Only suddenly her father was dashing for the entryway door, abandoning the woman with whom he'd not only committed a crime but was planning to run away. In spite of saying earlier that he'd wanted her, had he deserted Daisy in the same manner when she was a child? Was that the reason her aunt had been forced to raise her? Because he was a coward?

Without hesitation, Bishop flew after him, in pursuit.

Daisy managed to free her right arm and immediately went to work on the knots keeping her left wrist secured to the chair. Hearing grunts, groans, and flesh hitting flesh, she couldn't imagine her aging father was any match for a younger man who kept his muscles toned so he could defend women. Then all went quiet except for loud, angry voices trailing in through a door that she was relatively certain had not been closed, although she couldn't discern the distant words.

Finally freeing her arm, she quickly released the bindings around her ankles, jumped up, scurried outside, and nearly smashed into Bishop, who'd been loping up the steps.

His arms, steady and sure, came around her, his breaths harsh and heavy from his exertions, as he brought her in close. "Are you hurt?"

"No." Leaning back, she scrutinized his features. "But you are. You're bleeding." Just above his brow, a trail of blood coated the left side of his face.

"The valise clipped me, but I'm all right."

Looking past him, she saw her father was being held by two uniformed constables. Inspector Swindler was standing nearby. "What are they doing here?" she asked.

"I sent Swindler a message before coming after you, in case help was needed." Two constables edged past them, and Bishop called out, "She's on the far side of the parlor."

His gaze swung back to her. "I could have killed him," he said, his voice taut and seething.

Him needed no moniker, no identifier. But she had to give him one anyway. "He's my father."

Bishop's brows jumped together so quickly, so hard that she thought she might have heard the impact. "What the bloody hell? I thought he died."

"Yes, so did I. I need to visit my aunt. Now. Immediately."

"It can wait until morning, surely." Taking her arm, he pressed a kiss to the skin at her wrist that had been rubbed raw as she'd fought to free herself of the bindings.

"No, no it can't." She felt vulnerable and betrayed by someone else she loved and trusted. Was her heart as bad a judge of character as her mother's? Was no one in her life completely honest with her? "But first a word with Swindler."

He gave a nod before stepping to the side, but his arm stayed around her as they walked over to the inspector, who was asking questions of her father, questions he was stubbornly refusing to answer.

Swindler turned his uncompromising attention to her. "Miss Townsend, you seem to have had an eventful night."

"Indeed, Inspector, but it bore fruit." She told him everything she'd overheard and all she'd been told. She didn't stop when her father ranted and raved, called her vile names, and threw profanity at her. The moment she felt Bishop loosening his hold on her, she knew he was on the verge of taking whatever means necessary to quieten Lionel Townsend. She took Bishop's hand, keeping him in place, not willing to risk him doing something that might land him in a cell beside the man her mother had loved.

When her father was dragged away, she should have felt something—anything. She remembered how she'd sobbed when her aunt had told her that he was gone. Her dear papa, who would toss her in the air and always catch her. She had trusted him. Loved him. Missed him.

Now she hoped only to never set eyes upon him again.

It was well over an hour later, and she was weary beyond belief when Bishop's coachman brought his carriage to a halt in front of her aunt's residence.

"Shall I accompany you inside?" Bishop asked.

She didn't particularly want to be separated from him. Much to her surprise, she'd been nestled against his side during the journey, as though he couldn't bear the thought of not touching her. She'd expected him to be cross with her for leaving him in his bed, but it seemed he was presently too relieved that she still drew breath to confront her about her daring and inconsideration. "I appreciate the offer, but I need to speak with her alone. However, if you wouldn't mind, would you wait?"

"Of course."

The door opened, and she suspected he'd told the footman to give them a few minutes before seeing to their alighting from the carriage. As though he'd anticipated that she'd need a little time to settle herself before making her way into the residence that had served as her home for the majority of her life. She placed her hand in the waiting footman's and he helped her climb down. She looked back at Bishop.

"I'll be right here when you're ready to leave," he said, "or should you need me at any time beforehand, for any reason."

With a nod, she left him there, walked up the steps, unlocked the door, and entered. The foyer had always had the most wonderful echo. As a child, she'd often stood at its center and shouted up. She did so now, but not with the joy of her youth. Instead with the rage and disappointment of betrayal. "Auntie Charlotte!"

She called out three times before her aunt was scurrying down the stairs, lamp in hand to guide her way, her nightcap and dressing gown askew, her long plait draped over one shoulder tapping against her bosom, a bosom that had absorbed a good many of Daisy's childish tears.

"My dear girl, what is amiss? Oh, you look dreadful. Is it that rakehell Blackwood, did he—"

"No, we caught Mallard's murderer tonight."

Her aunt skidded to a stop and gently touched her arm. "Did he harm you?"

He'd very nearly destroyed her. *If you wish to lay the cause of your mother's death at someone's feet, perhaps you should lay it at your own.*

She'd struggled to regain her composure, her purpose, and to ensure that justice prevailed. She'd focused on Bishop and her need to do everything possible so he didn't pay for her father's sins. It was that which had finally brought her out of the pit of despair into which her father had so callously tossed her. "Why did you tell me my father was dead?"

Aunt Charlotte looked as though all the blood had been drained from her. "Why would you ask such a question, as though . . ." Her voice trailed off like she hadn't the strength to form further words.

"As though I know he isn't dead, but am aware that he is very much alive?"

Fury flashed. In all her years, Daisy could count on one hand the number of times she'd seen her aunt angry. "He called upon you, the scapegrace. Where? At your place of business? Bellingham will have something to say about this."

Her aunt was seething, and Daisy feared more was involved than a secret exposed. "He didn't come to me. As a matter of fact, fate had me calling upon him."

"Come into the parlor as I need some sherry." Aunt Charlotte didn't wait for a response but was marching briskly into the other room as though salvation waited within. Daisy followed.

"Don't turn on the gaslights, as what needs to be said is best done without brightness," her aunt ordered.

Daisy wanted this confrontation done with quickly, a hasty explanation provided so she could absorb and reflect upon the truth within Bishop's embrace, but her aunt had mothered her for twenty years, and thus, Daisy felt she owed her a little patience. She sank into the chair she normally occupied when they were together in this room and waited as her aunt offered her a small glass of the dark wine before gracefully lowering herself into the chair opposite her. The lamp had been left on the sideboard, the flame turned up, so they weren't completely hidden from each other.

"Firstly, I would like to know how it is that you called upon him," Aunt Charlotte said in the tone she'd used when Daisy was a child and she'd suspected her of any wrongdoing. *Cook has reported that three biscuits are missing. Have you any notion as to where they might have gotten off to?*

Only Daisy was no longer a child. Nor was she the guilty party here, the one who'd done wrong. "I had followed Mrs. Mallard to his residence. I found her actions suspicious, so I later returned and knocked on his door. He lied then regarding who he was. But tonight, our paths crossed again. At her residence. The truth bore out. My father. Risen from the grave. The grave in which you put him. Why did you lie to me?"

Her aunt took a sip of her sherry before lacing her fingers around the stem of the glass as though it gave her courage. Her eyes were watery when she met and held Daisy's gaze. "I didn't lie exactly. I never actually told you he was *dead*. I claimed he was *gone*. Gone from your life. And he was. Your uncle saw to that. You'd been in my care for all of three months when Lionel suddenly showed up one day and demanded you be given back to him. Bellingham offered to pay him a thousand quid per annum if he would stay away from you. If he made contact with you even once, the funding would stop, and we would take him to court to ensure I retained custody of you. Lionel was agreeable to taking the money. Extremely. Very quickly. I always believed it was his plan all along, a way to manipulate us into paying for his indulgences."

Dead. Gone. Semantics. However, the actions they'd taken were as false as the words. "But you had a headstone carved for him."

"Yes, I suppose that was terribly deceptive, but we were trying to spare you any further hurt. You were having nightmares and screaming in the dark. We didn't want you asking for your father whenever you visited your mother's resting place, and we weren't going to forbid you spending time at the cemetery when it might bring you some comfort or solace. You were just a child, and you wept for her. So often while in my arms, it was her you wanted." A lone tear trailed along her cheek. "There is a bond between mother and child that I believe it is cruel to deny. I wanted to offer you a haven where you could feel close to her, without wondering where your father was. Over the years, there were times when I wanted to tell you the truth about him, but at what age would it not have hurt to learn that he chose pound sterling over you?"

"Did he ever come to you in secret and ask about me?"

"No, darling. But if he had, I would have told him that you were remarkable."

Hot tears burned her eyes at her aunt's words. She loved this woman so incredibly much, and it made the lies hurt all the more. "He spied on me from time to time. That was how he recognized me."

"Perhaps he loved you in his own way, then, and missed you. I would like to think he came to regret the bargain he'd made. You do look very much like your mother."

"He mentioned that tonight. When he told me how much he loved her and assured me that I was responsible for her death."

The fury was back in her aunt's eyes, and Daisy imagined that an avenging angel had the same mien about her. "Don't you dare believe such rubbish. It's exactly like him to shift accountability for his actions to someone else. You were a babe. How in God's name are you to blame for what happened?"

"She was in agony after birthing me. She needed laudanum and then the opium to get through it."

"Poppycock. Countless women endure pain after childbirth, and they don't make their way to an opium den. He partook as much if not more than she. No. He

was striving to manipulate you, to throw off the guilt
like a cloak that is too heavy, to make you pity him.
It's what he does. He has always placed himself first,
above all else."

She thought of his running out of the residence
while his lover lay bound and gagged. Perhaps he'd
have come back for her. Perhaps he'd have devised
a plan to rescue her. But if he'd truly cared for her,
would he not have stood and fought for her? Bishop
had not left Daisy. He'd come for her. Even if her
father had gained the upper hand, she knew Bishop
would not have dashed off, intent on escape, but
would have remained in the battle until he drew his
last breath.

Her aunt scooted to the edge of the chair cushion.
"He'd have never taken proper responsibility for you.
I know at the moment you must hate me"—she held
out her aging and slightly wrinkled hand, absent of
jewelry because she'd been abed—"but you must understand that Bellingham and I believed we had no
other choice if we were to keep you safe."

Daisy studied that hand that had comforted—and
smacked on a rare occasion. But she couldn't reach
across the widening chasm to take it. Was it too much
to expect the truth from those she loved? She was floun-
dering, her foundation crumbling beneath her. What
she'd known to be her past wasn't actually her past.
She felt as though the truth was reshaping her into
someone she didn't know.

Her aunt withdrew her hand, her eyes a well of sad-
ness. "I fear, from the way you're looking at me, that
I've lost you."

Daisy shook her head. While it made no sense, she

was feeling abandoned, unsure of her place. Unable to trust that anything her aunt had told her since she'd walked into this room was true. "I'm feeling a bit untethered, I'm afraid."

Tears welled in Aunt Charlotte's eyes. "I think we both are. I prayed this moment would never come. I also prayed that if you ever learned the truth, I'd find the right words, but they escape me. Perhaps they simply don't exist."

They did, but Daisy thought she might choke on them if she uttered them. *Betrayal. Deceit. Lies.* They were a cacophony shouting through her mind.

Her aunt set her glass on the table—slowly and very carefully, as though it might shatter when it made contact with the cherrywood. Although perhaps it was Aunt Charlotte who was in danger of shattering. "Why don't you stay here tonight and get some needed sleep? Everything always looks better and brighter in the morning."

"I can't stay. I don't know if I can ever stay here again. I love you, Auntie. But I have to wonder what else have you not been entirely truthful about."

Her aunt's face crumpled, while another tear escaped and rolled along her cheek. "I always feared this day would come. Still, my darling, it breaks my heart to have broken yours."

BISHOP MOVED INSIDE her, slowly and with purpose, as though he was fully aware that Daisy was somehow broken, but he had the means to carefully piece her back together.

He hadn't been waiting within the carriage, but standing outside of it, tall and proud, even if he did look a bit rumpled from his encounter with her father. He'd taken her into his arms and held her securely as they'd journeyed to his residence.

But it wasn't until the pleasure danced through her, reaffirming that they were both alive, both unharmed, and she was nestled protectively against his side that the tears surfaced. She did nothing to stop them; she doubted she could have anyway. They were a force of nature, like lava flowing from a volcano, or a tempest tossing about a ship. They would have their way. They would conquer. And they would leave devastation in their wake.

He had to have been aware of the tears because they seemed to encompass her entire body, causing her to quietly shake with the potency of them. He held her all the tighter with those arms that he'd molded into power. If she believed in fate, she'd think that his efforts through the years had been leading to this precise moment when she was sapped of strength, when she was able to take some from him.

She was struggling to come to an understanding of who she was. The daughter of a murderer. What a legacy. Certainly not one to be shared. She wondered if Bishop's legacy, being the son of a murderer, was the reason that he'd decided to never take a wife. The reason that it hadn't mattered to him if his reputation kept respectable ladies away.

But her reputation was of paramount importance because how could she build her business if she was written about in scandal sheets? She needed to be trustworthy. How could anyone trust her when they would soon read about her father's actions?

"You are not him," Bishop said, his voice low as if

fearing she might shatter into a thousand shards that could never be reassembled. He brushed his lips over her forehead. "Nor are you a reflection of him."

"I don't know who I am."

"You are who you have always been. His evil intentions didn't shape you."

"I don't know how much you deciphered from the night, but the plan all along was to kill Mr. Mallard and make it appear that you'd done it," she said quietly.

"So I gathered. Do you happen to know if Mallard *ever* struck his wife?"

She wanted to spare him the truth, but she was feeling untethered because others had wanted to do the same for her. "He didn't. My father hit her, hoping you'd confront Mallard, make a scene, so you'd be suspected of doing him in."

"Christ." His arms tightened around her, his fingers trailing circles over her back in a soothing motion. "I delivered a blow to a man who didn't deserve it. I have no way to make amends."

She heard the genuine remorse reflected in his voice, remorse her father would never experience. "Perhaps you shouldn't feel that you need to save everyone. That's an awful burden to carry."

"Perhaps you shouldn't feel that you always need to go it alone."

"You paid me for my services. I was merely delivering what was owed. It's my business, Bishop. I can't have you traipsing after me when I may have to encounter situations you might not like."

His fingers went still, his hold loosened. He didn't like what she'd said. She was rather certain of it. He was gracious enough not to point out that, while she had told him on numerous occasions she was not in need of saving, tonight, in fact, she had been.

When she'd first seen him, she'd known a moment of exquisite joy and horrifying fear. If he'd been killed, she'd have never forgiven herself, never recovered. What she felt for him was overwhelming and terrifying. Had her mother felt this way toward her father? As a result, had she neglected to recognize his flaws?

Would a time come when Daisy would lose herself in Bishop? When she would do anything to please him, even give up who she was? Would it happen slowly over time or all at once?

Was she destined to repeat her mother's fate?

CHAPTER 24

THE Earl of Bellingham wishes an audience at 2 this afternoon at Bellingham House. A carriage will be sent for you at half one.

The missive arrived a mere two days after Daisy's encounter with her aunt. Last night, she'd again slept in Bishop's arms, but during the daylight hours, she returned to her office building and flat. She had yet to display in the window her *Open for Business* sign or draw back the draperies. Melancholy preferred the gloom, and she was too wrecked and raw to do much of anything except curl up with a book. She'd gone with *Jane Eyre* because it suited her mood. Reading a detective novel would have reminded her too much of her aunt and stirred up too many pleasant memories. She would eventually forgive Aunt Charlotte, she knew that. She was already edging toward exoneration but needed a little more time to come to terms with the notion that what she'd believed for twenty years had all been a falsehood. While she understood the reasons behind the lie that wasn't exactly a lie, the deceit still hurt.

However, one didn't dismiss the summons of an earl, even if he was one's uncle.

Thusly at precisely two o'clock that afternoon, his butler escorted her into Bellingham's grand library that carried the scent of books lovingly read. From behind his desk, he came to his feet, his posture reminding her of a ship mast: tall and stately and confident of its purpose and its ability to see it through. With a small smile that hinted he was truly glad to welcome her. "Ah, Marguerite, I'm so thankful you were able to make time for me in your schedule. It's a lovely day. Walk with me in the garden."

He didn't hug her or take her hand. He'd never been as demonstrative with his affections as her aunt. Daisy had always thought that the three older brothers had handed their effusive and expressive tendencies over to their sister, because she possessed a warmer and more welcoming air than they did.

Her uncle had a large, magnificent garden, but it didn't begin to compare with Bishop's. Here everything was trimmed, contained, and lined up like soldiers preparing to march into battle. Blossoms displayed various shades of a single color: red. There were more blades of grass than blooms. Whereas Bishop's garden heralded every color imaginable with riotous blossoms, wild and untamed, and yet the arrangement was majestic, a tribute to the wonder of nature.

"I recently had a visit from Scotland Yard in the wee hours. It's my understanding you were instrumental in their apprehension of a murderer," her uncle finally said quietly, as though he didn't want to disturb the bees buzzing around. "A murderer who happens to be my youngest brother."

The reason they'd come to him, no doubt. It wouldn't

do for a lord to learn such information from reading the *Times*. "I suppose you're going to chastise me for not telling you myself."

"No chastisement. I merely wanted to ensure you had recovered from the ordeal."

Physically perhaps, but mentally she still seemed to be a bit of a mess, because his concern, while flatly expressed with only a hint of true worry, managed to make her eyes sting. "It was all a bit unnerving, but I'm coping."

"As I would expect a Townsend to do. Still, it had to be difficult. I made no secret of not being in favor of you taking on this occupation, but it appears you're quite good at it."

"Is that a compliment?"

A corner of his mouth hitched up. "Sarcasm doesn't become you." He shifted his gaze to her. "I know I'm not the most effusive of creatures so when I offer praise, you may rest assured it is not false flattery."

"I like the challenge of what I do. The dull moments are few." Usually she enjoyed the unexpected aspects of being an inquiry agent—although her father's revelations may have dimmed her enthusiasm for surprising results.

"Not always easy, though, I suspect. Even when you're not encountering ghosts. I paid a call on your father in his cell this morning. He did quite a bit of blubbering, asking for forgiveness and such, assuring me he'd been taken in by a pretty face and a woman's wiles. I accepted none of his excuses. Murder, for God's sake." He shook his head, clearly disappointed and disapproving. "I can only be grateful that our parents are not alive to see what he has become. He has not aged well. I hate to contemplate what he might have spent these past twenty years doing."

"Duping people, apparently." She recalled the easy lie that had rolled off his tongue the morning he opened the door to her. "He seems quite proficient at it. Certainly Mrs. Mallard fell for him and his scheme. I doubt she is the first woman of whom he's taken advantage."

"I suspect you have the right of that. She has been charged as an accessory to his crime, a crime for which he will no doubt go to prison, if not the gallows. I shall, naturally, hire the best barrister in all the kingdom to defend him in hopes he will not make that long walk with the short drop, but I will not use my influence to spare him all punishment."

Daisy could not work up the enthusiasm to care about a man who had proven himself so remarkably dreadful. "I was in his company only a short while, but I saw no redeeming qualities in his behavior."

She and her uncle walked along in silence for several minutes as though each was contemplating the fate of the same man. Daisy wondered how different her father's life might have been if her mother hadn't died or if her uncle had handed Daisy over to him when he'd come to claim her. Would she have provided her father with a reason to become a better person, or would he have dragged her down into the mire alongside him? Would she be an inquiry agent now or someone without scruples who took advantage of people?

The quiet was disturbed by her uncle's clearing of his throat. "My sister came to see me yesterday, quite distraught by your reaction to the truth. To be honest, I was rather surprised you didn't show up at my door to vent your displeasure with me."

"I was somewhat drained after the confrontation with my father and then the conversation with my aunt. I planned to have my tête-à-tête with you after I regained my vitality."

He chuckled low, then sobered. "I won't apologize for what I did. I was the earl by then, but my obligation was to the whole of my family and to do right by each individual. With him, your life would have been misery. Of that I am convinced."

"I don't disagree, but still it was a shock after all these years of believing him dead to learn he was very much alive. And to learn of the great lengths you all went to in order to keep the truth from me. I was deceived by the people I trusted most. I'm struggling with that, Uncle."

"Perhaps we handled it poorly, but it was all done with good intentions. For whatever that is worth."

She felt a slight easing of the pressure from the weight that had landed on her chest with the arrival of the truth, but it still bore down on her, and she didn't know if she'd ever again be entirely comfortable spending time in the company of these people.

"Has Charlotte ever told you about the man she almost married?"

Nearly tripping over her feet, Daisy was acutely aware of her eyes widening and her mouth going slack. Perhaps because he'd anticipated taking her off guard, Bellingham had immediately ceased walking to study her.

"I thought not," he said quietly, reflectively. "She was

thirty. Considered to be permanently on the shelf at that age. *He* was an earl. I won't tell you which one, so don't bother to ask. Her dowry was five thousand. I know you considered that a pitiful amount when I named it as yours, but he is the reason. I wanted some reassurance that a man coveted you and not the coins.

"Be that as it may, her earl gained little by offering for her. The young swells were more interested in the younger, glittery debutantes. But she had caught his eye. He had no need of property for he had plenty of his own. He did not need her dowry as his coffers were full. He did not require political influence for he had it in abundance. Nor did he need to be associated with a powerful family, because at that time few were more powerful than his. I did not doubt his love for her, because she was the only thing of value he gained by marrying her. And she also loved him, immensely. Her face shone with her feelings for him. As you are well aware, my sister gives nothing in half measures. I knew he would ask for her hand before the Season was done, and I would grant it."

He looked up at the sky before lowering his gaze back to hers. "Then one night, a constable came to the door to inform us that your mother had been found dead in a rather dodgy part of London. Too much opium, they surmised. The constable hadn't even departed before my sister had roused all the footmen and ordered the carriages readied. Soon we were racing through the streets to make certain you were all right. When she saw you in that little cage they kept you in"—he shook his head—"she announced then and there that you would never again be let out of her sight.

"But her earl, you see, did not want to be responsible for another man's child. He gave her the choice—him or you."

He didn't need to tell her whom her aunt had chosen. Daisy felt the tears immediately burst forth, so many that she couldn't stop them from rolling down her cheeks, too many to brush away, although she tried valiantly. Her aunt understood broken hearts because hers had been broken. Daisy rather wished she didn't know the truth of it. But it was the lack of truth telling that had made her angry to begin with. She had to be willing to accept all the truths. Even when they hurt, and this one hurt more than discovering her father was alive. *Oh, Aunt Charlotte. It breaks my heart to have broken yours.*

Because she had. With her not reaching across to take the hand offered. By not staying the night. With the last words she'd tossed to her aunt. Yes, Daisy had been hurting, but now she had a clearer comprehension regarding how much heartache Aunt Charlotte had been experiencing as well.

Finally, her uncle handed her his pristine white silk handkerchief before looking back up at the sky. "'Tis such a lovely day. I suspect Charlotte is strolling through Hyde Park at this very hour, taking in the sun."

She was indeed, near the Serpentine. Daisy spotted her straightaway.

Although it was terribly undignified, and she was far too old to be doing it, she began loping over the green, waving her arm. "Auntie Charlotte!"

Her aunt turned and immediately quickened her

pace, her worry evident in the creases that deepened on her face. "My dear girl, whatever is wrong? What's amiss?"

They nearly crashed into each other, her aunt's hands folding around her arms, steadying them both—steadying Daisy as she had for almost her entire life.

"I'm so sorry," Daisy said. "Please forgive me for what I said the other night. I will stay with you whenever you want. I love you. I love you so very, very much."

With a soft smile, Aunt Charlotte skimmed her gloved fingers over Daisy's cheek. "My dear girl, I know all that. You'd had a shock, and I should have found a way to tell you sooner, more gently. You were correct. You had a right to know the truth of things. But why your change of heart now, so quickly, when I expected you to remain cross with me for at least a week?" She closed her eyes. "Bellingham." She opened them. "Bellingham told you, didn't he? About my earl. Blast the man. I wondered why my brother sent word that he would meet me at Hyde Park at this hour. He hates the outdoors. The only lord in all of England who does."

"Why didn't you tell me that you made that sacrifice?"

"Because it wasn't a sacrifice. And I never wanted you to feel that you were responsible for my spinsterhood. I can't imagine that life with him would have been any more rewarding than life with you. If he'd truly loved me, he'd have known how precious you were to me. The fact that he would ask me to choose—well, it made it very difficult to love him after that."

So she'd given him up, along with all the satisfactions marriage would have given her. She might even have brought her own children into the world.

"I'm not going to call you Auntie Charlotte any longer."

"Oh, no, not Aunt Charlie. I've never liked that moniker."

Daisy smiled warmly, lovingly, her chest expanding with everything she felt for this woman. "No, I have decided I'm going to call you Mum."

CHAPTER 25

⌒◯⌒

"ALTHOUGH Aunt Charlotte encouraged me to wed, I always thought she was secretly against marriage," Daisy said quietly, nestled against Bishop's side, her head resting in the nook of his shoulder. Following the reconciliation with her aunt that afternoon, she'd spent the evening with the dear woman in her residence before coming to Bishop after all the servants, except the coachman and footman, were retired for the evening. He had to have been waiting for her in the front parlor, drawing room, or foyer because, before the coach had even come to a stop, he was standing on the drive ready to hand her down.

She was fairly certain that he'd been able to tell that her melancholy over what she'd considered a betrayal on her family's part had dissipated, and that she was lighter of heart and spirit, because like children let loose to play after a morning of studies, they'd dashed up the stairs to his bedchamber, where their clothes had been rapidly discarded, and she and he had proceeded to make mad, passionate love. He read her moods, comprehended every aspect of her. Knew when to tease, when to seduce, when to listen, when to talk, what to say.

She wondered if this sense of understanding and completion was what it was like to discover a soul mate, because she experienced frightening moments when she felt as though she'd gone through life with some aspect of herself missing. The gladness that swept through her each time they were once again together was like a little ball of sunlight residing within her that glowed more brightly with his presence.

And she could tell him anything, had just finished sharing her uncle's revelation regarding her aunt's sacrifice. "If not for me, she might have married."

"You shouldn't feel responsible or guilty regarding her unmarried state. Ultimately, she would have been miserable with him, eventually might have come to me," he said quietly, skimming his fingers lazily along her arm.

"How did you deduce that?"

"They had different priorities, required different things for happiness. At least he was honest with her, I'll give him that. Too often I think people pretend to be what they believe the other person needs or desires. They choose harmony over honesty. I think it leads to a quiet misery."

She supposed having grown up witnessing an unhappy marriage, he'd given a lot of thought to what actions might have resulted in a happy one. From all accounts, her parents had been happy. Even if they'd eventually traveled a path they shouldn't have, one that had led to the demise of her mother and, in a way, the destruction of her father. Although based upon what she was learning about him, he may have always been destined for an unfortunate ending to his tale. "She doesn't seem to have any regrets regarding her choice."

Earlier, she and her aunt had enjoyed a lovely dinner and far too much sherry. They'd reminisced about their favorite moments together. They'd laughed, cried, and laughed some more. Her aunt had even told her about some of the men who had kept her company over the years. Like Bishop, she had devised alternate names for them: Green Eyes, Cuddles, Wicked Hands.

A week later, another dinner with her aunt. Another revelation. Another night of lying naked in Bishop's arms.

"She's recently begun seeing someone. A Mr. Paul Wiggins. I don't know why she didn't tell me sooner." Although neither had Daisy told her about her relationship with Bishop. She still hadn't. Lifting her head, she studied the lines of his face and refrained from tidying his mussed hair. "She shared that he was playing the piano in the musicale room at the Fair and Spare one night—when he caught her attention. He's a widower, a fine gentleman, and she rather likes him. I think he might be the fellow who performed the lullaby for us."

"He certainly fits the description."

"I may get a chance to confirm it at a ball in a couple of weeks. I think she invited him."

He ceased his stroking, and his expression went blank, his eyes unreadable. "I didn't think you were on the hunt for a spouse."

She laughed softly. "I'm not. The ball is being hosted by my uncle. Well, his wife really. For the past three Seasons, it's the only ball I've attended. Family obligation, don't you know?"

"Odd timing, considering your notorious father has been making an appearance in newsprint, and reporters haven't been shy about mentioning the family connection."

"It was planned months ago. I'm rather certain they're striving to give the impression that their lives are unaffected by the scandal of a murderous brother, and so they're keeping their chins up and going on as though it doesn't distress them. People will no doubt attend out of curiosity. It's bound to become a rather awkward affair and be a difficult evening for many of the family. I need to be there to lend my support. After all, it is my father who brought this shame upon the House of Bellingham. My absence would serve only to spark more gossip and conjecture."

His fingers began dancing lightly over her skin. "It won't be easy for you."

"It won't be easy for any of us, but you have friends in the nobility, so you must be aware that hiding is frowned upon."

He pressed a kiss to the top of her head. "You lot do seem to like to march into the breach."

He'd get no argument from her on that score. Tough decisions were made, and the music was always faced. Her chest swelled with pride as she realized her family had never taken the easy road, no matter the consequences. With the exception of her father. How kind of the Fates not to have placed her in his uncaring hands.

"Will you come here afterward?" Bishop asked in a low voice, filled with promises.

She sat up, her legs curled beneath her, one of them—from her knee to her toes—pressed against his side. "I was hoping you would attend."

"I've not received a single invitation this Season."

"Well, it's not fully underway yet." Although she knew that wasn't the reason.

"Marguerite, you know as well as I do that being named the party responsible for a number of divorces has brought my reputation into question, and I'm no longer welcomed into parlors much less ballrooms."

"Would it really hurt if people knew the truth about your involvement with the women? Those divorces are over and done. They're not going to be undone. And the three women you were recently seeing, well, one has reconciled, one has murdered, and one's husband is dead. You've not created a scandal in months, and I don't think anything is in your appointment diary for the near future. To be honest, I rather regret that we didn't dance in the ballroom at the Fair and Spare."

He cupped her face. "Then we'll return to the Fair and Spare. But I refuse to damage your reputation by making an appearance at a ball uninvited and dancing with you in such a public venue."

"But—"

"No buts." Taking hold of her, he flipped her onto her back and pinned her into place. "Now, let's share a different sort of waltz."

Lowering his head, he took her mouth and she welcomed him.

YOUR FATHER HAS *made an offer on a replacement for the ship lost at sea a few months back.*

After reading the missive once more, Bishop dipped his pen in the inkwell and began scrawling his response to his man of affairs. *Offer double.*

He didn't know what the deuce he was going to do with a ship. Lose money on it no doubt. Perhaps have it refitted as a yacht so he could travel the seas. Just he and Marguerite, alone for a few months, save for the small crew needed to manage it. Away from London during the Season when she would receive invitations to balls. Where she might be tempted to occasionally go in order to flirt and dance with other gentlemen.

He'd been surprised by the fierceness of the jealousy that had shot through him two nights ago when she'd mentioned attending a ball. They were not beholden nor committed to each other. They were simply . . . lovers of a sort, he supposed. He couldn't define quite what they were to each other. He knew only that, even though he was no longer a client, his innocence was clear, and no further reason existed for her to remain in his company, he wasn't yet ready to say farewell.

Unlike when one of his ladies finally got her divorce, and he wished her an abundance of happiness in the future. He never mourned when they ceased coming to see him. *She*, he would mourn.

Those evening hours before her arrival were the most torturous of his day. He'd increased the wages of his coachman and footman in order to ensure their continued discretion regarding her visiting him here. He was rather certain that with the exception of Perkins, the servants were ignorant of his having a late-night guest. He'd had his butler explain to the staff that, although no ladies were presently calling upon Bishop, he'd grown accustomed to having a bit of nourishment before retiring. Therefore, Cook was still preparing him a tray, while Tom would bring it up. But always before Marguerite arrived. The one time she'd shown up earlier than expected, Bishop had opened the door when Tom knocked and relieved him of the tray—to the footman's immense surprise, his eyes going as wide as saucers.

She was his secret. Delicious, gratifying, and delectable.

As she had no wish to marry and neither did he, the arrangement suited them. He was not wooing her. She was not flirtatious. Complete honesty resided between them. More open and honest than any other relationship he'd ever experienced, except perhaps with the Chessmen. Yet, her acquaintance seemed *more* somehow. More fulfilling, more enjoyable, more . . . necessary.

It was the last that had caused him to experience a measure of unease at the thought of her attending the ball. She might consider herself on the shelf, but there were men aplenty who wouldn't, men who might decide she would make the perfect wife and would take it into their heads to convince her of the same. With poetic words, earnest attentions, and promises of bliss.

"Sir?"

He jerked his gaze up to find Perkins standing before the desk, a pleat between his brows. Bishop hadn't heard him enter, wondered if the butler had said something before daring to use the sharp tone that had finally garnered his attention. He also realized he'd only written half the sentence he'd intended for his man of affairs. "What is it, Perkins?"

"A Mrs. Bennett has come to call."

He was not acquainted with a Mrs. Bennett, which could mean only one thing. He nodded. "I'll see her."

After Perkins left and Bishop began tidying his desk—he'd complete the letter later—he wondered why he didn't feel the sense of chivalry that usually accompanied the arrival of a woman in need of rescuing from a dragon of a husband. Before, he'd always felt as though he was donning armor and preparing to draw a sword in defense of the downtrodden. But instead, he suffered through an overwhelming sense of loss with the realization that helping this woman would probably mean one less night with Marguerite every sennight.

When everything was in place, he took his usual position in the center of the room. The woman following Perkins over the threshold possessed a sturdy frame, with ample curves that for some reason he imagined children burrowing against. Her hair was a mixture of salt and pepper, prematurely going white because she didn't appear to be much older than forty, if that. Not that age really mattered. Unhappiness cared little about years. "Mrs. Bennett, how might I be of service?"

"Are you the bishop?"

"It's merely Bishop," he repeated by rote, and stopped himself from continuing with any further explanation.

"Mrs. Winters shared that you helped her out of a difficult marriage last year and was most gracious while doing so."

Had Mrs. Winters formed a society of disgruntled wives? Was that the reason she was acquainted with another who needed to be sent his way? "Why don't you join me in this sitting area here"—near the door because for some reason he wanted her gone as quickly as possible once their business was concluded—"where we can discuss matters in more comfort? Perkins, send in tea."

Memories of Marguerite bringing it that fateful
night when he'd welcomed Mrs. Mallard swamped
him. With a sigh, wondering if he'd even notice who
delivered it this time, he joined his guest.

DAISY DIDN'T BOTHER to knock on the door to Bishop's
residence, but simply let herself in. She was entirely
comfortable here, and in a way had begun to think of
it as their little special place. She'd considered inviting him to her apartment, but her bed wasn't nearly as
large or comfortable. He'd have no room to sprawl out
as he did within his own, and she liked studying all
the various dips and curves of him when he was on
full display, as he often was after they'd made love.

While he always drew a sheet over her to provide
her with some warmth afterward, he left himself exposed as though his skin was on fire and he needed
to cool off. She would indulge herself with the sight
of him. But then it didn't matter if he was clothed
or unclothed, the unobstructed view of him always
made her go warm and tingly. He was so beautiful.
Sculpted muscles that he'd been very much an artist
in creating—although there'd been nothing artistic
in the reasoning behind his efforts. He'd wanted the
strength in order to stop the brutality. She experienced
moments when she wanted to tell her aunt every detail
of him. More, she wanted to tell all of England.

*He is not as you believe. If you only knew him as
I do.*

She was near the doorway to the library when she
heard the voices. The deep one, she recognized, but
then she'd be able to distinguish it from others in a
crowd of a thousand. Smooth, rich, and dark. It had

whispered sweet words and naughty ones in her ear. The other voice, feminine and soft but filled with purpose, was unfamiliar.

"It was my understanding you wouldn't ask why I wanted him out of my life," the woman said.

"Your reasons are your own. They matter not one whit to me."

With her heart hammering, Daisy moved into the doorway. She could see only the profile of what appeared to be an older woman. Bishop was leaning toward her, resting his elbows on his thighs, his hands clasped before him.

"To be clear, this will not be a pleasant experience for you. Divorce is granted—"

He came to an abrupt halt and jerked his attention toward Daisy, who was hovering there, trying to comprehend what she was hearing. No, it was obvious what she was hearing. What she didn't understand was the reason behind it.

"If you'll kindly excuse me for a moment," he said to his visitor, even as he was already unfolding his body before all the words were spoken, before she'd acknowledged his request. He crossed quickly over to Daisy, wrapped his large hand around her upper arm, and drew her into the hallway, a good distance away from that yawning doorway. "What are you doing here at this hour? Is something amiss?"

His brow was deeply furrowed, but all she could surmise was that yes, something was terribly amiss. "What are you doing with that woman?"

Unfurling his fingers, he released his hold on her. "Mrs. Bennett is in want of a divorce."

Her throat went so dry that it actually hurt to push

out the coming statement with conviction. "You're going to pretend to have an affair with her."

He studied her for what seemed an eternity before finally he smiled, the smile that had first taken her breath. She had a strong urge to smack it right off his face. "You're jealous when you have no reason to be."

Perhaps she could play cards after all, was not so easy to read because what she was feeling was not jealousy—well, maybe a touch of it—but confusion, hurt, and resentment all forged together into a blade that seemed to be piercing her heart. "She's going to be coming to you."

Apparently, accurately gauging the tone of her voice, he quickly sobered, all hint of teasing gone. "Yes."

"What about us?"

"This doesn't affect us. We will continue on as we have been doing."

Suddenly she found it difficult to breathe, as though she'd been stuffed into a corset four sizes too small. How was it that he believed this didn't affect them *at all*? She'd thought him a man of intelligence, a man who keenly understood women. But her *understanding* of him felt remarkably off-kilter. Disappointment and fury began simmering and weaving together like wisps of smoke striving to become solid. "What night will be my night?"

"Marguerite—"

"What. Night?"

His frustration was evident while he glanced around the corridor as though he might discover the answer hidden there. "I'll give her Thursday, I suppose. All the other nights are yours."

Until another woman showed up in need of assistance and Daisy would lose one more night. "What notation will you put in your appointment diary to identify me? Or have you already penned me in?"

"Don't be ridiculous, Marguerite."

"Don't be ridiculous? You are carrying on as though nothing of any substance exists between us. As though we are pretend as well."

"You know this is what I do. Help ladies forge a path to divorce. Their affairs are pretend, but not yours. Yet even so, we can't acknowledge our relationship in public. What we have is secret. It must remain so."

"Why? Do you think I would be ashamed to be seen with you? I wouldn't even care if all of London speculated that we were lovers. I can withstand the gossips believing I'm having an affair, as long as I am the only one with whom you are associating. But what I will not tolerate is being considered one of many women thought to be warming your bed. I have my pride, and I know my worth."

She knew how much helping women meant to him, that he was devoted to his cause, but she couldn't reconcile that he believed having a sullied reputation was the only way that he could offer assistance. "Become an MP, work to change the laws so it's not as difficult for a woman to get out of an untenable arrangement."

"I won't do this from a distance. I won't find it satisfying. I won't win."

She stared at him, struggling to comprehend why being intimately involved was so deuced important to him. Because of what his mother had suffered, yes. But there was more to it than that. "Win? What are you striving to win? Are you playing a game . . . with whom? Every husband who is not ideal?"

"This has nothing to do with *their* husbands." Anger rippled through his voice.

If not their husbands . . . dear Lord. His mother's husband. "Your father? That's it, isn't it? Somehow, it's your father. But how does any of what you're doing affect him?"

"Because when I'm written up in the papers as a fornicator, it brings him shame. Because he is reminded that he should have liberated my mother, not killed her. For him there is no path to redemption except through me. It was the reason he wanted me in the clergy. But I will not assist him in receiving absolution. He will rot in hell."

"Is he even aware of this game? At what point do you win? When he is dead? When your life has almost run its course? After you've sacrificed any chance of happiness at all?"

He lowered his head, his eyes blazing into hers. "What of you? Your mother chose poorly so you will not even entertain the idea of marriage. You have chosen to make no choice at all. I have *chosen* this path and I will see it through. I will ensure these ladies do not suffer my mother's fate."

"By being judge, jury, and executioner of a marriage without even knowing all the facts? I overheard you. You don't have any earthly idea what prompted her coming to you."

His jaw tightening, he glanced toward the doorway, before leveling his gaze once more on Daisy. "May we finish this discussion later? I have a guest."

A guest more important than Daisy. A woman he would sacrifice everything for, while sacrificing nothing for Daisy. A murder had shown her what a partial life with him would be like. Only she didn't want a partial life. She'd erroneously believed now that everything was resolved they could broaden their relationship.

"Why have you come at this hour?" he asked, almost repeating what he'd asked when he first saw her.

She held up the ecru envelope. "I brought you an invitation to the Bellingham ball."

"I already told you I would not attend. I will not be welcomed."

"You would have been . . . by me. That might have started a revolution that would have led to . . ." *A proper courtship.* She shook her head. "I don't know what it might have led to."

Carefully, as though it was made of delicate crystal that could easily shatter—when in truth, it was she who was on the verge of shattering—she set the card on a nearby table, beside a vase of daisies. "I'll leave it in case you change your mind."

"I won't change my mind."

She studied the lines of his face that she had traced with a fingertip, had kissed lightly, had pressed her lips against more firmly. "I know."

At last she did know. The young lad who felt responsible for his mother's death, who had been unable to save her, still resided within him. Every decision in his life was guided by that boy's regrets. She couldn't compete with the ghost of that woman or the frightened eyes of other ladies seeking help. She wasn't bothered by the notion that he wouldn't place her first but rather with the idea that all he would offer her was a secret life, never a public acknowledgment. "My apologies for barging in without thought and taking you away from your visitor. I'll leave you to her now."

"We'll discuss this in more detail later."

With a quick nod and a sad smile, she turned on her heel and strolled toward the door. She rather feared that, like her mother, she'd chosen poorly. But unlike her mother, she intended to correct her mistake.

CHAPTER 26

Normally Bishop divided his pacing between the foyer and the front parlor, waiting to catch the first sight of the carriage rumbling up the drive so he could rush out the door and be there to help Marguerite disembark, to feel her small hand being placed in his larger one and to have that sense that it was precisely where it belonged. To inhale her fragrance, to see her soft smile, to gaze into her blue, welcoming eyes. To have no need to wander through his garden seeking solace because solace arrived with her.

But tonight, he was outside, standing on the top step anxiously awaiting her arrival. He was extremely bothered by the conversation they'd shared earlier. More needed to be said, so much more explained.

He couldn't identify the precise moment when she'd become so important. Sometimes he wondered if perhaps Chastity had the right of it when he'd last seen her and she'd announced that he was in love, and he'd vehemently refuted it. Because he couldn't deny that he had moments when Martin Parker's words—*I cannot bear the thought of a world without her in it*—echoed through his heart with the resounding conviction and clarity that even a day without her was unbearable.

That afternoon when he'd looked up and seen her standing in the doorway, he'd resented Mrs. Bennett for occupying a chair in his library because her presence made it impossible to do exactly what he wanted: take Marguerite into his arms and carry her up the stairs to enjoy a delightful afternoon together.

But she was for after hours. After she closed her office for the day. After he cleared his desk. After the servants were abed. After neighbors had drawn draperies. After an hour when they might be caught.

Yet she'd brought him an invitation to that damned ball. As though he could attend without revealing any of his feelings for her. As though he could waltz with her and act like she meant nothing. As though he could watch her dancing with other men and ignore the tiny cracks forming in his heart. She thought they were pretending in his bedchamber? The greater pretense would happen outside of it.

Her business would thrive only if people thought she possessed sound judgment. What would it say about her judgment if she was seen in public with him? He needed her to understand that he was striving to shield her, even if she claimed to need no protection.

What was giving up one night a week when a woman might be saved? A sacrifice he was finding it incredibly difficult to want to make. But didn't the greater good outweigh the selfishness of one person? How different might his life have been if someone— anyone—had been willing to assist his mother? Besides, Mrs. Bennett had young children. They added to the importance of what he was doing. They would be affected if he turned away their mother, if they grew up surrounded by hatred, if tragedy befell the woman who'd given birth to them.

At the sight of the carriage turning into the drive, the tight bands around his chest loosened. He took a deep cleansing breath and slowly released it. She was here. They would talk, eventually laugh, and then he would take her to his bed and demonstrate that they most certainly were not a pretense. They were heated gazes, searing kisses, and scorching touches that resulted in a blazing torrent of sensations coming together to form a conflagration that ultimately encompassed the whole of them. Sated and lethargic, they would lie in each other's arms and talk in low voices about matters of importance and things that mattered not at all. Always there was the beauty of those shared moments before they drifted off into slumber for a spell.

He was already in place when the carriage drew to a stop. Reaching out, he pulled open the door and stared at the blackened abyss. Empty of warmth. Empty of joy. Empty of her.

"Apologies, sir," the footman who appeared at his side said. "Miss Townsend informed us that she wouldn't be coming tonight, wouldn't have need of the carriage any longer. We knew you'd be waiting, so thought it best to come here before going to the stables. Hence you would know of her decision."

She could have returned the carriage anytime during the late afternoon or early evening. But she'd waited for this hour, their hour, in order to send a distinct and an impossible-to-misinterpret message.

She wouldn't be coming to his residence in the

dead of night or otherwise. She was done with him. They, as a couple, would be no more.

With a nod, he did not slam the door shut, but it did click rather loudly. "As I expected." As he'd feared. He now realized the reason he'd had such a difficult time drawing in breath standing on that top step. He'd known she wasn't going to come. "Carry on."

He climbed up those steps with the difficulty of a man striving to scale a steep, rocky mountain. Once inside, he went straightaway to his library, poured himself a scotch, and tossed it back. After pouring himself another, he held it up to the lamplight, searching for any smearing that might indicate it was the same tumbler she'd touched that first night. But, of course, the glass was spotless. Perkins would have seen to it.

As though moving through treacle, he dragged himself to his favorite chair in front of the fireplace and stared into the empty hearth. He couldn't look around this chamber without seeing her here. As a matter of fact, he was fairly certain he was going to envision her in every room. Even in his strength training room that had once been his haven, where he could push himself until he was too exhausted to remember his mother's cries or his father's shouts or his own body trembling with his fear. Although, it had been a good long while since he'd brought forth any of those memories.

They still mattered, had helped shape him, but lately when he drifted into the past, he didn't drift far. His first sighting of Marguerite. Conversations. Smiles. Laughter. The way she moaned when he pushed into her, as though nothing had ever felt so exquisite. Her sigh when she nestled against him. The manner in which she jutted up her chin when negotiating with him.

Negotiating.

There should have been a fourth term in their damned agreement.

Do. Not. Fall. In. Love.

CHAPTER 27

❦

$\mathcal{D}$AISY had been cloistered in her office and apartments since the afternoon she'd walked out of Bishop's residence determined never to return. She'd had an evening of weeping, aching, and missing him. Of convincing herself that sending his carriage to him empty was the most effective way of delivering her message. For two days, she'd thought perhaps he might come for her, and she'd practiced the words she would use to drive him away. But he hadn't shown. Nor had he written to her or sent her gifts or attempted to cajole her back into his arms in any manner.

Just as well. She was done with him. With all men. They were naught but trouble.

Therefore, that morning, Daisy awoke earlier than usual, as though Perkins was hovering outside her door refusing to let her sleep in, went to her desk, and sketched a drawing. After leisurely enjoying her morning cup of jasmine tea, she dressed for the day and delivered the etching to a gentleman, paying him extra to deliver what she wanted that afternoon.

A few hours later, she stood on the bricked pavement and watched with satisfaction as two men hung above her door, the sign she'd commissioned that morning: *Townsend Investigative Agency.*

"Perfect," she declared when they were done and gave them each an extra shilling for their trouble.

Then she went into her office, sat at her desk, and observed through the windows, with the draperies drawn aside, as people wandered by. Many glanced up. Some stopped to stare at the new adornment. A little after four, a gentleman strode in.

"I warned you about putting up a sign, Miss Townsend," he announced. "I'm here to collect the additional lease fee."

A fee she had no intention of paying. "How good of you to call, Mr. Swift. Tell me, have you seen this article in a recent edition of the *Times*?" Turning the newspaper around and scooting it toward the edge of the desk away from her, she placed her finger on said article.

Warily, as though she might be presenting him with an adder, he approached and glanced down. "'Bout the arrest of a murderer? Aye, I read it."

"Did you notice this little sentence here that begins, 'With the aid of Miss Marguerite Townsend'?"

He lifted his gaze to hers. "What of it?"

"I've begun to make a name for myself, Mr. Swift. I need potential clients to have no difficulty whatsoever in finding me. Hence the sign."

"And hence the doubling of your lease fee."

"I think not. You argue that my presence will lower the value of your properties. I believe it will enhance them. If anything, I should be paying you less." He scowled. "However, I won't quibble with you about that matter. What I will say is that if you insist on my paying double, I shall pack up my belongings and move my business elsewhere, taking my sign with me, naturally."

He glared at her for a moment before finally relenting. "I suppose I could see my way clear to charging you only a quarter more."

Exhibiting no facial expression at all, she merely stared at him.

The gust of air he released was strong enough to send her wooden sign swinging. "All right, then, we'll keep things as they are."

"Very good."

He furrowed his brow. "Why the chain of daisies painted on the sign?"

"They serve as a reminder, Mr. Swift." That she was fully capable of rescuing herself. She also hoped that one day very soon, they would serve as a reminder that broken hearts did indeed eventually heal.

BISHOP TOLD HIMSELF that he was relieved things were over between him and Marguerite. Certainly, he'd never had a long-term relationship before, knew nothing of wooing. So her calling things off saved him the bother of eventually having to say, "We're done."

Although he couldn't imagine when he might have wanted to utter those words. After a month perhaps? Six? Twelve? A thousand?

Instead, he'd been like Mr. Parker, wanting to make things easy for her. Therefore, he hadn't gone to her building. He hadn't knocked on her door. He respected her decision. Even if it was tearing him up inside.

"You're awfully quiet this evening."

Bishop glanced over at King. The four Chessmen were occupying their favorite corner in the library of the Twin Dragons.

"Contemplating daisies again?" Knight asked, humor laced through his voice.

"A daisy, yes. Only one and there is no other like her."

"Sounds as though you've been keeping something from us," Rook said. "Who is she, then?"

"Someone I thought I could best at a game."

"I assume you lost."

"The fact that I'm here tonight with you instead of with her, I believe makes that an easy assumption."

"So tell us about this Daisy," Knight said.

"Her name is Marguerite. For now, that's all you need to know." He looked at King. "How did you convince Penelope you loved her enough so she consented to marry you?"

King's eyebrows shot up before he exchanged a quick glance with Rook and Knight. "Well, therein lies a story, doesn't it? I did a bit of groveling, but mostly I understood her past, accepted it, and vowed that I would do all in my power to ensure it never came between us."

But it wasn't Marguerite's past coming between them. How did he make his past no longer matter? It had woven itself through the very fabric of his soul, influenced every decision he made. Letting the past go would be like severing off a gangrenous limb. Where did one find the courage to do it?

"MARTIN, WHAT WAS the name of that inquiry agent you hired?" Louisa Parker asked as she perused the latest gossip rag while enjoying breakfast with her husband. It had become their morning ritual following a night in each other's arms. It had been somewhat humbling to discover that he'd avoided her because his desire for her was so strong that he hadn't the resilience to resist her otherwise, and he'd been terrified of getting her with child again and possibly losing her.

Sitting beside her, he looked up from an article in the *Times* he'd been reading and smiled at her somewhat abashedly. "Marguerite Townsend. Why, my love?"

As always warmth surged through her when he used one of his many endearments for her. "The on-dit here is that she helped to solve the murder of a Mr. Mallard—a man Bishop was thought to have murdered. Bishop had hired her to help prove his innocence, which she did remarkably well. Personally, I'm not at all surprised, as he's not the sort to go about killing people. However, there is speculation that she couldn't have assisted him without succumbing to his . . . *proclivities for pleasure*, as stated in this piece."

"That's ridiculous. She's an intelligent woman. She'd never fall under the spell of that scoundrel."

She gave him a patient yet perceptive smile. "Oh, Martin. They kissed. Quite passionately, I'd wager."

He looked as though she'd slapped him. "When?"

"At the brothel. In that room next to the one we were in."

He shook his head. "No. That's preposterous." He leaned toward her. "Isn't it?"

After she placed her hand over his, he turned his palm up and intertwined their fingers. Of late, they couldn't seem to go long without touching, and she adored him for it. "A woman's eyes do not glaze over, and her lips are not swollen if she hasn't just been thoroughly kissed by a man who is extremely knowledgeable when it comes to delivering a smooch that will take away a woman's ability to think and leave her with naught but the ability to feel."

"I rather hate to ask but how do my kisses measure up?"

"They make my entire body curl."

"A good thing, correct?"

"Martin, I do wish you didn't doubt how much I love you and how much I relish every touch, caress, and kiss you bestow upon me." They were presently taking precautions to ensure she didn't get with child, but she hoped at some future date they might again take the risk.

"I have a rather hard time believing I could be so fortunate."

"If you don't mind being late to the office, I'll be more than happy to try to convince you after breakfast."

He blushed. "I don't believe I have anything pressing on my schedule at the moment."

"Then I shall most definitely have you pressing against me. But first we need to think of a way to resolve this Bishop issue."

"I didn't realize there was a Bishop issue."

"I told you that nothing happened between us. Nothing physical at least. I'm fairly certain the same could be said for the other women who came to him. But he's not going to admit that. I don't know why, but he feels a need to assist in these difficult situations. However, there must be another way to do it, a way that would restore his reputation so he and Miss Townsend might have a chance."

"A chance?"

"At a future together. He could have simply gone on and let us continue with our plans to get divorced. Instead, he went to the extra effort to help us resolve the matter."

"He didn't have to do it by sending us to a brothel," he grumbled. He was still rather embarrassed and upset that Bishop had forced him into such a scandalous place when inviting them to dinner might have served just as well to get them talking again.

She smiled because she'd quite enjoyed the wickedness of such a disreputable excursion. "But think how much we will laugh about it in a few years' time."

"I can't see myself ever laughing about it."

However, she was rather certain that someday he would. For the moment, however, she was more concerned about Bishop. "Martin, I saw the way he looked at her each time she entered his bedchamber. As though the sun had suddenly burst forth from behind gloomy clouds to brighten the day. Do we not owe him for our present happiness? Should we not try to return the favor?"

"Mr. and Mrs. Martin Parker have come to call."

As a rule, Bishop despised interruptions when he was striving to pen a letter to his man of affairs because it required a precision that ensured the gent knew exactly what was required of him to meet his employer's exacting standard. Although he'd finally finished the letter regarding his instructions for the ship and sent it off, he had other matters with which they needed to deal. But at the moment, he welcomed the arrival of his guests. Truth be told, he missed his time with Louisa Parker. If anyone understood his current plight, it would be her, and he'd considered asking for her advice regarding his most recent thinking. Not that he was going to ask anything of her with her husband hovering about.

However, he was most curious regarding the reason for their visit. Maybe their reconciliation had taken a nasty turn and they'd decided to move forward with the divorce, and he needed once again to pretend to be her lover. But after he'd sent Perkins to fetch them and the butler escorted them into the room, Bishop knew no divorce was going to be forthcoming. They walked in as a united front, her all smiles and happiness, him proud and protective.

Bishop felt a satisfaction for his role in their reuniting as well as a pang of what suspiciously resembled envy. It was not an emotion with which he was accustomed to dealing. Still, he stood, knowing they required something of him. It was the only reason anyone—other than the Chessmen—visited. They needed his assistance in some way. "How may I be of service?"

"We saw in the newspapers the account of your recent trouble, you being suspected of murder," Louisa said.

"It reached a satisfactory resolution. No need to worry there."

"The gossip rags are speculating that Miss Townsend might have been unable to resist the lure of your charms."

He'd seen the gossip sheets. Part of the reason he was having troubling finding the words to write to his man of affairs was that he was constantly contemplating the words he needed to write to the editors of every publication in London regarding the ludicrousness of Marguerite being involved with him. She needed a sterling reputation to ensure she attracted clients and could continue doing something she not only loved but was incredibly good at it. However, he also needed to ensure he wasn't protesting so much that he added weight to the rumors and made them believable. "I intend to sort it."

"We thought we might be able to help."

"Louisa—"

"Hear us out."

With a nod, he swept his arm toward a sitting area. "Would you like to make yourselves comfortable? Shall I send for tea, or can I offer another libation?"

"No, thank you," Louisa said. "I don't think we'll be long."

The couple settled on the settee, sitting so their hips and thighs touched, his fingers intertwined with hers. It was difficult to reconcile that at one point they'd wanted to go their separate ways. Bishop lowered himself to the opposite chair.

"Do you recall when I mentioned something about how London Society likes nothing better than a good rake reformation story?" Louisa asked.

"I'm not going to reform."

"Not even to save Miss Townsend's reputation?" Parker asked sharply.

"If I stay away from her, it will give no credence to the gossip and it will all die down."

"Do you wish to stay away from her?" Louisa asked.

"That is beside the point."

"Do we need to arrange for the two of you to share a room together in a brothel?"

He laughed, thinking about what happened the last time they were in a room together in a brothel. "Absolutely not."

"Whether or not you want to be viewed as reforming or wish to see her is beside the point. What Martin and I have discussed, however, is a need for more women to be helped. His very first shop is rather small. It is comprised of a series of rooms that served as a demarcation for each department. But now that he has the larger stores, the first is used as a warehouse of sorts. We thought we could donate the smaller shop to your cause. You could oversee the administration of it or hire someone to manage the task. With the addition of doors and furniture, the building could become a haven for women in want of refuge. We could have solicitors available to advise them. In the process, you would become Society's darling." She smiled. Sweetly. Innocently.

Bishop shifted his attention to Parker. "I can't believe you'd want to remain with this conniving wench."

"Love does tend to make fools of us men."

With a tiny huff, she slapped playfully at his arm. "Martin!"

He grinned at her, she smiled warmly at him, and Bishop had to look away. If he wasn't there, he suspected these two would be going at each other with wild abandon. He'd already decided he shouldn't be the arbiter of divorce, creating a false scenario for a woman. Marguerite had been correct there—with some thought, planning, and effort, he could make a difference for a good many more women. It was what he'd spent all morning striving to outline and explain to his man of affairs. He'd already informed Mrs. Bennett that he wouldn't pretend to have an affair with her, but would help her pursue another avenue for acquiring what she wished to achieve. He'd also sent a missive to Mrs. Winters apprising her not to send any more ladies his way as he'd be unable to accommodate them.

He turned back to his guests to find their gazes on him and not on each other. "Actually, I've been searching for a building. Yours sounds perfect. If you've time now, perhaps we could begin working out some particulars."

"WHAT THE DEVIL game are you about now?"

Looking horrified, Perkins was rushing in two steps behind the shouting man who stormed into Bishop's library the following morning. It had been several months since Bishop had seen his father, not since the last divorce case when the old man had arrived to proclaim that Bishop was naught but an embarrassment as a son. His words had spurred Bishop on, determined to assist more women, and in doing so, bringing further mortification to his father. A game, Marguerite had correctly surmised, that the elder Blackwood didn't even know they were playing.

"My apologies, sir," Perkins began.

"It's quite all right. You're dismissed to tend to your other duties. I'll see to our charming guest." And it was quite easy to *see* him, because Bishop had begun working with the draperies drawn aside so the sunlight could filter into the chamber, and he could look out on his gardens whenever he wished.

Perkins quickly disappeared as though aided by a magician's hand. Bishop's father advanced, slapped his large hands on the desk, and leaned forward, fury turning his dark eyes black. "I offered double what that ship was worth and have been informed the papers are ready for me to sign. I am now obliged to deliver the requested funds. Why have you not made an offer on it?"

Because the missive he'd finally sent to his man of affairs had read: *Offer nothing. Let go anyone you have hired to keep watch of his activities. His business is no longer mine.*

"I have no need of a ship. I would think you'd be pleased."

His sire slammed his eyes closed, and his jaw went so tight that it was a wonder Bishop didn't hear bone cracking. "I haven't the funds. I told the owner I could get him an exorbitant amount. He promised to give me half." He opened his eyes, defeat mirrored in them. "I know you've been purchasing everything I want. Why not this?"

"Because I no longer care." *Because I want—need—you out of my life. I'm forfeiting the game for something much more important. I'm letting go of the anger and the hatred. However, they won't be replaced by their opposites. What I feel for you is absolute nothingness.*

"I was so certain you'd come through, I promised to pay what I offered if you didn't. This will put me in the poor house or worse, debtor's prison. Think of the shame that will bring you."

"Your actions have no bearing on how I regard myself."

"I'm your father, deserving of your respect."

"You may have planted the seed, but you've never been my *father*. The first time I saw you strike Mum"—he shook his head—"afterward, I begged her to leave you, for the two of us to run off together. I was only five, but I promised I would protect her. However, she loved you. Wouldn't abandon you."

His father shoved himself off the desk, walked over to the window, and gazed out. An eternity seemed to pass, and Bishop wondered if his father was traveling a path of memories. Finally he placed his hand on the glass, as though he wanted to reach through it and touch something significant. "Your mother loved her flowers. She would have fancied your gardens. I was not a good husband. I acknowledge that. But I didn't kill her." He looked at his son. "Truly, she fell down the stairs."

"I don't believe you." He'd even considered hiring Marguerite to get at the truth, but after twenty years, what evidence would remain? "However, even if you didn't push her, the way you treated her is unforgivable. If you ever barge into my residence again, I shall have you arrested for trespass. Recently, I've come to know an inspector at Scotland Yard rather well. I think he would accommodate my request without much bother. Now, if you'll be so good as to leave, we are done."

His shoulders slumped, with the mien of a defeated man, the elder Blackwood shuffled out. Bishop should have felt a measure of victory. Instead, he felt loss for all the years when he'd thought he'd been in control of his life, but that man had still maintained some power over him. No longer.

Breathing deeply, he could have sworn he inhaled the lingering fragrance of violets.

CHAPTER 28

"How is it that one can be both the darling of Society by assisting Scotland Yard in apprehending a murderer as well as a disgrace for possibly cavorting with the top-ranked scoundrel of the Season?"

Daisy rolled her eyes at Bellingham's eldest, Viscount Townsend, who would one day inherit the earldom.

"If you cared at all for your reputation, Cousin Rob, you wouldn't be speaking to me here within your family's ballroom." Where the elaborate ball was already underway. The orchestra, situated on the level above, had been enticing dancers onto the floor for at least an hour now.

"I care so little for my reputation, Cousin M, that I'm going to claim a dance with you in a bit. That I would associate with such a scandalous person should ensure I'm not bothered by mamas striving to marry their daughters off to me. Although to be honest, I hadn't really expected you to show."

After reading the speculation in the latest gossip rags, she'd certainly considered sparing herself the humiliation of suffering through cuts directly. But she'd not shared with her aunt that her heart had been shattered into a thousand tiny shards, and her niece not appearing would have made her worry. In spite of the fact that Daisy had been correct and was being approached by more clients, the victory seemed a tad shallow, since she was unable to share it with Bishop.

"Marguerite has more backbone than you, Rob," her cousin and his brother Jack said. "She's not going to let a few tawdry words dictate her behavior."

She was actually quite touched that all four of Bellingham's children, his three sons and one daughter, had been surrounding her since her arrival, forming a sort of moat that no one in the *ton* had yet found the courage to swim across.

"I think it's disgraceful that the gossip rags can print speculation with no proof," Adelia said. All of nineteen, she was expected to make a good match by the end of the Season. Her eyes warmed and she offered a secretive smile. "Although if you were to whisper in my ear the truth of the matter, I can hold a secret."

"The truth of the matter is no secret. There was never anything salacious between us. He was a client, nothing more."

"But so devilishly handsome. He has the look about him of a man who truly knows how to kiss a woman properly."

"When did you see him?" Phillip asked.

"What do you know of proper kissing?" Rob demanded.

"I saw him at a ball during my coming out Season, before he was so embroiled in scandal. As for proper kissing, I read romantic novels." She looked at her dance card. "When this waltz ends, I must take to the floor." Reaching out, she squeezed Daisy's hand. "Don't let any of these people make you feel less. You are a heroine, and that far outweighs being a tart."

Daisy laughed. "I'm not sure most of the *ton* would agree with you."

"It was a shock to learn Uncle Lionel is still alive," Rob said. "Weren't you at all afraid when he took you captive?"

"I knew he wouldn't harm me."

"Do you think he'll hang?" Phillip asked.

"Your father doesn't think so, but I suspect he'll spend considerable time in prison."

"As well he should."

"To be honest, I'm surprised anyone showed up here tonight," Jack said. "What with the family name being slung through the mud."

Another reason Daisy had felt it was important to make an appearance. The family had stood by her all these years. Now it was time to stand by them.

"Oh, my God," Adelia suddenly blurted, her eyes going wide. "It's him."

"Who?" Daisy asked, as she turned to look in the direction her cousin was staring, but she knew before she saw him because the room suddenly felt charged with electricity.

Bishop.

In his evening attire. So remarkably handsome. With a touch of arrogance, as though daring anyone to object to his presence. Guests weren't being announced, but at some point, he had descended the stairs or come in through the doors that led to the refreshment room. He was striding along the outskirts of the dance floor, dipping his head in acknowledgment here or there, but receiving no corresponding salutations in return. Only cuts.

He'd tried to tell her that he'd not be welcomed, but she'd refused to listen or acknowledge it, because she'd wanted him here, had wanted her damned waltz.

Then he was standing before her, with her cousins flanking her, two on each side. Out of the corner of her eye, she could see some of the dancing couples straining their necks to get a better look at what was going on in this little corner of the ballroom. At any moment, someone was going to crash into someone else, but she didn't care.

"Blackwood," Rob said sternly. "I think you're terribly obtuse, old chap, if you think my cousin wants anything at all to do with you. On your way now."

A corner of Bishop's mouth curled up, but he never took his eyes from her. "She doesn't like to be rescued, my lord. And she certainly doesn't need rescuing from me."

Oh, he was so wrong there. She'd missed him far too much, had contemplated going to him. Being a secret. For it was better than being without him. But she had her pride. And as she'd told him, she understood her worth. She deserved more than being hidden away.

He shifted his gaze to Rob. "Don't you have young ladies to charm?"

"I'm not going to leave you alone with Marguerite so you can try to woo her."

Bishop's attention came back to her. "I've never wooed a woman in my life. Wouldn't even know where to start."

Her heart did a strange sort of skip and jump. What was he confessing here?

"Then how the devil is it that you have all these affairs with married ladies?" Rob asked, his voice rife with disbelief as well as irritation, certain he was being mocked.

"I don't," Bishop said simply.

"But you swore you did. In the courts. Your admittance secured some wives a divorce."

"Yes, that could prove to be a bit of a bother should the truth come out and create a tempest, but then I have a very good solicitor, who assures me much can be forgiven when accompanied by true remorse."

She didn't think he was answering Rob at all but was speaking only to her. Words that carried weight, a message only she could truly hear and comprehend. A message that sent hope perilously spiraling through her.

He held out his hand. "Miss Townsend, will you honor me with a dance?"

She could feel all her cousins' eyes boring into her, and she desperately wanted one of them to bring her to her senses. But other than tackling her to the floor, she didn't know how they were going to stop her from following her foolish heart. She was rather surprised by the steadiness in her hand as she placed it in his, as though delivering it home. "I will, yes."

His gloved fingers closed around hers, and he moved her to the edge of the dance floor. Where they waited, her heart giving such hard lurches that she wouldn't have been surprised to learn that he heard it hitting her ribs. She had questions, but at the moment all she wanted was to absorb his nearness. She could see the speculative and assessing glances of the dancers as they swept by, and she was relatively certain a few were going to have sore necks on the morrow because of all the whipping around of heads that was going on.

"Chin up," he said, in a low, mesmerizing voice, the one he used when buried deeply inside her.

"It's the only way I know to hold my chin. It's the way my aunt taught me."

"Is her lover our pianist?"

Our pianist. How could he carry on a casual conversation as though everything between them was as it had once been? Yet it was something they'd shared. In so short a time, they'd shared so much. "He is, yes."

Although she couldn't see her aunt, she could feel her watching, knew she would jump into the fray to rescue Daisy from Bishop, if need be. But also knew she respected her enough to give Daisy the opportunity to rescue herself first. However, at the moment, as unwise as it was, she couldn't claim to want to be anywhere else.

The dance finally came to an end. Another tune began. Only a handful of notes had sounded before she found herself in Bishop's firm arms, gliding over the parquet, gazing into his eyes.

"I forfeited the game," he said quietly.

She furrowed her brow. "I beg your pardon?"

"You were right. Of course, you were. I was playing a game with my father, always trying to best him. I've ended my association with him completely. He's no longer in my life. When he walked out, I felt as though I'd taken my first free breath of air after spending years in a dungeon. The air smelled of violets. It smelled of you."

Oh, God. For a man who claimed not to know how to woo, he certainly gave a fine imitation of knowing precisely what to say in order to send her emotions into tumult. "Bishop—"

"I'm not quite finished. Those women who came to me were safe, but you weren't. You made me feel things I'd never felt before. Yet I couldn't seem to distance myself from you. I love teasing you. I love talking with you. I love walking at your side. I even loved when you were cross with me because of the things I said and didn't say to Swindler. I know you have no wish to marry, and I understand your reasons. Your father is a dreadful excuse for a human being. He and mine will no doubt become best mates in hell. I will not ask you to marry me, ever. What I would like to ask is that you give me the opportunity each day to allow you to choose me."

Tears began stinging her eyes. "Bishop—"

"Negotiations aren't quite done yet. I shan't interfere with your business. Nor shall I pretend to have affairs any longer. I intend to establish a residence where women can seek shelter. I shall declare to the world that you have reformed me. Should a day come when you don't wish to choose me, I shall respect your wishes and walk away, without so much as a whimper. Even if it kills me to do so. And trust me, Marguerite, it will kill me. I know that as surely as I know that flowers blossom. And rain falls. And there is no smile in the world as beautiful as yours."

The last was not true. That distinction belonged to his smile. She remembered the first time he'd bestowed it upon her, and it had been as though he'd delivered sunshine to her soul. But she needed more, because she'd weathered too many storms of late.

"Why?" she asked. "Why are you willing to do all this?"

"Because I love you. And it terrifies me how much you mean to me. You are everything. I can't promise that if you choose me, someday you won't realize you chose poorly. What I can promise is that you won't be shackled to me should that day arrive."

"The gossip sheets claim it is impossible for me to have been hired by you and not to have fallen under your spell."

"Yes, unfortunately, I saw that."

"They were so wrong. I fell under your spell long before you hired me."

He grinned, the grin that had first taken her breath. "How fortunate for me."

"It frightened me, what I began to feel for you. It seemed a perilous way to go. You were a scoundrel."

"A counterfeit one at best, eh?"

"Yes." Did anyone know him as well as she did? Did anyone know her as well as he did? All the conversations shared in dark carriages and a dimly lit bedchamber. Secrets uncovered. But from the beginning, it was as though they'd each seen the truth of the other, had not been fooled by the facades, but had seen beneath them to the very essence of their souls. "Will you marry me?"

His eyes widened. "Pardon?"

She poured everything she felt for him into her smile. "By choosing you, I'm not choosing poorly. I know that with everything within me, because I love you so very much. I need choose you only once, and it will be forever. So now the question becomes, do you choose me?"

"Every day until the end of time."

There, within the Earl of Bellingham's ballroom,

where somewhere, she was relatively certain, her aunt was looking on, Bishop took her mouth, and she melted against him. Never had anything in her life felt more right.

This man, here and now. This man, tomorrow and always.

She decided then and there that she was going to have to return to Mr. Parker every farthing he'd paid her, for without him, she'd never have discovered that with Bishop, she could have it all, everything that she'd never even realized she'd dreamed of one day possessing.

EPILOGUE

⌒⌒⌒

THE church was packed to the rafters, many guests smiling at the three-year-old dark-haired girl wandering slowly up the aisle while tossing with wild abandon the red rose petals from her small white wicker basket. Carrying a bouquet of red roses, Daisy trailed along, keeping a watchful eye on the little sprite who had a tendency to wreak havoc wherever she went.

Suddenly, the lass wandered over to a pew and held up between tiny fingers a solitary rose petal. With a loving, indulgent grin, the Duke of Kingsland took the offering and passed it over to his duchess.

Daisy placed her hand on the little girl's shoulder. "Remember, this is a game, Violet. To win, you must keep walking and throwing your petals until we reach the end of the path." Gently, she nudged the child forward toward the altar, where Bishop waited, smartly dressed and as handsome as ever, taking her breath as he always did, even if it also appeared that he was striving very hard not to laugh at the flower girl's antics. He'd warned Daisy that the child would be troublesome. "She's too much like her mother, strong-willed with a mind of her own."

Daisy had almost relented, but Aunt Charlotte had

insisted, and Daisy couldn't deny her aunt anything she wanted, even if the decision did result in the slowest procession to ever grace England's sanctuaries.

Not that anyone seemed to mind the occasional delay in getting to the matter at hand. After all, this marriage had been a terribly long time in coming.

Suddenly, Violet spied Bishop. "Papa!"

With her dark curls bouncing and her basket haphazardly spilling its contents, she raced toward him. He crouched and captured her when she leapt into his arms. Laughter and quiet murmuring made its way through the gathering as Bishop unfolded his body and stood, his daughter now cradled in his arms and raining flower petals over his head, much as her mother had once spilled chocolate. It had been predetermined that he would stand at the front of the church so their daughter would know her precise destination, and he could step forward if she began to wander.

Daisy hastened to join them. "Violet, you need to come stand with me now."

"I wanna be with Papa." She placed her head in the curve of his shoulder, her favorite place in the whole world, she'd recently declared, and Daisy knew there would be no getting her away from Bishop now.

He leaned over and bussed a quick kiss across Daisy's cheek, and she could have sworn she heard a few sighs from the ladies—married and not—in the crowd. It was a well-known fact among the *ton* that Besotted Blackwood was not shy about kissing his adoring wife in public, whenever the mood struck. "It'll be fine," he said, giving her a wink before settling himself in his reserved spot on the first pew, with Violet nestled on his lap.

Turning her attention to the groom, Daisy squeezed Paul Wiggins's hand. "I'm so sorry for the chaos. She's too excited by everything."

"It's a good omen to have a demonstration of such love during a wedding. Charlotte wouldn't want it any other way."

With a nod, Daisy took her place across from him and turned toward the door where her aunt stood, dressed in an elegant ivory gown, her arm entwined with that of her eldest brother.

The organist began playing "The Wedding March." Daisy's eyes filled with tears as people came to their feet and Bellingham escorted his sister up the aisle.

For some time now, Paul had been asking for her aunt's hand, but the stubborn woman had repeatedly responded, "At my age, what need have I for marriage?"

But his persistence had eventually paid off, although Daisy suspected that her aunt may have been influenced to finally accept the proposal after four years of witnessing how terribly happy Daisy and Bishop were, how marriage could transform and enhance a life, how *forever* wasn't something to avoid but rather to embrace.

Her cousins had never mentioned to a soul what Bishop had hinted at that night at the ball—that he'd had no affairs with married ladies. Although his confession had made it easier for them to like him and welcome him into the family. No charges of perjury were ever brought against him. His haven for women, Lily's House, named in honor of his mother, was generously supported—either through volunteering or funding, depending upon what their circumstances allowed—by the women he'd once assisted. His good works had endeared him to many of the *ton*'s matrons, although she assumed the letter that he'd had published in the *Times* regarding how a good woman could reform even the most rakish of rakes hadn't hurt to bolster his rapid acceptance back into Society. Even if it had upset a few fathers whose marriageable daughters had suddenly turned their attention to flirting with rakes.

Blackwood's Investigative Agency—Daisy had seen to having a new sign mounted after her name changed—was thriving, and she had hired a secretary to manage the office and arrange meetings with potential clients. She'd also added one male and two female sleuths to her staff. She had mixed emotions about the success of the business. While she continued to enjoy solving the mysteries presented to her—locating missing family members, proving infidelity, or occasionally assisting Scotland Yard with the cracking of a case—she was sometimes saddened that her skills were needed at all. That people hurt others, especially the ones they loved.

Her father had been found guilty of murder. While her uncle had done all in his power to spare him dancing in the wind, he'd not been successful. Her father now rested in the once-fake grave beside her mother. In the end, she'd mourned the loss of him.

As her aunt slowly continued her journey up the aisle, Daisy glanced quickly at Bishop, Violet now asleep in his arms. She realized what she'd mourned of her own father was that he'd never loved her as Bishop loved his daughter. That she'd never had the chance to adore her father as Violet adored hers.

She looked back at her aunt. The woman was fairly

glowing with happiness. Beneath the veil, her smile was bright, her eyes shining. Then she was standing beside Daisy.

"You look beautiful, Mum."

"Bosh. Don't make me cry."

Daisy hugged her. "I love you."

"I love you, too, my darling."

"Now, let's finally get you married." Just as she had earlier with her daughter, Daisy gently nudged her aunt toward the man whose love for this remarkable woman was evident in the adoration and appreciation that wreathed his face. Never would there ever have come a time when her aunt would have gone to Bishop. Not married to this man. Not married to Paul.

As Aunt Charlotte and her future husband began to exchange vows, Daisy looked back over at Bishop. The man she'd chosen. The man who'd chosen her. His gaze was focused on her.

"I love you," he mouthed silently and, after touching two fingers to his lips, blew her a discreet kiss.

While she knew it was impossible, still she could have sworn that she'd felt it, landing against her own lips as lightly as a butterfly perching upon a petal, beautiful and solid.

Then he smiled, a smile that promised when they were done here, he'd be taking her to bed to demonstrate exactly how much he loved her. Her cheeks warmed. The man could still make her blush. Which she thought was a fine legacy, indeed.

AUTHOR'S NOTE

$\mathcal{P}$RIOR to January 1858, divorce was granted through an act of Parliament, which limited it to the elite and wealthy. In order to make it more affordable to the masses, a law was passed moving the decision regarding divorce to the civil courts. However, one of the stipulations for a divorce being granted was that adultery had to be involved. Two witnesses were required for proof of adultery. It has only recently come to light that this aspect of the law resulted in an increase in women serving as inquiry agents, also known as detectives, to secure the proof necessary to dissolve a marriage. *Sister Sleuths* by Nell Darby is a fascinating read about how women worked as private investigators as well as undercover, sometimes unofficially, for the Metropolitan police during the latter nineteenth and early twentieth centuries.

As early as 1860, detective novels—which were very popular in Britain—often had women portrayed as detectives, which has led to speculation that there was more truth than fiction recounted in these early novels.

Strength training was popular during the Victorian era and as early as the 16th century, books were written with advice on how to increase strength using church bells with the clappers removed as weights.

I do hope you've enjoyed this story and will join me when the next Chessman meets his match.

Coming in the Summer of 2023 . . .

The Notorious
Lord Knightly

NEW YORK TIMES BESTSELLING AUTHOR

LORRAINE HEATH

BEYOND SCANDAL AND DESIRE
978-0-06-267600-9

Orphaned and sheltered, Lady Aslyn Hastings longs for a bit of adventure. With her intended often occupied, Aslyn finds herself drawn to a darkly handsome entrepreneur who seems to understand her so well. Mick Trewlove, the illegitimate son of a duke, must decide if his plans for vengeance is worth risking what his heart truly desires.

WHEN A DUKE LOVES A WOMAN
978-0-06-267602-3

Gillie Trewlove knows what a stranger's kindness can mean, having been abandoned on a doorstep as a baby. So, when faced with a soul in need at *her* door—Gillie doesn't hesitate. But he's no infant. He's a grievously injured, distractingly handsome gentleman who doesn't belong in Whitechapel, much less recuperating in Gillie's bed.

THE SCOUNDREL IN HER BED
978-0-06-267605-4

The bastard son of a nobleman, Finn Trewlove was a shameful secret raised by a stranger. When he came of age he spent clandestine nights with an earl's daughter that ended in betrayal. Lady Lavinia Kent is engaged in a daring cause inspired by the young man to whom she gave her innocence. When their paths cross again, they can't deny the yearning and desire that still burns between them.

LH3 0919